YACHT GAMES

COASTAL FURY BOOK 22

MATT LINCOLN

PROLOGUE

IT WAS A BRIGHT, sunny, and gorgeous afternoon when the jukebox decided to take its last breath. It was a busy time of day, during the golden time where the sun was just beginning to set. The air was still warm, but it was getting dark enough that customers had started to flow in steadily. So, of course, that was the precise moment that the jukebox decided to give out.

"The hell is that?" One of my regulars looked up from the glass of scotch he was nursing, his eyebrows knitted together in confusion at the unholy noise the jukebox was making.

It had happened out of nowhere. One moment, the bar was filled with the soft notes of old classic rock, and the next, the speakers suddenly doubled in volume and were letting off a screech that was only slightly more pleasant than the sound of nails on a chalkboard.

"Oh." Rhoda looked at the machine in confusion before stepping out from behind the bar to inspect it.

I watched her cringe as she got closer to the source of the noise before finally covering her ears completely. She spent a few minutes looking it over and messing with some of the settings before finally just giving up and yanking the plug out of the wall. The terrible noise cut off abruptly and plunged the entire bar into welcome silence.

"What's the matter with your jukebox?" my regular asked me as he went back to slowly sipping from his glass.

"Heck if I know," I scoffed. "The girls are the ones who helped me set up and program the thing. I've never heard it do that before."

I looked back at the jukebox. Rhoda was walking back to the bar now with a frown on her face.

"That was weird," she muttered as she tossed a look back at the jukebox over her shoulder. "I wonder why it did that all of a sudden."

"It's not raining or anything," Nadia added as she walked back to the bar carrying a tray of empty glasses. "It couldn't have been a short."

"I could probably figure it out, but..." Rhoda sighed as she looked around the bar. "We're pretty packed right now, and I don't want to plug it back in and subject anyone to that sound again."

"Let me try something," Nadia suggested as she set the tray down.

"Knock yourself out," I replied. I'd be happy if whatever she was thinking managed to fix it. The jukebox wasn't that old, so it would be a shame to have to buy another one so soon. And though I'd never really paid attention, the bar felt oddly quiet now without it humming softly in the background.

"I wonder if someone spilled a drink on it or something," Rhoda mused aloud as she took the tray and walked back toward the kitchen to stack the dishes in the dishwasher.

I looked back at the jukebox. Nadia was crouched beside it, fiddling with some panels on the side. There weren't any customers sitting near it, though. In fact, there weren't any tables that were close to it at all. I shrugged as I pushed the thought aside and went back to work.

Only a few minutes later, my favorite group of customers arrived. It was impossible not to notice them because they came into the bar as a group. They weren't necessarily loud or boisterous. On the contrary, they were a pretty respectful bunch of kids. It was just impossible to miss them, especially in comparison to the rest of my typical clientele, which mainly consisted of older retirees who just wanted to enjoy their drinks and unwind in peace. Nevertheless, it was no secret that the group of kids had grown on several of my regulars as well, especially since their presence almost always meant one of my stories.

"Hey, Ethan," Jeff greeted me with a smile and a wave as he and the rest of them headed over to their usual table.

I gave him a small wave in response before getting to work preparing their drink orders, which I knew from memory at this point.

"Your fan club is here?" Rhoda teased me as she wiped up a small spot of beer she'd spilled on the counter.

"In their usual spot," I replied as I finished preparing their drinks.

"I give it two minutes until one of them is begging you to tell them about the *Dragon's Rogue*," Rhoda snorted.

"Two minutes?" I repeated as I loaded the drinks up onto a tray. "That's generous of you."

Rhoda laughed, and I turned to pick up the tray. The kids were laughing about something when I walked up to the table.

"It's been a while," I remarked as I set the tray down on the table to distribute their drinks.

"It's rare we all get leave at the same time," Mac explained after thanking me for her drink. "And after the meltdown that *someone* had when they missed a story, we decided not to come unless we all could."

"It was not a meltdown," Charlie protested. "I was just *rightfully* upset that you guys ditched me, and I ended up missing a story because of it. What if that had been the day that Ethan revealed what happened to the *Rogue*?"

"Please," Jeff snorted. "As if Ethan would tell us that soon. This man loves leaving us hanging."

"Well, whatever," Charlie grumbled before turning to look at me. "The point is we're all here now, so —*what is that?*"

He made a face halfway between horror and confusion as the ear-splitting noise from the jukebox screeched through the bar once more. I snapped my head around to look at Nadia, who was frantically pressing something on the jukebox, all to no avail. Finally, she just pulled the plug again.

"What the hell...?" Mac mumbled as she turned around in her seat to look in Nadia's direction.

"Sorry!" Nadia called sheepishly. "I thought maybe one of the internal components came out of place. Obviously, that wasn't it."

"Aw, your jukebox is broken?" Ty asked sadly. "That sucks."

"Yeah, it does," I sighed as I looked mournfully over at the machine sitting sadly in the corner.

"It does sound quiet in here, now that I think about it," Mac noted.

"Let me have a look at it," Charlie offered as he took a long swig from his glass before standing up. "I used to fix cars with my uncle."

"That is not a car," Jeff snickered as Charlie walked toward the jukebox. "And weren't you just complaining about missing stories?"

"I can hear it just fine from here," Charlie called back dismissively as he knelt in front of the jukebox. "Just talk loud, Ethan!"

I laughed to myself as I walked back to the bar to get my own drink. I guessed there wasn't even a point in putting up a token protest at this point since it was already decided that I would be telling them a story. In any case, it was the least I could do as thanks for fixing the jukebox.

"So, what's today's about?" Mac asked me eagerly as I sat back down in the chair that Charlie had vacated.

"Let me think," I replied as I thoughtfully took a sip of my beer. The next logical story to tell would be the one that took place directly after the red room case. "This one doesn't have all that much to do with the *Rogue*, to be perfectly honest."

"Aw." Jeff pouted immediately.

"But it does have a lot to do with Holm," I continued before taking another sip of my drink.

That caused all three of them to perk up at once.

"You mean...?" Mac turned to look at the stool at the end of the bar.

"Not yet," I clarified. "Though the stories aren't that dissimilar, I guess. In any case, it all started with a body found washed up on the beach..."

1

"IF YOU'LL JUST SIGN HERE, you'll be all good to go, Mr. Bransen."

Wesley looked up at the nurse from where he was sitting on the edge of his hospital bed. She had a broad, almost scary-looking smile stretched across her face. It emphasized the wrinkles around her mouth and highlighted how her makeup began to crack around her nose and cheeks. She probably meant for the smile to appear welcoming, but it seemed like she was mocking him to Wesley. How could she grin that awful fake smile while she threw him out on the street? It made him sick.

"Thanks," he mumbled sullenly as he took up the pen that was attached to the clipboard. It was bright purple, covered in glitter, and it had a little fluffy pom-

pom at the top. The nurse was still grinning maniacally at him as he scrawled his name down at the bottom of the page.

"Great!" the nurse exclaimed, snatching the clipboard back the moment he was done leaving his signature, as though she was worried he might change his mind or something.

As if he had a choice. Wesley snorted beneath his breath. She actually looked *relieved* that he was leaving. Wasn't this her job?

"Alright, just give me one second, and I'll go and fetch a wheelchair for you," the nurse informed him as she turned away from him.

"Don't bother," Wesley replied gruffly as he got to his feet. He winced as pain shot up his right leg and back.

"Oh, careful!" the nurse warned.

She sounded concerned, but Wesley knew it was all just an act. She didn't care about him. Nobody did. They all just saw him as an annoying inconvenience, taking a hospital bed from someone who could actually afford to be here.

Wesley ignored her as he grabbed his coat from the chair it was thrown over before shrugging it on. After checking the pocket for his wallet and phone, he slowly trudged his way out of the building, doing his best not to limp too obviously in front of all the hospital staff. Wesley just knew they all must be laughing at him, and he wasn't about to give them the satisfaction of seeing him hobble away.

He managed to keep the display up at least until he got past the doors of the emergency room, at which point he gasped with pain and stumbled over to the nearest bench to take a load off before continuing. The frigid air cut against his lungs as he took several deep, harried breaths.

The doctors had said that there was nothing obviously wrong with his leg.

"Yeah, right," Wesley muttered bitterly to himself. If that were true, then it wouldn't hurt every time he put any weight on it, now would it? Damned doctors were just sick of having to deal with him. They were just like all the rest, a bunch of jerks who only saw him as a useless, annoying bum.

A woman passing by turned to look at him with wide, frightened eyes as he continued to mutter angrily to himself, and Wesley snarled at her. After watching her scurry off into the hospital, Wesley felt terrible. Was this what he'd become? The dirty man sitting on a bench, talking to himself and growling at passersby? It wasn't like he wanted to be mean, but he just couldn't stand the way they all looked at him now, like he was a sideshow freak or a cockroach on the sidewalk.

He sighed as he reached a hand down to massage

his leg. New York was freezing this time of year. There was even a bit of snow on the ground, and the cold only made the pain in his leg that much worse. The emergency room doctors had told him he needed to see a specialist. There was little they could do there, and Wesley would likely need surgery. Well, that was all great to know. If only there were a way he *could* go to a specialist or afford surgery.

Sometimes, Wesley just wanted to break down and cry. It was impossible to fathom that everything could change in the blink of an eye the way it did. A good job, a warm home, a loving fiancée… Wesley had once had it all. Then all it took was one drunk driver to run a red light at just the wrong time, and Wesley lost everything.

"Suck it up," Wesley scolded himself as he forced himself back onto his feet. He wasn't going to gain anything from sitting here in the cold. Since he couldn't stay in the hospital now, it'd be wiser to go and find somewhere warm before it got later and the temperature dropped even more.

He allowed his mind to wander as he shuffled slowly through the crowded streets of lower Manhattan. To think it had only been three years since he'd moved here from middle-of-nowhere Arkansas with big dreams about becoming a Broadway star. For a while, it had all gone pretty well, too. It was so surreal to think about just how far he'd fallen in that time.

Wesley's first thought was to find a subway station to settle down in. It wouldn't be comfortable, but it would help keep out the cold a little. He descended into the first entrance he spotted, and it wasn't until he made it to the bottom that he remembered that he needed to pass the turnstiles to get inside, and turnstiles required money.

Wesley patted the pocket on his coat where he had his tiny remaining funds. Eighty-four dollars and a handful of change. That was all Wesley had to his name, and he guarded it fiercely. His gaze slid over to the woman sitting behind the booth, just off to the side. She was talking with a group of people who looked like tourists, probably giving them directions or something. Wesley snapped his head back around toward the turnstile and made a split-second decision. He rushed forward and awkwardly lifted his leg over the metal bar. A jolt of pain burst up his thigh and across his back as he did, but he ignored it. He'd come this far, so he might as well see this through. After several painful seconds, Wesley finally managed to amble his way over the barrier and onto the platform. The moment he made it onto the other side, he quickly walked away, shoulders hunched as he hoped that the attendant wouldn't say anything to him, as it was unlikely she *hadn't* noticed the spectacle he'd just put on back there.

Wesley's eyes lit up as they landed on an empty

bench a few feet down the platform, and he walked over to it as quickly as he could before plopping down onto it. It was wooden, flat, and uncomfortable, but at least he was off his feet again, and the relief of not putting pressure on his leg was immeasurable.

Wesley took a look around at the platform. It was early enough to be still packed with people, but maybe later tonight, it would clear up enough for him to claim a spot over in the corner where he'd be able to sleep undisturbed.

"What are you doing here?!" an old, graying man croaked at him as he jumped up from behind a bench tucked up against the wall. Wesley hadn't even noticed him lying there.

"Whoa, sorry," Wesley muttered as he instinctively shot up to his feet again. A jolt of pain shot up his leg as he did. "I didn't know this spot was taken. I'll just—"

"No, no, don't worry about it," the man hurried to calm him. "I thought you were one of them filthy commies! My eyes aren't what they used to be!"

"Sure," Wesley replied.

The man did look pretty old. His face was wrinkled, and he had wiry gray and white hair sticking out of his head in every direction.

"Why don't you sit here?" the man suggested as he pointed down at the bench. "Could use some company. Most folks tend to give me space, which I appreciate, you know. Kids these days don't appreciate their elders, but they do here. I do like visitors sometimes, though, you know? Gets a little lonely sometimes. You going to sit or what?"

"Yeah," Wesley muttered as the man continued to ramble about respect and elders and the war.

The man clearly wasn't all there, but he seemed friendly enough, so Wesley didn't see the harm in sitting down with him. If nothing else, it would provide some relief for his leg.

"They hide in the shadows," the old man muttered. "Never know who you can trust. They come in the night when no one's expecting it. I've seen it happen myself."

"Who?" Wesley asked as he settled back against the hard, uncomfortable bench. "The commies?"

"Yes!" the old man replied. "I mean, no... don't try to confuse me, young man!"

"Sorry," Wesley chuckled. "And thanks for letting me stay here."

"Of course!" the old man exclaimed heartily. "We've got to stick together in times like these! Here, have some chocolate."

The man reached into a ragged backpack tucked back behind the bench. Though he'd had some oatmeal at the hospital before leaving, Wesley's stomach still watered at the thought of the chocolates, which he gratefully accepted.

"Helps keep calories up," the old man explained

helpfully. "Keeps you warm at night, too. We'll need the energy in case they strike tonight."

"Right." Wesley nodded as he tore the wrapper off one of the candies with his teeth. He wasn't sure who the old man thought might be coming for them, but he figured it was best to just go along with it.

"Anyway, the name's Logan," the old man introduced himself as he started in on his own piece of chocolate.

"Wesley," Wesley muttered in response.

"Good to meet you," Logan replied cheerfully. "So, what happened to your leg? I noticed you limping earlier. One of my platoon mates stepped on a landmine during an operation a few years back." Logan shook his head. "Is that what happened to you?"

"No, uh, it was a drunk driver," Wesley replied softly. "Hit me damned near head-on... Shattered both my legs. They both healed up eventually, but, uh," Wesley looked down at his right leg, "the right one never quite stopped hurting. My back, too. Lost my job since I couldn't go to work, so then I lost my insurance, so I couldn't fix my leg." He chuckled mirthlessly. "Lost everything in the past year, and now I'm here."

"That's a shame." Logan clapped Wesley on the back sympathetically. "But hey, you're still alive, right? So long as you've still got air in your lungs, you can't give up, right? You're too young to think about giving up."

Wesley turned to look at the old man, who was smiling kindly back at him.

"Yeah, I guess you're right," he replied as a shiver ran through him. Even down underground, the bitter cold cut through him.

"Of course I am!" Logan laughed. "Anyway, maybe we should find someplace to hit the hay. It looks like it's going to be a cold one tonight. Come on." The old man got shakily up onto his feet before turning to Wesley. "I know a spot not far from here. It should be pretty deserted this time of night, so we shouldn't have any problems. And it'll be dry!"

Wesley stared back at Logan warily. Just moments before, he'd been thinking about how nice the old man seemed, but that didn't necessarily mean that Wesley trusted him. He was, after all, still a stranger. A stranger whose first inclination had been to accuse him of being a communist and of plotting to attack him. Wesley wasn't keen on the idea of following him anywhere, especially not somewhere that would be "deserted."

"Come on, what are you sitting there for?" Logan asked as he leaned down to haul Wesley to his feet.

Wesley was shocked by just how much strength the man had. For someone that looked like they were in their seventies, the man was anything but frail, and he managed to yank Wesley at least partway off the bench.

"Snow's picking up!" Logan spat. "If we dally, we'll be soaked to the bone by the time we get there, and then it won't matter whether the place is dry or not. We will die of hypothermia in our sleep. That's why you should never sleep in wet clothes, you know. Even if you end up having to strip down and sleep in your skivvies, the best way to survive is..."

He continued to ramble on about survival tactics and how he'd used those methods himself back during "the war." Wesley had no idea what war he was referring to if it was even a real one that actually happened. In truth, he was barely listening to what Logan was saying at all. His mind was still stuck on the safety aspect of following this man to who-knows-where in the middle of the night.

I guess I've lived long enough, Wesley thought to himself, self-deprecatingly, as he resigned himself just to go wherever the man suggested. What was the worst that could happen? He could be killed? At that point, Wesley wasn't sure that would be the worst outcome. Since he was crippled, homeless, penniless, and without a single prospect or way out, what other hopes did he even have?

"Alright, fine," Wesley cut Logan off with a low, defeated mutter. Logan blinked in surprise, as though he'd completely forgotten that Wesley was there in his rambling. "You're right. Let's go before we freeze to death."

"That's the spirit," Logan replied cheerfully as he clapped Wesley on the shoulder. "Come on then, let's go."

Logan took off without another word, ambling away surprisingly quickly for a man his age. It was still, fortunately, at a pace that was slow enough for Wesley to keep up with his bad leg. That was good because Logan didn't stop or turn around once to make sure Wesley was even behind him. Wesley smiled ruefully as he thought about what a sight the pair must make, shuffling down the street in single file like this. He might have laughed if his teeth hadn't been chattering too much.

The walk seemed to drag on for an eternity, and all the while, Wesley's leg was screaming in angry protest. Logan slowed down briefly to greet someone in an alleyway that was, as far as Wesley could see, chock-full of other homeless people, but they didn't stay long, much to Wesley's dismay. He was about to just call it quits and collapse into the shadow of a doorway when Logan finally spoke up.

"Here it is!" Logan declared when they finally arrived at their destination after what felt like an eternity of walking. "The guard's not here, just like I thought. Perfect, no one will bother us then."

Wesley, who'd been so focused on the steadily increasing pain in his leg, finally looked up. It was an ordinary-looking parking garage tucked between two nice, well-kept buildings.

Part of Wesley wanted to ask if Logan was sure this was a good idea, but he honestly couldn't summon the will to care anymore. He sighed as he followed Logan onto the deck. To his surprise, the inside of the deck felt a little warmer, probably because it was insulated due to being sandwiched between the two large buildings.

"Over here should be good," Logan whispered conspiratorially as he led Wesley over to a spot in the corner of the floor. "The air vent is just outside of this back wall, so this spot is always the warmest." He beamed proudly, and Wesley was shocked to discover that he was right. The spot just in the corner did feel a little warmer. "Ground's not that comfortable to sleep on, but at least it beats sleeping outside, huh?"

Logan lowered himself onto the ground, and Wesley followed suit nearby.

"Well, let's get some shuteye," Logan declared as he lay down without any more preamble.

Wesley watched him for a minute, still uncertain whether it was a bright idea to just go to sleep next to this stranger in a very deserted parking garage. In the end, he just shrugged and lay down as well. As he'd thought earlier, if this were the end, then at least he wouldn't have to worry about his leg or any of his other problems any longer. As he closed his eyes, he wondered vaguely what the next day might bring.

He woke with a jolt sometime later, his heart hammering as the sounds of screams echoed in his ears. He realized quickly that the old man was shouting something about being under attack, and Wesley groaned. Had he really been shocked awake all because of the man's crazy delusions?

"Come on, Logan, nothing is—" Wesley grumbled as he sat up to help calm the man.

He stopped short as he opened his eyes and found Logan several feet away from him on the parking deck, kicking and struggling on the ground as a man dressed in black clothes stood threateningly above him.

"Hey!" Wesley barked as he attempted to get to his feet.

His leg protested at once, and he stumbled slightly as he attempted to go to his newfound friend's aid, but he pushed through the pain to get to Logan, who was trembling on the ground now as the assailant rained blows down on him with his fists.

"Get off him!" Wesley yelled as he shoved the attacker away.

Wesley had always been more of a "brains over brawn" kind of guy, which showed in the awkward strike against the man, but he wasn't about to just stand by and let him beat on Logan. "You think you're tough, attacking a little old man? You must feel like a big man!"

The assailant turned to look at Wesley, and Wesley found himself regretting his surge of bravado immediately. The guy was big, built like a linebacker, and looked furious. Wesley barely had a moment to react before the man suddenly lunged at him. Wesley swung his fists wildly, whispered remnants of a self-defense class he took during his freshman year of college coming back to him as he tried to recall how to throw a punch.

Wesley was shocked when his fist connected with the attacker's face. The man yelled with pain as he reached up to press his hands against his nose, and for a few seconds, Wesley wasn't even sure what he was supposed to do next. Then he shoved the man again before turning to check on Logan, who was still curled up on the ground. Before he could take more than two steps, though, something hard hit him over the back of the head.

The pain from the blow was immense. It felt like whatever had hit him had cleaved his skull right in two, and stars were dancing in his vision.

"Hey, careful!" a warbled voice above him hissed. "Don't kill him! He won't be useful if he's *dead!*"

Another voice responded, but Wesley couldn't make it out. His vision was going dark, and the pain in his head was starting to recede as drowsiness overtook him. He knew, logically, that he shouldn't fall asleep. He shouldn't just give up and let his eyes fall closed. He was so tired, though, and the pain was gone now, so he allowed the darkness to overtake him.

2

ETHAN

I sat down at one of the stools at the bar, then reached up to check my mic, pretending to adjust the collar of my shirt as I did.

"Can you hear me?" I muttered quietly as I looked around casually.

The bar was as glamorous as they came, every surface polished and shiny, made of glass and marble and sleek gray steel. It was located on the twentieth floor of a skyscraper here in downtown Miami, and it was also the location of our current stakeout.

"Loud and clear," Holm's voice rang out from the tiny receiver in my ear.

It was pretty impressive how far technology had come in just a few years. Gone were the days when our earpieces were bulky and noticeable, like big, plastic hearing aids. The receiver I was wearing now was only slightly bigger than an earplug, and unless someone looked directly into my ear, they probably wouldn't notice it.

"Any sign of her?" I asked as I flagged the bartender down to get a drink. He walked over right away.

"Nope," Holm replied from where he was located at the other end of the bar. He was sitting at a table by himself, pretending to be on a hilarious phone call as he spoke to me. "Nothing yet—oh, looks like we got something."

I turned to the entrance, where I spotted her at once. Julietta Morales, stunning at nearly six feet tall, with long legs and a sharp, angular face that made her look like a queen. She was wearing a form-fitting, black velvet dress that stopped at her thighs and impossibly high heels that looked like they'd be impossible to walk in. She was managing it somehow, though, and doing it quite effortlessly as she glided along the floor of the bar. She was flanked by several guards, which wasn't surprising, considering who she was.

As the wife of a drug lord, it only made sense that she would travel with her own protective entourage. Her husband, Guillermo Morales, had been making waves around the metro Miami area for the past few months. He'd appeared seemingly out of nowhere, and for nearly half a year now, had managed to import a massive amount of narcotics into the United States from Nicaragua. All of our efforts to catch him had fallen flat so far, as he always managed to evade us at the last moment. We'd finally caught a break when we received an anonymous tip that Morales's wife, Julietta, tended to frequent this upscale bar. We'd quickly devised a plan to come and find her, with the hopes that we'd be able to tail her back to her husband's location. Now that she was here, all I needed to do was figure out a way past her wall of guards.

To my surprise, I didn't end up having to do much because she suddenly turned and walked in my direction.

"Oh, crap," Holm muttered into my ear. "Is she onto you?"

"I dunno," I replied quickly before grabbing the drink that the bartender had just brought for me.

"That looks good." Julietta smiled coyly as she approached and nodded toward the glass in my hand. "What are you having?"

"You came all the way over here just to ask me what drink I was having?" I replied vaguely, still unsure whether she knew who I was and what I was doing here. I offered her a polite, slightly aloof smile as I waited to see where she would go with this.

"Is there a problem with that?" she replied as she slid onto the stool next to mine. Her skirt rode up as she did, exposing more of her thigh as she brazenly crossed one leg over the other.

Her guards were standing right behind us, which wasn't a good position for me to be in. I was tense and didn't want to turn my back on them entirely, but I couldn't make it obvious that I was nervous.

"Not really." I shrugged as I turned around on the stool, so my back was to the bar instead. "I guess I just don't see what's so interesting about a normal glass of scotch."

"I guess, if I'm being honest, it was the man holding the drink that drew my attention," she murmured as she raised a hand to flag down the bartender. He appeared at once.

"Get me my usual," she commanded regally before turning to look at me. "And another one for...?"

"Ethan," I replied calmly, though inside, my heart was pounding frantically at the sudden development.

"Another drink for Ethan, then," Julietta finished. The bartender moved to prepare the drinks at once. "I haven't seen you around here before."

"That's because this is the first time I've been here," I replied, an easygoing smile on my lips. It wasn't a lie. Ritzy rooftop bars weren't my usual hangout spots. For better or worse, the divey little spot Mike owned was where I could usually be found getting a drink.

"Are you from out of town?" she asked as she leaned toward me, letting her knee brush against my leg as she did.

"Yeah," I replied. "I'm up here on business. I thought I'd check out what Miami has to offer."

"Oh?" she asked as she leaned even closer, just inches away from me now. "And do you like what Miami has to *offer*?"

She smiled slyly at me as the bartender returned with our drinks. She was laying it on pretty thick, and though I could almost believe that she might have just been flirting with me, I couldn't quite shake the suspicion that there was something else hidden behind her eyes.

"I can't say it's been too bad so far," I replied casually. "Tonight, especially, has been pretty eventful."

She laughed in response as she reached for the glass the bartender had set on the table.

"Well, I have a feeling it's about to get a little better," she grinned. "*Agent Marston.*"

And there it was.

Rather than feeling worried, I felt oddly relieved. I'd had a feeling that she was just pretending, and the fact that she'd confirmed it meant I could now drop the pretext I'd been keeping up.

"Do you?" I asked as I glanced over to the guards still standing just a few feet away. There were two of them, bulky and probably decent fighters. Holm could probably get over here in a few seconds, but if the two goons had guns on them—

"Don't worry about them." Julietta smirked. "They won't do anything. Not unless I tell them to."

"And you're not going to tell them to kill me?" I raised an eyebrow at her.

"Of course not." She gasped at me in mock indignation. "At least not yet, anyway. We're having such a nice conversation, you and me. It would be rude to have them take you out now."

"How considerate of you," I replied dryly.

"You really shouldn't talk so much." She frowned at me. "You've got such a nice face, but you ruin it every time you open your mouth. No, just sit there quietly and listen for a moment, alright?"

"Alright," I replied flatly, still mentally calculating my best escape route should things go sideways.

She snorted.

"You really don't know how to follow directions, do you?" She shook her head.

"I don't take orders from people like you," I replied without hesitation.

"Don't you?" She snickered maliciously. "I think you do, actually, since you're here. And all I had to do was make one little 'anonymous' phone call."

"Wait," I muttered. "That was you?"

"Oh, you can't honestly be telling me that you had no idea this might all be a trap?" She tutted at me disapprovingly. "That's disappointing. I suppose there really isn't anything more behind that handsome face. No, Agent Marston, I'm the one who made that call. And while I'm at it, I suppose it can't hurt to tell you everything else since you won't be alive for very much longer."

"What do you mean by 'everything else'?" I demanded.

"Your plan was probably to use me to find my husband, correct?" She raised her eyebrows at me. "Along with your little partner over there. The one sitting at the booth pretending he's having the conversation of his life? I'm certain he can hear us, so why don't you tell him he can drop the act?"

I glanced over at Holm, who immediately put his phone away and looked our way.

"So, you wanted to lead us out here," I sighed. "Why? Are you planning on betraying your husband on your own?"

"Betray him?" She scoffed. "What's there to betray? You can't honestly believe that idiot is the one who's been running things, right?"

"What are you trying to say?" I asked her.

"I suppose you're just as dense as my stupid husband is," she huffed. "I'm telling you that I'm the one who's in charge here. Guillermo is a figurehead, a pawn. You can hardly count on men to do anything correctly these days, except maybe for taking the fall when you need them to. That's what I'm trying to tell you, Agent Marston. *I'm* the one you've been looking for this entire time."

I glanced over at Holm again.

"No," she snipped. "Whatever you're thinking, don't even try it. My men will have you both dead before either of you can even stand up."

"Is that right?" I smirked at her. "Did everyone hear that? It sounds to me like we've got everything we need."

"What?" Julietta snarled as she shot to her feet. "What is that supposed to mean?"

"Everybody down!" Agent Birn roared as he suddenly jumped up from one of the tables at the other end of the bar.

"Down, now!" Muñoz repeated the order as she drew her weapon and directed all the other patrons in the bar to safety, away from the scene.

"What is this?" Julietta gaped at me, fear and fury swirling together on her face.

"Looks like you're the one who underestimated us," I replied as Holm got up and pointed his gun at the two guards.

The guards stood in numb shock as they faced down the three agents. One of them reached for his waist, but I drew my gun and spoke up before he could do anything.

"I wouldn't do that," I warned.

Both guards looked at each other before raising their hands in the air and sinking to their knees.

"What are you doing?" Julietta screeched. "Get up!"

"It's over, Morales," I looked her dead in the eye as I slowly stood up to face her. "You were right. I'm not stupid enough to believe that this wasn't a trap. We had a feeling something was up when that call first came in, and from there, it didn't take us long to figure out that you were the one behind all of this. I figured you would come and talk to me if we came, and thanks to your little monologue, we now have you on the recording admitting to everything."

"You're going to regret this," she hissed as Birn, Muñoz, and Holm rushed in to apprehend her and the two guards.

"I doubt that," I replied as Holm pulled her arms behind her back to cuff them.

She continued to struggle and snap at Holm about not touching her, but I tuned her out as I plopped back down onto the barstool and downed the rest of my drink. Everything had ended as smoothly as it possibly could, all things considered. No one had been shot, and we'd even gotten a full confession. That didn't mean that it hadn't been nerve-racking, though. My heart had been pounding the entire time, worried that one of the two goons would suddenly strike or that Julietta would realize what was actually going on.

"That was good," Holm commended as he walked

back over to me. I could see Julietta and the two guards sitting by the entrance, being watched over by Birn and Muñoz. "You played the part of clueless detective pretty well. I almost believed it."

"Really?" I looked at him. "I thought it was kind of obvious that I was faking it. I mean, she did have a point. It would have been pretty stupid of us to just run in here blind, without any kind of suspicion that something shady was going on. I was worried she'd suddenly catch on that she was right."

"Well, lucky for us, she was too confident," Holm replied with a shrug. "She thought she was too smart for her plan to fail."

"That was her mistake," I agreed. "Now, we can wrap this case up."

The rest of the evening passed by in a blur as we got to work cleaning up the scene, which didn't take long as there wasn't actually much of a fight or even any shots fired. After getting Julietta and her men into custody at the police station, all that was left to do was head home.

It was well past midnight by the time I stumbled through the door of my houseboat, tired from the long day spent working on the case and ready to go to sleep. As I walked into my bedroom, I slipped my phone from my pocket, intending to check for any new messages or calls before having a quick shower. I was pleasantly surprised to find that I did, in fact, have a message from one Ava Finch-Hatton.

Ava was a distant relative of mine I'd gotten in touch with through Bonnie. Apparently, she'd posted on an ancestry message board looking for information about an ancestor of hers, which had led Bonnie to the discovery that we were both related to Jonathan Finch-Hatton, the original owner of the *Dragon's Rogue*. We'd exchanged messages a few times since then, and though my busy schedule made it difficult for us to meet right away, we were still planning on getting to it, eventually.

Her latest message was short, a funny reply to the last thing I'd sent her, as well as some information that she thought I might find interesting.

"I have some old documents that I think you might like. A few of them talk about ships, though I'm not sure if any of them are about the Dragon's Rogue. There are some drawings, too. To be honest, I really don't know much about any of them. I always thought they were cool, but it was never something that really drew my interest. I figure you'll appreciate them a lot more since you're super into pirate ships and all. Anyway, let me know when you might be free to meet up or even talk on the phone!

Love, Ava"

. . .

I smiled at the way she'd signed the message. It felt kind of weird, but I supposed we were technically family. She was my cousin a hundred times removed or something like that. In any case, the message had piqued my interest, as anything concerning the *Rogue* always did. I shot back a quick message promising to get back to her as soon as I had some free time and then headed off to bed, feeling much lighter than I had before.

3

ETHAN

A COOL BREEZE blew past me as I got out of my car in the office parking lot. It was a temperate sixty-six degrees, the coldest it ever really got in Miami, even in the middle of December. It wasn't cold by any means, but for someone who was used to nearly year-round sun and warm, balmy weather, the breeze was enough to send a chill through me, and I hurried across the parking lot and into the building.

Up in the office, I headed straight over to my desk. Holm was already sitting at his, talking with Birn.

"Speak of the devil!" Birn declared as he looked up at me.

"Uh-oh," I replied. "I'm assuming that means you were talking about me? Good things, I hope."

"Define 'good,'" Holm grumbled.

"Holm's feeling grumpy," Birn teased as he snickered at Holm.

"Hm? Why?" I asked as I looked down at my partner, who did have a bit of a sour expression on his face.

"He's moping that Julietta went over to you instead of him," Birn practically cackled as he clapped Holm on the shoulder.

"I'm not moping!" he countered defensively. "Just... I mean, there was a fifty-fifty chance, you know? We knew that she was trying to lead *both* of us there to take us out."

"And you're grumpy that she went for Marston instead of you," Birn snickered. "Well, no offense or anything, Holm, but—"

"Don't finish that sentence," Holm deadpanned. "Nothing remotely good has ever come after the phrase 'no offense.'" Holm turned pointedly away from Birn to look at me. "Anyway, how are you this morning, Marston?"

"Uh, great," I replied as Birn took his leave. "I got an email from Ava last night."

"Ava?" Holm furrowed his eyebrows at me. "Who— oh, Ava! What did she say? Did you two finally figure out a date to meet up?"

"Not yet," I sighed as I took my seat. "It's hard to find time between cases, especially since we never know when another one might pop up. Now might be a good time, though, since we just wrapped up the

Morales case. She said she had some documents I might be interested in, and as long as there's a lull—"

"Marston, Holm," Diane's voice suddenly cut me off. I looked up and found her standing at the end of the bullpen, calling to Holm and me. "Could I see you two in my office?"

"So much for a lull," Holm muttered as the two of us got up to follow Diane. She closed the door behind us as we stepped inside before taking a seat behind her desk.

"I've got a case for you, potentially," she dove right in after sitting down.

"Potentially?" I repeated as I took a seat in my usual spot during these briefings. "What does that mean?"

"Well, the details of the case are a little... strange," she replied. "A lot of it isn't adding up, and while it seems fairly likely that the case should fall into our jurisdiction, there are too many missing pieces for us to say with certainty until we get a little more information."

"What, so this might not be under our jurisdiction?" Holm asked, his face marred with confusion.

"Why don't I just explain everything?" Diane replied. "Several days ago, the body of an American man was discovered on a small island in St. Vincent and the Grenadines. Now, normally, something like this would immediately become our responsibility. However, several things about the body and the crime scene make this an unusual case. For one, Palm Island, where this man was discovered, is a tiny, private island only accessible by private boat. It's extremely exclusive, and by that, I mean that at any given time, there are only a couple of dozen people *total* on the island."

"I would imagine that would make it pretty easy to figure out who the killer is," I replied, sensing that there was a lot more to this than she'd told us.

"You would think," she scoffed. "Especially considering the state the body was in. The corpse had been absolutely brutalized. He was covered in bruises practically from head to toe, he had lacerations, and even his nose was broken. The extent of it was so bad that it would be unthinkable that it could have happened without any of the other people on the island noticing, and yet that's what happened."

"No one saw anything?" I raised an eyebrow at her. "They're obviously lying."

"Maybe not," she sighed heavily. "There's more to the mystery. No one on the island knew who the man was, and in fact, there was no record of how he'd gotten there. Of course, all the people on the island had purchased tickets to get there, but all of them were accounted for. No one had any idea who the dead man could be, not the guests nor the officials on the island. As he was found on the beach, it's believed that he might have been killed somewhere else and just washed up there. However, that's difficult to believe, too, since the nearest body of water is several kilometers away. He likely would have sunk before making it all the way to Palm Island."

"So, he just appeared out of nowhere?" I asked. "That is bizarre."

"There's more," Diane added, to my surprise. "Since no one had any idea who he was, the police ran a DNA test on him. It came back two days ago, and that was when they discovered that he was actually Logan Clearwater, a seventy-two-year-old military veteran who'd been reported missing over a year ago in New Jersey."

"A year!?" I balked, unsure if I'd misheard. "This man has been missing for a year, and he suddenly turned up dead on a random, private island out in the Caribbean?"

"Now you understand why we aren't sure who should be taking jurisdiction on this case," Diane sighed as she clasped her hands together on top of her desk. "There are a lot of confusing factors here. His disappearance may or may not have anything to do with the case as well. Apparently, when he was initially reported missing a year ago, his daughter told authorities that he had exhibited signs of dementia. It's possible he just wandered off on his own, and in fact, that was what the police believed happened until his body was discovered recently. Now, they're not quite sure what to think."

"So, what should we do?" I asked as I leaned forward in my seat pensively. The case was certainly odd, but I already felt invested. I wanted to know what happened to this man, and I wanted to find justice for him. "Can we investigate?"

"For now, yes," Diane replied. "The FBI seem interested in taking it from us, especially if it turns out he was actually abducted all that time ago, but for now, it seems like this falls more under our jurisdiction, so we'll proceed as normal."

"Alright," I replied, honestly relieved to hear that we weren't going to get booted off the case. "So, we're heading to St. Vincent?"

"Not quite yet." Diane shook her head. "For now, I'd like you to head up to New Jersey to speak with Clearwater's family. I'd like to get some more information about his initial disappearance before we move. After that, though, you probably will be heading out to St. Vincent and the Grenadines. I've already booked you a flight to New Jersey. It leaves tonight."

"Got it," I replied as I stood up.

"I'll forward the flight information and everything we know about the case to your tablets," Diane added as Holm stood up after me.

"We'll head to the airport now," I replied.

"Have a safe trip," Diane replied as Holm and I headed toward the office door. "Keep me updated on anything you find."

"Will do," I replied before saying goodbye and heading out. Holm and I stopped by our desks just long enough to grab our things before heading back out.

"I guess meeting up with Ava will have to wait for now," I remarked as we headed out of the building and into the parking lot, anticipation for the mission already rising in me like a flame. "Never a dull moment working as an MBLIS agent."

4

ETHAN

I REGRETTED my earlier griping about the weather in Miami the moment we landed in New Jersey, which was a shocking thirty-three degrees. I hugged the jacket I'd brought with me closer as Holm and I walked out of the airport. Though we often traveled for work, we usually didn't stray all that far from the warm, sunny shores of the Caribbean. As someone who lived and breathed balmy Miami air virtually year-round, there really wasn't any need for me to own a heavier winter coat. The jacket, which was soft leather and too warm to wear most of the time back home, felt like paper against the harsh wind that tore through me as we ventured into Atlantic City, where we'd landed.

Clearwater's daughter, Marjorie, lived all the way up in Burlington, which was a solid two-hour drive from the airport, so our first order of business was getting our hands on a car. It seemed a little wasteful since we'd likely only be using it for a few hours before heading down to St. Vincent and the Grenadines, but we had to get there somehow.

At least the ride itself was peaceful. The roads weren't particularly congested this time of day, and the further north we got, the more scenic our surroundings became. Lush oak trees that hadn't lost all their leaves yet painted the hills in shades of red, orange, and yellow. For a long period, there was nothing but trees and grassy fields as far as I could see. Then, suddenly, we hit the first stoplight I'd seen in nearly an hour.

"We're making good time," Holm noted as we drove into Burlington.

As we made our way through the streets of the small town, my first thought was how much it reminded me of the place in upstate New York where Tessa and I had now gone several times to visit Professor Slade at his museum. I was so used to being surrounded by the huge, towering skyscrapers of Miami that the tiny, old-world buildings that lined the streets here seemed like they belonged to an entirely different world. Holm was right, as well. Traffic had been exceptionally light on the way up here, which had allowed us to arrive in just under an hour and thirty minutes.

Marjorie lived in the kind of quaint, picturesque house that's often used as the backdrop for feel-good Christmas movies: a two-story Victorian-style made of brick, with an arched roof covered in shingles and even a white picket fence. The light blanket of snow spread over the front lawn to complete the pretty picture, and it was jarring to think that inside the warm, cozy-looking home was a woman in the throes of grief.

The front door opened as soon as Holm and I stepped out of the car. As we made our way up the short driveway that led to the front door, a small, blond woman stepped cautiously outside.

"H-hi!" she called nervously, wringing her hands as we approached her. Her eyes and nose were a little red, and it looked like she'd been crying recently. "I'm Marjorie. You must be, um... sorry, could you remind me of your names again?"

"Agent Marston," I introduced myself as I stepped forward to shake her hand.

"Agent Holm," Holm added before doing the same.

"Right, sorry," Marjorie mumbled as she brushed a lock of hair out of her face. "I'm not usually this scatterbrained, but, well, with the news..." Her face fell as she trailed off, and her eyes got shiny with unshed tears again.

"Thank you for agreeing to meet with us," I said as she sniffled and quickly reached up to wipe her tears away with the back of her hand.

"Oh, no, not at all!" she muttered. "If anything, I should be thanking *you*. You're the ones who are going out of your way to investigate his—what happened to him. Anyway, let's not just stand here in the cold. Let's head inside where it's warm." She turned around and beckoned us to follow her into the house.

The home's interior looked just as quaint as the outside, if a little messier. Toys and coloring books were littered around the floor, and a couple of half-eaten bowls of cereal were sitting on the floor in the living room, in front of the TV.

"Sorry about the mess," Marjorie laughed nervously. "My kids can get a little crazy. I should have cleaned up before you got here."

"Don't worry about it," I replied as she led us into the living room before leaning down to pick up the bowls.

"How many kids do you have?" Holm asked her as she hurried to the kitchen to drop the bowls into the sink.

"Um, two," she replied, smiling slightly as she answered. "A boy and a girl. Their father... he, uh, he died last year. It's been rough since then, and now *this*." A flurry of emotions flashed across her face, among them anger, sadness, frustration, and likely more that I didn't manage to catch in the brief instant that her face crumpled in on itself before she recovered. "Sorry, you didn't come here to listen to me unload like that. You're here about Dad." She ambled back over to the living room before sinking into one of the armchairs. "Please, have a seat."

"Thank you," I replied as I did as she suggested and sat down.

"So, um, where should we start?" Marjorie mumbled as she fidgeted with her hands.

"How about with his initial disappearance?" I suggested.

She pursed her lips and swallowed as I said that.

"Right, well, it was a little over a year ago," she replied quietly. "Fourteen months, exactly. I remember that it was right around Halloween. I was so busy getting the kids ready for trick-or-treating that I didn't even notice. I have no idea how long he was gone before I finally realized he wasn't in his room."

"He was living here with you?" I asked.

"Oh, yes," she replied as she reached over to pluck a throw pillow off the couch. She held it close to herself and played with the scraggly fringe along the edge as she continued her story. "He'd been having some issues lately. Normal stuff, you know? He had just turned seventy, and he was having some trouble remembering things. He couldn't drive very well anymore, either. So, he came to live with us. It was an adjustment, but the kids loved having their grandpa close." She smiled fondly again, the way she had earlier when she mentioned her kids.

"So, what happened the day he went missing?" I prodded, and the smile slipped off her face.

"I told him I'd be out with the kids for a while," she replied. "I was a little worried, to be honest, since his memory seemed to have gotten worse lately. He'd forget where things were. He'd forget where *he* was. Sometimes, he would even look at me like he wasn't sure who I was." She paused for a moment, a somber expression on her face. "Anyway, that day, he seemed fine. He told me to have a great time and bring him back some candy. I left his room to get the kids ready, costumes, coats, their little treat bags. It was only an hour or so. I went back to let him know we were leaving, and he was just... gone."

A hushed silence fell over the room as she stopped speaking.

"What did the police do?" Holm asked. "We read the report. They weren't able to find anything?"

"Maybe if they'd tried," Marjorie replied bitterly, her face twisting into an angry grimace before falling again. "No, I guess that's not fair. It *was* Halloween, after all. I'm sure they had enough to deal with. They told me as much, anyway, when I finally called to report my dad missing. I told them that he'd been exhibiting symptoms of dementia lately, but I guess a grown man wasn't much of a priority. It wasn't like it was a small child that had gone missing."

Though she said that, I could still hear the resentment in her voice. I couldn't blame her. While most people might agree that a missing adult is not quite as pressing an issue as a missing child, the fact that the man wasn't entirely in his right mind should have been a cause for greater concern.

"Anyway," Marjorie sniffled. "That was it. I followed up with them a few times, but they never had any information for me. It wasn't until three months ago that I heard anything back at all."

"Three months?" I repeated. "What do you mean? What happened three months ago?"

"Oh, the police didn't tell you?" She looked up at me in confusion. "They found him. They arrested him for trying to shoplift from this high-end boutique store up in New York, of all places. When they ran his prints, they discovered that he'd been reported as a missing person."

"So, what happened?" I furrowed my eyebrows in confusion. If he'd been found already, then how exactly had he ended up on Palm Island?

"They lost him again," Marjorie sighed as she reached up to massage her temple with the tips of her fingers. "I rushed up there, of course, as fast as I could. When I got there, they told me they would go and get him, only to come back a few minutes later to tell me that he was gone." She laughed sadly. "Apparently, there had been some kind of mix-up. Something about shift changes and a miscommunication about who was supposed to be watching over him. And he was gone again." She shrugged and looked up at me almost pleadingly. "It was like a slap in the face, to be told that they'd found him, and then suddenly he was gone again. I spent days looking for him, but New York is enormous and so full of people. It was like trying to find a needle in a haystack."

"I'm sorry that happened," I replied.

I couldn't imagine how awful that must have felt, to hear news about your missing loved one after nearly a year, only to have your hopes crushed at the last moment.

"Me, too," Marjorie murmured. "Anyway, ever since then, I've assumed that he was living on the streets somewhere. It made sense, the idea that he just walked out of the house on his own, got confused, and just got lost. The fact that he was shoplifting proves that he wasn't in his right mind. My dad was about as strict and straight-laced as they came. He would have never committed any kind of crime. In any case, I was shocked when I got the call that they'd found him... that they'd found his body off on that island." She shook her head slowly as she stared off into space. "For a minute, I wondered if they'd made some mistake, but they'd run his DNA. I didn't even know what to think. How could he have made it over there? He was home-less! And not in his right mind! He didn't have money to travel. It just doesn't make any sense!"

She had a good point. It really was bizarre that an indigent man without any resources would have been anywhere near the small, private island. Then again, if the man had been taken there against his will, the fact that he'd been homeless, confused, and without a family likely would have made him a very easy target.

"We're going to do everything we can to figure out what happened," I assured her. "To start, could you tell us which police station you went to that day? I'd like to speak with the officers who handled your father's arrest."

"Sure," Marjorie replied as she nodded fervently. She got up off the couch to retrieve her purse from where it was sitting on the table. "I've got everything written down here in my journal. I'll get you the address right now."

I was glad that we'd chosen to get the rental car after all. I had a feeling that our stay here was going to last a bit longer than we'd initially anticipated.

5

ETHAN

THE DRIVE from Burlington to New York City took a little over an hour, but getting to the police station took nearly three. New York City traffic was a force to be reckoned with, and I was woefully unprepared for just how extreme it would be. I'd been to New York before, of course, but on those occasions, I'd taken a cab or the subway, for the most part. Actually trying to traverse the city at street level was nothing short of a nightmare.

"I thought Miami was bad," Holm muttered as another driver swerved sharply around us, laying on the horn as he went.

"It is bad," I countered as visions of perpetually gridlocked streets flashed across my mind. "People here seem to take it personally, though."

I pulled off the road and onto a parking deck. We

were still several blocks from the station, but I didn't want to take the risk of trying to find a spot closer. I also just didn't want to drive for any longer than I had to. It was amazing that we hadn't been involved in a crash yet, and I knew that Diane was liable to kill us if we managed to wreck another car while in the field.

"You think we should find a hotel here?" Holm asked as I pulled the car into a spot near the exit. "Assuming it takes us an hour or so to speak to the cops, it'll probably start getting dark by the time we finish."

"That might be a good idea," I replied.

"I'll give Diane a call then," Holm replied as we both got out of the car.

Even from inside the parking garage, I could hear the sounds of the city: car horns, shouts, and the faint thrum of construction going on somewhere nearby. They were all sounds I'd heard plenty of times on the occasions that I'd come up here to see Tessa, and something about the din made me think of her. As Holm and I made our way down the crowded street toward the station, it occurred to me that it might be nice to pay her a visit if we ended up having some spare time.

I was brought back to reality as we passed a man sitting at the entrance of one of the buildings. Though the temperature was cold enough for pockets of snow to be on the ground, the man was wearing little more than a threadbare wool coat, and one of his shoes was missing its sole. He was slumped over and barely looked conscious, but his eyes were open, and his gaze briefly met mine as we walked past. I frowned as I wondered if that was the kind of life that Logan Clearwater had been living up until the day of his demise. Unfortunately, the homeless were a pretty prime target for becoming the victims of crime. They lived on the outskirts of society, and most people just passed them by without sparing them a second thought. Whoever had killed Clearwater might have specifically chosen him because he knew he was unlikely to be missed.

Then again, that only made the fact that he'd mysteriously turned up on a remote Caribbean island all the more confusing. After all, if your goal was to ensure that your crime went undetected, dumping the body somewhere where it was sure to be found like that was a pretty stupid choice. I tucked that thought away in the back of my mind for later as Holm and I entered the police station.

The inside of the station looked pretty dull in shades of white and pale gray. It was also quiet, and the only sounds that permeated the uncomfortable silence were the faint clicking of keys and the occasional low murmur. It didn't feel particularly welcoming, and my first thought was that I would hate to work in such a suffocating place. The female officer sitting at the desk up front looked at us with a cheerful smile as we approached.

"Good afternoon," she greeted us warmly. Her inviting demeanor was a stark contrast to the austere atmosphere of the station. "Did you need some help with something?"

"Yes, I'm Agent Marston," I replied as I pulled my badge out of my pocket to show her. "This is my partner, Agent Holm. We're with MBLIS, an investigative agency that takes on international crimes. We need some information about a man who was arrested by officers here about three months ago."

"Well, let me see," the officer responded as she turned to her computer and typed something in. "I'm not sure I have access to that kind of information... No, it looks like I don't. Hang on just a minute, and I'll get someone who can help you with that."

She smiled at us again before standing and walking off further into the back of the station. She returned a few moments later with another officer in tow, an older gentleman who, judging by the slight variation of his uniform, was a higher rank.

"Hello, I'm Sergeant Kopernick," the man introduced himself to us. "I heard that you had some questions. Why don't we go talk somewhere privately?"

"We'd appreciate that," I replied as I reached forward to shake the sergeant's hand.

After getting through the pleasantries, he turned and led us further into the station.

"So, what exactly did you want to know?" He turned to look at me as the three of us walked onto the busy main floor of the station.

Officers in uniform sat at neatly arranged desks set up in clean rows. It wasn't unlike the setup back at the office at home, but it seemed somewhat colder here. There was a tension in the air that I couldn't quite place, like a cord ready to snap at the slightest provocation. The faces of the officers working in the large room were strained with worry and stress.

Probably understaffed and overworked, I thought to myself as we walked by. It didn't excuse the fact that they'd lost track of Clearwater, but it did perhaps explain how it had happened. They seemed to be a bunch of officers already stressed out and exhausted. If they'd been tasked with watching over a seemingly harmless old man, it was possible he'd just slipped beneath everyone's radar.

"We need information about a perp who was held here for a short while," I answered. "We believe he's the victim of our current case. His name was Logan Clearwater."

"Clearwater?" The man frowned in confusion before cracking a smile. "I'm sorry, gentlemen. I'm afraid I will need a little more than a name to work with. We get dozens of new cases every day. Can you give me some more information? Dates, maybe? What kind of crime are we talking about here?"

He led us through a winding maze of desks as we made our way to a narrow staircase at the opposite end of the large bullpen we'd just passed through.

"Three months ago," I replied as we made our way up the stairs. "A homeless man was arrested for shoplifting from a boutique just a few blocks from here. He had dementia." I stopped short as we made it to the top of the stairs. "Your officers *lost* him after discovering that he was listed as a missing person."

Kopernick snapped his head around to look at me, his eyes wide with shock for a moment before his face lit up with realization.

"Ah, right." He pursed his lips together as he looked around awkwardly, as though afraid that someone might have overheard my accusation. "Of course, I remember Mr. Clearwater. That was a, uh... a terrible miscommunication. Something that never should have happened, of course."

"We're going to need some more details," I replied dryly.

I could tell by the look on his face that the sergeant knew precisely who I was talking about now, and I really couldn't bring myself to feel bad for him. Not when Clearwater was dead now, possibly due to his officers' ineptitude.

"Of course." Kopernick nodded stiffly. "Why don't

we go speak in my office?"

He clamped his mouth shut tightly after that and gestured for us to walk through a small doorway that separated the management offices from the rest of the station. After Holm and I stepped through, he guided us to an office a few steps away.

"Wait here, if you don't mind," he muttered quietly. "I'll go and get the arresting officer from the case."

He turned and opened his office door to let us inside before walking off, back down the stairs, and into the bullpen.

The sergeant's office wasn't quite as morose feeling as the rest of the station. Though still gray and utilitarian, a cartoon bobblehead set on the desk and a collection of colorful children's drawings taped to the wall behind the desk gave the small office a hint of life.

"Sorry about that, agents," Kopernick huffed as he returned to the office, accompanied by another man. The new officer was a bit younger, and he looked a little green as he stepped into the office. His eyes were wide, and the tendons in his neck were tense, as though he was very nervous about something. "This is Officer Naples. He was the one who brought the elderly man in." He turned to look at us. "That *is* who you're here about, right? Homeless old man, about six foot, seemed confused about where he was?"

"That sounds like him," I replied.

"That's what I thought," Kopernick replied as he

walked past us to his desk. "Please, have a seat, and we can talk."

"Thanks," I replied as I took a seat in one of the chairs opposite the desk. Holm did the same, while Naples moved to stand by the sergeant's desk,

"His daughter was pretty upset after the incident," Kopernick remarked.

"You mean after you lost track of him?" I asked dryly.

Maybe it was a little mean of me to phrase it so bluntly, but I was irked by the fact that they'd literally lost track of a confused elderly man who'd been in their custody. Maybe if they hadn't dropped the ball, Clearwater would still be alive today.

"Yes," Kopernick replied reluctantly. "That is, unfortunately, what happened. There was a miscommunication. An officer who believed that someone else had taken over watching him left for the day, and the officer who was meant to be watching him misunderstood and left the vicinity as well."

"And one of those officers was Naples?" I surmised as I looked over at the young officer. He stiffened under my accusatory gaze, and he looked like he wanted to run from the room.

"It was my fault," he admitted nervously. "I should have double-checked to make sure someone was watching him."

"Well, that's true," Kopernick muttered. "But there's

not much that can be done now, I'm afraid. In any case, what did you want to speak to us about? Has something happened to Mr. Clearwater?"

"He's dead," I replied flatly.

Both of their eyes went wide in unison as their jaws dropped open. It would have been funny if it was a remotely laughing matter.

"Are you serious?" Naples gaped at me. If he'd looked nervous before, he looked even worse now. His face was pale, and he'd broken out into a cold sweat.

"I'm afraid so," I replied. "His body was found a few days ago, and it was positively identified through DNA. The only thing is that it was discovered somewhere it really shouldn't have been. As far as we can tell, the officers here were the last people to see him alive, so it's important that we know exactly what happened that day."

For a few moments, there was nothing but tense silence.

"I see," Kopernick finally replied. "Well, it started around noon, if I recall correctly. Is that right, Naples?"

"Yes," he replied as he shifted uneasily from one foot to the other. "We got a call from this upscale children's clothing store that a man had stormed in and started trying to steal things off the shelves."

"A children's store?" I raised an eyebrow at him. "That seems like an odd choice. Did he have any kids with him?"

"No." Naples shook his head. "He was completely alone when we arrived, yelling about how he needed the clothes for his friend."

"He was probably confused," Holm muttered sadly. "So, you arrested him?"

"Well, yes," Naples replied. "He was pretty combative when we got there. He started throwing punches, and he was pretty strong for a guy that age. But we weren't aggressive or anything. And once we realized that he was having cognition issues, we took him out of the cell and let him sit out in the bullpen." He paused and then looked awkwardly down at the ground. "Then again, I guess doing that was part of the reason he was able to slip away so easily. We didn't want him in the cage with all the drunks and drugged-out users, so we brought him out to sit at my desk. He was actually pretty mellow once we got back to the station. He asked for a glass of orange juice and told us we were doing a good job." His face crumpled as he recalled what had happened, and I could tell that he felt guilty.

"So, what happened after that?" I asked.

"Like the sergeant was saying earlier," Naples responded, "there was a mixup during the shift change. I thought Officer Lopez knew that he was supposed to be watching him, so I left. I mistakenly assumed that someone else had already told him."

"When Ms. Clearwater arrived to pick him up,"

Kopernick continued, "we went to fetch him, and Lopez had no idea that he was even meant to have been watching him. Apparently, everyone assumed that someone else had passed on the information."

"And in the end, no one did," I replied flatly. I understood that mistakes happen, but it was a little ridiculous that they could have messed up this badly, and now a man was dead.

"I won't make excuses," Kopernick replied seriously. "This was our error, and I take full responsibility for the mistakes of my officers. I'm extremely saddened to hear about what happened to Mr. Clearwater, and if there's anything that we can do, we'll do it."

At the very least, they both had the decency to look ashamed about what happened. And it seemed that they genuinely felt remorseful, so I supposed that I couldn't hold it entirely against them.

"I appreciate that," I replied. "To start, could you give us the name and address of the store where Clearwater was arrested? I'd like to speak to the employees. It's possible that one of them saw or heard something from Clearwater that could help us figure out more about him."

"Sure," Kopernick replied as he tore a page off a notepad that was set on his desk.

As he scribbled down the information, I couldn't help but feel that this mystery just kept going deeper and deeper.

6

ETHAN

THE STORE that Kopernick had sent us to was a small, fancy shop in lower Manhattan. The moment I saw it, it occurred to me again just how strange a choice this would be for Clearwater to rob. Food, money, and adult-sized clothing would make sense, but overpriced toddler dresses? It was bizarre, and it made me think that Clearwater must have been having some kind of episode when he attempted to shoplift. In my opinion, it made the fact that the police had failed to get him home to his family all the sadder.

"Welcome to L'enfant!" an attendant called out to us as Holm and I walked into the store. She looked up at us from the tiny shirts she was folding with impressive precision and speed without ever faltering. "Can I help you find something this afternoon?"

"Not exactly," I replied as I walked toward her. The

inside of the store was just as ostentatious as the front facade. All the clothes were displayed delicately along low tables or hung on sleek metal racks along the walls. "My name is Agent Marston. This is my partner, Agent Holm, and we're with an organization called MBLIS. We wanted to ask about a man who was here a few months ago. He attempted to shoplift some clothes, and the police were called."

"Agents?" The young woman finally stopped folding, and the shirt she'd been holding crumpled into a ball on the table. "Like, in the FBI?"

"Kind of," Holm replied. It was a question we'd gotten before from people who were unfamiliar with us, and though not an exact comparison, it was an easy shorthand to explain the kind of things we did. "Our agency is called MBLIS, though."

"Wow, that's... scary," she muttered as she looked up at us apprehensively. "But, um, I just started working here a few weeks ago, so I don't know anything about an arrest. I can go ask my boss, Katrina, about it, though."

"Please do," I replied.

The girl nodded and scurried off toward the back. I could just make her out through the door at the back of the shop. She fidgeted nervously as she spoke to someone I couldn't quite see from where I was standing. A few seconds later, she walked quickly back to the front of the store, this time accompanied by another woman.

The woman who I assumed was her boss was tall, with sharp, defined features and long, platinum blond hair that she had pulled up into a tight, severe ponytail. She was wearing a gray wool skirt suit, and she walked with a poised and confident gait.

"Good afternoon," she greeted us with a smile, though it seemed oddly strained and unnatural. "Jolene tells me that you gentlemen have some questions for me."

"Yes," I replied as I looked around the store. There weren't any other customers inside, but talking about this out in the open didn't really seem like a good idea. "Is there somewhere else we can talk about this? An office, maybe? I wouldn't want to disturb your—"

"Agent, we are really too busy for this," she cut me off rudely. "Please ask me what you need to ask so we can move on with our day."

I stared back at her in stunned surprise for a moment, taken aback by her antagonistic response. I was used to suspects acting defensive, but it was a little strange to be hit with so much opposition from a mere witness.

"Alright," I replied. "Three months ago, you called the police on a man who was attempting to take clothes from this store without paying. We'd like to know what happened that day."

"Well, I'd much rather forget about it entirely," the woman huffed. "But if you must know, yes. That... abhorrent person rushed in here, in the middle of a busy morning, mothers in the store shopping with their little ones, and he just began grabbing things!" She scrunched up her nose as if just the memory of the man made her want to throw up. "Sticking his filthy hands into all of our clothes! And as if that wasn't enough, then he tried to just walk out the door with it all! Can you imagine? The nerve of him." She shook her head in disgust, and though she was technically in the right, I couldn't help but feel put off by her attitude.

"So, that's when you called the police?" I asked.

"Of course!" she exclaimed. "That vile man was terrorizing my customers! I guess I shouldn't be surprised, though. The entire street's gone down the drain ever since that homeless camp popped up a few blocks away!"

"There's a homeless camp?" I asked. "Is that where Mr. Clearwater came from?"

"Probably," she scoffed. "I knew from the moment I saw them the first time that it was only a matter of time until they spread everywhere, and just look!" She crossed her arms and rolled her eyes. "The city should have done more about them the moment they started to settle down in that old building! Then maybe we wouldn't have had to deal with one of them barging in here!"

"And where exactly is this camp?" I asked.

Her snobby attitude was grating on my nerves, and I was, frankly, ready to get out of here as quickly as possible.

"Four blocks down," she replied primly. "Just off Thirteenth Street. It's impossible to miss them. Especially considering the smell—"

"Okay, thank you so much for your time, Ms. Katrina," I cut her off before she could continue her abrasive diatribe. "We really appreciate it. Let's go, Agent Holm."

Holm nodded to the two women before turning to follow me out of the shop.

"Goodbye," the owner called as we walked away, and though it was only a single word, somehow it felt impossibly passive-aggressive.

"Wow," Holm snorted the moment we were back on the street. "She seemed nice."

"Yeah," I replied sarcastically. "Seems like a really kind and understanding person. Anyway, at least we got some useful information from her. If Clearwater really did come from that homeless camp, then the people there might know something about him."

"You think they'll be willing to talk to us?" Holm sighed. "People living on the fringes of society tend not to be the most friendly toward law enforcement."

"We'll just have to see," I replied as we made our

way down toward where the shop owner had directed us.

Though the fancy little store was located in a relatively upscale part of the city, it was jarring just how quickly the surrounding scenery seemed to decline just from one street to the other. As we got closer to our destination, I noticed that the buildings began to look a little less maintained and the roads a little dirtier. The kinds of people I saw walking around were different as well. Gone were the businessmen in their slick suits and the sharply dressed women carrying shopping bags on each arm. Instead, all I saw in the area surrounding the abandoned building where the homeless camp was were people who looked like they'd hit rock bottom.

The camp itself was only partially located inside the building, which was half demolished and appeared to have been victim to a fire at some point. The entire left side of the building was blackened and charred, and some parts of the wall and roof appeared to be missing entirely. A large scaffolding wrapped around the building, with several "condemned" and "do not enter" signs adorning its metal bars. That obviously hadn't stopped the homeless community from moving in, though, as I could see several of them sitting around the perimeter of the building, spilling out of its main entrance and even inside the alley just beside it.

As Holm and I approached the alley where most of

the residents appeared to be congregated, many of them got up and scurried away without a word. The ones who stayed barely seemed to notice our presence, not bothering to look up at us or otherwise move at all. It looked like Holm was probably going to be right about us encountering problems in our attempt to question the local populace.

We couldn't just give up, though. The odds were high that someone here knew Clearwater, or at least knew of him. Either way, we needed to do whatever we could to find out as much as possible. I stepped forward to address the crowd at large, but before I could say anything, someone called out from my right.

"Whatever you're thinking of doing, you probably shouldn't bother," the man said. He looked like he was in his late forties or fifties, and he was leaning back against the wall of the alley with a half-finished cigarette dangling from between his fingers.

"Oh?" I turned to look at him. "And why do you say that?"

The man let out a laugh somewhere between a wheeze and a cackle.

"Are you kidding me?" he snickered. "You two might as well have a couple of flashing neon signs over your heads that say 'COP'! Ain't nobody going to talk to a pair of police officers. Whatever foolishness you came here for, you might as well just turn around and leave." He closed his eyes and took a long drag of his cigarette.

"We're looking for someone," I explained.

"Well, good for you," the man cackled. "Still doesn't change what I said. Matter of fact, it might actually make it worse. Do you think anyone around here is going to squeal on one of our own? You must be crazy."

"It isn't like that," I protested as I tried to level with the man. "Someone's been killed—"

"Killed?!" the man exclaimed, laughing again as though it was the funniest thing he'd ever heard. "Now I know you're crazy. You're talking about murder here, and you really think anyone's going to get involved with that? Hell nah. You two should just turn around and get out of here."

"We're not going to just give up," Holm chimed in.

"That's right," I added. "We aren't just going to turn our backs on him. At the very least, we owe it to the man's family to get some justice for him."

"Well, that's damned decent of you." The man raised an eyebrow at me before taking another drag of his cigarette. "Been a while since I met a decent cop. I gotta say, I'm pleasantly surprised."

"We're not cops," Holm replied. "We're federal agents."

"Six of one is half a dozen of the other," the man scoffed. "But I guess that ain't so bad then. Now, let me ask you this: who exactly are you two looking for?

What makes you think someone here knows anything? I mean, take a look around." He nodded down the length of the alley. "Don't nobody here know much of anything, to be honest with you."

"Logan Clearwater," I replied. "Seventy-two years old, about six foot. We have reason to believe that he used to be a regular around here."

"Logan?" The man looked up at us in shock. "He's who you're looking for? Now that I think about it, it's been a while since I've seen old Logan around—" He stopped short, his eyes going wide as realization dawned on him. "Wait. You said that this was a murder case, right?" He looked expectantly between Holm and me.

"I'm afraid so," I replied. "His body was found a few days ago."

"No..." the man whispered, shaking his head sadly. "Damn, that's a shame. Logan was a nice man. A bit messed up in the head, you know? But he was a cool guy, always looking out for the newcomers, acting like he was everyone's dad."

"He sounds nice," I replied. "We heard that he was involved in some kind of shoplifting incident. Do you know anything about that?"

"Oh, yeah," the man rolled his eyes. "They blew all that out of proportion! Old Logan was just trying to help. We had this woman arrive a few months back. Nina, her name was, I think. Anyway, she was pregnant. I mean, this chick was ready to pop. It's not a good situation to be in when you're about to have a kid, no home, no money, no nothing. Anyway, Logan was worried about her. He kept mumbling to himself and anyone else who would listen about how she would get food? And diapers? And clothes? I swear Logan was more worried about this girl's baby than she was. Anyway, one day he gets into one of his weird moods. He used to get all loopy and start doing crazy stuff. So, he goes off to this store and just starts taking stuff for the baby, you know? Man, when he came back from the police station and told everyone about how he escaped, I could barely believe what I was hearing."

"So, he did make it back here after that?" I asked.

"Oh, yeah." The man laughed. "Hell, he wouldn't shut up about it for a while. Going on and on about how he outsmarted the cops and managed to slip away when they weren't looking. I always thought that part might have been a fib, but what do I know?"

I frowned. So, now we knew that Clearwater had at least made it back here after his arrest. That didn't shed any light on what had ultimately happened to him, though. If anything, it just raised more questions since now it seemed unlikely that either his initial disappearance or the arrest had anything to do with his death.

"Can you remember the last time you saw him?" Holm asked.

"Well, let me think..." the man muttered as he snuffed out the cigarette on the ground before reaching up to scratch his head. "It was a few weeks ago, I think. Yeah! I remember now; it was right after that other guy showed up."

"Another guy?" I repeated. "So, there was a newcomer?"

"Sure was." The man nodded. "Annoying, too. One of those yuppie types that think they're better than the rest of us. I could tell from the moment he got here, looking down his nose at everyone as if he wasn't in the same boat." The man rolled his eyes. "Anyway, Logan was nice to him, as usual. He invited him to stay in the parking garage over on the other side of the street. That's usually where he stayed. Logan liked his privacy."

"Over there?" I asked as I looked off at the garage beside the wide, dark alley on the other side of the street. I could see the silhouettes of a few people sitting inside the alley.

"Yeah, but you ain't gonna find anything there," he replied. "It's been picked clean by now. That's what happens around here when you're not around to guard your crap. It gets taken."

"I see," I replied disappointedly.

"I can't believe I never thought of that," the man muttered lowly. "Logan disappeared just as soon as that other guy showed up. I never made the connection, but do you think maybe that guy had something to do with it?"

I pursed my lips together as I thought about it myself. It was certainly possible. In fact, the strange circumstances actually made this mystery man our prime suspect, if he was really the last person that Clearwater interacted with before he went missing.

"A stranger shows up, and Clearwater disappears the next day?" Holm shot me a knowing look, and I knew that he was coming to the same conclusions that I was. "Certainly sounds like he might have had something to do with it to me."

"Y'all are all wrong!" a female voice suddenly rang out, breaking through our conversation.

"Dorris, did anyone ask you for your opinion?" The man turned to look at the woman, who stood up from where she was sitting just a few feet away to walk over to us. She was wearing a purple puffer coat, and her long dreadlocks hung down around her sharp face.

"Shut up, Carter," Dorris scoffed at him before turning to look at us. "That guy that showed up didn't kill Logan. The dude had a bum leg. He probably wouldn't have been able to take down a baby, much less a man like Logan. Logan was old, but he was a retired Marine. I saw him fight his way out of his fair share of scrapes in his time here."

"And you're absolutely sure the new guy wasn't the

one who killed Logan Clearwater?" I asked. "Are you saying that you know who did?"

"That's exactly what I'm saying," the young woman replied. "I know 'cause I was there that night. I saw them. It was two men who did it, just like they did with everyone else."

"What do you mean by 'everyone else'?" I asked as an uncomfortable feeling began to build in the pit of my stomach.

"I mean that this isn't the first time that someone's gone missing around here," Dorris replied firmly. "Someone out there is hunting us down."

7

ETHAN

"Dorris, don't tell them that bull—" Carter groaned.

"It's not bull!" Dorris snapped at him. "It's true! Just cause you'd rather sit here all day and pretend like it's not happening doesn't mean it isn't!" She turned to look at us again. "It's true. People have been coming here for a while now. They show up in the middle of the night and snatch people away. I've seen it happen before, and I saw it happen that night to Logan and the new guy."

"Okay, slow down a minute," I replied. "I believe you, but I need you to start from the beginning."

"There ain't nothing to say!" Carter insisted as he sat up to glare at Dorris. "People go 'missing' around here all the time. It doesn't mean anything! It's not like any of us got homes to come back to or anything.

People come and go. That doesn't mean there's some killer out there whacking people."

"Uh-huh," Dorris looked at him with disgust. "Keep living in denial. One of these days, you're probably going to end up just like them."

"Dorris," I called the woman's name to get her attention off of Carter and back onto us. "That's your name, right? We believe you. We want to hear more about it."

"See? They believe me." She made a face at Carter before turning back to us. "As I said, people around here disappear sometimes. And sure, sometimes they just leave, like Carter says, but sometimes it's different. When people leave, usually they take their stuff with them. They'll say goodbye, or even if they don't, someone will notice them leaving. That doesn't happen with the others, though. One day, we wake up, and they're just gone." She looked down at the ground as she hugged her coat tighter around herself. "I had a friend. We were thick as thieves. We shared everything with each other, and I mean everything. When one of us had cash or food, we always split it. We looked out for each other. He was my best friend..." She bit her lip as she swayed vacantly from one foot to the other, her eyes wide and haunted. "One night, he said he got a tip about a job opportunity. It wasn't much, but it was enough for him to make some cash. Then he left and just... never came back. I waited for a few days, thinking maybe he was just busy with the job. My dumb self was actually excited about it. But then days passed, and he just never came back to me."

"He probably took the money and ran," Carter grumbled beneath his breath.

"No, he didn't!" Dorris screeched at him. "Vince wouldn't have done that! We were in this together. Even if he decided to leave, he would have said something. I know there's just no way that he would just abandon me like that." She reached up and rubbed furiously at her eyes with the back of her hand. "Anyway, I knew right then that something was wrong, that someone must have taken him or hurt him or something. Then, that night out at the parking garage, I saw them with my own eyes."

"The people who've been attacking you?" I asked.

"Yeah," she confirmed.

"What parking garage are you talking about?" Holm clarified.

"Oh, there's this place across the street," she explained. "It shuts down at midnight and doesn't open up again until seven in the morning. There's usually a guard on duty, but sometimes they're asleep, and other times there's no one there at all. On those nights, sometimes a few of us will go over there to sleep. It's a little warmer than here and a lot drier too, on nights that it snows."

"I see," I replied. "And you and Logan both went there?"

"Not together," she replied. "But yeah. It was snowing pretty hard that night, so I headed over there. When I got inside, I saw that Logan and the new guy were there too. I didn't really feel like talking or anything, though, so I decided to just find my own corner to sleep in. I'd been sleeping for a little while when I heard them."

"The attackers?" I asked.

"Yeah," she replied with a shudder. "I didn't know at first what had woken me up. Then I heard the sounds. Like scraping and yelling. I got up and looked toward where I'd last seen Logan and the other guy at the other end of the deck. They were fighting against these two big guys, and they were losing."

"Do you remember what they looked like?" I asked anxiously.

This was our first significant lead. If this attack had only taken place a few weeks ago, then odds were high that these mystery men had something to do with Clearwater's death.

"No." Dorris shook her head, to my immense disappointment. "Sorry. The truth is, I was so scared that I ran as soon as I saw what was happening. I wish I'd stayed to help, but I'm five-foot-one. What the heck was I supposed to do against two grown men twice my size?"

"You did the right thing," I assured her. Though it definitely didn't help us, in reality, she probably would have gotten hurt if she'd attempted to do anything against the two men.

"Well, it doesn't feel like it," she muttered morosely. "Feels like I left two decent guys to die on their own. In fact, I felt so bad about it that I ended up going back to check on them later, and you know what I found? Nothing! They were gone, no bodies or anything! The moment I saw that, I knew that the same thing had probably happened to my friend, Vince. Suddenly, I start remembering all the other times folks around here suddenly disappeared without any warning. It's like Carter said, we always just assumed they'd decided to move on and find somewhere else to be, but now I'm not so sure."

I wasn't either. On the contrary, I suspected that she was right and that Clearwater had been stolen away. That much was evident from the fact that we'd found his body hundreds of miles away, out in the middle of the Caribbean. For what purpose he'd been taken, we still didn't know. On top of that, we also had another victim now, this "new guy" who had apparently been attacked alongside Clearwater. We'd found Clearwater's body, so where was this other man?

"Do you know what the new guy's name was?" I asked Dorris. "The man that was with Clearwater when they were attacked."

"No," she replied with a shrug. "No idea. The guy was only here for a day."

"Wesley," Carter spoke up from where he was still sitting on the ground. He'd lit up another cigarette and had already worked his way through half of it as he listened to our conversation. "His name was Wesley. I heard him and Logan talking before they headed off to the parking garage. No last name, though, at least not that I heard."

"Wesley," I repeated. It wasn't much to go off, but it was something. "Alright, thanks." I turned to look at Dorris. "So, did you ever report what you saw to the police?"

"Yeah," she snorted. "You want to guess as to how that went?" She rolled her eyes. "They told me they'd look into it and then basically shoved me out of the building. They don't care about people like us. Heck, they were probably relieved that there were two less of us for them to deal with."

"I'm sorry that happened," I replied, genuinely sympathetic that she'd had to experience that when she was only trying to get help for her friends.

She just shrugged.

"Not like I'm surprised," she muttered. "Police treat us like dirt. I'm surprised you two are going through so much effort to find the killer of some bum."

"Well, regardless of who or what he was, he

deserves justice," I replied. "We're going to make sure he gets it."

"Yeah, well, I really hope you figure out who did this," Dorris replied as she took a look around the crowded alley. "For all our sakes."

8

ETHAN

AFTER SPEAKING with Dorris and Carter at the home-less camp, Holm and I went to have some lunch and talk over what we knew. We also needed to call Diane to update her on everything that had happened so far.

We picked a spot almost at random. The extensive menu posted outside seemed to have a large variety of dishes available, so it seemed like as good a place as any for us to stop and recharge while we figured out what to do next. We were seated at a table on the second floor with a lovely view of the city. The sun was just beginning to set, and I could see people down on the street, rushing to their destinations. I noticed immediately that, rather than dwindling, the crowd appeared to have grown larger as the sun fell. I supposed that was why they called New York the city that never sleeps.

Holm offered to be the one to call Diane again, so I took the opportunity to look through the menu. The available selection really was enormous, and I wondered vaguely how the chef managed to keep up when customers could order such a wide variety of dishes. They even had breakfast foods available at all hours, which I found myself gravitating toward as I listened to Holm speaking on the phone.

"Okay," Holm declared a few minutes later as he set his phone down on the table. "Diane's all up to speed, and she got us a hotel not too far from here."

"That's good," I replied as I turned to look out the window. "Maybe we should just walk there. It looks like it's actually getting more congested the later it gets, and I'd really rather not move the car if we don't have to."

"Smart idea," Holm agreed as he turned to look at his menu just as a server walked up to our table.

"Good evening," the young woman greeted us politely. "Can I get you guys started on some drinks, or would you like a minute?"

"I'm actually ready to order," Holm replied as he looked up at me.

"Yeah, me too," I added.

"Oh, excellent," the young woman nodded as she slipped a notepad out of her pocket. "What will it be tonight then?"

I'd been tempted enough by the breakfast offerings

that I ended up ordering a steak and eggs dish, while Holm went a more traditional dinner route by ordering ribs. The server quickly jotted down our orders before rushing back downstairs to where the kitchen was. As we waited, Holm and I talked a little about our theories on the case so far. Though we both agreed that Clearwater had definitely been kidnapped, we couldn't agree to the "why" of the situation.

We were still discussing it when our food arrived, at which point we both fell silent as we dug into our meals. It was often easy to just forget to eat while we were out on a mission. When a new threat or challenge popped up unexpectedly every few minutes, there just wasn't often time to sit and eat like this. While we were investigating, most of our meals tended to be quick and usually of the greasy, fast food variety. It was a horrible diet to live on, but it was the only thing that worked most of the time.

"So, someone is hunting down New York's homeless..." I muttered as I stabbed my fork into a piece of egg and scraped it idly across my plate.

"Yep," Holm replied. "Though maybe not all of New York." He looked out at the street just below us. "Dorris said that she knew of several people that had mysteriously gone missing recently, right? Well, that means that they must all be from this same area."

"That's a good point," I replied. "Of course, there may be more she just doesn't know about, but I think you're onto something with that. Lower Manhattan may be the perps' main hunting ground." I set my fork down and leaned back in my chair. "Now, if only we could figure out what the purpose of this hunt is. It's not just to kill them. That much is certain because we would have found some bodies if that was the case. From how Dorris explained it, they just disappear entirely."

"So, the kidnappers are moving the victims to a secondary location," Holm surmised as he crumpled up a napkin inside his hand. "But then still killing them, anyway? Clearwater was dead, after all, and from the looks of it, he'd been beaten pretty badly, so what's the game here?"

"I wish I knew," I muttered as I tried to work out the most logical explanation as to why the perps would go through the effort of kidnapping the victims just to kill them. "It's not like they're doing this for a ransom. They're taking homeless people without any money, or likely any family."

"It really doesn't make sense," Holm sighed as he ran a hand through his hair.

"Maybe it's—" I started to say, but I was distracted by something outside the window before I could finish my thought.

"Hm?" Holm furrowed his eyebrows at me in confusion. "Maybe, what now?"

"Something's happening," I muttered as I watched

the suspicious scene unfold. A woman was standing at an ATM on the street below, flanked on either side by two large men. She was visibly nervous, even from a distance, which was what had caught my attention in the first place. She kept looking around nervously. Her shoulders were also tense and hunched up like she was trying to shield herself from something. The men, too, were acting strangely. They were also looking around, but it was different from how the woman was doing it. It seemed more like they were looking out for something, like they were making sure no one was looking their way.

"Do you see what I see?" I asked Holm, who nodded as he looked out the window toward the trio.

"Something's wrong," he replied. "The woman looks like she's scared."

"Yeah, she does," I agreed as I continued to observe their interaction. One of the men leaned down to say something to the woman, who shrunk in even further on herself as she took bills out of the ATM.

"I think she's being coerced," I noted with alarm as I stood up from the table, slapping a handful of bills down as I did.

Holm got up as well, and without another word, the two of us raced down the stairs and out of the restaurant.

We ran down the street toward where the woman and the two men were fortunately still standing. Now that we were closer, I could definitely see something was wrong. The woman stared down at the ground, refusing to make eye contact with either man. She was literally shaking as she stood between them. I moved forward to confront the men, but Holm beat me to the punch.

"Excuse me!" he called out firmly as he approached the trio. The two men frowned at him immediately, while the woman looked at him like he was a lifeline and she was out in the water. "Is something going on here?"

"What's that supposed to mean?" one of the men growled as he stepped aggressively toward Holm. He was puffing out his chest and doing a lot of tough-guy posturing, but I could tell it was all talk and that Holm would be able to take the man down quickly if it came to that.

"Yeah, why don't you just mind your own business?" the other man sneered.

The woman's face fell as though she was scared that Holm might actually do as they asked and abandon her.

"Okay." Holm raised an eyebrow at the two men. "Why don't you just give the lady her money back, and we'll let you two screw off with a warning?"

"A warning?" the first of the two men to come forward snickered. "Who the hell do you think you are coming over here and trying to threaten us?" I swiftly pulled my badge out of my pocket to show them exactly who we were.

"Federal agents," I replied dryly. "Don't try to deny that you were just coercing this woman into withdrawing money from her bank account to give to you. We saw it all go down, so why don't you just—"

"Hey, screw you!" the first man screamed as he grabbed the woman roughly by the arm before shoving her to the ground.

Holm leapt forward instinctively and managed to catch her just before she hit the hard pavement. The two men turned and took off with the woman's money, and I immediately gave chase.

"Stop!" I yelled as I ran at full force toward the two men.

The streets were crowded enough that I had to be careful as I weaved around all the bystanders, but I was still fast and quickly gaining on the two. The second man turned to sneer at me over his shoulder, an action that caused him to lose sight of where he was going. He crashed directly into a young couple walking hand in hand and tumbled to the ground right in front of me. The first man, the one that was holding the woman's money, stopped to turn around and look at his friend just as I reached down to grab him. It seemed like he wanted to come and help but thought better of it in the end and just took off to save his own skin.

I swore under my breath and considered letting go

of the fallen suspect to pursue the other one, but before I could even make a decision, a blur of movement and color flashed past me. It was Holm, sprinting at full speed toward the remaining suspect.

I watched as he caught up to the man at lightning speed. The suspect turned around, but Holm was already on top of him before he could even react, tackling him to the ground like a linebacker. The money thief cried out in pain as he hit the ground hard, and I breathed a sigh of relief, knowing that neither of the two thugs had managed to get away.

9

HOLM

HOLM DOVE FORWARD without even thinking about it. He'd honestly been struck dumb with shock as he watched the large man ruthlessly shove the defenseless woman to the ground, so it came as a surprise even to him when he suddenly found himself on the ground with his arms wrapped around her slight frame.

She'd cried out with fear and surprise first as she'd been pushed and then again as Holm had caught her. She was silent now, though, as she stared up at him.

"Are you okay?" Holm asked her as he quickly checked her for any visible injuries.

"I'm alright," she replied. There was a slight lilt to her voice as she spoke, and Holm thought he could detect a hint of Italian in her accent.

For a moment, the two just stared at each other. Then the woman suddenly seemed to come to her senses because she pulled herself out of Holm's embrace before getting unsteadily back onto her feet, the heels of her stiletto shoes clicking against the pavement as she did.

"I'm fine, but—Those men took my money." Her face crumpled as she looked off in the direction that the two perps and Marston had run.

"Don't worry," Holm reassured her as he jumped to his feet. "I'm going to get it back for you."

The words had scarcely left his mouth before he was off, sprinting at full speed through the bustling streets of Manhattan. He bumped into a few passersby on his way, but he didn't let that deter him in the slightest. He merely pushed them out of the way or dodged around them as he continued the chase.

It wasn't long before he could see Marston just up ahead. Holm watched as one of the two thieves careened directly into a pair of civilians before falling to the ground. Marston was upon him in an instant, tackling him harshly to the hard sidewalk before he could get back up. Since his partner had that perp under control, Holm decided to turn his attention toward the other guy. He'd paused for just a moment to check on his buddy but had quickly changed his mind and decided to go on without him. He'd been too slow to evade Holm, though, and only seconds later, Holm was right behind him.

The man turned around just as Holm jumped

toward him, and in the split second, before they collided, the perp's face was so comical that Holm could have laughed. The two of them tumbled to the ground in a graceless heap.

"Get off!" the thief yelled as he struggled to push Holm off.

Holm was too strong, however, and it was clear that the punk didn't have an ounce of any real fight training in his body because all his flailing around didn't bother Holm at all.

"Stop!" Holm growled as he punched the man once in the face.

It was only a single blow, but it had been so tactfully and precisely delivered that the man's eyes had immediately rolled back into his head as his neck lolled like a limp ragdoll's. Holm reached down to grab the wad of bills that was still clutched in the man's hand and snatched it away forcefully before getting back up on his feet.

"Wow," Marston commended him as he sauntered up to where Holm was standing. "You KO'd him in one punch. You really weren't about to let him get away, huh?"

"Not with the woman's money," Holm snorted as he looked past me. "Where's the other guy?"

"Oh, the cops came and took over," Marston replied as he nodded toward a pair of officers that were standing nearby, holding the suspect between them.

"They saw me chase the guy down. Speaking of which—"

Holm followed Marston's line of sight. Another cop was heading toward them now, jogging briskly from across the street.

"We can take it from here," the officer noted, and Holm couldn't help but feel that he sounded just a bit too snobby about it. It wasn't like they'd just swooped in to arrest the perps after he and Marston did all the work or anything.

"Sure," Holm replied as he stepped aside to allow the police officer to take custody of the man.

As annoying as the cop's attitude was, he really didn't care either way who ended up taking the perps into custody. After all, they weren't actually related to his and Marston's case. Furthermore, Holm had more pressing matters weighing on his mind. Namely, he needed to get the victim's money back to her. He turned back in the direction from where they'd come and was shocked to see the woman standing just a short distance away. She was ambling up to them a little awkwardly, the high heels she was wearing making it difficult for her to maintain a steady gait as she approached them as quickly as she could.

"Oh, thank goodness you're alright!" she exclaimed as she finally caught up to the two of them.

She was panting slightly as she walked up to them, and there was a light sheen of sweat on her forehead, as though she'd run here after them. Her hair was askew, and she looked a bit disheveled, but Holm still couldn't quash the thought that she looked stunning all the same. She was wearing a short, black velvet dress over a pair of dark, sheer stockings that showed off her long, shapely legs. Over her dress, she was wearing a turquoise green wool coat that was cinched at the waist to the point that Holm could clearly make out her curvy figure even with the coat on. Wisps of golden brown hair fluttered over her face in the breeze, and Holm had to fight the urge to brush them aside so he could better see her face.

"I was worried something bad might happen," she continued. "I was so shocked when you appeared, and I just stood there. In any case, are you both alright?"

Her voice yanked Holm harshly back into the present, and he felt his face flush red hot as he realized he'd been staring at her.

"We're fine," Holm replied automatically as he stepped forward to offer her the money back. "Here, I managed to get this back from them."

"Thank you!" she exclaimed as she delicately took the wad of bills from his outstretched hand. Her soft fingers brushed lightly against his as she did, and Holm felt a jolt of electricity pass through him even at the faint contact.

Get it together, Holm, he scolded himself mentally. He wasn't some hormonal teenager, so why was he acting all love-struck and goofy? All she'd done was kind of touch his hand for a second. There was no reason for him to be getting worked up.

"You really didn't have to do that, though," she murmured demurely as she tucked the money into the leather purse that was slung over her shoulder. "It's only some money. I would have been much more distraught if anything had happened to either of you. The fact that you two risked your own safety to save me is more than enough. Really, I have no idea how I can thank you."

She smiled up at Holm, and he felt as though his heart skipped a beat. He could have sworn that he could see stars shining in her green eyes, and for a moment, he was struck too dumb to speak.

"It was nothing," Marston stepped forward to reassure her. "We're federal agents. Stopping criminals is part of our job."

"Federal agents?" Her eyebrows shot up as she regarded the two agents with wide, awestruck eyes. "Wow, I've never met anyone like that. Is that an interesting job?"

"That's one way of putting it," Holm cut in before Marston could reply again.

Marston raised an eyebrow at Holm, and a slight, knowing smirk played at his lips.

"Is that right?" the woman smiled, having completely missed the quick, nearly unnoticeable interaction that had taken place between the two men. "Oh! How rude of me. You two did so much to help me, and I haven't even introduced myself yet. My name's Aurora Marino."

"Agent Marston," Marston stepped forward immediately. If Holm was being entirely honest with himself, the action irked him. "And this is my partner, Agent Robbie Holm." Marston gestured toward Holm with a grin. "You should have seen the way he took down the guy who took your money. Tackled him to the ground single-handedly. Isn't that right, Holm?"

"It wasn't such a big deal," Holm replied, already feeling bad that he'd been rather bitterly cursing Marston in his mind just moments earlier.

"Well, I appreciate it all the same," Aurora replied, a shy smile gracing her lips as she looked at Holm. "It was all so scary. One minute, I was minding my own business, just walking down the street and admiring the city's architecture. Before I even knew what was happening, those two men had cornered me against a wall. They offered to take me on a city tour, but I declined. I was doing just fine exploring on my own, and in any case, I got a bad feeling from the two of them the moment they came up to me. They kept insisting, though, and eventually, they got angry. They told me that I had better do what they said if I didn't want to get hurt. Then they dragged me to that ATM and told me to take out as much as the machine would let me. It was awful." Her face crumpled like a withered flower as she bit her lip nervously.

Holm felt horrible for her as he listened to her recount the frightening string of events. Honestly, it wasn't surprising that Aurora had been targeted. She was a woman walking alone, clearly wealthy judging just from her clothes and the expensive designer bag she was carrying, and her accent, though faint, was noticeable enough for anyone to assume that she was probably a foreign tourist. Everything about her made her easy prey for those kinds of lowlifes.

"I'm glad we ran into you when we did," Holm remarked.

"So am I," Aurora replied, and there was a hint of something in her voice that went beyond mere gratitude. A faint, pretty blush dusted the tops of her high cheekbones as she looked at Holm, and he could swear that he could feel himself flushing as well.

"Why don't you escort Aurora back to her hotel, Agent Holm?" Marston suddenly clapped Holm on the shoulder, that same sly smirk from before planted firmly on his face once again. "After what happened, I'm sure she'd appreciate it."

"Oh, I wouldn't want to impose," Aurora replied immediately, putting her hands up in protest. "I mean, that would be lovely, but I'm sure that you must be busy. I've already taken up far too much of your time."

"Not at all," Holm hurried to reassure her. "It's

completely fine, really. You wouldn't be imposing at all."

"Yeah," Marston agreed. "Actually, the timing is perfect because I needed to go and send some, uh, reports back to the office. I can just meet you at the hotel later, Holm."

"That sounds great," Holm agreed at once, not even bothering to put up a token protest.

There were no reports to send, so Holm didn't have any idea what Marston actually intended to do, but he certainly appreciated his friend's willingness to make himself scarce while he took Aurora back to her hotel.

"Well, if you're sure it's fine." Aurora smiled up at Holm again. It was a dazzling enough sight that Holm felt his heart do that unsettling skipped beat thing again, but he didn't really mind. Truth be told, Holm doubted that he could get tired of seeing that smile.

"Of course," Holm replied, unable to keep a small smile from forming on his own face. An instant later, he thought he heard a snort coming from Marston's direction, but he covered it quickly with an awfully convincing cough.

"Well, I'll head off then," Marston declared as he turned to walk away before calling back over his shoulder. "I'll meet up with you at the hotel later!"

Holm watched him go, torn between appreciation that his partner had been considerate enough to bow out and annoyance at the knowledge that Marston was probably going to poke fun at him later over the eyes he and Aurora had been making at each other.

"Should we go then?" Aurora asked him brightly, and all thoughts of Marston were immediately discarded as he turned his attention back to her. "I'm staying at the Four Seasons. I'm actually not sure where that is from here. I wasn't really paying attention as I was wandering, and then those men dragged me around, so I got even more lost."

"Don't worry," Holm replied. "I'm sure we can figure it out between the two of us." He took his phone out of his pocket to plug the hotel's address into a GPS app. "Looks like it's about a twenty-minute walk that way." Holm turned until the map was oriented in the right direction. "We could take the subway if you don't want to walk that much."

"No, I'd rather walk," she replied quickly, a sly smile that was unnervingly similar to Marston's spreading over her face as she moved to stand close at Holm's side. "I could go for a nice walk right now. And besides, that'll give us some time to chat together." She shot him that dazzling, toothy smile again, and Holm vaguely wondered if it was healthy for his heart to experience this many unusual palpitations.

In the end, the walk wound up taking nearly thirty minutes, as neither of the two was in any rush. They chatted about anything and nothing as they strolled down the street together, and eventually, the topic of conversation circled back around to what had happened earlier with the thieves.

"It's my first time in New York," Aurora smiled ruefully. "I have to say, if nothing else, it's certainly been a memorable experience."

"That's one way to put a positive spin on it." Holm laughed.

According to the GPS, they were only a few blocks from the hotel now, and a heavy, reluctant feeling settled over him with every step closer they took.

"Well, I always try to look for the silver linings," Aurora replied. "There are a lot of horrible things in this world, but that doesn't mean we should be sad all the time or let the bad things control us. There's always something to be gained or learned, even from a bad experience."

"That's a nice outlook to have on things," Holm remarked, genuinely impressed by her hopeful demeanor.

In his experience, it was rare to find someone like that who hadn't been jaded to the point of always expecting the worst. On someone else, he might have considered the trait naïve, but Aurora seemed so genuine that he couldn't bring himself to think badly of her.

"I suppose that is a little foolhardy, though," Aurora laughed, as though having heard Holm's thoughts. "Sometimes, I forget just how unkind the world can be.

Take today, for example. The first time I tag along with my father on one of his business trips, and I get myself into a mess like this." She sighed as she looked up at the sky. "I have a difficult enough time convincing him that I'm not a helpless little girl anymore, and then I go and practically get myself kidnapped."

"That could have happened to anyone," Holm argued. "Guys like them are slick. They keep an eye out for people who clearly aren't locals and then dig their claws in. You didn't do anything wrong, so you shouldn't blame yourself for what happened."

"Thank you," she replied as they strolled past a restaurant that had a large canopy tent set up outside the front doors.

Tables lined the sidewalk, and an enticing aroma wafted out onto the street. Holm wished they could stop and get something to eat, or even just a drink. He wasn't really all that hungry since he and Marston had just eaten, but he would have welcomed any excuse to continue his easygoing conversation with Aurora. They'd already stretched this walk out for longer than was really necessary, though, and he was technically still working. He couldn't just abandon the case and Marston to go on a date.

"In any case, I think I'll just keep this little incident a secret," Aurora continued. "He's in New York working on a huge distribution deal, and the last thing I want to do is stress him out any more than he already is."

"What does he do, if you don't mind me asking?" Holm asked curiously. From the way she was talking about huge business deals and, frankly, judging from the expensive clothes she was wearing, Holm couldn't help but wonder just how big this business of his was.

"He owns a wine company," she explained simply. "Well, he and my uncle are co-owners, but my father is the one who runs the business side of things. I'm already inconveniencing him by tagging along on holiday while he's doing work, so I think I'll wait until after his deal goes through before I tell him about what happened."

"Maybe that's for the best," Holm agreed. "And try to steer clear of guys like them from now on. A beautiful woman like you is bound to be an easy target. You probably stand out wherever you go."

The two of them came to a stop in front of the massive hotel building. Aurora looked up at Holm with a shocked expression, and for a moment, Holm worried that he might have been a little too bold. Then she blushed again, her cheeks turning a lovely pink that looked nice against her green eyes.

"Well, I don't know about that," she mumbled bashfully as she reached into her bag. She pulled out a sleek black pen that looked more expensive than a pen had any business being, as well as something that looked kind of like a small dishtowel. "But just in case something happens again, here." She wrote something on the cloth with the pen, and as she handed it to Holm, he realized that what he'd mistakenly assumed was a dishcloth was actually a handkerchief.

Holm's first reaction was surprise that anyone carried handkerchiefs anymore. His second was pleased satisfaction as he read what Aurora had written on it. Scrawled across the embroidered cloth in looped, neat cursive was Aurora's name, and beneath that, she'd written her phone number.

"You should call me sometime." She smirked at him boldly. "That way, I'll have your number too. You know, just in case I need to call for help again."

She zipped her handbag back up and walked smoothly past Holm, tossing him one last sly look over her shoulder as she glided past. Unlike before, when she'd looked awkward and gangly as she attempted to run toward him in her heels, now she walked like a queen as she headed effortlessly through the front doors of the hotel, leaving Holm standing alone on the steps with her soft handkerchief clutched in his hand.

He didn't even try to hold back the smile that formed over his face as he watched her disappear through the entrance. As he rubbed his thumb along the raised embroidery of the handkerchief and willed away the shot of adrenaline that had come coursing through him as she'd handed it to him, he felt determined to ensure that he and Aurora would meet up again.

I SPENT a few minutes wandering around aimlessly after leaving Holm and Aurora together. More than once, as I walked, I laughed to myself as I recalled the way the two of them had stared at each other like a couple of lovesick kids. It wasn't really like Holm to flirt like that while we were on missions. Heck, usually, he was the one making fun of me for my "string of girl-friends" or whatever it was he always liked to say. Not that he never flirted, of course, but Holm generally just tended to focus on the case while we were out in the field. That was why I'd been shocked when he'd not only openly showed interest in Aurora but actually seemed to get irritated when I spoke to her as well.

I grinned as I walked beneath a metal scaffolding set against the side of a building. Vendors had set up tables full of wares beneath it, but I hardly paid them any mind, even as they called out to me to have a look. It wasn't often that I got to see Holm acting jealous, and I fully intended to tease him about it later. Still, I wasn't a jerk, so I'd backed down the moment I'd realized that he seemed interested in speaking with her.

I sighed as I thought about it. Aurora was very pretty, and to be completely honest, I'd had every intention of chatting her up myself until I noticed how well she and Holm were hitting it off. So, I'd given him a little push. Not that he needed it. Technically, he had been the one to catch her when the perp shoved her to the ground, and he'd been the one to get her stolen money back. By all accounts, Holm was the hero of that story.

As I continued to make my way down the street in the vague direction of Holm's and my hotel, it occurred to me that now might be a good time to call Tessa. Holm would probably be occupied with Aurora for at least a little while, and it wasn't like I had anything else to do. Of course, the blabber about reports had been a complete fabrication, and honestly, not a very convincing one. Neither Holm nor Aurora had put up any kind of protest to my leaving, though, so I figured they were both eager for me to leave.

I slipped my phone out of my pocket and dialed Tessa's number by heart. In the age of contact lists, it was one of the few numbers I actually knew by memory.

"Hello?" She answered on the second ring, and as usual, just hearing her voice instantly made me feel at ease.

"Hey." I smiled at the phone. "How are you?"

"I'm doing great." She laughed. "Just got finished getting some amazing shots. The weather cleared up just in time for me to make use of the sunset lighting."

"That's awesome," I replied. Just hearing how excited she sounded made me feel excited for her as well.

"Right?" she replied brightly. "Anyway, what's up? Is there a reason you called me?"

"Do I need a reason?" I replied coyly as I stopped to lean against the wall of a building. "Can't I just call because I want to hear your voice?"

"Oh, someone's being smooth today," she replied jokingly, though I could hear a tremor of something else in her voice as well, and I could perfectly imagine her blushing as she tried to play my comment off.

"Actually, there is a reason I'm calling," I continued. "Holm and I are in New York right now. We're gathering information over a case victim, and we ended up here."

"You're in New York right now?" Tessa asked, her voice flat and low and not remotely what I was expecting. It wasn't like I thought she'd be leaping for joy, but I didn't think she'd sound upset about it.

"Uh, yeah," I replied nervously, suddenly feeling

unsure about whether I should have even called. "Is that a problem?"

"You're in New York right now?" she repeated, to my immense confusion. "Yes, that is a problem, Ethan! Because I'm not in New York right now!" I jumped as the tone of her voice suddenly changed from quiet and sad to loud and angry. "Oh, all the terrible timing..."

"I'm sorry?" I muttered, unsure how else I should respond.

"No, it's not your fault," Tessa rushed to assure me, and a weight lifted off me as soon as she said that. At least now I knew it wasn't me she was angry at. "It's just —it's so hard for us to find time to meet up between both our hectic schedules, and now, the same day that you're actually where I usually am, I'm not there." I heard her groan over the phone, and I laughed. The fear that she'd been pissed off earlier was gone entirely now, replaced instead by somewhat smug satisfaction that the reason she was angry was actually that she wouldn't be able to see me.

"Did I just hear a laugh?" Tessa demanded in mock indignation. "Is this a laughing matter to you, Marston?"

"Not at all," I laughed. "You're just really cute when you're pissed off."

"Yeah, well, I guess that's fine then," she murmured, and this time I was sure that she was blushing on the other end of the phone call. "Anyway, I'm happy you called, but I need to get back. I'll call you later, okay?"

"Sure," I replied, feeling bittersweet as we said our goodbyes.

I sighed as I dropped my hand down to my side and leaned my head back against the building wall. So much for meeting up with Tessa. As funny as her reaction had been, I'd have been lying if I'd said that I didn't feel the same way. It was a bitter irony that Tessa was somewhere else on the rare occasion my work had actually brought me up here.

I tucked my phone back into my pocket and pushed myself off the wall. As disappointing as it was, I wasn't going to gain anything from sitting around moping about it. As I started to make my way back toward where our hotel was, I noticed that I'd inadvertently made my way back to the police station. I stopped walking as I passed the front door. I hadn't intended to come back here quite yet, but now that I was here, I supposed that I might as well stop by. I wanted to ask them about what Dorris had said about reporting the abduction and about whether other similar crimes had taken place within the past few months.

I turned and made a beeline for the front door, intent on having the sergeant make good on his offer to do whatever he could to assist us. However, the moment I walked through the door, all my plans went awry.

"Somebody's been kidnapped!" a man standing in the lobby of the station shouted at the top of his lungs. "Aren't you listening? Isn't anybody going to do anything about this?"

"Sir, you need to calm down," one of two officers standing on the other side of the bulletproof divider urged the frantic man.

Even though the man was screaming and causing a scene, I noticed that neither of the officers seemed particularly concerned about what he was saying.

"No, I will not calm down!" the man continued to yell. "You are not listening to me! My friend is missing! We were attacked! By a couple of lunatics that came at us in the middle of the night!"

"Sir, how much have you had to drink today?" one of the officers asked as he looked at the man disparagingly.

The man making the claims looked like he was about to lose it completely, so I stepped in before he could start shouting again.

"What did you just say?" I asked as I moved to stand between him and the cops. "About being attacked in the middle of the night?"

"Just what I said," the man barked. "We were attacked! We were just sleeping there, minding our own business, when I got woken up by the sounds of my buddy screaming for help. Man, who are you, anyway?"

"Agent Marston," I replied as I pulled my badge out of my pocket.

"Well, finally!" the man exclaimed. "It's about time someone gave a crap about what I'm trying to say here, and I guess if the cops aren't going to do it, then it's up to the feds."

"Hey, don't humor him," one of the officers behind me called. "He's a frequent flier here if you know what I mean. The guy's probably drunk off his ass."

"Man, shut up!" the victim snarled at the cop. "What, just because I've been arrested a few times, all of a sudden that means it's okay for someone to beat on me and kidnap my buddy? Is that what you're saying?!"

"Whoa, hold on a second," I cautioned the man as he took a single threatening step toward the glass barrier. "Look, I believe you, okay? Don't worry about them. Just focus on our conversation, okay?" The man threw one last glare at the officers before turning to look at me expectantly.

"Okay," I breathed. "You said they came up to you in the middle of the night, right? Tell me, are you and your friend homeless?"

"What?!" the man exclaimed angrily. "What is that supposed to mean? Are you trying to decide if we're worth your time? Are you saying that just because someone's homeless, it means it's okay for someone to go and do something to them?"

"That's not at all what I'm saying," I insisted as the man turned his rage onto me. It was pretty evident that the guy had anger issues. The fact that his friend was missing, and he was likely in a panic, certainly didn't help matters. "I promise, it's relevant. I'm here in New York investigating the death of another homeless man, okay? We have reason to believe that someone is deliberately targeting the homeless population—"

His face scrunched up in fury, and he opened his mouth as though he was about to let out another indignant howl, but I pushed on before he could get a word in.

"I'm telling you that I want to help you," I continued. "Whoever took your friend is most likely the same person responsible for the murder, do you understand? If you tell me what happened, I might be able to catch whoever this is, but the only way that's going to work is if you calm down and work with me."

I saw him tense the moment he heard me tell him to "calm down." His upper lip twitched, and I braced myself, fully expecting him to blow up again. To my surprise, however, the man took a deep breath before deflating completely like a balloon, his shoulders sagging as he looked back at me begrudgingly.

"Fine..." he mumbled quietly. He still looked angry, but at least he wasn't yelling anymore. "Thanks. Sorry about losing it like that, it's just—" He turned to glare venomously at the two officers. "It's just frustrating coming for help and being treated like you're nothing but trash."

"Hey, listen—" one of the officers spoke up in response, but I cut him off with a stern look before he could rile the man up again.

"I get it," I assured him. "I do. Don't worry. I'm going to help you figure this out."

11

ETHAN

HOLM MET BACK UP with me at the station rather than at the hotel. After my conversation with the enraged homeless man, I'd called Holm to let him know there was a change of plans and to meet me here instead of at the hotel.

The man, who had later introduced himself to me as Stephan, was currently sitting inside one of the small conference rooms at the station. Typically, we would have used one of the interrogation rooms while interviewing a witness or victim, but Stephan had vehemently opposed the idea.

"Oh, hell no!" he'd exclaimed the moment he'd laid eyes on the small room. "There's not a snowman's chance in Hell that I'm going to let a bunch of pigs stick me inside some tiny little box. Do you think I'm stupid? If I go in there, there ain't no telling if I'm going to come out again. No, sir."

He'd continued to kick up a fuss, much to the dismay of the officers at the station, who had already been reluctant to humor his claims in the first place. It had taken a solid amount of first convincing and then threatening on my part, but ultimately, it had been the sergeant who stepped in to make good on his promise to do anything he could to help us. He'd set the other officers straight and then personally offered to set up one of the conference rooms for us.

"That one cop was pretty nice," Stephan remarked as he bit into the chicken sandwich that one of the officers had procured for him. He'd wolfed down half of it the moment it had arrived, along with about half of the soda that had come with it. "I haven't had all that many good experiences with cops, but he was decent. He came and helped us right away."

"Yeah," I muttered as I exchanged a look with Holm. "That was pretty nice of him."

Stephan was calm, so I didn't want to rupture the illusion he had of the sergeant. Of course, Holm and I both knew that the real reason he was helping us was that he knew he was partially responsible for what ultimately happened to Clearwater, and he was on a mission to do some damage control. Dorris's testimony that they had ignored her pleas for help only added another damning nail to the coffin. Ultimately, the sergeant was only helping us because he knew that he was in hot water, and he probably believed that doing this would alleviate some of his culpability.

"Okay then, Stephan," I prompted him. "Can you explain to us exactly what happened?"

"Sure," he replied after taking another long gulp of his soda. "Me and my buddy, Roy, were sleeping out by the docks. He found a nice spot out at a construction site. He found out that they always clear out by eight. Something about noise restrictions and them not being able to work after that. Anyway, there's a fence up around it, but there's a spot that they never bother to lock, so we just went on in and found a spot. It's not a bad setup, you know. Not the best, but at least it's peaceful. Ain't swarming with bodies like everywhere else. So, we go to sleep, right? Minding our own business, just trying to get some rest, when what do I hear but some rattling and foot-stomping." He paused for a moment to shake his head, an unreadable expression on his face.

"You wanna know what I thought?" He looked back and forth between Holm and me. "I thought that it was the construction workers coming back. Or the cops. Someone who was about to get my ass put behind bars, you know what I'm saying? So, I hop up real quick and try to get my buddy Roy to wake up, but his drunk self is out cold. Then I see these two guys walking over, and I get to my feet and start apologizing.

I'm standing there, asking these guys to please not say anything, we're leaving, sorry we're in here..." He clenched his jaw as he stared angrily down at the table. Then, without warning, he suddenly balled up his fist and smashed it down onto the surface of the table. "I should have punched his face in right there! I'm pleading with them not to rat us out to the cops like a moron, and next thing I know, he's jumping at me, swinging his fists in my face."

"They didn't say anything to you?" I asked.

"No," Stephan grumbled bitterly before frowning. "Actually, though, there was something. Yeah, now that I think about it, one of them did say something. It wasn't to me, though. After I got up and started talking to them, I remember one of them saying something like 'should we abort?' or something like that. Then the other one said, 'No, the last ones were duds, we need replacements,'" like what the hell does any of that mean?" Stephan's face scrunched up in confusion. "At the time, I was panicking too much to think about it, but now that you mention it, it was really weird." He pursed his lips together and looked up at us. "Does that mean something?"

"It might," I replied as I thought about the implications myself.

The phrase, "the last ones were duds," in particular, made my skin crawl. Did that mean that there were two *more* victims that we didn't know about? Or was it possible that the cryptic message referred to Clearwater and Wesley? If so, what did it mean that they were "duds"? Was it possible that was the reason Clearwater had ended up dead? There was some reason that he'd been kidnapped instead of just outright murdered. Whoever had taken him might have decided that Clearwater was deficient in some way and made the decision to kill him off after all.

"So, what happened after that?" I asked.

"I fought back," Stephan replied angrily. "I wasn't about to let them just take me." He snorted cockily, but then his face fell, and his eyes took on a sad, almost vacant expression. "I left him behind. I fought them off of me and started to run and left my friend there." He clenched his jaw and shook his head in disgust at himself. "I can't even say that I forgot about him. I was thinking about him even as I was hauling ass away from there. Some tiny part of me was saying to go back and help, but I—" He stopped short as he bit down hard on his lip.

"If you'd done that, they might have gotten you both," I tried to reassure him. "And then you wouldn't be here to be able to ask for help. You'd both be gone or dead."

"Yeah," Stephan sniffed aggressively as he nodded his head. "Yeah, you're right. That's one way to look at it. If I'd gone back, then we'd both be screwed. Yeah, running was the right move." He was still nodding incessantly, and I could tell that he was trying to convince himself not to feel bad about leaving his friend behind. I hadn't been lying when I'd said he'd made the right choice, though. Ultimately, the fact that he'd run and saved himself benefited our case since we wouldn't have had a lead otherwise.

"Do you think you could show us where this happened?" I asked him.

"Sure I could," Stephan declared vehemently as he got to his feet. His chair scraped loudly across the floor as he stood. "Come on; I'll take you there right now!"

I blinked up at him in surprise. I hadn't explicitly meant right this very moment, but I supposed that there was no reason why not.

"Alright," I replied as Holm and I stood up after him. "Let's go."

The three of us left the conference room and headed back out into the lobby of the police station.

"I'll show you exactly where it was," Stephan grumbled under his breath, quietly enough that I had to strain to hear him. "We're going to catch those stupid sons of..." He trailed off as he continued to mumble angrily under his breath. I could understand how he was feeling, especially after what he'd told us earlier about leaving his friend behind.

I was surprised when Stephan suddenly descended a flight of stairs into a subway station.

"Where exactly did this happen?" I asked in confusion. I had been under the assumption that this had happened nearby since he was at this particular police station.

"Down by Pier 36," Stephan replied gruffly.

"Oh." I looked up at him in surprise. I wasn't super familiar with New York, but I knew enough to know that Pier 36 was quite a ways from here. I could vaguely remember that being the starting point for most Statue of Liberty cruises. "Why did you come all the way here to report it then?"

"You think I did that for fun or something?" Stephan snorted as we got down to where the turnstiles were. "I *tried* going to another station. I tried going to about three other stations, actually. Same damned thing in each one. They all told me to screw off, called me crazy, treated me like I was dirt just because of how I looked. Tell me, how messed up is that?" He turned to look at me morosely, and I felt a pang of sympathy for him. I couldn't imagine how frustrating it must have been to ask for help and be turned down again and again.

"This one," Stephan replied confidently as a train pulled up into the station.

A swarm of people shoved their way out the moment the doors opened, but Stephan was unperturbed as he stepped forward, seemingly unconcerned about the fact that he was colliding straight into people. Then again, it didn't seem like any of the people he was running into cared very much either, so I supposed that it didn't really matter either way.

We sat down and rode the subway several stops until we made it down to our destination. Stepping out of the subway station and onto the street felt like entering an entirely different city. Gone were the tall, glimmering skyscrapers of Manhattan, replaced instead by old buildings made of brick. Black metal fire escapes ran up and down the sides of the buildings. I could see potted plants, bicycles, and even clotheslines on some of the landings.

"That's gotta be a safety hazard," I muttered to myself as we walked by. It was certainly pretty, though, in a way that was completely different from the New York I was more familiar with.

"Hmm?" Stephan grunted over his shoulder at me. "What did you say?"

"It's nothing," I replied.

"Well, then quit muttering to yourself and come on!" Stephan groused. "We're almost there. It's just through here."

He took a right and turned into what looked like a small park. Trees and other small buildings surrounded it, so it didn't get much light, but it was still a nice little area. A few kids played hopscotch on the nearby sidewalk, with chalk clutched in their tiny hands as they laughed and pushed each other.

However, as we continued toward the harbor, I was

once again struck by how quickly the street changed. The green, grassy park became a stark, rough-looking dump from one block to another. Gone were the children, and in their place were groups of indigent people, sitting or lying on the ground. Some were inside worn, shoddily repaired tents, while others were just out in the open, looking out over the water or looking at nothing at all.

"This is it," Stephan declared. There was an odd mixture of both pride and sadness in his voice as he looked out over the area, and I could scarcely imagine what he was actually thinking.

"Normally, we just sleep over there, beneath the bridge," he noted as he pointed off toward a small alcove that was created where the lowest part of the bridge met the highest part of the ground. There were several tents, sleeping bags, blankets, and other assorted types of makeshift bedding all crammed in together up there. "There was no room, though. Roy suggested we find someplace on our own to sleep. He'd managed to snag a really nice tent from one of the church ladies that come around sometimes to hand out food and stuff, and he didn't want anyone else taking a piss on it or something, so we went down that way."

He nodded out toward the other end of the dock, where there were significantly fewer people. In fact, there was only one person over there. By how he was repeatedly looking down at his phone before looking around at his surroundings in bewilderment, I assumed that he must be a lost tourist, not one of the local homeless.

"Right here," Stephan declared as he led us over to the back door of one of the riverfront buildings. There was a small outcropping over the top of the doorframe, which I imagined probably provided some amount of cover from the elements. "The tent was right here... Someone must have stolen it, I guess. I can't say I'm surprised. It was a pretty nice tent. Almost new. I ran after the attack and didn't come back until this morning. The tent was still here then, but it's gone now."

"I'm sorry about that," I replied. It was just adding insult to injury to have lost his friend and then lost the closest thing he had to a shelter.

"Man, I don't care about that," Stephan croaked, and I was shocked to hear his voice crack as he spoke. "I just need you guys to find Roy. He and I have been through it together, and then I went and just left him like he was nothing." He sniffed harshly as he reached up to scrub at his eyes with the palm of his hand. He rubbed so hard that the skin on his face was raw and red when he pulled his hand away, but when he looked at us again, his eyes were dry, and his face was set into a hard line. "I need you to find him."

"We're going to try everything in our power," I

assured him before turning to look at Holm. "This kind of sounds like trafficking to me. What do you think?"

"Trafficking?!" Stephan scoffed in disbelief. "You mean like when women get snatched and forced to become prostitutes? Roy? Who in the hell would want to do that?"

"Yes, it's similar to that," I replied. "But sex trafficking isn't the only kind of trafficking there is. It's possible that he was taken for some other reason."

"He does have a point, though." Holm frowned as he reached up to stroke his chin thoughtfully. "Grown men aren't usually a prime target for trafficking. In fact, they're pretty much the opposite. Women and children are much more at risk, and though impoverished and homeless women are at greater risk, the same doesn't really apply to men."

That was true. Women were the most common target of trafficking since sex trafficking was the most prevalent form that existed within the United States, closely followed by children of both genders. Men were a different story, though. Men were more difficult to overpower than women and children, so they weren't prime kidnapping targets. Of course, there were always things like organ trafficking. Though mostly considered an urban legend, it wasn't entirely baseless. Even that was questionable, though, as homeless men would likely not be in the best physical health. Then again, a group that was illegally harvesting organs from random people off the street probably wasn't taking much consideration into the quality of their goods.

I turned to Holm to share my theory with him but stopped short when I remembered that Stephan was still here with us. Though I did believe that he had the right to be present and hear what was going on with a case that he was personally involved with, I didn't think throwing out gory, unconfirmed theories was the best way to go about it.

"Regardless," I said instead, "the only way we'll know for certain is if we find out for ourselves, and I think the best way to do that will be a stakeout."

"Here?" Holm raised an eyebrow at me. "You think they'll strike again in the exact same spot?"

"I have no idea," I admitted. "Actually, the fact that the two accounts that we know of both took place so far apart makes me think that there's a good chance they won't. We don't know where they'll strike next, though, so this is our only shot at the moment."

"That's true," Holm sighed. "So, how—"

"I'll help!" Stephan suddenly declared, loudly enough that I jumped in surprise. "Use me as bait! I can help."

"That is not a good idea," I stated plainly. "For about a hundred reasons. First and foremost is that we can't allow a civilian to put himself in harm's way for our sake. I appreciate the offer, but—"

"Oh, screw all that!" Stephan exclaimed angrily as his eyebrows scrunched together in an unpleasant grimace. "Do you want to catch this guy or not? They're looking for homeless guys like me, right? You said that yourself. How do you expect to find them otherwise? This can work!"

He made a good argument. If we wanted to hunt down someone targeting homeless men, then leaving some kind of bait, for lack of a better word, really was the logical choice. Of course, what I said still stood. We couldn't just let Stephan do something that dangerous.

"Man, come on," Stephan huffed impatiently. "Look at me. Seriously, look. Do you think I'm the kind of guy that anyone gives a crap about? Do you think anyone will care if you put some bum in danger? You know they won't. You saw yourself how the cops treated me when I asked them for help. Come on. Let me help with this. That's my friend they have! If I don't do something to help him, nobody will."

He'd run the gamut of emotions from angry to desperate as he pleaded with us to allow him to join the operation. Obviously, I still had my reservations, but the more I thought about it, the more I realized that he was right. No matter how I felt about it, nobody was going to help this man, and taking him up on his offer might actually be the best way to catch the kidnappers as soon as possible.

"Fine," I replied after several long moments of

contemplative hesitation. "But you need to do exactly as we say, got it?"

"Yeah, yeah, yeah," Stephan replied excitedly, sounding very much like a kid who was just agreeing on the surface and had absolutely no intention of actually following through. "I've got a friend, Miles, who can help out. We'll set it up just like it was before."

"Wait." I looked back at him in shock. "You want to bring someone else in? No, look, one is already dangerous enough."

"Don't worry," Stephan brushed me aside dismissively. "It'll be fine, trust me."

He looked excited as he spoke, as though the thought of getting back at the kidnappers thrilled him. It was, admittedly, an emotion that I was familiar with. Getting back at a wrongdoer by putting them in their place and bringing them to justice was an incredibly satisfying feeling. All that being said, I couldn't help but feel extremely worried that something was bound to go wrong, especially now that Stephan apparently intended to bring someone else into the mix. I sighed and resigned myself to making the best of the situation, knowing that it was our best chance at catching the people responsible for all of this.

12

ETHAN

I WATCHED with mounting trepidation as Stephan and his friend Miles made a big show of looking for a secluded place to sleep later that night. After finalizing the details of our plan, we'd outfitted Stephan with a bug so we could listen in while we kept watch from the cover of our car, which we parked in a parking lot adjacent to the harbor where Stephan and his buddy were planning to go to sleep. Or rather, pretending to go to sleep to lure out the kidnappers.

"Man, all these people just lying around," Stephan grumbled just a little too loudly to feel natural. "Makes me sick! Is it too much to ask for some space to move?" His friend just nodded along as Stephan continued to turn his nose up at the other indigent people gathered on the street nearby. "Come on, Miles! Let's find somewhere else to sleep! I can barely even see where I'm walking with all of these people lying around."

The irony of that particular statement was that there wasn't actually anyone lying around, at least not where he was standing. I stifled a groan of dismay as I watched him put on the bizarre show. It was apparent that he was trying to attract the kidnappers' attention. A little too obvious.

"No one's going to approach him while he's acting like that," I sighed. "They're going to know it's a setup."

"Maybe not..." Holm shrugged, but it didn't even sound like he believed himself. "Maybe they'll just think he's crazy. He definitely looks crazy, talking like that."

"Maybe we should just tell them to cut it out," I muttered to myself. "What's the likelihood that the kidnappers are even watching right now? We don't know how they find their victims. Heck, we don't have any guarantees that they'll even show tonight."

"I have a feeling they will." Holm frowned. "Remember what Stephan said? When he and his friend were attacked, the kidnappers said something about needing replacements because of some 'duds.'"

"What about it?" I took my eyes off of Stephan to look at Holm.

"Well, they only got one, right?" He shrugged. "Stephan's friend. That means that they probably need at least one more."

"So, there's a solid chance that they'll come rooting around again," I surmised. "Especially if they're on some kind of time crunch, which seems likely given the fact that they were looking for replacements, anyway."

"Yep," Holm replied. "You've got a point, though. I doubt that whoever is doing this is finding targets by skulking around homeless camps. More likely is that they're scoping things out after dark once everyone is asleep, and hitting targets that look isolated enough that no one else will notice."

"Well, hopefully, they're desperate enough to come straight back here," I muttered. "At least here we can intervene. If they decide to strike somewhere else, we'll have no way of knowing, and they'll probably grab another victim."

"That's another thing," Holm sighed as he leaned back in his seat.

I looked back out the window to monitor Stephan. He and Miles were setting up a tent that we'd procured for them. It was bright orange and sure to stand out, and the plan was to place it somewhere conspicuously far away from the rest of the group. We hoped that the kidnappers would be drawn in by the prospect of an easy mark and move in.

"Why men?" Holm continued. "The homeless part, I understand. As sad as it is, no one really notices or cares when something bad happens among homeless communities. But what I can't figure out is why they're being kidnapped, and not just mugged or killed outright."

"I've been thinking the same thing myself," I replied. "A sadistic freak who just wanted to hurt someone wouldn't go through the trouble of struggling with the men to kidnap them. He'd just beat them or kill them wherever they were. It's obviously not ransom either."

"Well, it *could* be sex trafficking," Holm noted with a disturbed grimace. "If these were women disappearing under the exact same circumstances, that would be our very first guess. All the signs are there. The only thing that doesn't fit is the gender."

"I was actually thinking it could be organ harvesting," I admitted with a frown.

Holm turned to look at me in shock before an expression of understanding settled over his face.

"That's not a terrible conclusion," he muttered as he chewed thoughtfully on his lower lip. "How likely is that, though?"

"Not likely at all," I replied as I continued to monitor Stephan and his friend.

They'd dropped the weird act, thankfully, and were now sitting on the ground together, playing with a deck of cards.

"It's practically unheard of," I continued, "since it's difficult to pull off and not all that profitable unless you know what you're doing. Most organs that are illegally harvested aren't removed well enough surgically to remain viable."

"Guess we'll just have to ask our kidnappers when we find them," Holm muttered under his breath.

We stayed like that for a while, tossing theories and suspicions back and forth as the night wore on. At some point, Stephan and Miles had stopped talking. I couldn't hear anything through the wire we'd planted, so I assumed that they'd actually fallen asleep for real. It wasn't until about three in the morning, when the entire dock along the harbor was quiet and still, that something happened.

A large black van rolled slowly down the street right past where Holm and I were parked. It was moving slowly enough that I could make out the faces of the two men sitting in the front seat of the car. The one in the driver's seat had long, scraggly hair that looked like it hadn't been washed in a while. The one sitting in the front passenger seat was skinnier than the other man, with a long, hooked nose and gaunt, sunken cheeks that made him look emaciated. He reminded me a bit of a skeleton, and I was on edge the moment I laid eyes on him.

"That's weird." I pointed out the obvious to Holm.

"Seems like an odd time to go for a drive," Holm agreed as he followed the car with his eyes. It was heading directly toward the harbor where the homeless camp was. It disappeared around a corner, past where Stephan and Miles were in their tent. I tensed for a moment, then deflated when nothing happened.

"Maybe they really were just out for a drive in the middle of the night," I mumbled as I turned to Holm with a look of confusion. I didn't really believe that, but the fact that they'd just carried on past what was intended to look like prey on a silver platter had thrown me for a loop.

"Should we follow them?" he asked as he sat up straight in his seat. His eyes were wide and alert as he looked out toward the spot where the van had disappeared around a corner. "Just because they didn't go for Stephan doesn't mean that they won't try someone else."

"You have a point," I agreed as I moved to turn the key in the ignition. "They'll notice if they suddenly see a car following them, though. We should get out and tail them on foot."

"Got it." Holm nodded as we both opened the car doors in unison.

No sooner had we stepped out than I heard a roar of an engine as the van suddenly made its way back around before coming to a screeching halt right in front of the tents. The moment it was at a stop, both men jumped out of the car and rushed for the tent.

"Let's grab whoever's in there and go," a new, unfamiliar voice came through the earpiece I was wearing as the men stopped in front of the tent. I was surprised by how clearly I could hear them. "The bosses need more as it is. We really screwed up with the last two, and if we don't grab another one fast, it'll be our asses on the line."

"Dammit!" I hissed as I took off at a sprint.

The men had likely had their sights set on the tent from the beginning, just as we'd expected. They'd likely driven past initially to ensure the coast was clear before going in for a strike like they were now, quickly and ruthlessly. My feet hit the floor hard as I raced down the mild incline to the harbor, reaching for my firearm as I went.

"Stop!" I yelled as I yanked my gun from my holster, but the two men were already at the tent, tearing it open brusquely.

"You thought you were gonna get me twice!?" Stephan's voice suddenly roared from inside the tent as one of the men ripped the flap open. Stephan lunged at the kidnapper hard enough to knock him off his feet. After seeing his buddy go down, the other kidnapper suddenly reached inside his pocket for something.

"Don't move!" I barked as I caught up to the scene, my gun held aloft toward the man.

He looked back at me in shock, his eyes wide as he caught sight of the gun. Then Miles stumbled out of the tent, looking sleep-addled and confused. He stepped directly between the man and me before he had time to take stock of the situation, and the kidnapper pounced on the opportunity he saw. He lunged forward and grabbed Miles around the neck before taking out what was inside his pocket. It was a syringe, though I could only guess what was in it.

"S-stay away," the man stammered as he looked between me and his buddy on the ground, who was still grappling with Stephan.

Holm had arrived and was just pulling his gun from his holster when a loud bang cracked through the air, and Stephan screamed in pain. The scraggly-haired kidnapper threw him off like a doll, the smoking gun that he'd just used to shoot Stephan still clutched in his hand.

"Gun!" Holm yelled as he pointed his own weapon at the armed kidnapper.

The man was fast, though, and he swung around to shoot at Holm quick as a flash. Both guns went off at once. Holm dove to the ground as he fired and narrowly avoided being struck by the assailant's bullet. The kidnapper wasn't as lucky, and he howled with anger and pain as Holm's shot struck him in the shoulder. He didn't let up, though, and quickly began to scramble to his feet.

I was too fast for him, and I fired two shots before he could lift his arm to shoot at Holm again. He fell once more with a strangled cry as the bullets hit him.

The gun he was holding clattered to the ground, and he didn't move again once he was down.

Behind me, the skinnier kidnapper that I'd been fighting with before took advantage of the momentary distraction to act. He plunged the syringe into Miles's neck before shoving him forcefully toward me. I was still holding the gun in one hand, so I awkwardly twisted my body around to catch Miles with the other. He was completely out cold by the time he slammed into me, and his dead weight was enough to cause me to stumble backward. Then the kidnapper turned and took off.

"Crap," I muttered as I gently set Miles down on the ground and checked for a pulse.

It was there and strong, so whatever the kidnapper had injected him with had only knocked him out. I sighed with relief as I turned to check on Holm, who was crouched over Stephan. Unlike Miles, Stephan didn't look so good. His skin looked clammy, and his face was twisted up into an awful, pained grimace. He was breathing heavily, too, as he clutched his hands to his side, where a spot of red was rapidly spreading.

"Looks like he got him in the ribs," Holm said before looking over at me. "I'll stay and call for an ambulance. You go and catch the other guy."

I nodded only once before jumping to my feet, but it was too late. As soon as I'd stood up, I heard the roar of an engine, and a moment later, the same large black van we'd seen before came speeding down the street past us. As he went, the bastard actually took the time to roll his window down and begin shooting at us. I clenched my jaw in anger as I lifted my gun and fired back. Just after I did, the kidnapper yelled with pain, and the car swerved sharply for a moment. It wasn't enough, though, because he didn't stop. After taking a moment to regain control of the vehicle, he leveled out again and sped off.

My shoulders sagged with disappointment as I watched him get away. We'd been tantalizingly close to catching them, and though we'd managed to take down one, the other had slipped away by using one of the victims as a shield, like a coward. Ultimately, the safety of Stephan and Miles was what mattered the most, though, so I was at least content with the fact that we'd managed to keep them safe. With that in mind, I turned and walked back to where Holm and the two men were.

"You let them get away, huh?" Stephan groaned laboriously. "Didn't you say you were a fed? What kind of fed... lets bad guys get away?" He screwed his eyes shut and pursed his lips together as he pushed through the pain he was feeling.

"Sorry about that," I apologized sincerely, even though I knew he was just teasing. "I never should have agreed to let you be part of the mission. That was stupid on my part."

"Oh, don't start with that nonsense now," Stephan hissed. "We saw them, right? Now, we know what they look like. And we heard them too." He opened his eyes and tossed me a pained but cocky smile. "I did good, right? Holding that microphone you gave me up to the edge of the tent. I heard them coming and knew you'd be listening."

"That was smart," I commended him. "And it's definitely going to help us find them again."

"Good," Stephan sighed as he lolled back onto the ground to look up at the sky. "Good. Whatever it takes to get Roy back."

13

ETHAN

I LOOKED out the airplane window pensively as we touched down in St Joseph and the Grenadines. After the debacle of the previous night, we'd reported everything that had happened to Diane. After taking it all in, she'd decided that the best course of action was for us to head out as soon as possible. Since that was where Clearwater's body had been found, we needed to look at the crime scene before we decided anything else.

Thanks to what happened last night, we knew a few things for sure. The first was that homeless men in New York were definitely being kidnapped for some kind of nefarious purpose. If the eyewitness testimonies we'd received from several of the homeless people we encountered hadn't been enough, what we'd overheard the kidnappers saying had made it undeniable that something strange was afoot. They'd mentioned a boss, which meant that they weren't the ones ultimately calling the shots. They'd also implied that a steady supply of bodies was something that these bosses expected, so it was evident that these men were serving a purpose for someone. Exactly what that was still remained to be seen. After meeting with our liaison, our first goal would be to examine the body and then examine the crime scene, if there was anything left of it. If I recalled the report correctly, the body had been found on the beach on Palm Island, and beaches were very good at destroying evidence. Between the shifting sand and the tide that washed everything clean every night, I had my doubts that we would find anything significant there.

I was brought out of my thoughts and back to the present as the other passengers around us began to get up to collect their luggage from the overhead compartments. Holm and I were sitting in the back, and though we didn't intend to waste time, we weren't exactly in a hurry, either. Not when our current goal was to examine a body that wasn't about to go anywhere.

"Do you have the address of the hotel?" I asked Holm as I leaned back in my chair to wait for everyone to get off.

"Yeah, it's here," Holm replied as he reached into his bag to pull out his tablet. Something small and blue came out with it, and it fluttered to the floor of the plane as it came unstuck from the tablet.

"Dammit," Holm hissed as he leaned down quickly to snatch the thing off the ground. He dusted it off and then turned it over a few times as if checking it for dirt. "Great. There are probably only a few things nastier than the floor of an airplane."

"What is that?" I asked curiously as he folded the object back up to put it in his bag. It looked like a napkin to me.

"Oh, nothing really," Holm replied casually enough that I might have believed him if it hadn't been for the slight flush on his face as he said it.

I frowned for a moment as I wondered what could have caused such an odd reaction, and then it hit me.

"Oh, there's a stain right there," I fibbed as I pointed toward the object just as he was putting it back inside.

"Hmm? Where?" Holm asked with alarm as he unfolded the thing and looked it over. The moment he did, I slipped it smoothly out of his fingers to get a better look.

"Aha, I knew it." I smirked knowingly at him as I read what was written on the piece of cloth: the name Aurora and a ten-digit telephone number. "That woman from before gave you this, huh?" I could see now that it was a handkerchief, embroidered around the edges in a cutesy way.

"Who raised you?" Holm grumbled at me as he snatched the handkerchief back. "Do you always go around grabbing stuff that doesn't belong to you?"

"Don't dodge the question," I replied impishly as Holm carefully placed the handkerchief back in his bag. "She gave it to you, right? Are you planning on calling her?"

"That doesn't really make any sense," he replied sadly. "I mean, we've left New York. And she was just visiting there from Italy, remember? The chances we'll be able to meet up again are microscopically small, so what's the point in delaying the inevitable by getting my hopes up with a call that won't lead to anything?"

After that, he fell quiet, and I started to feel bad about teasing him. I'd only been poking fun, thinking he would return in kind like he usually did, but this time, he seemed actually upset about it. He'd had flings before. He'd had one just recently, actually, with a woman who he'd fallen out of contact with pretty quickly after we'd returned home from our mission. He hadn't seemed all that broken up about that, which was logical. The nature of our jobs had us flying all over the place at the drop of a hat, after all. Any time we connected with someone, we always knew that it wasn't bound to be permanent. I supposed the only real exception to that rule was Tessa, but I quickly moved away from that particular line of thinking before I could delve into it too deeply. This was about Holm, not me.

"You never know." I shrugged encouragingly. "The world is smaller than you think. We've proven that time and time again. You might still see her again. Isn't she super loaded or something? I'm pretty sure she mentioned her father was the owner of some big company. If you want to meet up with her, she can just fly out."

"Haha," Holm deadpanned at me in response. "Yeah, no big deal. I'll just casually ask a woman I've met once in my life to fly across the ocean to come to see me. That'll go over like a lead balloon."

"Maybe not," I replied. "I've dropped everything at a moment's notice to—" I stopped myself short as I realized that my mind had drifted back to Tessa again.

It was true that I'd thrown caution to the wind and literally flown to different countries while on adventures with Tessa, but I was hesitant to bring that up in the context of Holm's issue with this Aurora person. Tessa was a great friend, and aside from me, she was the person probably the most interested in the *Dragon's Rogue*, but she was not my girlfriend, and if I said anything that even hinted at that, Holm was going to rib me over it forever.

"Yes..?" Holm raised an eyebrow at me.

"The point is that you never know," I ungracefully changed the subject. "She obviously likes you. There was no denying it with the way you two were making eyes at each other."

Holm's ears went bright scarlet at my remark.

"If she's got enough money to throw around casually," I continued, "she might very well be willing to fly across the ocean to meet you."

"How romantic," Holm replied sarcastically, but I could tell by the way that his ears got even redder that some part of him was secretly pleased by the idea. "Can we go already? It's our turn to get off."

I laughed as we got up to grab our things. Holm made it too easy to tease him. Although, in fairness, I had the advantage of having known him for quite a long time. I knew all of his tells easily by now, so I could always suss out when he was lying or trying to avoid something. Still, as fun as it was to mess with him, I didn't want to do it at his expense. I hadn't realized until that moment just how smitten he was with this Aurora woman. As we got off the plane and shuffled along with the rest of the crowd that was heading to pick up car rentals, I wondered what it was about her that had made Holm fall like that.

Luckily, Diane had prearranged the booking of a rental car for us at the same time. Apparently, she had also ensured the absolute highest possible insurance available was purchased along with it. I couldn't help but feel sheepish as I climbed into the driver's seat, knowing that the reason she'd done that was due to my and Holm's recent tendency to damage cars while on missions.

"Damn, it's hot." I breathed a sigh of relief as I peeled my jacket off and blasted the AC in the car.

"It's not really," Holm countered. "It's pretty mild, actually. It just feels hot because we were just in New York surrounded by snow."

"I much prefer this," I replied as I leaned back in my seat to enjoy the cold blast from the air conditioner.

It wasn't that I hated snow or anything like that, but the bright sun and warm, baking heat was what I was used to. Still, even Miami couldn't compare to the gorgeous climate that could be found out here. Miami could become blisteringly hot, and the humidity made going outside feel extraordinarily wet and miserable. The islands just south of the coastline could always be counted on to be warm, sunny, and pleasant, though.

"The hotel isn't too far from here," Holm noted as he plugged the address into the car's navigation system.

"It's a pretty small town," I replied as I pulled the car out of the lot and onto the road. "I don't think anything is very far from here."

Like most of the other Caribbean islands we'd visited, St. Vincent and the Grenadines was small enough that the entire thing could be traversed by car in a matter of hours. However, what was unique about this country were the dozens of tiny outlying islands scattered around the perimeter of the larger one, which was where we had landed in the capital of Kingstown. Our ultimate destination was, of course, Palm Island, which was where Clearwater's body had been found. It was also one of the aforementioned tiny islands that could be found on the outskirts of the main island of St. Vincent. The only way to get there was by boat, so we had no other option but to fly into Kingstown.

It was just as well, though, since Holm, Diane, and I all had a suspicion that Clearwater might not have been killed *on* Palm Island but possibly just dumped there post-mortem. If he had been killed there, someone would have almost certainly seen something. Of course, it was also possible that anyone who had seen something was just refusing to come forward. If that were the case, it added an entire layer of complications to the already puzzling case.

"What if the people on Palm Island killed him?" I mused out loud, not really expecting an answer.

"Hmm?" Holm turned to look at me. "Who? You mean the tourists?"

"I'm just thinking out loud," I replied pensively. "But picture this: a group of people on a small, deserted island. One day someone turns up dead, and everyone else claims that they have no idea who he is, never even seen him."

"Sounds like an Agatha Christie whodunnit kind of story," Holm replied with a frown. "If I hadn't heard anything else about the case, my first inclination would be to think that someone on the island killed him and, for some reason, everyone was choosing to cover it up."

"Exactly," I muttered. "Not that I for sure think that's what happened, but I am curious."

The drive from the airport to the hotel wasn't very far, but it did take a fair amount of time in the car. The center of town was swarming with tourists, and they and the locals alike consistently blocked the road as they made their way to and from the large cruise ships that were docked just along the shoreline. As a result, the line of traffic moved painfully slowly down the street.

"I don't know why I thought there'd be *fewer* tourists during the winter," Holm remarked as he fiddled with the radio, apparently trying to decide between a station that was playing upbeat bubblegum pop and one that seemed to be playing an endless stream of ads. "It actually makes sense to come down here this time of year. It's nice and warm on the islands, while back in New York, I felt like I started to freeze any time I stood still too long."

"Yep," I sighed as I stared out over the water. It was still early enough that the sky was slightly pink, and the water beneath the horizon glittered like it was covered in crystals. "That's what's so nice about the Caribbean. It's warm and pretty year-round."

The crowd finally cleared up enough for us to drive at a decent pace about a mile away from the center of the city, but by then, we'd basically already arrived. The hotel we pulled up to was surprisingly nice. It was right on the beach, and I was pretty sure that I could see a pool from where we parked. That wasn't to say that Diane would typically put us up at some dump, but it was normal for us to stick with more budget places while traveling. After all, we weren't on vacation, and when we often had to move at a moment's notice, it made sense to stay somewhere cheap.

"I'm surprised Diane sprung for a place like this," I remarked as I got out of the car. "Seems fancier than the places she usually sends us."

"That might just be because we're in Kingstown," Holm replied as he reached into the car to grab his bag. "I mean, we passed by some pretty luxurious-looking places on our way here. Not that this place is bad, or anything, but maybe there just aren't any 'bad' hotels in St. Vincent?"

"You might be onto something," I replied as I grabbed my bag from the trunk and slammed the top closed.

Now that I thought about it, this was a pretty small island. Logically, most of the hotels would be overlooking the water. Heck, virtually everything was over-looking the water, and considering a large amount of the city's revenue likely came from tourism, it was no shock that even the budget hotels would cater to tourists.

The front doors of the hotel opened into a large, open lobby. I could practically see my reflection on the shiny, marbled floor, and the lone desk set at the end of the lobby made the room feel even bigger.

The woman standing behind the desk greeted us with a large, friendly smile.

"Hi! Welcome!" she exclaimed brightly. "How can I help you this morning?"

"Hey, we were hoping we could drop off our bags," I replied as I glanced down at my phone to check the time. It was still several hours before the three PM check-in. "I know it's too early for us to check-in, but we were hoping we could just leave our stuff until later."

"That is no problem at all," the young woman replied as she turned to her computer. "And actually, I believe we have some rooms already available for check-in. What was the name?"

"Marston," I replied. "And Holm."

"Okay..." the receptionist hummed as she typed something into the computer. "Yep, it looks like I can get you guys in right away. Not a problem. Now, usually, there would be an extra fee for early check-in, but if you two would like to sign up for our mailing list, I can waive that for you."

"Uh, sure," I replied as I looked over to Holm, who just shrugged in agreement.

It was unlikely that we'd ever be here again, so whatever coupons or offers they planned to send us would definitely go unused. I didn't mind putting up with some spam mail in exchange for the convenience of being able to check in early, though, so I took the pen that the receptionist offered me and quickly filled in the form she presented me with my name and email.

"Perfect!" She smiled after Holm and I had both finished filling out the forms. "Here are your keys. The same card can be used to get into the pool and the gym. Breakfast is complimentary, of course, and available between six and eight. If you have any questions, please don't hesitate to ask, okay? Oh! And before I forget—" She reached over to a stack of pamphlets that were set up in clear, plastic containers off to one side of the reception desk. "There are a lot of amazing places to visit here. Is this your first time in St. Vincent?"

"Uh, yeah," I replied vaguely.

No doubt she was about to give us the spiel she probably gave to all the tourists that wound up staying here. Of course, we were here for a much more serious reason than casual sightseeing, but I didn't feel like giving her all the gory details was necessary.

"Well, welcome!" She grinned happily. "You're going to love it. Anyway, as I was saying, there is a lot to do right here in Kingstown, but there are also a lot of excursions available." She pointed down at the pamphlets as she spoke. "A lot of first-timers get so caught up just being here that they never leave the main island, but I'd recommend you check out one of the smaller islands out in the Grenadines. You can reserve a spot on a boat, and if you book through our hotel, you'll get a discount as well!"

"Thanks," I replied a bit stiffly as I took the pamphlets from her. She was so enthusiastic as she tried to upsell us that I almost felt bad. She was really just wasting her time. "We'll have a look."

"Great!" she replied. "Like I said, please let me know if there's anything else you need. Your rooms are 206 and 207, down that hallway and up the elevator."

"Thank you," I replied before turning to make my way off in that direction.

"It's a shame we won't get to do anything in here," Holm noted as he took one of the pamphlets from me. "Actually sounds kind of fun."

"She certainly seemed enthusiastic about it," I replied as we stepped into the elevator.

"Oh... Palm Island is on here," Holm muttered as he looked down at the pamphlet in his hand.

"What?" I asked as the elevator came to a stop on the second floor with a rumble and a chime. "Really?"

"Yeah," Holm replied as the two of us stepped out. "Gorgeous marvel of the seas... pristine beaches, yadda yadda—oh, that's creepy."

"What?" I asked as we made our way down the hallway.

The dark green carpet beneath our shoes swallowed the sounds of our footfalls, muffling the noise so that the long corridor felt eerily silent.

"Virtually untouched by man and nearly impossible to reach," Holm read off the paper. "Only accessible by private ferry." He shuddered. "I know it's supposed to sound luxurious and exclusive, but it just seems foreboding to me, considering the circumstances."

"I know what you mean," I replied as we reached the doors to our hotel rooms. The combination of missing people and a plethora of deserted, nearly inaccessible islands was frightening. Holm was right. Rather than sounding like a peaceful getaway, the island's description made it sound a lot more like an ideal murder location. "Hard to get to also implies that it's hard to leave. So, anyone there would be stuck."

"You think that's what happened to Clearwater?" Holm looked at me questioningly. "Trapped on a nearly deserted island with no chance of escape? I mean, it's possible, but why?"

"That's the big question." I sighed. "Anyway, let's put our stuff away and get settled. The faster we get down to the station, the faster we can get some answers."

"Alright," Holm replied as he turned to step into his own hotel room. "Meet you back out here in five?"

"Five it is," I confirmed before unlocking the door to my own room. The inside was bigger than I expected it to be and just as nice as the outside of the hotel. I supposed it made sense. Kingstown was a resort destination and popular cruise stop. It wasn't surprising that even the budget hotel rooms were decadent.

I set my bag down on the table at the end of the room before taking a moment to stretch. Sitting in cramped airplane seats, even for just a few hours, was always uncomfortable. Not for the first time, I recalled that we'd once had our own jet. We'd been flying commercial for so long at this point that it had just become routine. The Hollands were gone now, though, and our finances weren't in ruins anymore, so I'd have to see about talking with Diane about getting it back, or maybe just getting another one.

That would have to wait for another day, though. I tucked the thought in the back of my mind to be shelved for later, then went to work making sure I had everything I would need to start investigating. Once I was ready, I set back out to meet Holm.

14

ETHAN

THE CENTRAL POLICE Station in Kingstown was actually quite remarkable. The vast, two-story building of stone and brick sat imposingly over the city. Jutting up from the center of the roof was a bright red tower that made the large structure look a lot like a castle.

"Wow," Holm remarked as the two of us stepped out of the car just in front of the station. "You don't see something like that every day."

"No," I agreed as the two of us walked toward the entrance of the building. Though signs of Dutch and British influence were evident in the architecture of other buildings we'd passed on our way here, nothing I'd seen so far had been quite as impressive as the police station.

As we walked up to the entrance, I noticed an officer wearing a white uniform standing outside, just beside the door. I half expected him to stop us or ask us to identify ourselves, but to my surprise, he merely nodded at us before turning his attention back to the street ahead. As we stepped inside, I realized that although the outside was grand and unconventional, the inside of the station looked remarkably normal. I supposed that shouldn't have come as much of a surprise, but the building's archaic exterior had left me expecting something different.

A long desk was set up just past the main entryway. Several uniformed officers sat at intervals along the desk, in a setup that looked a lot more like a DMV or a bank than a police station. A few of the officers were busy speaking with people, so I made a beeline toward the first man who wasn't helping anyone else. Before I could get to him, though, a stocky, bald man stepped up behind the officer.

"The agents are supposed to be here later this afternoon," I heard the bald man say. I could tell from his uniform that he was of a higher rank than the men sitting at the long desk. A captain, maybe. "Two of them. Call me as soon as they're here, alright?" The officer nodded, and the bald man turned to speak to one of the other officers. He had just started relaying the same message when I walked up to him to interrupt.

"Hello," I spoke up. There was a steady thrum of noise in the room as the sounds of voices, ringing phones, and computer keyboards all merged into one continuous din, so I had to raise my voice slightly. "I didn't mean to eavesdrop, but we're the agents you're expecting." The man blinked at me in surprise. "I'm Agent Marston, and this is my partner, Agent Holm. We're with MBLIS."

"Of course," the man replied, still looking a little shocked at my sudden appearance. "Sorry, you caught me off guard. I wasn't expecting you until a little later."

"We figured we'd come down as early as possible," I replied. "That gives us more time to get out in the field and have a look at what's going on."

"Of course," the man nodded before offering us a kind smile. "Anyway, I'm Captain Larose. I've been overseeing this case personally since Mr. Clearwater's body was discovered. Here, let's go and speak in my office so we can talk comfortably."

He gestured for us to follow him and then led us forward into the depths of the station. The place was just as big on the inside as it looked and confusing to boot. After walking through a bullpen full of desks, down a long hallway, through what looked like another bullpen, though one devoid of any officers, up a flight of stairs, and through a twisting series of corridors, we finally came to a stop outside the captain's office.

"Sorry about the trek," he chuckled as he pushed the door to his office open. "I know it's a bit of a far walk. The building was first constructed back at the end of the seventeen-hundreds. Building techniques were different back then, and definitely no elevators or escalators."

"We don't mind," I assured him as the three of us stepped into his office.

A bit of exercise had never been a deterrent for either me or Holm. I was a little worried about getting back out of here, though, and I quickly went over the path we'd taken here before it could slip from my mind entirely. As I did, I took a look around the captain's office. It reminded me a bit of Diane's, actually: neither extremely personalized nor overly utilitarian. It looked comfortable but professional, with a sturdy set of cushioned chairs set in front of a large oak desk.

"Well, I'm glad to hear that," Larose replied as he circled the desk to sit in his chair. "Please, have a seat. Oh, and let me call Officer Da Silva in here. She'll be accompanying you while you're here on the island."

"Great," I replied.

The captain seemed to be on top of things and cooperative, which was a relief. It made our jobs infinitely more manageable when we didn't have to worry about being hindered by the local law enforcement, an experience we'd gone through on more than one occasion. Larose reached into his pocket and pulled out his phone before quickly scrolling through it. A second later, he held the phone up to his ear.

"Hello, Officer Da Silva?" He spoke firmly into the phone. "Yes, that's actually why I'm calling you. They're here now... Yes, if you wouldn't mind. Thanks." He ended the call just as quickly as he'd made it before tucking the phone back into his pocket and turning to look at us. "She's on her way. Anyway, as I said earlier, I've been personally overseeing this case ever since we discovered who Mr. Clearwater was. It was obvious to me that something strange was going on." He frowned, his mouth twisting into a thin, concerned line as he stopped speaking for several moments.

"People die here, of course." He looked up at us, and I could see the trepidation in his eyes. "Tourists, I mean. Outsiders. We get a lot of older folks coming out on cruises. That's not very uncommon at all. Then, of course, we have the stupid ones who have a bit too much to drink and have a little accident, fall and hit their head, or whatever. It's sad when it happens, but it's explainable. This..." He trailed off, his eyes going hard as he slowly shook his head. "I've never seen anything quite like this."

"We appreciate you taking such a deep concern in the case," I replied honestly.

"Of course," Larose muttered. "As I said, death is one thing. What happened to Mr. Clearwater, though, that wasn't a run-of-the-mill death. He was—" He stopped as a sharp knock came abruptly at the door. Larose looked up. "Come in!"

The door swung open at once, and a prim, confi-
dent-looking woman stepped into the room. Her dark
hair was tied into a braid that trailed down over her
shoulder, and she had a sharp, piercing gaze that
seemed to penetrate straight through me.

"Captain," the woman addressed Larose.

"Oh, Officer Da Silva," Larose greeted her back
before turning to look at us. "Agents, this is Yvonne Da
Silva. Officer Da Silva, this is Agent Marston, and this
is Agent Holm."

He gestured to each of us in turn. As he did, Officer
Da Silva nodded curtly, her gaze still hard and pene-
trating. Her eyes were a shockingly pale blue, almost
gray, and I found myself unwilling to look away.

"It's nice to meet you," she replied as she looked
toward both Holm and me.

"Why don't we get another chair in here?" Larose
suggested as he began to stand up. I did as well, ready
to offer her mine in case we couldn't find a third one,
but Da Silva spoke up before either of us could get far.

"No need," she replied firmly, her tone steady and
commanding. "I'll just stand. Let's not waste time on
that when we have pressing issues to deal with." She
turned to look at Holm and me. "The agents even got
here early, so we shouldn't waste what little extra time
we have."

I could tell that Da Silva was a no-nonsense kind of
woman. She'd barely bothered with introductions and

was now rushing us to get to the details of the case. Frankly, it was an attitude that I could get behind.

"Well, alright then," Larose replied. "Let's get right to it. To start, how much have you been told about the case?" He turned to look at us.

"As far as details, not much," I replied. "We know that Clearwater was found on the beach on Palm Island. We know that he was covered extensively in bruises, and we know that the other guests on the island claimed not to have any idea what had happened. We don't know much beyond that."

"We also read that Palm Island is tough to access," Holm added as he recalled what we'd read on that pamphlet earlier. "It's uninhabited, and you can only get there by private boat. Is that right?"

"Partially." Da Silva raised an eyebrow. "You're right about it being hard to get to, in a way. Realistically, anyone with a boat can get there. It's not like there's a gate around it or anything. As far as getting there *legally*, it is privately owned, so the only people who are allowed to dock there are the companies that have travel agreements in place with the owners."

"But that doesn't mean Clearwater got there legally," I concluded. "In fact, it's very likely he didn't, considering no one seemed to recognize him."

"That's what I've been thinking as well." Da Silva nodded. "Though I'm not sure I believe that no one on that island saw what happened. And it's not the 'untouched paradise' that all the tour guides make it out to be." She scoffed and shook her head. "Palm Island is a giant resort for the super-wealthy. It's pretty, yes, but there's nothing natural about it. It's a huge man-made island. It costs an arm and leg just to get the privilege of going there, and it's always full of tourists. The odds that someone managed to commit a murder without anyone noticing anything are incredibly slim."

"Especially considering how quickly news spread once the body was discovered," Larose added. "From what we'd been able to gather from eyewitness reports and security footage, the body was initially found on the beach in front of one of the vacation houses at around six in the morning. Just twenty minutes later, guests from all over the island were swarming to the crime scene to get a look."

"That's disheartening," Holm replied, his face twisted into an expression of disgust.

"It's also suspicious," I replied as I realized what Larose was saying. "No one saw or heard anything while a man was being brutally beaten to death, but it only took twenty minutes for basically the entire island to hear about his death after the fact? That is weird."

"It definitely caused quite a stir," Larose muttered.

"I suppose I can't fault anyone for that," Da Silva replied as she crossed her arms. "I can only imagine how that must feel. You're on an island with no imme-diate escape, and you've just been informed that someone's been murdered." She heaved a heavy sigh. "I probably would have panicked as well. All that being said, though..." She suddenly tensed her shoulders as her face took on a furious expression. "That still doesn't excuse what those morons did next!"

"Which morons?" I asked as Da Silva reached a hand up to rub at her temple.

"The proprietors of the main ferry that takes people over to the island," she replied with a groan. "Apparently, they decided to move the body a few minutes after it was found. They said that they didn't want there to be a panic among the guests on the island." She huffed and shook her head bitterly. "Right. It's more like they didn't want to put off any guests from coming to the island in the future. A dead body is a pretty strong deterrent. They probably thought it would be bad for business. So, because of them, both the crime scene and the body were contaminated by the time police finally arrived on the scene."

"Officer Da Silva was one of the first on the scene," Larose explained as Da Silva took a few long, steadying breaths.

"Don't remind me," she grumbled. "They really just dragged him away and shoved him in a back room. Any fingerprints or DNA particles that might have been on him are gone, just like that!" She snapped her fingers before placing her hands on her hips. "Then again, there probably wasn't much there, to begin with.

There's a good chance that Mr. Clearwater was killed somewhere else, and his body just happened to wash up onshore. If that's the case, the water would have destroyed any evidence long before he was even found."

"We'd considered the possibility that he was killed somewhere else as well," I replied as I looked over at Holm. "It makes sense if we assume that the other guests are telling the truth about not having seen anything."

"That's right," Da Silva agreed. "Unfortunately for us, that means that there are a dozen different places he could have been killed. There are tons of small islands in that area. He could have been killed on any one of them and then dumped into the ocean."

"Which means we're no closer to figuring out what happened," I sighed. "Nevertheless, we should still head down to Palm Island to have a look for ourselves. There might be a piece of evidence that was overlooked in all the chaos."

"Of course." Da Silva nodded curtly. "Have you had a chance to see the body yet? I imagine you'll want to do that first."

"Not yet," I replied. "We just landed and came straight here, actually."

"We should definitely go and have a look then," she replied. "So you'll have a better understanding of exactly what it is we're dealing with. We can head down to the coroner's office now, if that's alright with you, Captain."

"I think that's a good idea," Larose replied. "I can call ahead and let them know that you're coming."

"Alright," I replied as Holm and I stood up.

"It isn't very far," Da Silva noted as she promptly headed out the door, barely pausing to make sure that we were following behind her before continuing down the hallway toward the stairs. "We can walk there in about five minutes. Did you drive here?"

"Yes," I replied as I hurried to keep up with her. She walked with bold determination, her head held high and her strides long as she moved through the station with ease.

"That's alright," she replied before I could say anything else. "We'll have to come back here anyway after we're finished examining the body. We might have time to head to Palm Island, depending on how long we take at the coroner's office."

"Sounds good," I agreed.

I'd thought earlier that Da Silva struck me as a very serious woman, and now I was sure of it. Her tone wasn't mean, but it was concise and straight to the point. Truth be told, I found her commanding attitude rather alluring.

"This way," she informed us as we finally stepped out of the station and onto the street.

On the way here, I'd been too busy focusing on the

road to pay much attention to what was around us, but now that we were walking at street level, it occurred to me just how unusual Kingstown was, at least in comparison to other Caribbean islands I'd been to. Prior experience had taught me to expect brightly colored buildings, streets lined with food vendors, and wide-open spaces filled with lush greenery and palm trees. In actuality, Kingstown reminded me more of Scotland, which we'd visited a few months prior, than it did any of the other islands we'd had cases on.

The police station wasn't the only imposing building made of stone and brick on the street. On the contrary, most of the architecture looked European in influence. Just on the other side of the road was a huge church made of dark, square stones, with brightly colored stained glass windows and a towering spire topped with a cross. Spiked, wrought-iron fences encircled several of the buildings on the street, and though there was plant life to be seen, the palm trees we came across were few and far between.

It was, however, just as crowded and busy as every other island I'd ever visited. That was the thing about these tropical locations. Most of them were so small and closely knit that people only really used cars when traveling long distances. People walked where they needed to go in their daily lives, something that would be almost unheard of in Miami, or most places in the US, for that matter. The lack of traffic fumes was abundantly evident in how fresh the air was, as well. I could practically smell the salt of the ocean as I breathed in, and the sky above us was a stunning shade of bright blue.

"Here we are," Da Silva announced as we came to a stop in front of our destination.

In contrast to the much grander buildings around it, the building we were standing in front of was small and nondescript. It was painted a pale terracotta orange, and if it hadn't been for the large banners hung just out front, I might have just assumed that it was an ordinary residential home.

"Memorials, cremations, funeral services," I muttered to myself as I read the banners that were slung just above the entrance.

It wasn't surprising to discover that the city's coroner doubled as their funeral home director. Kingstown was small enough that it probably wasn't practical for them to have a dedicated coroner. This wasn't a major metropolitan city where murders were commonplace, so it was only natural that the person most knowledgeable about dead bodies would be the local morgue director.

"The body's been here since it was recovered," Da Silva explained as the three of us stepped into the small building.

A bell rigged to the top of the door let out a little jingle as we stepped inside. It was a light and joyful sound, but somehow that only made the place feel all the more austere. This was a building dedicated to death, after all. Most people only came here during the worst times of their lives.

"I made sure no one else was allowed to touch it after I discovered how badly it had been handled before I got to the scene." Da Silva pursed her lips and shook her head, clearly still aggravated as she thought back to what had happened on Palm Island. "After we learned that he was American, I made sure that he was left undisturbed." She paused as she turned to look at us. "I knew that the FBI or someone would want to come in to take over, and I was right. So, don't worry, the body's in the same condition that I found it in."

A door opened from somewhere further into the building just then. I couldn't see very far past the front desk that bisected the lobby from the rest of the funeral home, but just a moment later, a small, graying man shuffled up to the front desk.

"Hello," he greeted us with a small smile. He had watery blue eyes, and every line on his face seemed to wrinkle and crease as he spoke.

"Good morning," Da Silva replied without hesitation. "Officer Da Silva. This is Agent Marston and Agent Holm. We're here to see the body of Logan Clearwater. Actually, I was here just yesterday. I'm the officer in charge of the case. I spoke with someone else, though."

"Yes, I was just on the phone with someone from the station," the man replied. "I'm sorry. The person you spoke with must have been my son. He's the one in charge, actually, but he isn't here at the moment."

"Will he be gone long?" I asked, trying to hide my disappointment at the news. We'd been making such good time as far as hitting the ground running early. I didn't want to have to wait now that we were already here.

"Oh, I imagine so," the old man replied. "There's a bit of drama going on with one of our families right now—some issues with the graveyard they want to have their dearly departed loved one buried in. Don't worry, though. I was the director here for thirty years. The name's Walt. Whatever it is you need help with, I'm sure I can be of assistance."

"I hope so," Da Silva replied curtly. "As I said, we're here to examine the body of Logan Clearwater. That would be the American who was found on the beach over on Palm Island."

"Of course." The old man nodded slowly as he gestured for us to come around the counter and follow him into the back of the funeral home. "How could I possibly forget a case like that? It's not every day something like that happens, and what with the condition of the body..." He clamped his mouth shut and gave a slight shudder.

A cold, unsettled feeling fell into the pit of my

stomach at his visceral reaction. Someone who'd been a funeral director for thirty years had to have seen a lot on his time, so I couldn't imagine what kind of condition the body must be in if it could evoke this kind of reaction.

"Follow me in here, please," the man directed us as he stepped through a door that led down into a steep set of stairs.

I grabbed onto the railing as we descended. The steps were narrow and high enough that I felt like I might trip and snap my neck at the slightest misstep.

"I should warn you, the corpse is in quite a shocking condition," he continued. "Then again, I'm sure a pair of agents such as yourselves must have seen quite some awful sights before."

"Unfortunately, yes," I replied as we made it down into the morgue. It was freezing and dark, and I fought the urge to shudder as I looked at the rows of cabinets lining the walls.

"Right over here," Walt called as he shuffled over to one of the metal tables in the center of the room. "I took the liberty of bringing him down when I got the call that you'd be coming."

"That's fine," Da Silva replied, though judging by the constrained tone of her voice, it seemed like it was very much not fine.

I recalled what she'd said about how she'd diligently made sure that no one touched the body, and I assumed that she must be upset that the man had moved the body while she wasn't there to supervise.

I walked over to the body on the table. It was covered head to toe in a thick gray sheet that looked like it was made of some kind of plastic. Walt appeared to hesitate for just a moment before pulling the sheet off, starting from the head. Even though he'd been right about Holm and I having seen our fair share of disturbing sights, I was still caught off guard by what awaited beneath the sheet.

Clearwater had been brutalized. There was no other way to describe what had happened to him. It took me a moment to even be able to recognize what color his skin was naturally because he was so covered in bruises and cuts that he looked blue and purple from head to toe. One side of his face was heavily swollen in a way that could only have resulted from blunt force trauma. Aside from that, though, his entire body was slightly bloated and puffy, likely from being in the water.

I clenched my jaw as I looked down at Clearwater's corpse in revulsion and anger. I could understand now why Walt had hesitated. Clearwater was very obviously an old man, older even than Walt. The hair on his head was completely white, and heavy wrinkles were evident in the parts of his face where I could still make out his wrinkles. His daughter had told us that Clearwater had been in his seventies already, a war vet with dementia. Just what kind of monster could do something like this to a confused, helpless old man? None of us said a single word for several long, somber seconds.

"Cause of death?" I asked flatly when I finally made my peace with the horrific sight in front of me.

"From what we can tell," Walt replied just as seriously, "It was likely blunt force trauma to the head." He reached down gingerly to move Clearwater's head around so we could see the extent of his injuries. "Although it's difficult to be sure, considering just how bad the damage is, he has several head injuries that would definitely be fatal. You can see the impression marks just here." He pointed directly to a spot on Clearwater's temple, just above his ear. "The way it's caved in like that indicates that he was struck there quite powerfully with something hard and blunt, maybe even kicked."

"Somebody kicked this man?" Da Silva snapped angrily, her eyes alight with fury as she looked up at Walt. "Which means he was already down, right? If they kicked him in the head?"

"I'm afraid so," Walt replied, his mouth twisting into a concerned grimace as he spoke. "As I said, it's impossible to be completely sure. He has quite a few injuries that would prove fatal if untreated. Really, it's just a matter of which one killed him first. The water certainly didn't help. It likely washed away a lot of evidence."

"He looks like he got beat to hell and back," Holm muttered as he leaned down to examine the body more closely. "Usually, in a case this severe, the motive would be something personal."

"You're right," I replied as I reached up to stroke my chin thoughtfully. "This is overkill. These kinds of injuries don't happen unless the assailant is angry. But that doesn't make any sense…"

"Why not?" Da Silva turned to look at me, and for a moment, I was caught off guard by her clear, gray eyes.

"Well, everything we've learned about this case leads us to believe that a stranger snatched Clearwater," I explained. "We've learned of other, similar reports back in New York, which is where Clearwater was last seen before he turned up here." I looked back down at the body in confusion. "We don't know *why* he was taken, but if it really was a stranger, then why take it this far? If the motive wasn't personal anger or revenge, then why are his injuries so severe?"

"Maybe Clearwater wasn't the target of the perp's anger," Da Silva suggested. "Statistically, serial killers go after a 'type' that looks like the true object of their rage because, for some reason or another, they can't go after the real person. So, you wind up with someone who really wants to kill their mom, for example, but instead, he targets women that look like her."

"I see what you're saying," I replied. "So, you think

that whoever's doing this is using substitutes for whoever it is he really wants to kill."

"That would explain why they were all men," Holm added. "Instead of women or kids, like we were thinking before."

"It would," I agreed. "But that still leaves a few questions unanswered. Why go through all the trouble of bringing them *here* of all places? If the goal is just to kill someone, why not do it in New York? There's also the fact that the men who were taken were of several ages and ethnicities. That kind of throws a wrench in the theory that they're being used as substitutes. The only thing they really have in common is the fact that they were all homeless."

"That's a good point," Da Silva conceded as she crossed her arms and frowned down at the ground in deep contemplation. "You said that there had been other reports, right? So, where are these other people? Several missing men and only one turns up dead, beaten nearly beyond recognition?"

"That's a good question," I replied.

"Unless we just haven't found their bodies yet," Holm suggested as he looked between Da Silva and me. "We're operating under the assumption that Clearwater washed up on shore, right? What if whoever did this just did a crappy job of disposing of the bodies? For all we know, they're all sitting at the bottom of the sea right now."

I frowned at the thought. I didn't want to think that it was already too late for us to do anything about the other missing men, but I had to admit that what Holm was saying was very likely. This entire situation was strange, and I couldn't think of what could have happened to these men that would warrant transporting them out of the country like this.

"Hey," I looked up at Walt as a thought suddenly occurred to me. "Were all of Clearwater's organs still in his body?"

I heard Da Silva gasp quietly behind me as Walt moved forward to check the chart next to the table.

"Yes, looks like they were," he replied as he scanned over the document. "Oh, but one of his lungs was collapsed, and his spleen was ruptured."

I cringed involuntarily at the revelation. Covered head to toe in bruises and with two damaged organs to boot, I just knew that Clearwater's final moments had been complete agony. I took a deep breath to collect myself as I swore to find whoever had done this to him.

"Were you thinking that he'd had his organs harvested?" Da Silva asked me.

There was a faint twinge of disbelief in her voice, not that I could blame her. Holm and I had discussed the possibility briefly a few days before, though we'd almost immediately dismissed it. It was, after all, practically unheard of—more of an urban legend than anything. The more we found out about this case, though, the less sure I was what I should think.

"I was," I admitted as I took a few steps away from the table. The sight of the mangled body and the smell of antiseptic and formaldehyde was beginning to make me feel sick. "I guess that's ruled out, though."

"I'm sorry I couldn't be more help," Walt murmured as he gently covered the body back up again.

He handled Clearwater's body with such care and attention, and I found myself feeling grateful for the small gesture. It was the absolute least that Clearwater deserved after what had happened.

"It's a shame, all of it," he continued. "I've been a mortician for decades now, and I've seen pretty much everything. Death I can handle, but *this*." He shook his head. "Evil is what I can't handle. The kind of evil that it would take to inflict this on anyone, let alone an elder like him. I just can't understand it."

"Neither can we," I replied quietly. A long beat of silence followed that was neither comfortable nor uncomfortable.

"Come on." Da Silva was the first to speak up. "We can still get to Palm Island with plenty of daylight to spare if we go now." She turned to look at Walt. "Thank you for taking the time to speak with us."

"We really appreciate it," I added.

The small man smiled and waved his hands at us dismissively.

"No, no, don't mention it," he assured us. "As I said, I only wish I could have done more. I wish you luck in finding who did this."

"Thanks," I replied before turning to follow Da Silva back up the stairs.

Her back was stiff, and her shoulders were tense as she walked ahead of me. I wondered if she was still thinking about the condition of Clearwater's body. I knew that I felt incensed just remembering it, so I imagined she must feel angry as well. Children and the elderly made up the most vulnerable populations, so it always seemed especially heinous when either was the victim of a crime. I was going to make sure whoever did this paid for it.

15

ETHAN

I LOOKED out over the water as the wind whipped through my hair. The boat that Da Silva had secured for us to get to the island was small but fast, and I could feel the ocean spray hitting my face as I leaned down against the railing of the boat. The water below looked unbelievably clear, and for a second, I longed for the opportunity to go for a dive.

It had been a while since I'd gone on one, either for work or for pleasure, and I spent a few seconds racking my brain to try to remember when exactly the last time had been before stopping myself short. Just thinking about it was bumming me out. I kept the thought in the back of my mind for later, though. Once this case was over, I was definitely going to find a reason to go out on a dive again. It had been some time since I really focused my energy on finding information related to the *Rogue* as well, so maybe it was time to go treasure-hunting again.

"Hey, so, you sure they won't kick up a fuss or anything?" the man captaining the boat called over the sound of the splashing water as he roared over the surface.

"Well, I'm not entirely sure," Da Silva replied with a shrug. "Are you that worried about it?"

"I wouldn't say worried!" The captain cackled. "To be honest, it might be kind of funny if they do. Bunch of uptight jerks. They get so mad if anyone so much as sails close to the shore, let alone docks there. Snobs!" He let out another chuckle before continuing. "I mean, sure, I get that it's a private island and all, but there's no need to be rude, you know what I mean? The rich tourists come down here from the States and Europe, and then they look down their noses at the locals. How are you going to come to the Grenadines and then act like the people who actually live here are beneath you, you know?"

"They're really that hostile?" I asked curiously as I turned around to face him, leaning back against the edge of the boat as I did.

"Not *all* of them," the captain replied with a slight shrug. "I had a nice American couple who wanted to go on a little boat ride just yesterday. Nice people, and they tipped well, too. But the kinds of people who come over to these exclusive islands..." He scrunched up his face in mild disgust. "They're a different breed of people. The kind of people with so much money that they think their money can buy them whatever they want, like they can own other people even." He shook his head, and the impish smile that had been on his face just moments earlier was gone, replaced instead by a sober, almost chilling frown.

"Like they can own other people..?" I repeated quietly to myself, so softly that I was sure no one else had heard me over the sound of the rushing water.

That was an oddly fitting choice of words, though I was sure that it had only been a coincidence on the captain's part. Still, my brain instantly went into overdrive as I considered the implications of what he'd said. A rash of missing men and an island full of people so affected by their own wealth that they believed they had the right to possess people? I felt like I was getting close to figuring out how this was all connected to Clearwater, but there were still too many pieces of the puzzle missing for me to make a definitive conclusion.

"Well, here we are," the captain declared as he began to ease the boat into a small dock. "And there they come."

I walked over to the helm where he was standing to see what he was seeing. Sure enough, a group of people dressed in crisp black uniforms was marching over to the dock like they were on a mission. A woman headed the group with platinum blond hair that was styled into big, exaggerated curls that looked like they required a copious amount of hairspray to stay intact.

"Excuse me!" she called as the captain brought the boat to a stop right up against the wooden dock. Her mouth twisted into a wide, unpleasant smile as she shouted, and I decided after hearing just that one word that I did not like this woman. "Hi! Yes, you there at the wheel. This is a *private* beach. Do you have the proper documentation to be docking here?"

"I'll handle this," Da Silva declared airily as she walked to the edge of the boat. She stepped off gracefully, pausing only for a moment to brush off her white police uniform before striding over to the blond woman. The woman, to her merit, dropped the saccharine sweet smile the moment she spotted Da Silva's police uniform.

"Well, hello—" the blond woman greeted Da Silva, her voice dripping with false sincerity.

"Officer Da Silva," our liaison cut her off brusquely. "I'm here with federal agents Marston and Holm of MBLIS. We're investigating the death of a Mr. Logan Clearwater who was found here approximately two weeks ago now."

"Please keep your voice down," the blond woman hissed at Da Silva before looking around anxiously. She looked as though she was worried someone would overhear, but the only people I could see anywhere nearby were a couple of girls sunbathing several yards away. "That was an... unfortunate incident, and while I appreciate—"

"You're right," Da Silva cut her off again as Holm and I stepped off the boat. "It is unfortunate, which is why we will be investigating the crime scene as soon as possible."

"Well, listen here," the blond woman huffed as she put her hands on her hips.

Holm and I had caught up to Da Silva by now, and I could see her raising an eyebrow at the squat woman.

"I understand that you have to do your jobs," she continued, "but this is still a private island! You can't just barge in however you want and start making demands!"

"Demands?" I scoffed at the woman.

She snapped her gaze away from Da Silva to look at me, the expression on her face one of pure indignation.

"I would hardly call wanting to look at the crime scene a 'demand,'" I countered. "A man is dead, Ms...?"

"Gail Fletcher!" the blond woman sniffed as she yanked at the nametag that was pinned to her top.

"Ms. Fletcher." I smiled at her. "This island is a crime scene. A man who was brutally beaten to death was discovered here. Surely, you're not saying that you're going to impede our investigation, right?"

Her face puckered up like she'd just bitten into a lemon.

"W-we have guests on the island!" she protested, as though I was supposed to care more about the comfort of her wealthy guests than about a man who'd been murdered. "If they see a bunch of cops poking around, they're going to become upset!"

"We're not cops, first off," I replied plainly, letting the pleasant smile slip from my face as I answered her. "We're federal agents. Frankly, I don't give a crap about your guests. If you really plan to stand there and block our way, just know that you'll not only be interfering in a police matter but in a federal one as well." I paused for just a moment to let that sink in. "I can assure you that the United States government doesn't take kindly to people who impede criminal investigations."

Fletcher opened and closed her mouth several times without actually saying anything. Her hands were balled into fists, and with the way she was pouting, she looked like an overgrown toddler.

"Fine," she finally sniffed, lifting her chin so she could look down her nose at me. "I suppose that's a reasonable request. Of course, I'll have to insist that I accompany you during your time here on the island. Just in case you need anything, of course."

"Who even are you?" Holm snorted as he tossed her a dubious look.

Fletcher looked at him like he'd just slapped her across the face.

"I-I, well, I'm the manager here at the marina!" she stammered in response as her face started to glow red. "I'm in charge of overseeing transportation. You can understand why I was so shocked to see that dinky little boat pull in. It definitely isn't one of *ours*."

"Ha!" the captain guffawed from where he was still standing on the boat. He turned to look at me. "See? That's exactly what I meant. Even the help acts like— well, you remember what I told you."

"What? The help?" Fletcher squawked as she glared up at the captain, who just laughed harder, having clearly gotten the reaction he was looking for.

I couldn't blame him for messing with her. The woman was abrasive, and I really wasn't looking forward to having her tail us the entire time we were here.

"And just what is that supposed to mean?" Fletcher demanded as she continued to look up at the captain, who deliberately ignored her as he turned to look at us instead.

"I'll be waiting here whenever you need to go back!" he announced cheerfully.

"Thanks!" I called back before looking over to Da Silva and Holm. "Come on, let's go." I turned on my heel, hoping that maybe we might just slip away from the obnoxious Ms. Fletcher. I knew it was a long shot, though, so I wasn't surprised when she suddenly spun around and called after us.

"Now, wait just a minute!" she snapped as she quickly trudged toward us.

I didn't bother to slow my pace or even turn around. I supposed that I couldn't really stop her from following us, but that didn't mean I had to pay her any mind.

It dawned on me just how deserted the island really was as we walked. I couldn't see any sign of a gas station, grocery store, or heck, even a road. The only actual structures I could see were fancy resort bungalows and small seaside cafes and bars. The beaches themselves were pretty empty as well, with plenty of space for each of the guests I could see lounging on beach chairs or lying out on oversized towels. It was a far cry from the beaches I'd seen back in Kingstown. Though those had been beautiful and pristine as well, they'd been far more crowded with tourists and locals alike. It was evident from just a look that the people here weren't local. In fact, they all looked like movie stars, with plastic, perfect bodies and brilliant white smiles that just looked fake, somehow. Even though the temperature was warm and balmy, I had to fight the urge to shiver. Something about it all seemed uncannily wrong, like the entire island was a display home. Everything looked pretty but fake at the same time.

"The body was over here," Da Silva informed us as she suddenly stepped off the smooth, man-made path and onto the sand. This stretch of beach was pretty deserted, though a small villa was just a few yards away.

"Could you please not talk so loudly about that?" Fletcher whispered as she looked around again as though checking for witnesses. She'd lost her posse along the way, so it was just her with us now. It was little comfort, though, as she was annoying enough on her own.

"He was here, face down according to the man who found him," Da Silva continued at full volume, completely ignoring Fletcher's request. If anything, she might have spoken slightly louder.

"And who was that?" I asked as I looked down at the spot on the beach.

"Glendale, I believe his name was," Da Silva replied as she turned to look at the small villa behind us. "He was staying there. He came down to do some exercise by the water, and that was when he found the body." She suddenly twisted around to look at Fletcher. "Isn't that right?"

"Huh?" Fletcher stared back at Da Silva in wide-eyed befuddlement.

"It's just that you seem to know a lot about the island," Da Silva replied, her voice coated with sarcasm. "And you seem to be extremely concerned about us talking about the particulars of the case, so I can only assume that you must know quite a great deal about it."

"Oh, w-well, I—" Fletcher mumbled incoherently for several moments before looking down at her feet. "Well, yes, that's what happened. Mr. Glendale called management to report that he'd discovered the body at around five in the morning. He was on his way down to the beach to have a walk when he spotted it. He thought it was just a drunk at first, but then he saw all the bruises and the way his face was—" She clamped her mouth shut as she suddenly stopped talking, her face pale and a bit sweaty.

"He called you and not the police?" I raised an eyebrow at her.

"Well, not me *personally*," Fletcher replied. "But yes, he felt letting that one of the staff know right away about what he'd found was the best course of action, and it's a good thing he did, too."

"Because that made it all the easier for you to cover it up?" Da Silva asked brazenly as she glared down at the shorter woman.

Fletcher looked up at the officer in shock.

"How dare you!" she blustered. "We would never do such a thing! Did it ever occur to you that we were the ones most equipped to handle the situation, given the circumstances? There are no police here, Officer! We're the ones who have to run around cleaning everyone's messes! If I recall, it took several hours for the police to arrive once we had called them!"

"It's an island, Ms. Fletcher," Da Silva deadpanned. "We had to take a boat here. And in the time it took us to arrive, you managed to put your hands all over the body while moving it, destroying any potential evidence, not to mention ruining the crime scene as well!"

Fletcher looked up at her in fear, like a kid who'd just been scolded.

"W-well, like I said," Fletcher mumbled anxiously. "I wasn't personally involved with handling the body. That was all someone else..." She was back-pedaling now, obviously trying to cover her own ass and shift the blame onto someone else. "In any case, we had to do something about the body. By the time anyone from the staff showed up, there was already a crowd trying to get a look!" She huffed as she crossed her arms over her chest. "Completely ridiculous. It had barely been ten minutes since Mr. Glendale had called to let us know about what he'd found, but it seemed like half the island was already there! I get that gossip spreads fast, especially in a tiny place like this, but I don't understand why anyone would actu-ally *want* to see something as atrocious as a dead body!" She shuddered as she hugged her arms tighter around herself.

"Morbid curiosity, I suppose," I muttered in

response as I looked up and down the long stretch of beach.

There was absolutely no way we were going to find anything useful, not if half the guests had been traipsing around the crime scene. Even if they hadn't, it had been days since the body was discovered, and we were standing on a beach. Sand, by its very nature, shifted and moved around. That was to say nothing of the tide as well, which would have surely washed away anything that natural erosion hadn't managed to take care of.

"How did Clearwater end up here?" I asked.

"There are boats just offshore," Holm noted as he nodded out toward the water.

There were, in fact, a few large boats on the horizon. From where we were standing, I could just barely make out the figures moving around onboard, probably drinking and partying it up.

"There's nothing else around for miles," he pointed out. "If I had to guess, I'd say he was probably killed on a boat and then thrown overboard."

"That's impossible!" Fletcher rounded on him, her voice shrill and unpleasant. "All the boats here are property of the island! Well, more or less, anyway. There's no way he could have been on one without someone noticing!"

"You're not wrong about that," I muttered.

She blinked at me in surprise, clearly shocked at how easily I'd agreed.

"It is difficult to believe that no one saw anything," I clarified, "either on one of the boats or here on the island."

I turned around to look back toward the villa. The spot we were in was pretty out of the way, so it was possible the Clearwater might have been killed quickly and dumped before anyone noticed. However, what was impossible was the idea that he had sustained so much damage without anyone noticing.

"The victim was beaten until he was literally black and blue," I continued. "There's not a chance that happened without someone noticing."

"Well, it certainly wasn't anyone here!" Fletcher insisted vehemently.

Honestly, I believed her. Right now, everything pointed to Clearwater having been killed somewhere else and dumped here. How and why that happened was still a mystery.

"What about Mr. Glendale?" Holm asked as he gestured toward the villa. "Is he still here? We'd like to speak with him."

"I'm afraid not," Fletcher replied, though she sounded more relieved than sorry about that fact. "He left just a few days after the body was discovered. Not that I can blame him."

"I spoke to him immediately following the

discovery of the body," Da Silva assured me. "We ruled him out as a suspect. There was no motive and no evidence that he was involved in any way."

"Well, of course not!" Fletcher crowed. "As I told you, there's no way any of our guests were involved in... something like that." She scrunched her nose up like she'd just smelled something foul. "Now, was there something else you wanted to see? If there is, can we hurry up and get to it? I haven't got all day, you know."

"You're free to stop following us anytime you like," I replied dryly, hopeful but doubtful that she would actually acquiesce and go away.

"I don't think so," she replied snobbily. "I'm not going to interfere with your investigation, or whatever it was you called it, but I'm not going to let you waltz around as you please, either."

"Right." I sighed with frustration. This woman was the worst, and just listening to her was giving me a headache. "In any case, I think we're about done here." I ignored the look of glee that crossed Fletcher's face as I turned to look at Da Silva and Holm. "I don't think we're going to get much else from being here. By now, all the evidence has washed away, our key witness is long gone, and from the looks of it, the people in charge don't actually know anything useful."

Out of the corner of my eye, I noticed Fletcher stiffen at my last barb, and I fought the urge to smile in satisfaction.

"I agree." Da Silva sighed in resignation. "As much as I hate to admit it, I don't think there's much left for us to see or do here. I say we head back to the station to regroup. We can go over what we know and come up with a new plan of action."

"Took the words right out of my mouth." I smiled at her, and to my surprise, the ever-present stern expression on her face melted away just slightly as she offered me a small smile in return.

"Perfect," Fletcher sniffed, completely ruining whatever small pleasure I'd felt at seeing Da Silva's expression. "Well, I'll escort you back to that little boat you arrived on." She turned around dramatically before trudging off, her head high in the air as she walked.

"Must be exhausting to be so uptight all day," Holm muttered to me, so quietly that I was sure no one else could hear. To my surprise, though, Da Silva responded before I could.

"She'd probably ease up a little if she removed the stick she has lodged up her backside," she quipped in response, not nearly as quietly as Holm had spoken.

I darted my eyes over to Fletcher. Her shoulders had tensed, and I realized that she definitely must have heard Da Silva. I was equal parts mortified and impressed by how brazen Da Silva's comment had been, and I had to bite my lip to keep from smiling.

"Well, here we are," Fletcher grunted when we

arrived back at the dock a few minutes later. "It was a pleasure to—"

"Gail!" someone suddenly shouted from behind us. I turned around and spotted another worker wearing the same black uniform running toward us.

"What is it, Raj?" Fletcher looked back at him in shock. The kid was a little out of breath.

"There's a problem over in guest services," the employee explained. "Some people said that they left their luggage on one of the boats, and they're pitching a fit. The lady said that she had some really expensive purses in her suitcase, and she's accusing Linda of trying to steal them."

"Oh, for goodness' sake!" Fletcher groaned as she threw her hands up in the air. "If it isn't one thing, it's another." She frowned as she turned to look at us again. "Like I was saying, it was a pleasure helping you. Please have a safe trip back."

Her words were pleasant, but the tone in which she said them made me think that what she actually wanted to happen was for us to sink to the bottom of the ocean as quickly as possible. She didn't wait for any of us to answer before pivoting on her heel and scrambling away to deal with whatever drama was going on. The young man who'd come to deliver the message continued to pant heavily for a few moments, watching over his shoulder as Fletcher scurried away. Then, to my immense surprise, he suddenly stood up straight, his breathing completely level as he turned to face us.

"Hey, sorry about that little act," he muttered sheepishly. "I needed to get her to leave."

"Oh," I replied, too stunned to hold in my surprise. "So, that was all a lie?"

"Uh, yeah," the kid replied as he awkwardly reached up to rub the back of his neck. "There's no crisis. I mean, a crazy lady was screaming about us stealing her bag, but she found it in the end, so it's fine."

"Alright," I replied, still confused about what the kid was up to. "So, why did you want to get rid of her?"

"Oh, right," he replied quietly. He looked around, just like Fletcher had done, only this time the kid seemed genuinely nervous about it. "Well, uh, I couldn't really talk to you earlier. Not with Gail going off like she was. Actually, I wasn't sure if I should talk to you at all. It's kinda crazy, and I'm not really sure what it is I'm trying to tell you."

"Son," Da Silva cut him off sharply. The kid clammed up immediately. "You're rambling. I need you to take a deep breath and start over from the beginning. How about a name, first off?"

"Oh, yeah, sorry." The young man shook his head nervously. "Right, I'm Raj. I've been working here for a few months now. Anyway, I just wanted to let you know that, well, the people who come here are kind of weird."

"Weird?" I parroted. "What do you mean by that?"

"I don't know." The kid bit his lip. "I'm not sure how to explain it, to be honest. It's just... some of the people that come here are really scary. Not all of them. Most of them are pretty nice, even though they're super-rich. But sometimes, we'll get this one group that just creeps me out, you know?"

"I think I do," I replied.

It was difficult to ascertain what the kid was trying to say when he was being so vague, but I felt I could understand the feeling of just not trusting someone. Knowing when to trust your gut was an invaluable skill for a federal agent and one that had saved my life on more than one occasion.

"What exactly is it about these people that you think is creepy?" I asked.

"Well, just the way they act," he mumbled nervously. "They never look me in the eye, and they act like I'm not even there. I mean, they expect me to help them and stuff, but at the same time, it's like they don't actually see me as a person, I guess. They always arrive at weird times, too, usually in the middle of the night. That in itself isn't strange since people sometimes go out boating and don't come back till after dark, but... I don't know. Something about them just puts me on edge. You know that feeling you get when you can just tell someone's up to something bad?"

"Yeah, I think I do," I replied. The picture he was painting was alarming, and I didn't like where this was going.

"Well, anyway, there were some of them around the day that the dead guy was found," Raj explained. "There were a lot of them, actually. I remember because one of them had made some weird comment about my muscles." He scrunched his face up in displeasure as he recalled the memory.

"Your muscles?" I furrowed my brows in confusion.

"Yeah," the kid muttered in response. "It was weird. One of them made this comment about how I looked like I could throw a punch, and then the other one laughed. Like there was really nothing funny about it, but they were both laughing like it was the most hysterical joke. It was so weird. And usually, if someone said something nice about your muscles, it would feel good, right? Well, this didn't feel like a compliment. I don't know. It kind of felt like an insult or like they were laughing at some inside joke. Whatever it was, it freaked me out."

"And you think these people might have had something to do with Clearwater's death?" I asked. I had to admit, the story he'd just told me was more than a little off-putting, but being a weirdo wasn't really proof that you were a murderer.

"Well, I'm not trying to accuse anyone or anything," Raj replied hesitantly. "I mean, I don't have proof or anything, but the thing is, they were all gone the day after we found the body."

"What?" I replied with alarm.

On either side of me, Da Silva and Holm both stiffened in reaction to the kid's revelation.

"Yeah," he muttered. "The night before was the night that they made those creepy comments. It was a group of them, four or five, maybe. But the next day, I noticed that I suddenly didn't see them around. Honestly, I was relieved. I felt really skeeved out the entire time they were around, so I remember just feeling happy that they were gone. It wasn't until you showed up today that I started to think back on it."

"Do you remember any of their names?" I asked urgently.

What he'd just told us was all circumstantial information. It might have been all a coincidence, but I tended to believe that the most reasonable explanation was the correct one. I doubted such a huge coincidence could occur on such a small island.

"No, sorry," the kid replied, much to my disappointment. "They never told me, and I never asked. I tried to steer clear of them, to tell you the truth. Actually, I—"

"Raj!" a now-familiar, shrill voice screeched from the other end of the beach. I could have groaned in displeasure as I looked up and saw Fletcher standing here, hands on her hips as she stared ruthlessly at the kid. "What do you think you're doing? Get over here now!"

I glared at her, irritated both that she'd interrupted our conversation and that she was speaking to her employee like he was a misbehaving child. Raj, however, looked petrified.

"S-sorry," he mumbled as he bowed his head. "I gotta go."

"Wait!" I called, but he was already off, rushing over to where Fletcher was standing, now glaring viciously at us instead.

"Poor kid probably doesn't want to lose his job," Da Silva grumbled bitterly. "Damn, and we were getting such good info." She sighed as she reached a hand up to stroke the length of her ponytail. "What do you think the odds are that the lovely Ms. Fletcher will give us the names of the guests who were here that night?"

"Less than zero," I snorted as I turned around to head back onto the boat.

"Yeah, that's about what I was thinking, too," Da Silva replied. "I'll make a call and see about getting a warrant. With how long those usually take, though, there's a good chance we'll have solved the case by the time we get one."

"I know that feeling." I sighed as the three of us climbed back onto the boat.

"Back so soon?" the captain asked as we all sat

down in the circle of seats set at the front of the boat. He had a bag of store-bought cookies in one arm and was in the process of devouring one as he spoke to us.

"Afraid so," I replied.

"Well, I'll get you back to Kingstown then," he replied cheerfully as he stowed the bag of cookies on a shelf under the helm. "We should be back just before nightfall if we make good time."

"Great," I called back as he started the boat back up.

"So, where do we go from here?" Holm wondered out loud. "I mean, there's no way that lead from the kid is a coincidence, right?"

"That was just what I was thinking," I replied. "Seems to me like we've got a few potential suspects. The kid, Raj, said four or five, right?"

"He did," Da Silva confirmed. "If only he had any clue at all about their identities or where they are now."

"We'll figure it out," I replied confidently as I felt the boat shift beneath us. A moment later, the familiar, pleasant sound of splashing water reached my ears as we took off, away from Palm Island and back toward Kingstown. "Raj said that they come once in a while, which means that wherever they are, there's a solid chance they'll be coming back. The moment they do, we'll be there to grab them."

16

ETHAN

THE THREE OF us fell into a comfortable silence after that. Maybe we should have been a little more anxious about the fact that there were still so many questions left unanswered, but honestly, it was difficult to feel distressed when we were out here on the water. The ocean breeze swept over me like a calming wave, and in any case, there was no use in getting all worked up while we were out in the middle of the sea. It wasn't like I could do anything until we got back to shore anyway, so I might as well enjoy the ride there.

It came as that much more of a shock, then, when the marina at Kingstown finally came back into view. The sky was just entering that peaceful twilight stage. Streaks of orange and purple stretched across the sky, and it all would have been quite a lovely sight if it hadn't been for the commotion going on down on the docks.

"What's happening over there?" Holm asked just as I was wondering the same thing. He stood up and walked to the end of the boat to look, and I followed after him.

"Is it a fight?" I asked curiously.

We were just entering the marina now, and as we did, I could more clearly make out the faces of the people standing along the dock. The crowd was definitely in some kind of frenzy, but I couldn't actually see anyone exchanging blows.

"I don't think so," Holm replied as he craned his neck to get a better look. "It looks like—oh, crap!"

I looked around in alarm as he suddenly exclaimed, and it only took me a moment to realize what it was he was talking about. A man was up on the roof of one of the restaurants overlooking the water. He was stumbling around, almost as if he were drunk, and he had something small and shiny clutched in his hand.

"He's got a gun!" I exclaimed through clenched teeth as I ran to the side of the boat.

"What's going on?" Da Silva shouted as she looked up at Holm and me in alarm from where she was sitting.

"Armed man on the roof of one of the buildings," I replied as I continued to the edge of the boat.

Out of the corner of my eye, I watched her jump to her feet. The boat hadn't even made it all the way into the dock yet, but I still leapt over the railing and onto the wooden surface several feet below. Holm and Da Silva followed closely behind me, and the three of us stayed low to the ground as we quickly moved toward the building.

Now that we were closer, I realized that the man on the roof was shouting. The people on the ground were shouting up at him too, and it all culminated into a chaotic jumble of noise.

"Just put it down!" a dock worker in a dark gray tank top shouted up at the crazed man. "Whatever happened, you can fix it. This isn't worth it!"

"Cliff, will you shut up and get down!" another similarly dressed worker hissed from behind a large bollard he was using as cover. "The guy's nuts. You're going to get yourself shot!"

I was actually inclined to agree with the man and was about to shout at the sympathetic Samaritan to fall back and hide when the man on the roof started screaming in earnest.

"I didn't want to!" he screeched, and there was a profound pain in his voice that could only be described as grief. "They made me do it! I swear I didn't want to do it!"

The man was actually sobbing as he yelled, and though I felt some sympathy for whatever it was he was going through, I couldn't let my guard down, not as long as he was still waving that gun around wildly.

"We need to do something," I muttered to Holm. "I'll distract him, alright? In the meantime, you two go into the restaurant and—"

"—should have put a bullet in his head to make sure he was dead." A furious voice suddenly caught my attention.

I spun around to find the source, and my eyes landed on a stocky, muscular man who was standing just a few feet away. He was looking up at the man on the roof with a mixture of disgust and what looked like fear. It was a bizarre combination that was only made more suspicious by what he'd just said.

"Let's just do it now, before he says anything else," the man standing next to the first one muttered in response.

The second man reached for something at his waist, but before he could grab it, I stepped forward.

"What did you just say?" I demanded to know.

Both men turned to look at me with twin expressions of shock.

"Nothing," the first man replied reflexively.

I could tell that he regretted speaking at all the moment he opened his mouth to reply.

"Repeat what you just said," I ordered as I took a step closer to them.

I could feel Holm and Da Silva just behind me,

ready to back me up. For just a second, neither man moved, and then the taller of the two, the one who had been about to reach for something at his waist, suddenly turned on his heel and fled.

"Stop!" I yelled as I chased after him.

A jolt of anxiety coursed through my veins as I did because it struck me at just that moment that I was putting my back to the gunman on the roof. I didn't have any choice since I couldn't exactly chase this man without looking away from the building. Nevertheless, the situation was unbearably nerve-racking as part of me waited to be struck in the back with a bullet.

The man was fast but a little clumsy as well, as evidenced by the fact that he was crashing into everyone he passed. Fortunately for me, he slowed down a bit every time that he did, and in just a matter of seconds, I was upon him, tackling him forcefully to the ground. He let out an enraged scream as he struggled to push me off. He twisted his arm around to reach for something at his waist again, but I shoved his wrist down hard onto his back in a way that it was not meant to bend. He cried out in agony, and I quickly did the same with his other hand so I could get him into a pair of cuffs.

"Hold still!" I ordered as I got the cuffs into place.

He was still struggling valiantly, but I had a firm grip on him. As I got him under control, I looked around quickly for Holm and Da Silva. It only took me a moment to spot them, and when I did, I was struck numb with horror. Da Silva and the other suspect were both locked in an intense battle with one another as each wrestled to wrench the gun away from the other. I made to stand up, but the moment I did, my suspect thrashed frantically, and I pushed him down onto the ground reflexively.

I cringed as I heard a gunshot, and I looked up again, terrified at what I might find. I breathed a sigh of relief as I realized that both Da Silva and Holm were fine. The suspect was on the ground at Da Silva's feet. Holm was standing just a few steps away, his own gun still pointed directly at the fallen suspect.

"Are you okay?" I called toward them as I glanced up at the roof of the building.

It didn't seem like the gunman had even noticed what was happening because he was still pacing back and forth along the roof, moaning and shouting as he waved the gun around.

"Fine!" Da Silva replied as she ran over to where I was crouched on the ground over the suspect. "Can't say the same for him, though."

She tossed a glance over her shoulder to where the other suspect was prone on the ground, either dead or quickly headed there. Holm reached down to check the man's pulse before reaching into his pocket to grab his phone.

"I'll call for backup and an ambulance," he said as he hurried over to where Da Silva and I were.

"We need to do something about that one," Da Silva declared as she looked up at the man on the roof.

My heart was pounding in overdrive as I tried to decide what I should focus on for the moment. So much had happened in just the span of a few seconds, and we still weren't out of the woods yet.

"I'll stay here and keep an eye on him," Holm offered as he looked down at the man I had hand-cuffed. "You two go and handle the situation on the roof."

He'd just barely finished speaking when a loud bang rang out through the surrounding air. I swore as I looked up at the man on the roof. He was screeching now, and the hand holding the gun was shaking. Down on the ground, the few people who had been trying to reason with the man began to scramble away from the building.

"I'm sorry!" the gunman cried, fat tears rolling down his sunburned face. "I didn't mean to do that! Dammit, dammit! I just want this to be over!"

"We need to go now." I turned to look at Da Silva, who looked back at me with wide, alarmed eyes.

She nodded, and the two of us took off at a run toward the restaurant entrance. Inside, I could see several people ducked under the tables, shaking as they nervously looked around.

"How do we get up to the roof?" I yelled at an employee who was crouched beneath a bar at the right side of the restaurant.

"T-through that door over there," he replied as he lifted a shaking hand to point toward a door at the far end of the restaurant marked "employees only." "I have no idea who that guy is. He just barged in and—"

I took off before the man could finish. I didn't have time to listen to his explanation, not when the man had already fired the gun once and could do it again at any moment. Da Silva and I burst through the door and into the stairwell. The muscles in my legs burned as I took the stairs two at a time, running as fast as I could up to the roof. I stopped for just a moment when I finally made it up to the door that led into the roof. The man was very clearly unstable, and sudden noises or movements might be all it took to set him off.

I slowly pushed the door open. I was trying to be discreet, but an unfortuitous gust of wind chose that moment to blow across the roof. It caught against the door and yanked it open, causing it to slam hard against the wall just beside it. The gunman spun around to look at us, his eyes wide and crazed.

"Who are you!?" the man shouted as he rounded on us, the gun in his hand glinting as he pointed it toward us.

"Whoa!" I yelled as I threw my hands up defensively.

There was no way I'd be able to grab my gun before he got the chance to fire, and even if I could, I didn't want to shoot the man. Even though he had a gun, he didn't actually seem aggressive. On the contrary, he seemed scared, panicked even. "It's okay. We're here to help you."

"That's... is that true?" the man muttered as he looked frantically between Da Silva and me. He looked like he didn't really trust us. His gaze was a bit unfocused, and it was evident to me that the man wasn't at all in his right mind.

"Yes," Da Silva replied calmly. "Look." She gestured down at her own uniform. "I'm a police officer. Whatever it is that happened to you, we can help. Just put the gun down and—"

"No!" the man yelled as he raised his gun higher.

Da Silva instinctively reached for the gun at her hip, and the man's eyes went wide with panic. His finger twitched against the trigger, and I slid between the two of them on instinct.

"Wait!" I shouted, every muscle in my body tense as I stood between the pair of them. "Don't shoot."

"I'm not giving up the gun!" the man whined like a kid who'd been told he couldn't have a toy. "I need it. I need it, okay? It's the only way I can defend myself from them."

"Okay, that's fine," I called back as calmly as I could. "Can you tell me your name?"

"R-Roy," the man muttered after a moment of hesitation. "It's Roy. My name is Roy."

Roy? I thought to myself, my mind flying back to the conversation I'd had with Stephan, the homeless man who had begged us for help in finding his kidnapped friend back in New York. Was it possible that it was just a coincidence that his friend had also been named Roy?

"Who is 'them'?" I asked as I took the tiniest of baby steps toward him.

"Those people," the man replied in a horrified whisper, his eyes going wide and blank as his entire body began to tremble. "Those horrible people... they made me do it. They made *us* hurt each other. Kill each other!" The man screwed his eyes shut as he suddenly began to hit himself in the head with the butt of the gun. "I can't get their faces out of my head! Some of them were just kids! Little punks that should have been in school, not there! And the old man! I can't take it. I don't want to think about it anymore!"

"Okay," I tried to reassure him, but I was so alarmed and confused myself that I could barely maintain my own composure. What the hell was he talking about? People being killed? An old man? I froze as a thought occurred to me. Was it possible that he was talking about Clearwater? If he really was the same Roy who'd been snatched, then he might have encountered Clearwater after being taken to wherever the kidnappers took him.

"It's going to be okay," I insisted as I took another step toward him. If I could just get close enough, I could take the gun, and then we'd all at least be a little safer.

"It's not," the man whimpered as his shoulders suddenly sagged. He looked straight back at me, and the expression I saw on his face was haunting. His eyes were devoid of light, and he looked like all the fight had left him. Then, he lifted the gun in a flash and pointed it at his own head. "It's not going to be okay. I can't take back what I did."

"Don't do that," I pleaded with the man.

My ears were ringing, and my heart was beating so fast that I almost felt lightheaded. I was confident in my abilities, but I had to admit that I was out of my depth here. Though I had some hostage negotiation training, I'd never been in a situation quite like this, and I was terrified that I would say the wrong thing and cause this interaction to end in tragedy.

"Please listen to him," Da Silva added quietly. "We understand that something bad happened to you. We hear you, okay? But you don't have to do this."

"I don't know what else to do." Roy broke down crying. The gun glittered in the light as it shook in his trembling hands, and I felt a cold bead of sweat roll down the side of my face as I watched it like a hawk.

"Every time I close my eyes, I can see them. The people who took us, the people they made me kill. The blood on my hands. I can't sleep. I can't even eat. I don't want to live like this!"

"You're right," I quickly agreed with him. "But this isn't the way. You want to get back at the people who did this to you, right?"

I really didn't know what I was saying. I knew what I wanted the outcome of this to be, and I knew that I needed to convince him not to do anything brash, but truth be told, I really didn't know how I was supposed to get us there. I was just grasping at straws, trying whatever might convince him just to put the gun down.

"The people who took you," I continued. "If you die right now, then they'll never face justice. Don't give them the satisfaction of winning."

Roy looked back at me in silence for a second. His hand was still shaking, and it looked like he was really thinking deeply about what I'd said to him. The anxiety I felt was mounting with every second that passed. The man was standing very still, and I started to calculate the odds that I'd be able to rush him and knock him down before he could pull the trigger. He was several steps away, so the chances weren't good. There was also the possibility that doing so might accidentally cause him to squeeze the trigger instead. As it stood, my best option was just to wait it out.

"I think... you're right," the man mumbled as he slowly moved the gun away from his head. I breathed a sigh of relief. "This is what they would want. This *is* what they wanted. They threw me away. They left me for dead. This is exactly what they would have wanted." His mouth twisted into a furious grimace as he spoke, the tone of his voice growing angrier with every word.

"That's right," I replied cautiously as I took another step toward him. He wasn't pointing the gun at himself anymore, which was good, but now it seemed like he was becoming angry and hostile instead, so I still needed to proceed with caution. "You beat them. Now, if you help us, we can help you get some justice against them."

The man looked up at me and seemed startled to find that I was now standing only a scant few feet away from him. He blinked at me in surprise for a few seconds before looking down at the gun in his hand. I tensed, uncertain about what he would do next.

"Okay," he muttered as he slowly held the gun out to me, much to my relief.

I took it quickly from him and then turned to hand it over to Da Silva. The moment the gun was out of his possession, the man shrank down on himself, cowering as though he was afraid I might suddenly change my mind and attack him.

"It's alright," I assured him. "Everything's fine now. Let's get down off the roof, okay?"

"Y-yeah," the man stammered, and for the first time since I'd run up here, I could see a hint of life in his eyes. "Let's get down."

17

ETHAN

I RAN a hand through my hair as I sank into one of the chairs in the bullpen back at the station. There was a hum of noise all around me as officers went about their regular duties, typing, making phone calls, talking, and rushing into and out of the station. It was a strangely comforting sound, and I allowed myself a second to close my eyes and just clear my head. Holm was sitting beside me, just as quiet as I was. We were seated around Da Silva's desk. She'd gone off somewhere to prepare a room for us to interview the rooftop gunman in.

It was challenging to wrap my head around everything that had happened in just a single day. We'd just arrived in Kingstown early this morning, and already it felt like we'd been here for so much longer.

The suspect that Holm had shot was dead. His

heart had stopped beating before the ambulance even arrived. It had, of course, been a clean shot. He'd been trying to snatch Da Silva's gun away from her, so Holm had been acting in her defense. Honestly, that was the very least of our problems. More pressing was the issue of our gunman, who'd only much later revealed his name to be Roy Taft. Even though it didn't seem like the incident with him on the roof was directly connected to our case on the surface, I knew in my gut that there was a link.

"Are you sure?" Da Silva had asked me skeptically after we'd finally gotten control of the situation and were deciding what to do next. "Look, as far as we know, this is an isolated incident. An unwell man climbed up on a roof and put a lot of innocent people in danger. What exactly makes you think that this is related to your case?"

"There's no way this is a coincidence," I'd insisted fervently. "Look, he said his name was Roy. That's the same name a witness gave us back in New York. And I know you didn't hear them, but those men talked about killing him. I know it's crazy, but I'm sure this is all connected somehow. I just need a chance to talk to him calmly while he's not threatening to hurt anyone, or himself, on the roof of a building."

Da Silva had still looked uncertain, but in the end, she'd relented.

"Alright," she'd sighed. "I'll talk to the captain

about it. But this is on you, Marston. If we end up wasting our time chasing a baseless lead–"

"We won't," I'd responded confidently. "I know I'm right."

Before we could interview him on what had happened to him, though, he'd had to go to the hospital. Once he'd calmed down and I was able to get close, I'd realized that he was in only slightly better condition physically than Clearwater's body had been discovered in. He was covered in bruises, cuts, and extreme sunburn.

Unfortunately, Roy had been less than eager to comply with our requests that a doctor see him. He'd at first insisted that there was no way he was going, and then after that had only agreed to go if I stayed with him. It might have seemed like a bit of an odd request on the surface, but in truth, it was normal for victims of traumatic events to cling to people who helped them immediately following the trauma. Then, after a few hours, he'd decided that he'd rather be alone after all, so I'd agreed to his request and given him privacy to finish out the rest of his checkups. By the time I'd made it back to the station, night had fallen. I had wolfed down a bag of chips and a bottle of strawberry-flavored sparkling water that I'd found in a vending machine and then sat down to wait for everything to be in place for us to conduct the interview.

"He said that someone forced him to kill other

people?" Holm asked out of the blue, quietly enough that any of the officers working nearby wouldn't over-hear him.

I opened my eyes and lifted my head to look at him. Holm had been down on the ground watching over the remaining suspect, so he hadn't heard any of what Roy had said.

"Yeah," I replied quietly as I thought back to that moment on the roof.

Chills ran down my spine as I recalled how distressed Roy had seemed. He'd been crying as he explained what had happened to him, and though he'd been so panicked that I hadn't been able to make much sense of what he was saying, I could tell from how upset he was that it had been bad.

"Do you remember what Stephan said?" Holm muttered. "About how he overheard the men who attacked him and his friend talking? They said some-thing about the last two victims they grabbed being 'duds.' Do you think that has something to do with what he said?"

"Maybe," I replied as I leaned down to rest my chin on my hands. "Probably. There's no chance this is a coincidence, but I can't figure out what they could have meant. They're forcing the men they kidnap to... what, kill other people? That's already weird enough, but how would one be a 'dud' at that?"

"Maybe they just refused to do it?" Holm suggested.

"Maybe it's like a suicide mission kind of thing. They kidnap men and then force them to carry out hits on their behalf? That way, the guys in charge never have to get their hands dirty, and if something goes wrong, it's the victim that ends up dead."

"And maybe that's what happened to Clearwater," I surmised. "If he messed with a gang or something, then it would explain why he was beaten so badly."

"Are there gangs in the Grenadines?" Holm turned to look at me.

"Not really," Da Silva's voice suddenly cut through the conversation.

I lifted my head at the sound of her voice and found her standing just a few feet away. I'd been looking down at the ground as I contemplated what Holm had said, and I hadn't noticed her approaching. Now that she was here, though, I found myself unable to look away. She had taken down her ponytail and removed the top part of her police uniform to change into a black t-shirt with the station's logo on it. It wasn't a huge change, but the way her hair fell around her face and the way the shirt hugged her curves made me feel, for a moment, like I was looking at a different person.

"Sorry that took so long," she grumbled as she flicked a lock of hair over her shoulder. "I wanted to get cleaned up since it seemed we might still be here a while yet between Roy and the suspect. Dumb idea to have white uniforms. They get dirty if you so much as look at them the wrong way." She shook her head disapprovingly. "Anyway, we can go and speak to Roy now. He's back from the hospital, and I got him settled into one of the interrogation rooms. He seems to be doing a lot better now, less jumpy than he was earlier."

"That's good," I replied as I stood up. "And what about the suspect?"

"We can interrogate him afterward," Da Silva replied as she turned around to lead Holm and me to where Roy was waiting. "He's in a cell right now. So far, he hasn't said anything, as far as I'm aware."

"That's fine," I snorted. "We'll get him to talk. We always do."

The rest of the walk to the interrogation room was silent, and even though we were on our way to speak with him, my mind still raced with wild notions and possibilities. I knew this was all connected somehow, but no matter what theory I came up with, it seemed like something didn't quite add up. By the time we made it to the room, I was practically bursting with questions.

Da Silva pushed the door open slowly and quietly.

"Mr. Taft?" Da Silva called quietly as the three of us stepped inside. Roy was sitting at a round table in the room, an empty can of soda on the table and another clutched in his hand.

"H-hey." He looked up at us as we entered.

He still sounded a little anxious, but he didn't look nearly as crazed and panicked as before. He also looked a little cleaner, though the dark bruises and bright red burns on his face were still as clear as before.

"Hi, Roy," I greeted him as I moved to sit at the table with him.

Obviously, this room was probably used more to interview victims and witnesses than to interrogate suspects because it wasn't as austere as a standard interrogation room. Rather than the typical bare room and metal furniture, the room we were sitting in felt more like a simple meeting room. A round, wooden table sat in the center. Two large windows at the end of the room made the small area seem more open, and though it was nighttime now, I could imagine that they must let in a fair amount of light during the day. Over- all, this room didn't feel as scary or intimidating as a standard interrogation room.

"How are you feeling?" I asked as Roy began to fidget with the empty soda can.

"Uh, better," he replied before swallowing nervously. His Adam's Apple bobbed, and he reached a hand up to mess with the sleeve of his shirt. "Sorry about what happened back on the roof. That was really embarrassing, huh?" He pursed his lips together and looked down at the table.

"You don't have anything to be ashamed about," Da

Silva insisted. "You went through something terrible, and it's good that you were strong enough to pull yourself together in the end."

"Thanks," Roy mumbled, though he didn't sound very convinced by her reassurances.

"I know you said you don't want to think about it," I continued. "But we really need to know what exactly you were talking about back on that roof."

"No, yeah, I mean, it's fine," Roy replied awkwardly. "Yeah, I did say that, but, uh, I was feeling really upset then. It's fine. I can talk about it, seriously."

"Alright," I replied warily.

He was rambling a little, muttering as he forced his way through his answers. I was concerned about whether he really was okay to talk about it, but I had to ask. The sooner we got answers, the sooner we could do something about the men who did this and about any other victims they might still be holding captive.

"You said that someone forced you to do bad things," I pressed. "That they forced you to kill other people. Who were you talking about?"

"I... it's a really long story," he replied quietly. He was still looking down at the table, and his shoulders were hunched. "I don't even know *who* they are. Not really, anyway. All I know is that they're powerful and rich." He paused for a moment as he lifted his head to look up at me, his expression twisted into one that was equal parts agony and anger.

"How did you end up with them?" I asked.

"Well, I'm from New York," he muttered, and my heart sank.

Holm and I turned to look at each other, and Roy caught on right away.

"What?" he asked as he looked nervously between the two of us. "What does that look mean? Why are you looking at each other like that?"

"Roy," I replied slowly, "we think maybe you weren't the only victim. Actually, the reason we're here in St. Vincent is that we're investigating the disappearance and death of an American man. We've since learned that he, along with several other men, were all snatched from New York in a similar manner. Do you have a friend named Stephan?"

Roy snapped his head up to look at me.

"Yeah, I do," he replied, his eyes wide with surprise. "We met in New York after I ended up on the street. Why? Is he okay? Did he get grabbed too?"

"He's fine," I quickly assured him. "Actually, he asked us to look for you. After those men took you, he went to the police."

Roy looked at me with a stunned expression for a few moments before his eyes started to water.

"He did that for me?" he asked, his voice falling and rising in pitch as he spoke. He shook his head as he looked down at the table. "He's a real one. He really went and talked to the cops just to find me... So, he's okay, though?"

"He is," I confirmed.

"Actually, he felt bad about running away," Holm admitted, and Roy scoffed.

"It's good that he did," he muttered. "I would have too, especially now that I know what they had planned." He shuddered. "If he knew the things I'd seen, he wouldn't feel bad about running."

"We're going to get you back home as soon as possible," I promised. "For now, can you tell us more about the place where you were kept? Were there other men being held captive with you?"

"Yeah." Roy nodded his head jerkily. "A lot. And you're right. Snatching is a good way to put it, I guess." He chuckled, but there was no joy in his voice. On the contrary, the sound was empty and hollow. "I was sleeping one night, a few weeks ago, I think. It's hard to tell how much time has passed. Anyway, all of a sudden, these two guys grabbed me. I tried to fight, but they hit me over the head, and I fell back asleep. Next thing I know, I was inside a cage."

"A cage!?" I raised my eyebrows in shock.

"Yeah." Roy shrugged. "That's pretty much what it was. It was so dark at first that I couldn't really tell where I was. There were a lot of other guys around, though, and a kind of fence that we were all sitting inside. I could see a door, but I couldn't reach it past the metal fence. It wasn't until a few days later that I even realized we were on a boat."

"None of the other men told you what was happening?" I asked. "Did everyone arrive at the same time?"

"I don't know," Roy replied. "I don't think so, though. In fact, now that I think about it, I know some of them had been there longer. They had scars, spots where I could see bruises that had already healed up a little. I tried asking them what was going on, but no one would tell me. No one would even speak to me, except a couple of other guys who I think got there the same time I did." He smiled sadly. "I get why they didn't want to talk to me. After I found out what they had planned for us, I knew why no one would tell me anything. They were just trying to give themselves the best chance, I guess."

"The best chance at what?" I asked nervously, a horrible, sinking feeling settling into my gut.

"Survival," Roy replied flatly as he crunched the empty soda bottle inside his fist. "One night, one of the guards came down. They'd show up once a day to bring us something to eat, but this day, he told me and another of the guys to follow him out of the cell. The other guy who was nice to me, Wesley, I think his name was, started asking questions. He wanted to know what was happening, who they were, where we were. The guard just hit him and told him to shut up." He took a deep, shuddering breath as he looked off at a random spot on the wall. "I thought about running. There were so many of us and only one of him. I didn't get why no one was trying to fight, but I was too scared to do anything alone, so I just did what he told me."

"And what happened after that?" I asked, the foreboding feeling in my stomach growing even more potent with every moment that passed.

"He took the two of us up this rickety set of stairs," Roy explained. "When we got to the top, I realized why nobody had tried to run or fight back." He looked away from the wall and directly at me. "We were on a boat, out in the middle of the ocean. Even if we had tried something, there's no way we would have been able to get very far. That wasn't even the worst part, though."

Suddenly, there was a shift in Roy's demeanor. He ground his teeth together and clenched his fists closed. "It was all the people. Up on the deck, there were so many of them. They were wearing fancy dresses and tuxedos, holding glasses of champagne, and eating these little slices of cake." He began to laugh again, and once again, the sound was hollow and cold and bitter. "I thought I was dreaming or hallucinating. It was like I'd walked into some movie star's birthday party. They were all wearing fancy clothes, laughing and talking, and here I was, covered in dirt and wondering just what the hell was going on."

"So, when you came up to the main deck of the

boat, there was a party going on?" Da Silva asked, her face contorted into a mask of confusion and horror.

"Yeah." Roy nodded. "They all turned to look at the other guy and me and started cheering and clapping. I wanted to scream and ask for help or something, but all I could do was stand there, staring. I could feel in my bones that something was wrong with this scene. It didn't make sense. Nothing made sense. They were all laughing and clapping and talking and—"

He let out a pained, guttural groan as he bowed his head and yanked harshly on his hair. When he spoke again, his voice was quiet and flat. "The guard pushed the other guy and me into this circle in the middle of the deck and told us to fight. I didn't know what he was talking about. I looked at the other guy for help, but he was already coming at me." Roy stopped for a moment to wipe the tears out of his eyes with the back of his hand. "That's why no one wanted to tell me what was happening. They didn't want me to be prepared. It's easier to kill your opponent if you can catch them off-guard."

The room fell silent as he stopped speaking. I could feel the blood rushing through my ears as I digested everything he'd just told me, unable to comprehend what it was I was hearing.

"When you said they were forcing you to kill people..." I muttered. "They were forcing you to fight each other?"

"Yeah," Roy replied with a short nod. "We were the entertainment for their parties."

Suddenly, it was like the missing piece of the puzzle fell into place. The reason that all the victims were men, the reason they hadn't just been killed outright, even the comment about Clearwater being a "dud" suddenly made sense. If their goal was to pit these men against each other in some kind of perverse modern-day gladiator games, then a seventy-year-old man probably hadn't provided much of an exciting fight.

"I won, obviously," Roy laughed sadly. "I could hear them making bets about who would win, how long it would last. Some of them were even throwing out pointers. Hit him in the head! Kick him in the ribs! Then I heard them using the word 'survivor.' That's when I knew that only one of us was going to get out of this alive." He clasped his hands together and went back to staring into the distance. "I didn't want to die. I didn't want to hurt any of them, but I didn't want to die!" He let out a gasping sob as he turned to look at me. "I know I killed them, but it wasn't my choice! They made me do it!"

"It's okay." Da Silva stood up and reached her hand across the table to grasp his in hers. "You aren't in trouble if that's what you're afraid of, okay? I promise you. The police aren't going to come after you for what happened. You were a victim in this."

Roy nodded, but he didn't respond. He was crying openly now, and I couldn't begin to imagine what he was feeling. Taking a life was something you couldn't come back from. As a federal agent, there'd been times when I'd had to choose to take someone's life for the sake of defending a victim or myself but to be forced to kill innocent men who hadn't done anything wrong was inconceivably cruel.

"After the fight..." Roy sniffled. "After the other guy was... *gone*, they all clapped and went back to their business like they'd just watched a piano recital or something. I begged the guard to let me go. I'd done what he wanted. I'd killed that man! But he told me it wasn't enough. He said that there were still more fights left, and then he dragged me back down to that cell below deck." He took a deep breath and wiped his eyes clear. "No one would look at me then, except for Wesley and the old guy. They kept asking me what had happened, where the guard had taken me. I told them, and they didn't believe me at first. I convinced them it was the truth, though, and when the other guy never came back, they knew I was telling the truth. After that, Wesley tried to rally everyone to fight back. He said that there were more of us than them and that we could all take them if we went up against them together. No one listened, though." Roy frowned. "Maybe he was right. If we had, maybe we wouldn't have had to keep killing each other."

"The old man," Holm suddenly spoke up. "Do you remember his name? Or what he looked like?"

"Uh, no," Roy replied. "He didn't talk much, but he was always sticking right with Wesley. He had white hair, a little taller than me. No, wait, I think I remember Wesley saying his name a couple of times. Logan, I think it was."

"Clearwater." I turned to look at Holm, who looked back at me with a knowing expression on his face. Without a doubt, the connection was undeniable now. Roy had been kidnapped by the same people who had taken Clearwater and had probably been one of the last people to see our victim alive as well.

"You were right," Da Silva murmured somberly. "It wasn't a coincidence."

Usually, I would have taken satisfaction in having a hunch proven right, but I felt anything but smug at the moment. In this particular situation, it would have been better, for Roy's sake, if I'd been wrong about him being one of the victims.

"Wesley was the name of the man he went to the parking garage with," Holm noted. "That's what Dorris said, right?"

"Yeah, I think so." I nodded. Finally, we were getting to the root of what had happened to Clearwater. I turned back to Roy. "Do you know what happened to the old man?" Roy went pale, and for a second, it looked like he was going to throw up.

"Not exactly," he muttered as he looked down at the table. "All I know is that one night, the guard came down and took them up."

"Wesley and Clearwater?" I asked in alarm. "Together?"

"Yeah," Roy replied somberly. "They were best friends, or at least it seemed like that. The old man didn't seem like he always knew what was going on, and Wesley looked out for him. Then they went up, and only Wesley came back down."

I clenched my jaw in fury. This was possibly one of the worst of all the explanations of what had happened to Clearwater—killed not by some unnamed attacker but by his own friend? It was horrific.

"Wesley was really quiet after that," Roy muttered. "I thought he was sad at first, but then I realized that wasn't it. He was *angry*." Roy shuddered. "He said that he was going to find a way to escape, and he asked me to help him."

"So, that's how you got away?" Da Silva asked. "You escaped?"

"Yeah," Roy snorted. "We had to. One of the other guys found out about what we were planning to do, and he threatened to snitch. He said that we were going to ruin everything for them."

"What?" I looked at him in shock. "He didn't want you to fight back? Why?"

"Some of the guys believed that the rich people would set us free, eventually." Roy shook his head, his mouth twisted into a disgusted smirk. "That's what they kept saying. Win enough fights, and eventually, we'd win our freedom. It was a load of bull, though. No one was ever set free! They just pushed and pushed until they eventually died, and they always did. There's only so much that someone can take before their body just can't handle it anymore. The other guys didn't want to hear it, though. They wanted to believe that they'd make it out as long as they kept playing the game, and Wesley was going to mess that up for them." Roy paused to take a deep breath. "So, he killed him."

"What?" I shrank back in surprise. "Who killed who?"

"Wesley killed the man who threatened to snitch," Roy clarified. "They got into a fight, and Wesley won. When the guards came down the next day, no one said anything. Not Wesley or any of the other men. We all stayed silent, the way everyone had the first day I woke up down there. The guard dragged the man away, and we just went on as usual. The next time we stopped, Wesley had a plan. He told me that when the guard came down to get that day's fighters, we'd push past and run up. Then we'd jump overboard into the water."

He smiled, and this time, there was a hint of genuine humor in it. "That was his big plan, just jump overboard and swim to the nearest shore, I guess. I thought it was so stupid. 'We're going to die if we do that,' I told him. But then he told me we were going to die anyway if we just sat there, and I realized he was right. At least this way, we stood a chance, maybe. So, one night, they came down to get us, and just like Wesley said, we ran. We pushed past the guard and took off up onto the deck. As soon as we got up there, I froze. All those people in their dresses and suits looked at me in surprise, and I didn't know what to do. Wesley screamed at me to get it together, and then he grabbed one of the women."

"One of the, uh, party guests?" I asked, unsure how I should address the people who'd been running these bizarre games.

"Yeah." Roy nodded. "He grabbed her and dragged her to the edge of the boat, and then he jumped off. I really didn't know what he was doing. He never said anything about taking a hostage, but it was too late to back out, so I jumped off the edge too. It turned out it was all a distraction. He let her go as soon as we hit the water and then started swimming the other way. He only dragged her down with him so they'd all be too distracted rescuing her to come after us. Someone started shooting at us from the boat, but they missed. It was dark, and I guess they couldn't see what they were doing." Roy sighed, his shoulder sagging as he recalled the story. "We were lucky the water wasn't very cold.

We swam for a while until we were far away from the boat, but then we stopped. It was nighttime, and Wesley said if we kept going, we might accidentally swim farther away from the shore."

"So, you just stayed there all night?" I looked at him, both shocked and a little impressed at their determination to survive.

"Yeah," Roy replied. "As I said, it wasn't very cold. The sun started rising a few hours later, and we could see what looked like land. We started swimming toward it, but it was slow going." Roy sighed with frustration at the memory as he drummed his fingers against the table.

"Wesley had a bad leg," he continued. "He kept getting tired, and he kept wanting to stop to take breaks. We'd lie on our backs and just float for a while, but every time we did, we'd drift around, and even if I wasn't swimming, I felt exhausted. I just wanted to get to the shore. It took us so long that we didn't get back until after the sun had gone down again. I threw up the moment we were back on solid land. My entire body hurt like hell, and I just wanted to lie down and go to sleep. The next thing I knew, it was morning, and we were on the beach. Wesley was gone."

"Gone?" I repeated.

"Yeah," Roy confirmed as he leaned back in his seat. "I was scared at first. I thought maybe he'd been pulled back out to sea or something, but I didn't see him in the water. I didn't see him anywhere. I looked for him for a little while, but when I couldn't find him, I just started walking. I-I didn't want to leave him behind or anything, but I just wanted to find help. I wanted to get back to civilization."

"You didn't do anything wrong," I assured him when it started to look like he was about to break down again. "You were just trying to survive."

"Yeah," Roy murmured. "Anyway, for a little while, there were only trees. I just kept walking straight, and eventually, I found a street with cars and buildings on it."

"Did you call the police?" Da Silva asked him. "I don't recall hearing anything about this."

"No," Roy replied. "I wanted to, but... at the same time, I didn't want to talk to anyone. Every time I tried to go up to someone, I kept thinking, *what if they're one of them*? There were so many people on that boat. They all looked like normal people, and I kept thinking that if I talked to the wrong person, I might end up back there, back in that little cell, back on that deck full of blood and death."

Roy was shaking now, his eyes wild as he looked down at his own hands. "I didn't know what to do. I wanted to talk to someone, but at the same time, I didn't want to talk to anyone. I just wanted to stop thinking, to stop feeling. I just wanted *everything* to stop." He took a deep breath before reaching up to rub the back of his neck. "I passed by this pawn shop, and there was this gun in the window. I wasn't thinking of anything in particular, but when I saw it, all of a sudden, I knew I had to have it. I don't know why. I guess I felt safer with it. So, I went in and just... took it."

"The shop owner didn't have anything to say about that?" Da Silva asked.

"I didn't hurt him or anything!" Roy insisted. "I really just walked in and grabbed it and ran. It was inside a case, but it wasn't locked or anything. He shouted at me to stop, but I just kept running. I hid in an alley behind a restaurant for a little while. Maybe a couple of hours or maybe just a few minutes. I don't know. Everything was really fuzzy then." Roy looked down at his hands as if going back to that moment. "When I realized what I'd done, I felt sick. What the hell had happened to me? I was stealing and hiding next to a dumpster? I didn't even know where I was. Wesley was gone, and I didn't know what I was supposed to do from then on. Every time I closed my eyes, I could see the faces of the men I'd killed. I could see all of those people on the boat, laughing and smiling while we literally beat each other to death. I couldn't think clearly, and the next thing I knew, I was on the roof."

"You mean earlier today?" I asked him in surprise. "So, this escape, it only just happened yesterday then?"

"Uh, yeah, I guess so," Roy replied quietly. "Funny, it feels like it happened so much longer ago."

"So, just last night, these people were—" Da Silva muttered before stopping herself short. "Roy, how many men were still on the boat when you escaped? In the cell, I mean?

"Oh, uh, maybe ten or so?" he replied with a shrug. "It was hard to keep count when they were constantly getting replaced. After a while, I stopped trying."

"I see," she replied.

Her voice was low and tight, and I knew exactly what she was thinking. The situation was much worse than we thought if just last night, as many as ten victims were still being held captive.

"Roy," I addressed him seriously. "What you went through wasn't in any way your fault. The fact that you escaped and survived the way you did proves how strong you are. I know you feel like you can't move past what you were forced to do, but you can't keep punishing yourself for it."

Roy opened his mouth to protest but then closed it without saying anything.

"What am I supposed to do?" he asked me. His voice was small and weak. "I killed people with my own two hands. How... how do I get over that?"

"You don't," I replied honestly. The truth was that there was no "getting over" taking a life. "But you can learn to live with it, make peace with it. And I promise you that we're going to find the people who did this. They aren't going to get away with what happened."

Roy looked up at me, his eyes watery with unshed tears as he nodded meekly.

"Okay," he sighed. "I'm happy to hear that."

I looked back at him sympathetically, my heart aching for this poor man. He'd been through some-thing indescribably evil, and I really wasn't sure what else I could do for him. There was one thing, though, that I could do, and that was to start with interrogating the suspect that we currently had in custody.

18

ETHAN

My FACE FELT hot as I looked through the large pane of glass that separated the viewing room from the interrogation room. We'd only just finished speaking with Roy, and I was still so enraged by what I'd learned that it felt as though my entire body was alight with fire.

"So, what do we think about this one?" Da Silva sneered as she looked at the suspect through the glass.

We still weren't sure who he was. His prints hadn't pulled anything up in St. Vincent, and though we'd sent to have them run through the US database, they still hadn't come back. It didn't help that it was the middle of the night.

"He isn't one of the party guests," Holm replied as he sized the man up. He was stocky, muscular, with shortly cropped blond hair and a square, ugly face. "He said something about how they should have made sure Roy was dead, right? That makes me think he and his buddy were guards."

"I agree," I replied. "He was probably talking about the night that Roy and Wesley escaped. They must have assumed that he and Wesley drowned. That's what he meant by making sure they were dead."

"So, he's just an employee, basically," Da Silva scoffed. "Just a grunt for the ones who are actually running this little operation."

"I wonder how loyal he is," I remarked as I analyzed the man. I couldn't tell how intelligent he was without speaking to him, but I got the feeling that he was more the brainless goon type than someone who actually had a plan.

"Well, I guess it comes down to how generous those rich party guests were," Da Silva replied. "They were the kind of people who are willing to play with people's lives quite literally, so I have a feeling these guards were being paid quite handsomely."

"If that's the case, he might be easier to break than I thought," I replied. "After all, money's not a motivator anymore, not now that he's been arrested. With gangs, members are loyal to one another out of fear and a bastardized sense of fraternity. Muscle for hire, like him, are generally only loyal to their employer so long as the money flows. If we can convince him that telling us what he knows will benefit him, he'll probably roll over."

"I agree," Holm replied before turning to look at me. "So, how do we play this?"

"Straightforward, I think," I replied. "We tell him what we know, based on what Roy told us. We make it clear that there's no weaseling his way out of this and that the best outcome will come from him cooperating with us."

"I think that's a good plan," Da Silva agreed with a curt nod. "Let's go then."

She turned then and walked quickly toward the door that separated the two rooms. Holm and I followed her as she pushed the door open and stepped inside.

The suspect looked up at us as we entered, and his face went through a surprising range of emotions in just the span of a few seconds: surprise, panic, fear, anger, and finally, feigned nonchalance as the three of us sat opposite him at the metal table. Unlike the room we'd just been in with Roy, this room looked a lot more like the standard interrogation room I was used to, with stark white walls and a dull gray floor. A simple metal table and metal chairs sat in the center of the room. There were no windows either. All these aspects were specifically meant to evoke a negative reaction from whoever was being interrogated.

"Good evening, Mr...?" I addressed the man as Da Silva and I calmly sat down across from him.

The man just bared his teeth at me. I was sure it

was meant to look threatening, but it really just made him look pathetic.

"No name then?" I continued nonchalantly. "Well, that's alright. I'm not all that interested anyway, to tell you the truth."

The man frowned slightly, clearly annoyed by my slight, but he still didn't speak up. Just then, a sharp rapping came at the door to the interrogation room. Da Silva stood up at once and strode over to the door. She opened it, but I couldn't see who it was on the other side. She closed it just a moment later, and when she turned back around, she had a satisfied smirk on her face.

I noticed at once that she had a small stack of papers in her hand, and as she passed by me to get back to her chair, she handed the documents to me. I looked down at them curiously, and I understood at once why she'd been smirking so cockily. It was a criminal record. At the top was a prison photo of the suspect, and underneath was a rap sheet about a mile long.

"Devin Hicks," I read the name off the sheet. The suspect went still for just a moment as I said his name. "Well, Mr. Hicks, it looks like this isn't your first run-in with the law." I scanned down the list of crimes. "You were arrested for trying to carry out a hit on someone?" I looked up at him.

"Looks like he didn't learn from his mistakes,"

Holm added. "Since he's still out here helping get people killed."

"No kidding," I muttered. Hicks still hadn't said anything, and my patience was wearing thin. I slammed the papers down on the table between us. "Alright, enough with the crap. We both know what we know, Hicks. We spoke to Roy, the man that you and your buddy were planning on killing back on the docks."

Hicks fidgeted uncomfortably but still didn't speak up.

"We know about how he and the other man you were holding captive escaped by jumping overboard," I acknowledged. "We know how you were forcing them to fight each other like a disgusting human dog-fighting ring. We know all about how you've been snatching homeless men from the streets of New York. So, don't think for a single second that there's any way you're going to wriggle your way out of this. We're far past that at this point."

I paused to let all that sink in, and Hicks finally turned to look at me, a petulant grimace on his face.

"Well, then what the hell do you want from me?" He growled. "You know everything already, so what do you want?"

"We need information on the people running it," I explained. "Right now, all we know is that they're all very wealthy and that these fights take place out on the water. What we need are details."

"And what makes you think I'm gonna tell you any of that?" Hicks snorted.

"Well, it didn't seem to me like you were really all that invested in this little scheme," I replied. "After all, you're not the one forcing these people to go up against each other, right? You're just doing what you're paid to do, and now that you're not receiving your pay, there's no reason for you to stay loyal to those people." I looked him in the eyes. "Am I wrong?"

For several moments, Hicks just looked back at me in contemplative silence. Then he let out a snicker.

"Yeah, I guess that's true," he muttered. "And you're right. This is all just business to me. I'm not like those freaks that get off on watching guys beat each other up." He made a disgusted face.

"And that's supposed to make you better than them?" Da Silva glared at him. "Aren't you the one who was rounding them up for the slaughter?"

"Settle down, sweetheart," Hicks scoffed, and I could swear that the temperature dropped several degrees as Da Silva directed all the force of her fury upon him. "And no, actually, I'm not the one who gets them. My job is more like a bodyguard. I make sure the fighters stay put where they're supposed to, and I also make sure that none of them try to attack any of the clients during the fights. A couple of other guys are in charge of actually going and finding guys to bring back. I'm really not involved in that at all."

For some reason, the straightforward way he explained everything was really pissing me off. He told us everything we wanted to know, but I felt angry at how remorseless he seemed. He was talking so casually about kidnapping innocent men and forcing them to fight each other for the amusement of wealthy lunatics as if it was all nothing to him.

"As I said before," Hicks continued, "it wasn't personal. I'm doing a service that I was hired to do, and damn, did those rich weirdos pay me a lot."

"Is that right?" I asked him acidly. "Well, then it's too bad you'll never see another one of those payments again."

Hicks glared at me, and even though I knew it was probably a bad idea to antagonize him, it was worth it to be able to wipe that obnoxious, smug smile off his face.

"We want names," Da Silva suddenly interjected, her voice straightforward and icy. "And locations. Tell us where we can find these people who hired you."

"Calm down, honey," Hicks snickered at her. "I don't even know—!"

He suddenly yelped as Da Silva stood up and leaned across the table to grab him by the collar of his shirt.

"That's Officer Da Silva to you," she hissed at him,

quietly enough that I had to strain my ears to hear what she was saying. "Speak to me that way again, and you might find yourself sharing a cell with a couple of drunks just itching for someone to punch. Now, answer my question."

"I-I really don't know!" Hicks yelped as Da Silva roughly pushed him back down into his chair before sitting back in her own seat. "The clients, they don't exactly give us their names and contact information, you know? The only one I even have any contact with is the organizer, and he calls himself 'the Master.'"

"The Master?" I parroted as I raised an eyebrow at him.

"Yeah." Hicks snorted. "Lame as hell. He thinks he's James Bond or something, I swear. He insists on using codenames and codewords for everything. It's stupid, but so long as the money keeps coming, I'm not about to argue."

"Great," I replied as I reached up to stroke my temple with the tips of my fingers. "So, where can we find this person?"

"I told you, I don't know," Hicks replied. "All I know is where they'll be docked before the next party. We're supposed to meet him—" He suddenly stopped and tossed me an odd look.

"Yes?" I prodded.

"What's in it for me?" he asked me as his lips stretched into a cocky smile.

"Excuse me?!" Da Silva exclaimed as she fixed him with a terrifying glare.

"W-well," Hicks stammered, cowering for just a moment beneath her hateful stare. "It's only fair, right? That's how business transactions work. I have something you want, so it's only right that I get something in return."

"This isn't a business transaction," Holm sneered.

"I disagree." Hicks snorted as he leaned back in his chair and crossed his arms. "Sure, you might be right about me not being loyal to those rich freaks, but that doesn't mean I'm stupid. I'm not about to just give up *everything* for nothing in return. I scratch your back, you scratch mine. You know what I mean?"

"Yeah, I think I do," I sighed as I clasped my hands together and leaned forward onto the table. "You want to cut a deal."

"See, this one gets it," Hicks laughed. "Tit for tat, fair trade, and all that. It's only fair, right?"

"Shut up and get to the point," I deadpanned. "What did you have in mind?"

"Immunity," Hicks replied immediately.

"Ha!" Da Silva let out a wicked cackle. "There's not a chance. Try again."

"Hey, I had to give it a shot, right?" Hicks shrugged. "Alright then, how about a reduced sentence, minimum security, with regular visitation privileges?"

"You're no stranger to jail time, are you, Hicks?" I

quipped, and he frowned at me. "I'll tell you what. You give us the information, and I'll make sure it's known that you cooperated with the investigation. I'll recommend leniency, but that's it. No guarantees."

"No guarantees?" Hicks snorted. "Then no deal. You can just figure it out on your own."

"Okay," I called his bluff. "Then I'll make sure that it's put down on record that you *didn't* cooperate with the investigation, that you deliberately impeded us, and that you were directly involved in the abduction and murder of countless innocent men."

Hicks pouted up at me like a kid, his shoulders sagging as he realized he'd been backed into a corner.

"Damn, you don't have any mercy, do you?" Hicks mumbled sourly at me.

"About as much mercy as you had for the men who you were complicit in torturing and killing," I bit back. "So, do we have a deal or what?"

Honestly, I was loath to cut his monster any kind of deal at all. If I had my way, he'd rot in prison for the rest of his miserable life without any type of considerations. That being said, I knew that agreeing to this would allow us to find the group faster, which was my priority right now. They still had a lot of men captive, and according to Roy, they were actively holding these death parties, so right now, what mattered most was finding and rescuing them.

"Yeah, fine," Hicks grumbled. "I'll tell you where the boat is."

I took out my phone and jotted down the marina's address where the boat would be docking. Once that was done, Holm, Da Silva, and I all stood and left the room.

"I'm glad that's over," Da Silva muttered once we were all out in the hallway outside the interrogation room. "He was grating on my last nerve. I was about half a second away from punching him in the face."

"I understand the feeling," I agreed. "We got what we wanted, though. We know where they'll be tomorrow night."

"Now, all we have to do is—" Da Silva began to respond, but before she could finish her thought, she was cut off by Captain Larose, who was rapidly approaching us.

"Da Silva!" he called as he walked toward us. "Agents, something's happened!"

"What is it?" I asked, alarmed by the tone of his voice and the concerned look on his face.

"Another body," he replied, and I felt my blood run cold. "Another body's been discovered!"

19

ETHAN

"ARE you sure it's related to the case?" I asked a few minutes later after the four of us had reconvened inside Larose's office.

The news that another body had been found on the island had come as a shock, and even though it was late, we'd rushed straight up to Larose's office to discuss the new development. Da Silva and I were sitting in the two chairs in front of the captain's desk while Holm stood off to the side, leaning against the wall at the left side of the office.

"To be honest, I'm not sure what to think," Larose replied. Rather than sitting at his chair, he stood by his desk, pacing nervously as we discussed the facts of the case. "The circumstances are all fairly different, but I find it difficult to believe that the murder is unrelated, given the timing."

"So, what are the circumstances?" I asked. "Was this body found on Palm Island too?"

"No." Larose shook his head. "Actually, it was found here, in Kingstown. On the beach of one of the resorts."

"I see," I replied. "No offense, Captain, but are you sure it's not possible that the timing was just a coincidence? That doesn't sound all that similar to Clearwater."

"I thought so as well, at first," Larose admitted as he picked a paperweight off his desk and turned it over in his hands. "That was until I got the details about the condition of the body. Apparently, he was very, very badly beaten. Covered head to toe in bruises, and what's more, he had thirty-three stab wounds all over his abdomen and face."

"How many!?" I exclaimed in surprise.

"Well over thirty, according to the coroner's report," Larose replied. "I'm still working on getting all the information, but as it stands now, it's evident that whoever killed him did not hold back. It honestly seems like they were trying to inflict as much pain as possible."

"Do we know the identity yet?" Da Silva asked. "If he's another missing person, then maybe he is one of the victims."

"Well, we do know who he is," Larose replied cautiously.

"Why do you sound so uncertain about it?" I asked suspiciously.

"Because that's another way that this body differs from Clearwater's," he explained. "The man who was killed was Eugene Marguerite. He was a diamond tycoon from South Africa, here on vacation as far as we can ascertain."

"A diamond tycoon?" Da Silva repeated. "Well, that's a pretty far cry from the homeless men that have been targeted so far."

"Unless he wasn't one of the victims," I remarked as a thought suddenly struck me. "A wealthy diamond tycoon doesn't fit the description of the victims, but he does fit the description of the—"

"Party guests," Holm finished, his eyes wide with realization.

"Wait, you think he might have been one of the people who was actually paying to hold the fights?" Da Silva looked at me in shock. "I guess you're right. That does make more sense. But then who killed him?"

"I don't know," I replied. "Maybe there was some kind of internal argument? This is something pretty serious that they're all involved in, and a couple of the victims just escaped recently. Maybe they're panicking and trimming the fat to ensure that their secret stays just that." I turned to Captain Larose. "Where did this happen? We'll head there now and have a look at the body and the crime scene."

"The Blue Lagoon Resort," Larose replied. "Officer Da Silva, do you know where that is? Or should I send you the address?"

"I know it, Captain," Da Silva replied quickly before turning to look at Holm and me. "Come on. It's not very far from here. You can follow behind me in your car."

"Alright," I replied as I stood up to leave.

"Keep me updated on what you find," Larose called as the three of us walked to the door.

"I will, Captain!" Da Silva replied before turning and heading quickly down the hallway.

"Blue Lagoon resort..." Da Silva murmured as she, Holm, and I made our way back out of the police station. "That's one of the nicest hotels in Kingstown. Maybe *the* nicest. It's definitely one of the most expensive, that's for certain."

"Have you been there before?" I asked her.

"Me?" She turned to look at me with a disbelieving expression on her face. "Definitely not. That's not the kind of place that's really accessible to the locals if you know what I mean. Strictly tourists with more money than sense. In my opinion, the place isn't actually all that nice, but it's the most exclusive resort on the island."

"That certainly sounds like the kind of place where we might find someone rich enough to play around with other people's lives," I replied as we stepped back outside.

It was late and pitch-black enough to see the plethora of stars sprinkled across the sky clearly. I'd begun to feel tired a little earlier, but the news of a fresh body had shot a bolt of adrenaline straight through me, and I felt wide awake.

"This is bad," I muttered.

"In what way?" Holm asked me as we walked over to where we'd parked the cars. "I mean, I know a dead body is never a good thing, but why specifically?"

"They might be destabilizing," I explained. "If they're starting to have infighting and taking one another out, it might mean whoever was in charge, the 'master,' is losing control. If things fall apart, they might disband, and we won't be able to catch them."

"We'd better hurry, then," Da Silva declared as she yanked open the door to her patrol car. "Let's go."

She climbed inside, and Holm and I followed suit in our own car. I followed closely behind Da Silva, who turned on her lights and sirens as she sped down the street toward the resort. The road was virtually empty this time of night, so we made excellent time as we raced our way up to the northernmost part of Kingstown, where the resort was.

When we arrived, I immediately understood why Da Silva had described the hotel the way she had. The best way to describe the place was *gaudy*. The entire thing was huge, sparkling white, and surrounded by a tall, imposing, bleached limestone wall that, in my opinion, just looked ugly. It all reminded me of a tacky Las Vegas hotel that was trying its best to give off the impression of luxury but falling flat in the process.

I could see a pair of police cruisers with their lights flashing as we drove into the main parking lot. A few pockets of curious onlookers had formed around the perimeter, some still in pajamas and dressing gowns as they looked over at the police cars. I followed behind Da Silva and parked the car next to hers. As we got out, a police officer standing near one of the cruisers turned and walked over to us.

"Hey, Da Silva," the officer greeted her with a nod as he approached.

"Hey, Blackstone," Da Silva replied before turning to Holm and me. "These are Agents Holm and Marston. They're the ones working the Clearwater case with me."

"Nice to meet you," the officer, Blackstone, greeted us. "I wish it was under different circumstances. Anyway, the body's down on the beach." He lowered his voice as he took a quick look over his shoulder at all the bystanders. "Officer Claymore is down there now. I think Rogers is with him too."

"The area's been secured?" Da Silva asked.

"Yeah," Blackstone replied. "It wasn't that hard since it's a privately owned beach and all, but there were a few nosy guests, as you can see." He turned to toss another look over his shoulder at the small crowd.

"Thanks," I replied. "We'll go and take a look."

"Good luck," he replied as he turned away to walk back toward his car.

I realized then that they were likely positioned there to keep the other guests from wandering down to the beach. The three of us walked past the parking lot and into the resort's main complex. It consisted of a few buildings encircling a large courtyard. I could see a wide-open area leading down to the beach just ahead. From where we were, I could just make out the silhouettes of several figures in the darkness.

The closer we got to them, the more clearly I could make out their features: two more men dressed in police uniforms, as well as a man and a woman who were dressed casually. There was a dark lump on the ground between them, and I didn't have to think very hard to guess what that probably was. One of the officers turned to look at us as we approached.

"Da Silva, you're here," he greeted her as we made it to the spot where they were standing. "The captain called me."

As I suspected, the odd shape on the ground was a corpse lying on its back and covered in blood.

"We came as quickly as we could," Da Silva replied as she looked down at the body. "So, what do we know?"

"Only as much as the witness told us," the officer replied.

"There was a witness!?" I exclaimed as I snapped my head up to look at him.

"Oh, I mean the man who found the body," the officer clarified. "As far as I'm aware, he didn't actually see the murder take place."

"I see," I replied, unable to hide the disappointment in my voice. A credible witness would have been an enormous benefit.

"And the body was found how long ago?" Da Silva asked.

"Um, about an hour ago," the woman in street clothes chimed in before the officer could respond.

I turned to look at her, and she fidgeted nervously beneath my gaze.

"Uh, sorry," she added. "I didn't mean to cut in like that. My name's Dominica. I'm one of the managers here at the resort. The, um, gentleman who found the... the, uh... the—" She looked down at the body for just a second before looking sharply away. Her face was pallid, and she looked like she was about to throw up.

"The body?" I offered helpfully.

"Yes, that," she confirmed with a shaky nod. "He came over to the front desk after finding the, um, *him*." She nodded her head jerkily toward the corpse. "And he told us about what he'd just found. It was a little after one in the morning. That's when my employee called me to tell me what was going on. I can show you the call log on my phone if you want to see the exact time."

"That's okay, I believe you," I replied.

The woman was a nervous wreck. She was stammering her way through her explanation and was very clearly doing everything in her power to not even glance in the direction of the body.

"We would like to speak with the man who found the body, though," I added.

"He's over in the lobby with Blackstone's partner," the officer replied. "He was pretty shaken up when we arrived."

"I bet he was," I muttered as I crouched down to get a closer look at the dead man.

It was difficult to tell because his blood had stained his clothes such a dark shade of red that they nearly looked black, but I could see hints of pure white in the tiny spaces that had somehow been spared. The man looked like he was in his thirties or forties, but again, it was difficult to tell when his face was completely covered in blood, not to mention mangled from the various stab wounds all over it.

"Whoever did this was angry," I noted as I looked over the man's body. "It's overkill. The guy was probably dead long before the killer stopped stabbing."

"Well, that kind of pokes a hole in your theory

about it being infighting, doesn't it?" Da Silva asked thoughtfully. "Taking someone out to keep them quiet is one thing, but could it have warranted this level of anger?"

"I don't know," I replied as I continued to examine the corpse. I wasn't a forensic analyst like Bonnie and Clyde, so I couldn't be entirely sure what I was looking for, and I found myself wishing they were here right now to point out anything I was missing. "I think—" I stopped short as my eyes caught on something that struck me as a little odd.

"His pants are undone," I noted as I stood up straight.

"What?" Holm replied as he stepped forward to take a look. "That's... interesting."

It was definitely a strange detail, mainly because the belt around his waist was also undone. The blood and mess had made me miss it at first, but now, I couldn't unsee it. An unzipped fly was one thing, but the man's belt was also undone.

"Maybe the killer interrupted him while he was in the middle of taking a leak?" the officer suggested with a confused shrug.

"I guess that might be plausible," I replied as I took another look around the beach in the area immediately around the body. "If he were drunk, maybe. The hotel is just steps behind us, though. Why do it here when he could have just gone inside?" I paused as my eyes landed on something black a few feet away, half-buried in the sand. It was dark enough that if I hadn't specifically been looking for something, I might have just assumed it was a rock or a piece of trash. I walked over to it and knelt before reaching down to pick it up. The sand fell away to reveal a single black leather high heel.

"I think maybe our victim wasn't out here alone," I muttered as I gently brushed the sand off the object, careful not to touch it any more than I already had, lest I accidentally wipe away any prints or otherwise contaminate what was possibly a piece of evidence. Da Silva rushed over and quickly pulled a folded evidence bag from a pocket on her utility belt before carefully placing the shoe inside.

Of course, it might have just been a coincidence, but considering the dead man's compromised position, I doubted that.

20

ETHAN

"You're sure no one else came forward about what happened?" Da Silva turned sharply to the manager, who jumped in surprise.

"I-I'm sure!" she replied. "The man who came forward was the first we heard about it."

"That doesn't mean someone else wasn't here, though," Holm muttered. "We need to see the resort's security footage. We have to find out if the man was with anyone before he was killed."

"Oh, sure, that's fine," the manager stammered. "But there aren't any cameras that overlook this part of the beach. The area just outside the entrances is as far as they extend."

"That's fine," I replied as I stood up and walked back over to the group. Da Silva took the shoe from me and placed it into an evidence bag she procured from one of her pockets. "We just need to see where he was, and with who, in the moment before he came out here. That alone might give us something to go on."

"Okay." The manager nodded frantically. "Follow me to my office. We can go over the security footage there."

"We can call to have someone come to collect the body," the officer added. "If you're all done here."

"Yeah, we'd appreciate that," I replied. "Maybe the coroner can find something we missed. By the looks of it, though, the cause of death seems pretty obvious."

The officer nodded, and Holm, Da Silva, and I turned to follow the manager and the other man back toward the building.

"I'm Sal, by the way," the man introduced himself sheepishly to us as we made the short walk back to the hotel. "I'm one of the assistant managers. I wasn't here, so I don't know what all happened, but Dominica called me and asked me to come down to meet her."

"Well, when I heard there was a dead body on the property, I wasn't sure what I was supposed to do," Dominica muttered bitterly. She sounded irritated that Sal had even brought it up. "Just because I'm the one in charge doesn't mean I always have all the answers."

She shot Sal a look as we made it to the doors of the building, which opened automatically as we stepped close to them. As we stepped inside, I spotted another police officer sitting on a bright orange leather couch next to a man who had his head in his hands.

"That must be the guy who found the body," Holm whispered to me.

I nodded in response before calling out to get Dominica's attention.

"Just a minute," I called to her.

She stopped in her tracks and turned to look at me before glancing over to the pair of men sitting on the couch in the lobby, and her eyes lit up with understanding. She and the assistant manager hung back while Holm, Da Silva, and I walked over to the couch.

"Oh, hey, Da Silva," the officer greeted her as he looked up.

"Hi," she replied before jerking her head toward Holm and me. "Agents Marston and Holm."

"Nice to meet you," the new officer replied before looking back down at the man, who still hadn't lifted his head. "This is Mr. Schwartz. He's the one who found the victim out on the beach."

The man's shoulders tensed and rose a few inches as the officer spoke his name. He looked like a turtle that wanted to disappear into its shell.

"Hello, Mr. Schwartz," I replied softly as I slowly sat on one of the chairs perpendicular to the sofa. "I'm Agent Marston. Can I ask you some questions about what happened?"

"I don't know what happened," the man replied

quickly. "I didn't see anything or do anything. I was just taking a walk!"

He snapped his head up to look at me as he spoke, and I realized that he was a lot younger than I'd initially presumed. Maybe it was because my idea of the ultra-rich usually consisted of someone older who'd spent years accumulating their wealth, but I was surprised to see that the man looked like he was barely in his twenties, maybe even late teens.

"Okay," I assured him as he blasted through his explanation at lightning speed. "I believe you." Really, I couldn't make any concrete decisions yet about what I did or didn't believe, and I couldn't rule him out just yet, but I needed to get the kid calm if I was going to get him to talk. "Just slow down and tell me exactly what happened."

"Okay." The young man nodded and licked his lips before continuing. "I was down at the beach. My girl-friend and I got into a fight. I booked this whole big trip for us, and she's been in a bad mood the whole time! She said she would just fly back home early, and we ended up arguing. Then she said she was booking her own hotel room, which I told her was stupid because my dad had already paid for us to stay in this really nice place so it would be a waste, and I didn't want her staying in some nasty roach motel either. It's not safe for a woman to be on her own, you know? And then—"

"Mr. Schwartz." The officer cleared his throat pointedly.

"Oh, uh, sorry," the kid murmured sheepishly. "I did it again, huh? Anyway, yeah, she took off on her own, and I got really upset, so I decided to take a walk to clear my head. I know it's kind of a pansy thing to do, walking around on the beach by myself, but I just wanted to chill for a minute. Anyway, I was walking down there, and I saw this guy on the ground. At first, I thought he was just drunk. It seemed weird to me to see someone passed out drunk in a fancy place like this, but whatever, not my business how he wanted to party. I was just going to avoid him, but then I saw—" He cut himself off and bit his lip. He clenched and unclenched his fists, and he looked like he wanted to be anywhere but there at that moment.

"Yes?" I prodded him to continue.

"Blood." The kid let out a full-body shudder. "I thought maybe I imagined it, but the more I looked, the more it seemed like he wasn't sleeping. Who sleeps on their back with their arms all spread out like that, you know? I got a little closer, and... I don't know. It's kind of hard to remember after that, honestly."

"You blacked out?" I asked as I leaned forward in my seat toward him. ·

"Not really," he replied with a shrug. "It's weird. It felt like someone else was in control of my body, I guess. I remember standing there and looking at the body for a while. I'm not sure how long I did that for, and then I returned to the hotel and told the girl behind the counter what I saw. I just kinda sat down then until the police showed up."

"Alright," I replied. It sounded like he'd been in shock. It was common for people who witnessed horrifying things to block out negative experiences as a form of mental self-defense, so it didn't surprise me that he couldn't remember the details. "And you didn't see anyone else around?"

"Huh?" Schwartz looked up at me with a confused expression. "You mean when I found the dead guy? No, he was alone, and so was I. The whole beach was empty, actually. I mean, I don't remember seeing anyone else there." His eyes suddenly went wide. "W-why are you asking? I mean, I swear I didn't do anything."

"That's not why I'm asking," I assured him. Honestly, I believed that he was telling the truth. He didn't seem like he was lying, anyway. "Thank you for speaking to us, Mr. Schwartz."

"Is that everything?" He looked between the officer and me. "Can I go now? I really need to call my girlfriend."

"Well, we might have some follow-up questions later," the officer replied. "But for now, you're free to leave."

"G-great," Schwartz replied as he got awkwardly to his feet. He nodded at me before scurrying off.

"Seems like he got in over his head," Holm noted as the young man disappeared out of sight.

"No kidding," I replied. From the looks of it, he was just an affluent kid trying to impress his girlfriend on his dad's dime. I was sure that the last thing he'd expected to have to deal with during his vacation was a corpse. "Anyway, let's get back to that security footage."

"Right this way," Dominica replied, and we continued our procession over to her office.

We followed her back past the front desk and through a door marked "staff only." The area immediately beyond the door was decidedly less opulent than the lobby, with plain white walls and a dark blue carpet, but it nonetheless looked clean and well-kept. Inside the area was a row of lockers, a chair and a table, and at the very back, a small room partitioned off by curtained glass walls. The door at the front of the room read "Manager's Office."

Dominica stepped inside and flicked on the light switch as the rest of us piled in after her. It was surprisingly roomy inside, probably about as big as Diane's office, and modestly decorated. It was clean and professional, and everything from the solid but straightforward chairs and the sturdy desk at the head of the office made it evident that everything had been specifically chosen for maximum efficiency with a minimum of fuss.

"Let me just pull up our security feeds," she muttered nervously after walking around to her desk to turn on her computer. "One o'clock in the morning was when Mr. Schwartz found the, uh..." She swallowed anxiously, apparently still too squeamish about addressing the body. "So, I'll start backward from there."

"Do you know who you're looking for, though?" Sal spoke up as he moved to stand behind Dominica.

As he did, Holm, Da Silva, and I waited patiently just on the other side of the desk. I was too jittery to sit down, so I remained standing as I watched her work.

"We don't know who he is yet," Sal pointed out.

"No," Dominica agreed. "But it's not like there are that many guests walking around the grounds at one in the morning. Not as many as earlier in the day, anyway. If we take a look, we might find someone that looks like him."

"Are the cameras in the courtyard?" Da Silva asked. "That's the quickest path down to the beach, right? I'd check there first."

"That's a good idea," Dominica smiled at her in response before going back to her computer. "Let's see... oh, oh my goodness, I think we have something."

"Really?" I stepped forward in surprise. "Already?"

"Well, I'm not sure," she replied as she turned the

computer monitor, so it was facing us. "It's hard to be sure it's him, what with all the blood."

I looked down at the screen. A portly man wearing a white shirt and pants walked through the courtyard with a woman on his arm. The woman was wearing a black long-sleeve dress with matching black high heels.

"I think that's him," I replied. "And if it is, then I was right. He's not alone."

"They sure seem pretty giggly," Da Silva noted as she raised an eyebrow at the couple.

They were both wobbling slightly as they made their way across the courtyard and toward the beach. The woman was clinging to him for dear life as she stumbled her way onto the sand in the shoes she was wearing.

"They look drunk," I agreed as they stepped out of view of the camera. "Can you check the footage of the bar just before this?"

"Sure," Dominica replied as she turned the screen back toward her before leaning down to type something into the computer. "We have a few angles... here! Here they are, sitting at the end of the bar."

She turned the screen back around to face us. The same couple from the courtyard was sitting side by side at the end of the bar with their heads close together as they spoke and sipped from their drinks.

"So, they had drinks," I muttered. "Got drunk and

stumbled down to the beach. Judging from the victim's state of undress, I'm guessing they started to get frisky. And then—"

"He's dead, and she's missing," Da Silva finished for me as she lifted the evidence bag with the shoe in it. "So, the plot thickens." She looked back and forth between Holm and me. "So, what do we think? Did she have something to do with it? Was she killed as well? Or maybe snatched after our John Doe was murdered?"

"Hard to say," I replied as I looked back down at the screen. "If she *did* have something to do with the death, I'm assuming she had an accomplice. She looks like a strong breeze could knock her over. Somehow, I doubt a woman of her size could overpower the victim on her own."

"I don't know." Da Silva shrugged. "He was covered in knife wounds. The playing field evens out a bit when the weaker party has a weapon. Not to mention the, uh, *compromising position* that the victim was in."

"You think she seduced him and then killed him when his guard was down?" Holm looked at Da Silva in shock. "Damn, that's cold-blooded."

"It takes cold blood to be a murderer," she quipped back. "And it wouldn't be the first time a woman got rich by killing off her wealthy partner. Her motive might have been as simple as robbery."

"Do you know if this woman is a guest at the

hotel?" I turned to look at Dominica, whose eyes went wide with fear at my question.

"I-I'm not sure," she muttered. "Maybe? Probably, actually. The resort prides itself on its exclusivity. If they were at the bar, she would have needed a key to get in. Oh, unless he invited her... Wait, give me a minute to look through more of the footage. I'll try to see if I can trace her back to one of the rooms."

"You have that many cameras?" I looked at her in surprise.

"We have them in the centers of the hallways, right where the elevators are," she explained as she went back to searching the computer. "I won't be able to see the exact room that she's in, but if I find out which hallway, I can probably use the guest records to figure out the rest."

"That would be great," I replied as I crossed my arms and willed myself not to fidget nervously.

Dominica looked up at me with a small smile before turning back to the computer. I really wanted to pace or tap my foot or something. It was nerve-racking just to stand there waiting while she combed through the footage.

"You okay?" Da Silva suddenly asked me quietly.

"Hmm?" I turned to look at her in surprise. "Yeah, why?"

"You seemed kind of tense," Da Silva replied with a shrug. "Which I guess is normal, considering the circumstances, but, I don't know, you were staring off into space there for a second."

"Really?" I laughed. "I'm not usually that easy to read. I don't really like waiting, to be honest. I much prefer to take action myself than wait around for someone else to find the answers."

"Mmm, I understand that." She nodded thoughtfully, speaking quietly enough that we wouldn't be overheard. "I'm the same way, honestly. I don't like leaving things to others if I can help it. If you want something done right, you'd better go out and do it yourself, you know? On the other hand, rushing in without all the facts can just as easily lead you to disaster."

"He knows all about that," Holm replied as he took a step toward us. "Sorry, I didn't mean to eavesdrop, but you two are having this conversation like a foot away from me."

"What do you mean, *I* know all about that?" I scoffed. "Last I checked, you've been right there with me the entire time."

"Well, someone's gotta bail your ass out when you get into trouble," Holm replied nonchalantly.

"Now, children, don't fight," Da Silva deadpanned as she shook her head. "Instead, why don't we think about how we're going to find our Cinderella with the missing shoe?" She held the evidence bag up to where we could all see it.

"I'm not surprised she lost it," Holm noted. "With the way she was stumbling around on the sand in that video, I'm surprised she didn't lose both of them." I was about to respond, but Dominica called out from behind the desk before I could say anything.

"I think I know who she is," she announced as she leaned further toward the computer. She wasn't sitting as she typed, so her back was bent at an odd angle that looked very uncomfortable. "At first, I was trying to retrace her steps from the bar, but look." She turned the monitor toward us.

"She came back inside!" Sal exclaimed, his voice a mixture of horror and confusion. "Look, you can see her walk back into the hotel and a few minutes after that..." He reached down to fast-forward the video. "You can see Mr. Schwartz go outside."

"She walked back into the hotel on her own, just a few moments before the body was discovered," Dominica reiterated.

"Well, that's definitely suspicious," I remarked snarkily as I leaned down to watch the video again. "Can you zoom in on her face here?"

"Uh, sure," Dominica replied as she reached down to click on something with the computer mouse. A moment later, the picture enlarged, and though it was a little blurry, I could still make out the tears on her face as she stumbled shakily back into the lobby.

"She's crying," I muttered. "And she looks like she's trembling, too.

"That's not the behavior that I'd usually expect from someone who's just committed a murder," Da Silva noted. "Though not totally out of the ordinary. Guilt is a powerful thing, after all. She might have panicked and felt remorse about killing him."

"Maybe," I replied as I watched the video. Her shoe was missing, and she was hugging herself as she walked, her hands clutched tightly against her own arms. "I don't think she looks guilty, though. If anything... she looks *traumatized*."

"Like someone who just witnessed a murder," Holm concluded. He turned to look at me, and I knew we were thinking the same thing.

"So, you think this woman saw what happened?" Da Silva asked me. "She knows who killed the victim?"

"It's possible." I nodded. "We only know what the cameras show. She was all smiles when she left with the victim, and now, just a little while later, she's stumbling back inside by herself, looking like she's just seen a ghost." I turned to look at Dominica. "Do you know who the guest is?"

"Yes, I think so," she replied as she looked up at me from where she'd been typing. "Ms. Willow Helshire. She's up on the fourth floor. She's been staying here for a few days now. The security cameras show her leaving that floor, and there are currently only two women checked in as single guests on that floor."

"So, the woman in the video must be one of them," I replied. "Which room is she in?"

"Four-fifteen," Dominica replied as she stepped out from behind the desk. "I'll take you up there."

Holm, Da Silva, and I followed the manager out of the office and back out into the hotel's main lobby. Sal came as well, though I had a feeling that he was just tagging along for curiosity's sake. He'd said himself that he really didn't know much about what had happened. I guessed that I really couldn't blame him, though. The addition of a mystery woman was starting to make this all feel like a scene out of a drama.

As we all crowded into the elevator, I thought about what we might find up in room four-fifteen. Maybe our killer, though I highly doubted that. The expression on her face as she'd hurried back through the doors had looked haunted, and she just didn't look like someone who'd just stabbed a man several dozen times.

The elevator came to a stop on the fourth floor with a gentle rumble. The hallways were narrower than I'd expected them to be in a resort this upscale, and it was a tight squeeze as all five of us spilled out of the elevator and into the hallway. At the head of the group, Dominica was striding forward toward the room in question, her back stiff and her shoulders hunched with tension. I counted the rooms on the left side of the hallway as we walked past. Four-oh-nine, four-eleven, four-thirteen, and then finally four-fifteen, where Ms. Helshire was staying. Dominica lifted her hand to eye level before hesitating for just a moment. Then she balled her hand into a fist and rapped sharply against the door.

"Hello?" she called firmly. "This is the management. I have the police here. You need to come out and speak with us!"

I cringed internally at the caustic way she'd demanded that Ms. Helshire open the door. I understood that she was stressed about the night's events, but screaming commands at a witness and possible victim wasn't usually the best method of getting them to cooperate. For several seconds, there was no response to Dominica's shout.

"Hello!" she called again as she banged on the door. "If you don't come out, I'm afraid I'm just going to have to open the door myself."

She reached down and plucked a large set of keys from where it was hanging off the hook attached to her belt. The keys jingled loudly in the quiet hallway, and though her face and voice were firm, her hands shook with nerves as she fumbled slightly with the keys.

Before she could find the one she was looking for, we heard a muffled sound from just on the other side of the door that sounded like a lock being turned. It was followed just a moment later by a slight creak as the door opened just a few inches. A woman's face peeked out through the gap, her platinum blond hair falling over her gaunt, pale face as she looked warily at each of the people gathered outside her room door. Her hair was down, and she was wearing a thick sweater now, but the woman was undoubtedly the same one we'd seen on the security footage.

"Ms. Helshire?" I asked as I looked down at her. Even though I wasn't speaking very loudly, she still flinched at the sound of my voice.

"I suppose you're here to talk about Bill," she muttered as she anxiously rubbed her hands together.

"Was that his name?" I asked.

"That's what he told me." She shrugged before taking another look around at the group of us and then down the length of the hallway. "Why don't you come in then? I'd rather not have all of my neighbors hear about this if you don't mind." She turned and walked into the room without another word, her head bowed. I followed in after her, as did the rest of the group.

The first thing that hit me was the overpowering smell of cigarettes. It struck me as odd since the hallway hadn't smelled like that, and smoking rooms were usually all located on the same floor of a hotel. The inside of Ms. Helshire's hotel room was mostly neat. The bed was still made, aside from a few rumples in the comforter, and her suitcase was neatly placed beneath the window. The cleanliness of the room made the mess on the table all the more jarring. Several empty bottles of alcohol were sitting on top of it, as well as an assortment of cigarette butts. A crumpled piece of cloth was wadded up on the floor just beside it, and it took me a moment to recognize that it was the dress she'd been wearing in the security footage.

Ms. Helshire trudged over to the table and picked up one of the half-finished cigarettes, as well as a sleek metal lighter. She flicked the flame on and ignited the cigarette with a sharp, forceful inhale, sucking in a considerable amount of smoke before finally breathing out again. Beside me, I felt Dominica stiffen. Her managerial instincts were probably screaming over the fact that she was smoking like a chimney in a non-smoking room, but she restrained herself from actually saying anything to Ms. Helshire about it.

"So," Ms. Helshire muttered flatly as she plopped down into one of the chairs beside the table. "You wanted to talk? About what happened?"

"Yes, if you're okay with that," I replied gently as I moved to sit at the edge of the bed, which was the closest spot to where she was. The only other chair at the table had been thrown down onto the ground and was lying on its side.

"Why wouldn't I be?" she replied, her voice as flat and lifeless as before.

To an untrained observer, it might have seemed

like she didn't care or wasn't interested. I had a feeling the dead tone of her voice was more of a self-defense mechanism. Her eyes were half-lidded and had a faraway look in them, and though some of that was likely due to the alcohol, I was sure that she was trying very hard to distance herself from what had happened down on the beach.

"I didn't do anything wrong," she added, "except maybe agree to give that pig the time of day."

"He wasn't a nice guy?" I asked.

Out of the corner of my eye, I noticed Da Silva saying something to Dominica and Sal, who left the room a moment later. She must have told them to clear out so the victim wouldn't feel pressured.

"No," Ms. Helshire snorted. "Then again, there's not really any such thing, in my experience. I've been around the block a time or two. You don't get to be my age without having your fair share of encounters with men." She shook her head slowly. "And they're all trash."

"I see," I replied warily.

I wondered vaguely if I should let Da Silva take over. Ms. Helshire didn't seem very keen on the idea of, well, men in general, so maybe Da Silva would be more successful in speaking with her.

"He walked right up to me at the bar," Ms. Helshire continued as if she hadn't even heard me. "Made some stupid little comment about how he couldn't take his eyes off me and then rubbed his hand down my back." She shuddered at the memory. "Creep. I was about to tell him to screw off, but then I noticed the watch he was wearing."

She lifted her own delicate wrist and stared down at it as though she could see the watch in her mind's eye. "Cartier. White gold with a silver dial and sapphire crystal hands. It was gorgeous, but more than that, I could tell it was *expensive*." For the first time since our conversation started, the corners of her mouth lifted into a small, faint smile as she looked up at me. "So, I figured I'd keep the man company. Get him drunk enough that he wouldn't remember any of it the next day, and then help myself to his wallet. Or maybe to that watch."

The way that she just confessed to her actions without a hint of remorse was kind of eerie but not unusual for someone in shock. Right now, her brain was on lockdown, only processing the most basic thoughts, so it probably didn't even occur to her that she should lie about her plan to rob the victim.

"So, that's why you went down to the beach with him?" I asked.

Frankly, I didn't care about her plan to take the guy's watch. I just needed to know what she saw during the attack.

"Yeah," she replied quietly. "I suggested we go back to his room, but he insisted that we go do it on the beach. I guess he got some weird thrill out of the idea of doing it out in the open. Seemed like a pain to me, honestly. Who wants to deal with sand getting all up in your–Anyway, by that point, I'd already committed, so I decided to go along with him."

"And down at the beach," Da Silva chimed in as she crouched down in front of Ms. Helshire. "The two of you were…"

"We weren't doing *much,* to be honest," Ms. Helshire scoffed. Her voice still sounded flat and weak, but I noticed that she seemed a little more lively with Da Silva. "It was a bit of a disaster. Alcohol can do that to a guy, you know? Not that I was all that disappointed. Anyway, we were sitting there, and that's when…"

She suddenly trailed off. She bowed her head again as her breathing began to grow more rapid.

"When you were attacked?" Da Silva asked, and Ms. Helshire nodded.

"He came right toward us," Ms. Helshire croaked. She sounded like she wanted to cry. "I thought it was a security guard at first, coming to tell us to take it inside, but then I realized he wasn't wearing a uniform. But even worse than that was his face."

"His face?" I repeated, and Ms. Helshire nodded.

"He looked so *angry,*" she replied. "He was snarling like a wild animal. I remember thinking maybe his kid saw us or something. I just didn't understand why he would look so mad, but I knew I was scared. He was walking at us so fast, with that horrible look, and—" She shook her head frantically as she buried her face in her hands.

"He attacked you?" I prodded after giving her a few seconds to calm down.

"Not me," she whispered as she took her hands away from her face. "I was sure he would, with how angry he looked, but he didn't even look at me. He walked right past me and went for Bill. He pulled this big knife from behind his back and just started stabbing him, over and over and over."

"And the man, Bill," I replied. "How did he react when he saw the attacker? Did he look like he knew him, or did he say a name, anything like that?"

"It all happened so fast," Ms. Helshire replied. "I can't remember. All I know is, all of a sudden, Bill was on his back, and the killer was on top of him, stabbing him over and over. I think Bill yelled for help, but the man stabbed him in the neck, and then he couldn't yell anymore. Then I started screaming, but I couldn't run. I don't know why. I wanted to run away, but my legs wouldn't move."

"That's a normal response to a scary situation," I assured her. "You don't have to feel bad about that."

Most people were familiar with the phrase "fight or flight," but in reality, there was often the third option, "freeze." The same fear response caused deer to come to a stop in the middle of the road in front of a car instead of running away. Often, a person was just too scared to do anything but stand there.

"Pretty dang stupid, if you ask me," Ms. Helshire replied bitterly. "I just stood there waiting for my turn to die. It wasn't until the man finally looked at me and told me to shut up that I actually moved. Then my foot got caught in the sand, and I fell. I thought I was dead right then. I was on my back with no way to defend myself. But then... he didn't do anything."

"He didn't attack you, you mean?" I raised an eyebrow at her.

"No." She shook her head slowly. "And not just that, he walked over to me and helped me up."

"What?" Da Silva looked at her in shock.

"Yeah," Ms. Helshire replied breathlessly. "He walked over to me and grabbed my hand, and pulled me up. Even asked me if I was okay. I thought, well, I'm not sure what I thought. I felt like I was dreaming or something. He was all covered in blood. He'd just murdered Bill, but he was asking me if I was okay after I tripped." She looked up at Da Silva and me. "What kind of lunatic does that?"

"Did he do anything after that?" I asked. "Or say anything?"

"Yeah," Ms. Helshire replied, her brows knitting together as she spoke. "He said he was sorry I had to see that and that Bill was a bad person that needed to be scrubbed off the face of the earth. Then he said he had no reason to hurt me, not unless I told someone." Her shoulders sagged as she slumped back in her chair. "So, then I just left. I walked back here, back to my room. I took a shower, and I had a few drinks." She looked over at the empty alcohol bottles on the table. They were the miniature kind that could typically be found inside hotel mini-fridges, but there were still enough of them to make anyone drunk. "Smoked a little, too. I'm sure I will be getting a massive credit card charge a few days after I check out. That's fine. I don't care about that, to be honest with you." She was staring off into space again, her expression blank.

"Ms. Helshire," Da Silva addressed her gently. "I know this is painful for you to remember, but do you recall seeing what the attacker's face looked like? Did he have any identifying features that you can remember? Tattoos, piercings, maybe?"

"He looked normal." Ms. Helshire shrugged slowly. "White guy, maybe five-ten? It was dark, but I think his eyes were blue?"

"That's very helpful." Da Silva smiled encouragingly at her. "Was there anything else about him that stuck out to you in any way?"

"Not really," Ms. Helshire replied as she brushed a lock of hair out of her eyes. It looked a little knotted like she hadn't bothered to comb it after taking her shower. "Wait, there was something. He walked kind of funny."

"Funny?" I repeated as I leaned my elbows down against my knees to lean toward her. "In what way?"

"When he was coming to help me up," she replied. "He kind of wobbled like he had a limp."

"Did he look injured?" Da Silva asked.

"I'm not sure," Ms. Helshire replied apologetically. "Sorry, as I said, it was dark."

"That's alright," I replied before turning to look at Holm, who had remained in the room but was standing off to the side. "Maybe the victim managed to injure him during the attack."

"No," Ms. Helshire replied without hesitation. She looked down and gave a slight shudder. "That much, I'm sure of. It all went by so fast, but I know for sure that Bill didn't even have time to react. The guy was on top of him in a flash. Poor bastard still had his pants undone." She snorted. "Doesn't get much more humiliating than that, does it?"

"That was still a very helpful description," Da Silva replied kindly. "It'll definitely help us narrow down the pool of suspects."

"Well, I'm glad, I guess," Ms. Helshire replied flatly.

She reached over to the table and grabbed one of the nearly empty bottles before holding it up to her lips and draining what little liquid was left inside. Da

Silva stood up slowly as she did. She nodded her head for me to follow her, so I stood up as well.

"I'm going to talk to her about maybe getting some help," Da Silva whispered to Holm and me once we'd taken a few steps away from Ms. Helshire. "She's clearly still in shock, and if she doesn't stop drinking soon, she's going to hurt herself. While I speak to her, why don't you go talk to the manager about possibly finding out who this 'Bill' guest is?"

"Sure thing," I replied.

I looked back once at Ms. Helshire before turning and leaving the room. She hadn't screamed or cried the entire time we spoke to her, but that didn't mean she wasn't upset about what had happened. On the contrary, her mostly silent demeanor was a bad sign that she was in a worse state than she seemed on the outside.

Dominica and Sal were waiting just outside the door when we came out of the hotel room.

"I can try to see if we have any 'Bills' listed as guests at the moment," Dominica spoke up before I could say a single word. "Sorry, I didn't mean to eavesdrop."

"Yes, you did," Sal raised an eyebrow at her. "I mean, to be fair, we both did."

Dominica glared at him.

"Anyway," she huffed, "we can go and check now. And it's not like it was all that hard. They were talking right in there."

She and Sal continued to bicker as they led Holm and me down the hallway, back toward the elevator. We stepped back inside, and as the elevator doors closed, I thought about how this case might connect to everything else. Really, the only similarity this murder had with Clearwater's was the fact that both bodies had been found on the beach. Considering how different the cases were, it was possible they weren't even related. I doubted that, though, since the timing was just too perfect to be coincidental.

The elevator hit the ground floor with a ding, and the four of us stepped back out. As we walked back over to Dominica's office, we passed a pair of sleepy-looking guests.

"Man, can you believe what happened?" one of the men chortled to the other. "There were cops everywhere."

"Well, yeah," the other man responded. "Someone got murdered. I heard the killer used a chainsaw."

"What?" the first man scoffed skeptically. "Yeah, right."

"It's true!" the other man exclaimed. "Anyway, do you want to try that one lobster place..."

And then they were gone, around the corner that led to the guest rooms. Just like that, the heinous murder that had occurred just a few hours ago was reduced to little more than idle gossip, quickly super-seded by a discussion on where to have lunch the following day. It was crazy to think about, sometimes. Awful, unbelievable things happened every day, and most people never even noticed. And even when they did, it hardly warranted taking up a fraction of their attention before they were off to their own business again. I shook the thought away. That was just the way life was. Now wasn't the time to get introspective.

"Okay!" Dominica declared as she pushed open the door to her office. She sounded a lot more confident than she had just a little while ago when she'd been unable to even say the words "dead body." The thrill of solving a mystery was infectious, so maybe she was just emboldened by the idea that she held the key to discovering the victim's identity. "Let's see here, if I take a look into our guest records..."

She continued to mumble to herself as she clicked away at the computer. She remained standing again, probably too agitated to sit. I couldn't blame her, as I felt restless as well. The fact that the killer was still at large, and we had no idea who he even was, made me feel like I had to go after him right now. The last thing I wanted to do was have a seat and twiddle my thumbs.

"No 'Bills'..." she sighed defeatedly as she drummed her fingers along the desk.

"Try 'William,'" Sal suggested, an edge of sarcasm to his voice, as though he thought that should have been obvious.

"I was just about to!" Dominica muttered after

frowning at him. "Oh, looks like we've got three of those. That *is* a pretty common name. Now, how do we narrow this down?"

"I don't suppose you have age and height listed in there?" I asked, though I already knew the answer.

"Yeah, no," Dominica replied. "We don't typically ask guests for that information when they're making their booking."

"We could just round them all up and see which one looks like the body?" Sal suggested.

"What?" Dominica turned fully around to look at him in disbelief. "The b-body is dead, you moron. None of them are going to look like him!"

"Ah, right." Sal smiled sheepishly.

"No, that's actually not a bad plan," I replied.

"Excuse me?" Dominica spun around to look at me.

Even Sal was staring back at me in confusion.

"Page them down here," I explained. "Call up to their rooms and tell them you need to have a word. Heck, they don't even have to come down. Whoever doesn't answer is our victim."

"That makes sense!" Dominica exclaimed, wide-eyed as she reached for the phone on her desk. She glanced over at the computer, likely to check the room number before punching it into the phone. "This is going to tick off whoever isn't our Bill."

She pursed her lips nervously as the phone rang. I

could hear the telltale click when someone picked up on the other end.

"Ah, hello?" Dominica replied. "Yes, is this Mr. William Foundry? Yes... Yes, I realize it's late. I'm very sorry. I just wanted to let you know that we're, um—" She looked up at us in a panic. "We're comping you a free dinner during your stay here. Yes, at one of your restaurants. Yes, I'm sorry about calling so late. Thank you, have a wonderful night." She slammed down the phone before looking up at us. "He was not pleased to be woken up."

"Are we going to get in trouble?" Sal asked, looking genuinely concerned.

"No," Dominica replied, though she didn't sound very convincing. "Well, if anyone complains to corporate, we'll deal with it then." She glanced over at the computer again before punching another number into the phone. "Okay, William Marino is next."

She held the phone up to her ear, and I waited with bated breath. It rang, and rang, and rang for what seemed like a full minute.

"He's not answering," Dominica muttered shakily as she set the phone back into the receiver.

"Well, he could just be a deep sleeper," Sal noted nervously.

"Let's just try the third one," Dominica decided as she picked the phone up again.

This time it only rang for a few seconds before

someone answered again. She went through her spiel about the free dinner again before ending the call.

"He didn't seem as annoyed," she sighed with relief before setting the phone back into the cradle. "I think he was still awake. And that means…"

She glanced back at the computer.

"Number two is most likely our victim," I finished. "William Marino. I'm assuming you have an ID on file for him?"

"A passport, yes," Dominica replied as she looked at the computer screen. "It says here that he's visiting from Italy, apparently."

"We're going to need a copy of that," I replied.

Dominica nodded as she got to work typing something into the computer again. There was still a lot left to uncover, but it seemed like we were finally getting somewhere.

21

ETHAN

WHEN I OPENED my eyes blearily the following morning, I knew that it was already late in the day. I didn't even have to look out the window to know that the sun would already be high in the sky. After all, we hadn't actually made it back to our hotel until nearly three AM the night before. I'd immediately collapsed into bed, exhausted from everything that had happened just during our first day in St. Vincent.

I rolled over and grabbed my phone from where I'd left it charging the night before. It was nearly noon, which meant I'd slept for even longer than I'd thought. Usually, I would have kicked myself for sleeping in so late and losing so much of the day, but today was a different story. On the contrary, I wanted to be as well-rested as possible. Tonight, at midnight, we were supposed to go and meet the boat that the guard had told us about.

I reached up to drag a hand down over my face as I thought about everything that had happened. We'd found both one of the victims and one of the perps on the same day. Of course, the suspect we'd arrested had only been a pawn, hired muscle meant to do the dirty work of the real people in charge. Then there was the deceased William Marino. Before heading to bed, Holm and I had forwarded all the information we had on him back home to see what we could find out about him. Until we got some results back, all we could do was focus on the mission.

I slid out of bed and grabbed a clean change of clothes out of my bag before heading into the bathroom to get cleaned up for the day. Even though we weren't technically in a rush, I still hurried through everything. There were just so many loose ends we'd yet to tie up that I felt too anxious to do anything slowly. We not only had the group of wealthy lunatics to contend with now but also, potentially, a solo killer as well, if there was a connection there. Ultimately, only about twenty minutes had passed by the time I'd finished getting changed and ready.

It seemed like Holm had woken up at approximately the same time I had because there was a message on my phone from him when I went to check just after getting dressed, informing me that Da Silva was on her way and that he was finishing up getting ready. I tucked the phone into my pocket and then left the room.

I headed down into the lobby to wait for Da Silva and Holm. As I made it down to the ground floor, I spotted a table at the far end of the main lobby. A coffee machine sat at one end, next to a basket full of small, individually wrapped muffins, right beside a note encouraging guests to help themselves. I made a beeline for the table the moment I saw it. I grabbed one of the disposable paper cups stacked up in a tall tower beside the coffee machine and poured myself a cup of coffee, partially to wake myself up but also because I just wanted to have something to do.

I took a swig of the coffee before pulling my phone out of my pocket. It was only about ten minutes past noon now, which meant that we still had a solid twelve hours until we were meant to go and stake out the docks. Of course, we would be spending some of that finalizing the plan, but that would still leave several hours of downtime. I frowned as I put my phone back into my pocket.

"Oh, coffee," Holm's voice suddenly cut through my thoughts as he appeared beside me. He reached past me to grab one of the cups before holding it under the coffee dispenser.

"How'd you sleep?" I asked as I drained the rest of my small cup.

"Like a rock," Holm replied flatly as he moved his head from side to side to stretch his neck. It popped as he did. "Man, I can't believe everything that happened. The first day in St. Vincent, and we really hit the ground running."

"We were up for nearly twenty-four hours," I replied as I balled up the paper cup in my hand and tossed it into the trash bin just beneath the table. "We got on the flight at five AM and didn't get back to the hotel last night until three."

"Damn," Holm muttered as he lifted his cup to his lips. "No wonder I was so tired. Anyway, it looks like we've got some time to chill now, though."

"Yeah," I grumbled. "A little too much."

"I don't know," Holm muttered. "Considering what we're going up against, the more prep time we have for that, the better."

"Yeah, I guess that's true," I replied just as the front doors to the hotel opened. Da Silva stepped through, and I noticed that she was back in her full police uniform, pristine and white. Her hair was up in a neat ponytail again as well. She took a glance around the lobby before spotting us, then headed over to where Holm and I were still standing by the coffee machine.

"Ready to get started?" she asked as she came to a stop in front of us.

"Ready," Holm and I both replied in unison.

"Alright," she replied eagerly. "Let's get going then."

The next several hours passed by in an anxious blur. At first, everything seemed to drag on for too long. Then, as the sun began to set and the meeting time finally approached, it seemed like time was moving all too quickly.

"It's almost midnight," I informed Holm and Da Silva after glancing down at my phone.

We were in the rental car, sitting right out in the open on the edge of the dock. After careful consideration, we'd decided that hiding in plain sight was the best way to go about this. They would be expecting the two guards we'd apprehended to meet them here, so they likely wouldn't think it was suspicious if they saw a car here on the docks. Once they arrived, we'd jump out and restrain them before they could get away.

Of course, we weren't here without backup. Just a few yards away, in the marina's parking lot, another set of officers was standing by in a similarly unmarked car. They were far enough away that they likely wouldn't be noticed by whoever ended up coming off of that boat, but still close enough to come to our aid if we ended up needing assistance.

"Something's coming," Da Silva noted as she looked out through the front windshield of the car.

Sure enough, a medium-sized boat was floating slowly through the marina, directly toward where we were parked. It was definitely big enough to have a cabin below deck, but it wasn't big enough to be the

yacht the victim had described. The boat was undoubtedly heading toward us, though, and I tensed as I
watched it slowly pull up to the edge of the marina
before coming to a stop. For a few seconds, nothing
happened, and then a tall man suddenly stepped out
of the helm and walked to the front of the deck. He
looked straight out at our car, and he was close enough
that I could see him squinting as he looked in our
direction.

"He can't see us in here," I muttered. "The lights of
the marina are too bright outside. He's probably just
seeing a glare from where he's standing."

"Should we get out?" Da Silva asked.

"Not quite yet," I replied. "Let's wait until he's off
the boat first. If we reveal ourselves now, they might
still be able to bolt."

"Got it," Da Silva replied.

The three of us sat tight as the man on the boat
continued to peer down at us, bobbing his head up and
down and from side to side as if trying to find an angle
at which he could actually see into the car. Finally,
another man joined him on the deck. He was waving
his arms around impatiently, gesturing back at the
boat toward something. The taller of the two men
threw his hands up in confusion before pointing down
at the car.

"They're probably wondering why their contact
isn't coming out," I realized.

I quickly assessed the situation. If we continued to stay here, they might get spooked and decide to leave. If we revealed ourselves too early, though, we'd likely end up with the same result. Luckily for us, we didn't need to decide because the taller of the two men climbed down off of the deck of the boat just a moment later.

"Got one," I murmured triumphantly as I slowly put my hand against the handle of the car door, ready to jump out at any moment.

While apprehending both would be preferable, so long as we could capture one, we'd be able to get the information we needed, even if the other managed to escape. The man walked toward the car warily. As he got closer, I could more clearly see the perplexed expression on his face. Behind him, the other man was also starting to climb off the boat.

"Wait for it," I muttered as I watched the second man like a hawk. He was almost on the dock now. Just a little more, and they'd both be off the boat, and the playing field would be a lot more level.

"Now!" I yelled as soon as the second man was off the boat as well, and the three of us each threw open the doors in unison as we leapt out of the car.

"Freeze!" Da Silva yelled as she yanked her gun from her hip, so fast that the suspect standing closest to the car didn't even have time to react before he was staring down the barrel of a gun. "Don't move!"

The suspect standing closest to us went stock still, looking like a deer in the headlights as he stared directly at the gun in his face. However, the second suspect paid no mind to Da Silva's warning and immediately reached for something behind his back. The next instant, chaos erupted along the dock as several things happened at once.

First, Da Silva, who had noticed the second suspect move, screamed out in warning as she turned her gun away from the closer suspect to fix it onto the other man. Then they both pulled their triggers at once. The closer suspect, seizing his opportunity the moment it presented itself, jumped to the side, away from Da Silva's line of fire. Just steps away from me, Holm also yelled as he pulled his own gun from his holster. However, my focus was fixed solidly on the first suspect, who was reaching for something behind his back from where he had crouched just feet away from Da Silva.

I jumped toward him, knocking him to the ground before he could draw whatever he was reaching for. A flash of movement and color blurred overhead as Holm took off in the direction of the boat, probably to go after the other suspect. The man I'd pinned to the ground struggled beneath me, his one free arm flailing wildly as he tried to punch me from the awkward angle I had him restrained in. My knee was pressed to his back, and I could feel something hard and solid there.

I reached down, just beneath his shirt, and was unsurprised when my hand gripped around the cool metal of a gun. I quickly yanked it out from the waistband of his pants before launching it as far away as I could. The suspect realized what I'd just done and roared with anger. Above me, three gunshots suddenly rang out in quick succession.

I snapped my head up to see what had happened, panic seizing me as I tried to figure out if it had been friend or foe who had fired those shots. I was relieved to see that both Da Silva and Holm were still on their feet, which meant that, at the very least, they hadn't been shot. The suspect was still standing as well, though, which meant that I couldn't relax just yet.

Unfortunately, the sound of gunshots had pulled my attention away from the suspect I was grappling with for just long enough that he was able to twist around and pull himself free of my hold. He shoved me off roughly, and I hissed as I landed hard on my elbow. I could feel the skin on my arm scrape away as I slid against the hard ground of the dock. A sharp ache bloomed from the middle of my forearm, and I knew that the fall had left me with a nasty cut, at the very least. I didn't have time to inspect it right now, though. The suspect had already jumped back up to his feet, and he was rapidly scanning around the dock for his gun.

I jumped to my feet before he could find it again, and I lunged at him. He braced himself, likely expecting me to try to tackle him again. I knew better than to try the same tactic twice, though, and at the very last moment, I switched gears and lifted my fist to punch him across the face.

The suspect let out a pained grunt as the force of the punch caused him to stumble to the side. I moved in to punch him in the stomach, but he recovered remarkably fast and reared back around to hit me before I could get close enough. I lifted my arms just in time to block his strike, but the pain of the blow still resonated through my forearm, lingering for an exceptionally long time in the spot where I'd just scraped it against the ground. I gritted my teeth together against the pain and took a step backward. The suspect was right on top of me, though, and he moved in again to punch me in the stomach. I twisted to the side, but I wasn't quick enough, and his fist struck me right in my obliques.

I crumpled slightly as my muscles screamed in pain. The suspect wasn't showing any mercy, though, and he came at me again without hesitation. Instead of standing back up to face him, I went in the opposite direction and crouched down to avoid his next blow. He stumbled forward as his next punch connected with nothing but empty air. From where I was crouched, I quickly straightened my legs and head-butted him directly in the stomach with the full force of my body weight.

The suspect made a pained, choked-off gurgling noise and flopped straight back like a log of wood. He gasped for breath, his mouth opening and closing like a fish out of water. I leaned down to cuff him, and I froze when I heard a rash of footfalls running toward me. I spun around quickly, yanking my gun from its holster as I did.

"Oh, it's just us!" one of our backup officers declared as he skidded to a stop in front of me.

My shoulders slumped in relief as I put my gun back away. The other officer raced past me and knelt to get the suspect under control. While he did that, I turned to check on Da Silva and Holm. To my relief, they both looked fine, and they were both standing over the other suspect, who was similarly cuffed on the ground.

"Sorry," the officer I'd nearly shot apologized. "We ran as fast as we could. I guess everything's been handled, though."

"It's fine," I replied before nodding down at the suspect. "Just make sure he doesn't get away. There's another one over here, with Officer Da Silva and Agent Holm."

"I'm coming," the officer replied as he fell into step

beside me.

Together, we raced over to Da Silva and Holm, who were watching over the suspect.

"Get this off of me!" the suspect growled as he rocked angrily from side to side.

It was all he could do with his hands cuffed behind his back, and it might have been funny if I wasn't still worried that there might be more suspects on board the boat.

"We need to check onboard for anyone else," I said as I caught up with Da Silva and Holm.

"Let's go." Da Silva nodded, and the backup officer knelt to keep the suspect still as the three of us climbed deftly onto the boat.

I drew my gun from my holster and stayed low to the ground as we moved toward the short set of stairs that led down into the cabin below deck. I could see clearly from one end of the deck to the other. There was no one above deck, which meant that if there were any more suspects in here, they were downstairs.

I dove in without hesitation. There wasn't anywhere to take cover anyway, so if anyone was lying in wait down here, it wasn't like I could hide.

I was mildly surprised to find that the cabin was completely empty.

"What the hell...?" I muttered as I slowly lowered my gun.

The place was a complete dump. Pieces of old

furniture, fishing equipment, and even trash were strewn about the small space, but there was no one else on board despite the amount of stuff.

"It's clear," Da Silva declared as she too lowered her gun.

"Yeah..." I replied, my voice thick with confusion.

"What's wrong?" she asked me as she suddenly took a nervous look around the room. "You see something I don't?"

"No," I muttered. "More like I don't see anything at all. That's weird, right? I was sure there'd be... something. Someone."

"Or some*ones,*" Holm emphasized. "The guard we arrested said he would meet up with the kidnappers to pick up the victims, right? So, where are they?" I took another look around the room. It was irrefutably empty. A pigsty for sure, but void of human life, and yet...

I counted in my head as I walked the length of the room, using my own stride as a unit of measurement.

"It's too small," I mused aloud.

"Pardon?" Da Silva cocked her head at me.

"The cabin," I explained as I looked up at the wall in front of us. "It's too small. I mean, not all boats are built the same, but I've spent enough time on and around them that I can tell this cabin isn't as big as it should be."

I strode forward, climbing over a stack of papers

and what looked like a broken printer of all things. I made my way to the wall. I knocked on it, and not only did it sound hollow, as I expected, but the thing wobbled slightly as I pushed against it.

"It's a false wall," I informed Holm and Da Silva urgently as I spun around to look at them.

They both jumped into action at once, climbing over the deliberately placed piles of trash to get to the wall. I pushed and prodded at it experimentally. It wasn't particularly sturdy, but it wasn't light either. Between the three of us, though, we were able to lift and shove it out of the way enough to create a gap that allowed us to see what was behind it.

"Oh my—!" Da Silva gasped before clapping a hand over her mouth.

She was the closest to the gap, and as she took a step backward, I was able to catch a glimpse myself. I understood her alarm immediately.

Hidden in the tiny gap behind the door, in a space that couldn't have been more than two feet wide, several men were slumped over on the ground. They were tied up, gagged, and clearly unconscious. I could count at least six at a glance, though it was difficult to tell with the way they were all jammed together in the tiny space.

"We need medical down here now," I stated as my eyes roved over the terrible scene. "We've got at least half a dozen victims."

22

ETHAN

I DOWNED my second cup of coffee of the day in a single go before setting the ceramic mug down on the counter. I was standing in the Kingstown Police Station break room, drinking strong coffee out of a mug with a big smiley face on it. I hadn't actively chosen it. I'd just grabbed one at random from the cabinet above the counter before filling it with my sorely needed boost of caffeine. I glanced down at my phone to check the time. It was just before eleven. By this point, my sleep schedule was well and truly destroyed, not that it had ever been all that consistent, to begin with. Whenever we were out on a case, it was impossible to keep anything consistent.

We'd been out until quite late the previous night as well. Of course, our priority after finding the victims had been to get them medical attention. Waiting on the ambulances and then making sure that everyone was accounted for had taken over an hour. It had been challenging because we wanted to keep the entire thing as under wraps as possible. The last thing we wanted was for some news agency to catch wind of what had happened. If the news suddenly started reporting what happened and the group responsible found out, they'd no doubt lie low or disband entirely, and then we'd be completely out of luck in our attempts to catch them.

I'd wanted to interview the two suspects we'd arrested last night as well, but by the time everything had been said and done with the victims, it had been well into the wee hours, and in the end, we'd decided just to call it a night. Holm and I had hurried down to the police station as soon as we'd woken up, which was how I'd ended up there in the break room, sucking down cups of coffee as we waited for our chance to interrogate the two suspects we'd arrested.

"This case isn't letting up at all, is it?" Holm sighed as he fell into one of the chairs in the break room.

"Not at all," I replied as I reached for the coffee pot again. "Except for that downtime we had yesterday, and even that wasn't what I'd consider relaxing."

I picked the pot up but then set it back down. The restless night had left me feeling tired, but I knew I shouldn't drink too much coffee, either. Excess caffeine would make me jittery and cause me to be just as unable to focus as too little caffeine. Instead, I walked over to where Holm was and sat down next to him. As soon as I did, my phone went off. I reached into my pocket to grab it and frowned down at it in confusion as I realized who it was.

"Diane's calling me," I informed Holm before answering the call and holding the phone up to my ear. "Hello?"

"Agent Marston, have you received the information about William Marino?" Diane asked me without any kind of preamble.

"No," I replied. "Should I have?"

"I just forwarded it to Captain Larose," she replied. "If he hasn't mentioned it yet, I'm sure he will at any moment. The agents in the intelligence department ran a background check, though apparently, it wasn't very hard to find information about him."

"Why is that?" I asked.

"Because he's a billionaire," she replied point-blank. "Well, *was* a billionaire, I suppose. Anyway, he owned a prestigious wine company in Italy, *Vino Marino*.

"I've never heard of it," I replied with a shrug.

"I'm not surprised," she scoffed. "Apparently, their lower range bottles go for a couple thousand each, and that's the cheap stuff. It's not exactly the kind of thing the average Joe is regularly purchasing."

"Damn," I replied in shock, my eyebrows rising into my hairline as I heard the price tag. "Wait, did you just call me an 'average Joe'?"

Holm snapped his head around to look at me, an amused expression on his face. I realized he might be missing something important, and I quickly put the phone on speaker so he could hear as well.

"Oh, don't take it that way," Diane snorted. "I hadn't heard of it either. In any case, the guy was a pretty big deal. His family was informed early this morning when we first figured out his identity, and they're on their way there now."

"Should we be worried about that?" I asked warily.

If the guy was as big a deal as Diane was making him out to be, then his family might be a pain to work with, especially if he was actually one of the perps, as I heavily suspected. I couldn't imagine the family of a freakishly wealthy, well-to-do business tycoon would want it getting out that Marino was engaging in gladiator tourism.

"Honestly, I can't answer that one way or another," Diane replied. "The man I spoke to, his brother, seemed more saddened by the news than angry or defensive. Nevertheless, you should, of course, proceed with caution."

"Got it," I replied. "We'll make sure to keep that in mind."

"Good," Diane replied. "In any case, you should discuss this with Captain Larose and your liaison. Keep me updated."

"Will do," I replied before saying goodbye and ending the call.

"So, we know who William Marino is?" Holm asked.

"Yep," I replied. "And now, I'm more sure than ever that he was one of the people who was attending the fight parties as a guest."

"Well, that much was pretty obvious," Holm replied. "Now, we just have to figure out who killed him."

"Maybe one of our suspects has an idea," I replied. Just as I did, the door to the break room opened, and Da Silva stepped inside.

"Okay," she announced as she stepped briskly into the room. "They're ready. We're interrogating Daniel Chen first. That's the shorter one that pulled the gun first. Oh, your director called, by the way, we've figured out who William Marino is."

"Yeah, I just got off the phone with her," I replied as I slipped the phone in question back into my pocket.

"Oh, great," Da Silva replied a little tersely. There was an odd, strained expression on her face, and she seemed anxious. "The family should be here in—" She glanced down at the watch wrapped around her slim wrist. "About an hour now. Great. That's great. Well, that gives us enough time to interrogate at least one of the suspects before they arrive."

"So soon?!" I looked up at her in shock. "I thought they just left?"

"They did." Da Silva cracked a rueful smile. "Apparently, they chartered a private flight to bring them straight here. I guess you save a lot of time when you don't have to worry about security or other people boarding."

"You seem nervous about them getting here," I noted as I stood up off the chair.

"I'd be lying if I said I wasn't," she muttered. "Captain Larose is nervous about it. He's worried about how they might react once they hear the details of the case, especially once they realize we're looking at Marino primarily as a suspect of our main case." She pursed her lips together. "Money can get you a lot in this world. I think he's worried they might try to retaliate against the department or MBLIS."

"Don't worry about us," I replied. "If they do try something, then it wouldn't be our first time dealing with wealthy, vindictive people using their money to try to ruin us."

"The Hollands really did come close to bringing

MBLIS down," Holm murmured, his voice low and his eyes haunted.

"But they didn't," I countered before turning back to Da Silva. "We'll figure it out, don't worry. In any case, we're wasting the limited time we have before they get here."

"You're right." Da Silva nodded. "Let's go. Chen's already waiting in one of the interrogation rooms."

Holm stood up then, and the two of us followed Da Silva out of the break room and down a side hallway. Once again, I was struck by just how big this station was, and I tried to memorize the route we were taking as we walked further through the winding corridors. On the way there, we passed a heavy metal door with a small window in it, set with thick glass. As I walked by, I could see cells against the wall at the other end of the room, some filled with prisoners wearing orange clothes. I wondered vaguely if the other suspect was waiting in there for his turn to be interrogated.

"Here we are," Da Silva noted as we finally arrived at another fortified steel door, similar to the one I'd seen before that led into the holding cell area.

She had to punch in a code for the door to open with a hiss, and it was obvious that the police took security exceptionally seriously here.

"The station's really big," I mentioned off-handedly as she led us through the door.

"Yes, it is," she laughed as she looked fondly up at the high ceilings of the building. "It's not uncommon for rookie officers to get lost in here when they first start. I know I did. The layout can be a bit confusing because a lot of the building actually used to be barracks. A lot of these areas used to be dormitories."

"Oh, that does explain why it's so big," I replied.

"Yes." She nodded as she continued down the long hallway. "Some two hundred years ago, when St. Vincent first gained its independence from France and Britain, the Police Force Barracks was one of the first things built, both as a beacon of our nation's independence and for practicality." She paused as she came to a stop outside one of the rooms. "We were on our own after all, so we needed to build up a police force that was capable of enforcing order. A lot of the new trainees stayed right here in the police station."

She took a look around again as if imagining what it might have looked like back then. "Of course, things change over nearly two centuries. A lot of the space was converted from barracks into something else, mostly holding cells and offices, but we do have a few nice interrogation rooms as well."

She finished her explanation of the station's history with a small, slightly proud smile before turning back to face the door. She reached up to punch a code into a keypad identical to the one she'd used to gain access to this hallway. The door opened with a click, and Da Silva pushed on it to step inside.

The room we walked into was tiny, maybe ten by ten feet max. Two simple chairs took up the majority of the space in the room. They were facing the left wall of the room, into which a large glass window was set.

"Daniel Chen." She said the suspect's name, and her voice was low and serious when she did.

I turned to look through the glass into the room where the suspect was sitting. I hadn't been able to see them very well out on the dock, but the man was covered in tattoos, even over his face. He was wearing a set of pale orange clothes, and one of his ankles was cuffed to a thick bolt that was fixed to the interrogation room floor.

"American, forty-nine years old," Da Silva explained as she reached down to pluck a folder from one of the chairs. "He has priors for possession and distribution, the most recent of which landed him a ten-year stay in prison. He finished his sentence about a year ago, but we weren't able to find any kind of work history since his release."

"After ten years?" I scoffed as she handed me the folder. "I'm not surprised he doesn't have any work history. After that long in prison, any work skills he had are obsolete, and most people won't want to hire an ex-con, anyway." When I glanced down at the prison intake photo, I was surprised to see a bare-faced man looking back up at me. "Looks like he made some friends while he was in prison."

I looked up through the glass again. That explained the facial tattoos. Though I wasn't highly familiar with prison gangs and their tattoos, I knew enough to recognize them.

"After ten years, he probably didn't have a choice," Holm added. "For that amount of time, you'd have to join up with someone just to survive."

"So, he's out of prison," I sighed as I set the folder back down and looked back at Chen through the glass. "No work, no way to get work, and with ten years' worth of anger and resentment built up inside of him."

"So, he ends up working for a group of rich weirdos," Holm finished. "As a kidnapper for hire."

"That about sums it up, I think," I replied as I turned to look at Da Silva. "Do we know anything else about him?"

"No." She shrugged. "The last official record we can find of his whereabouts is from the day he was released from prison."

"Okay," I replied. "Well, that's fine. We caught him red-handed with a boat full of drugged-up victims, so it's not like we don't know what he's been up to since then."

"Are we ready to go inside then?" she asked, stepping toward the door that separated the tiny viewing room from the actual seated interrogation area. She paused and looked at Holm and me for confirmation.

"Yeah," I replied.

Holm nodded in agreement, and Da Silva turned to push open the door that led into the larger room.

Chen's gaze slid over to us as the three of us stepped inside. He barely spared me a glance, but his face twisted into a scowl as his eyes landed on Da Silva. She and Holm had been the ones to arrest him, so I guessed that he must have remembered her face from the docks.

"What the hell do you want?" he sneered as the three of us sat down at the table across from him.

"We have a few questions we'd like you to answer, Mr. Chen," Da Silva replied calmly as she folded her hands together in her lap. She looked relaxed as she leaned back in her seat, making it clear that she wasn't intimidated by Chen's ugly frown.

"Yeah?" he snorted, his upper lip curling up as he eyed her angrily. "Well, I'd like you to suck my—"

"That's really not necessary," I cut him off before he could finish whatever disgusting sentence was about to come out of his mouth.

He looked away from Da Silva to focus his attention on me.

"And who the hell are you?" he grumbled.

I'd only passed by him for a moment as I was

making my way onto the boat, so I wasn't surprised he didn't recognize me.

"Agent Marston," I replied simply. "With MBLIS. I'm sure you haven't heard of us, but my partner and I work for an organization specializing in investigating crimes that cross international borders. Knowing that, I'm certain you must know why we're here."

Chen's face first went red and then white as I explained. His eyes flicked over to Da Silva's and Holm's before finally coming back to meet mine, as though he wasn't quite sure where to look. Finally, he settled on just staring down at the table without saying a word.

"There's really no need to be coy or anything," I sighed as I folded my arms over my chest. "We found the victims right there on the boat that you and your partner were on. Surely, you don't think you have a chance of squirming your way out of that, right?"

He glared up at me hatefully, but I could see the panic in his eyes behind the anger. He knew that I was right.

"Mr. Chen, we're in a bit of a time crunch right now," Da Silva huffed, glancing down at her watch impatiently. It was a flippant gesture, probably meant to rattle him into getting flustered enough to talk. She wasn't actually bluffing, though, as Marino's family would likely be arriving shortly. "If you aren't going to cooperate, just say that. We can always go and speak to your accomplice instead."

That seemed to catch Chen's attention because he suddenly lifted his head and looked at her anxiously.

"That's not a bad idea," I replied. "Who knows? Maybe he'll have a little more sense. After all, whoever talks first is at an advantage." I leaned forward against the table to look Chen directly in the eyes. "Cooperating with an investigation always looks good to the judge, you know."

Of course, he did. As someone who had been to prison before, he would know all about the court system and the importance of taking advantage of every little thing you could to make things go in your favor. For a moment, it seemed like my words had convinced Chen because he spent several seconds looking back at me thoughtfully. Then he snorted before crossing his arms petulantly over his chest.

"Heh, you think I'm afraid of prison?" He scoffed before shaking his head at me. "I spent a decade of my life behind bars. Your little threat isn't going to make me snitch." He sneered at me in disgust before turning away.

"That's strange." Da Silva frowned at him in mock confusion before turning to look at me. "I would have thought someone who's been to prison for, what, a third of his adult life would want to avoid going back." She shrugged. "Maybe that's just me. Oh, well. Let's go and speak to Mr. Calvert then." She stood up from her chair gracefully. "I just hope for your sake he doesn't have anything negative to say about you."

"Good luck," Chen sneered. "He's not going to rat me out. He's not going to squeal to some pigs."

"Are you sure about that?" she asked him seriously as she leaned down to put her hands on the table, staring down at him almost threateningly. "According to what we know about him, Calvert's never even been arrested before. He froze up out on the docks as soon as he saw us. He isn't like you, Mr. Chen. You know that."

Chen was still scowling up at her, but there was a note of wariness in his expression.

"You really think that some clueless young man who's never even had a taste of the prison system is going to uphold some sort of code for your sake?" she asked him mockingly.

"That's a lot of faith to have in someone," I added as I stood up as well. "Anyway, I guess we'll find out—"

"Wait," Chen grumbled, so quietly that I almost missed it. He tapped his index finger against the table nervously and chewed on his lip. "Alright, you've made your point. Get on with it already."

"Well, thank you for your cooperation," I replied as I sat back down, the barest hint of sarcasm in my voice as I spoke.

His lip twitched as he looked up at me, as though he wanted to snarl, but he kept his composure.

"Why don't we just cut to the chase then?" I started as I leaned back in my seat. "We know a group of wealthy individuals hired you to find and kidnap homeless men for them to use in some kind of sick fighting game. We need to know who these people are and where we can find them."

"Well, too bad for you," Chen snorted. "I haven't got a clue who those bastards are. Our job is to find the targets, bring them back, and hand them off. Sometimes, we get pulled into guard duty too when they're short-handed, but I don't know who any of them actually are."

"Really?" I asked him skeptically. "You have no idea?"

"Really," he bit back sharply. "Believe me or don't, that's the truth. I only know that their leader is a guy who calls himself the 'Game Master' or some stupid crap like that, damned lunatic. He meets up with us about once a month, usually before or after one of their creepy little parties. He gives us our pay, tells us our quota for the month, and then splits on that fancy boat. I don't ask any questions. I just do what I'm told and get my money."

"I see," I replied, not bothering to hide the disgust I felt at his response. "So, you don't even know who you're working for? You're just out collecting victims for a total stranger in exchange for money?"

"Hey, think whatever you want." Chen shrugged dismissively. "Work is work. It's not like I'm doing this for fun."

"And where do you usually meet with him?" I asked.

"Wherever they happen to be at the time," he explained. "That's the reason they do this whole thing way out here in the Grenadines. There's a bunch of small, private islands they can sail out to. We'll meet them out there to hand over the targets. Then, when they're done with their party, they'll usually have someone bury the bodies out on whatever island happens to be closest."

"So, the bodies of the victims are just scattered all over the Grenadines?!" I exclaimed in horror and anger. As if brazenly using people and killing them off wasn't bad enough, the fact that they were then just discarding them wherever they just happened to be somehow made the entire thing feel all the more grotesque.

"I guess." Chen shrugged. "Anyway, that's how it works. There's supposed to be another party any day now, so we were just going to wait there at the docks until I got the call telling us where to meet them." He paused for a moment, then looked up at me with a sly smile. "You know, I could maybe help you out after all.

You said you wanted to find out where they were, right?"

"I did say that," I replied hesitantly, nervous about where he was going with this.

"Well, I should be getting a call sometime soon," he explained. "Once they call, they'll give me the address of where to bring the newest batch of guys. Too bad the cops took my phone when they arrested me." He turned to glare at Da Silva. "And if any of *you* answer, they'll know for sure that something's up."

"Let me guess," I replied flatly. "You want a deal in exchange for taking the call and passing the information on their whereabouts along to us?"

"More or less," Chen replied with a shrug. "I mean, at this point, it's no skin off my nose if I flip on them, right? I'm going back to jail either way. I might as well use what I can to my advantage."

"That's one way of thinking about it." I looked down at him in barely concealed disdain.

It was ironic how easily he was talking about betraying them now when he'd been going on and on about not being a snitch just moments earlier. Regardless, I was loath to cut him a deal. I'd already made one with one of the other suspects, and frankly, I wanted Chen to face the maximum penalty possible for everything he had done. Once again, though, I knew that my priority needed to be the safety of the victims. So long as there were still men out there that needed help, I had to do whatever was necessary to find them as quickly as possible.

"Fine," I replied. "Play along during the call and help us find out where they are, and in exchange, I'll make sure you get a reduced sentence."

Chen opened his mouth as if to argue for more, but I cut him off before he could say anything.

"That's it," I spat. "That's the deal. Either take it or leave it."

Honestly, the promise of a reduced sentence was already pretty generous, and I'd jumped straight to that because of the rush I felt to get this deal wrapped up so we could continue with the case. Chen must have known that as well because he clamped his mouth shut before twisting it into a satisfied grin.

"Fine with me," he replied smugly. "So, can I get my phone back?"

"We'll arrange for an officer to stay with you until the call comes in," Da Silva cut in at once. "He'll keep the phone for now. Once the perps call, then you can answer."

"Seriously?" Chen scoffed. "So, I get to have one of you pigs babysitting me until then? Great. Oh, well. I guess it's a small price to pay to have my sentence reduced."

He smirked again, staring at me as though he'd won. I ignored him. As irritating as it was that he would be getting a deal, he was still going to prison. I bit back the urge to make a snide comment and instead just stood up.

"I think we're finished here," I declared as I turned to look at Da Silva and Holm.

"I think so as well," Da Silva replied before looking down at Chen. "Someone else will be in shortly."

"Great," he deadpanned before leaning back in his chair, lolling his head back to look up at the ceiling as the three of us filed out of the room and back through the tiny viewing room before finally making it back out to the hallway.

"Did we *have* to cut him a deal?" Da Silva grumbled as the three of us stepped back outside.

"Should I not have?" I asked her genuinely, worried for a moment that I might have misstepped in doing so.

"No, it was the right call," she sighed defeatedly as she reached up to fiddle with a small necklace that was hanging at her collarbone. "I just hated seeing that smug grin on his face."

"Let him smile all he wants," Holm snorted. "A deal isn't a free pass out of jail. He's still going back behind bars, and another ten years instead of the, say, thirty he deserves still won't be a walk in the park. Regardless of how long he's in there, he'll be an old man by the time he's back out."

"Well, when you put it *that* way..." Da Silva laughed at Chen's expense.

I could understand her consternation, but Holm had a point. As smug as Chen had seemed in there, we were still the ones who had come out on top.

"Let's go get ready to interrogate the other suspect, Calvert," Da Silva suggested as she glanced down at her watch. "Depending on what he has to say, we might be able to squeeze him in before Marino's family arrives."

23

HOLM

As it turned out, Da Silva had been wrong about them having enough time to do anything before the Marino family arrived. The first thing the trio had done was head back down to the first floor of the station so Da Silva could arrange for someone to go and sit with Chen until the call came in. She'd only barely finished doing that when a commotion broke out from the main lobby at the front of the station, near the entrance. Holm couldn't quite make out what was being said from where he and Ethan were standing, but he could hear a distinctly female voice screaming in anger.

"What the hell is that?" he muttered as he craned his head to look further down the hallway.

He couldn't quite see the lobby from here, though

he noticed that several other officers in the hallway were doing the same.

"Maybe we should go see what's happening," Da Silva suggested warily, her eyebrows knitted together in concern as she too looked down the hallway that led to the lobby.

"Let's go," Marston agreed without hesitation before taking off at a stride.

That was unsurprising since Marston was always willing and ready to jump in headfirst at the first sign of danger. Of course, Holm was always right there with him since he wasn't about to just leave his friend and partner high and dry, but Holm did think it wouldn't kill Marston to be a little more cautious about it.

The three of them rounded the corner into the lobby just a moment later, and Holm stopped dead in his tracks the moment he laid eyes on the scene. He stopped so suddenly that he nearly tripped, so shocked by what he saw that he literally could not believe it, and for just a split second, he wondered if he was dreaming or maybe just hallucinating. There, standing in the middle of the lobby, her eyes ablaze with anger, was Aurora, the woman he'd met just a few days ago in New York. The woman whose embroidered handkerchief Holm still had tucked neatly in his travel bag back in his hotel room.

"Look, I don't mean to be rude," Aurora stated calmly, though the dangerous look in her eyes indicated she was anything but calm. "But surely, you can understand my frustration. My father is beside himself! Look at him!"

"Stellina, please." The man beside her sniffled. His eyes were bloodshot, and his nose was red and runny. It was clear he'd been crying. "I'm fine, really. The officers are just doing their jobs."

"Their jobs?" She looked back at the man incredulously. "The job of the police is to help people! Uncle Will is dead. They should be helping us!" She snapped her head back around to look at the officer manning the desk, who shrunk back a bit beneath her glare. "Instead, they're telling us something about how we can't even see our own family because of some investigation! My father flew here from New York after receiving a phone call that his only brother was dead! Don't you have any compassion?"

"Ma'am, please," the officer replied calmly. "I'm not entirely sure what the issue is, but I can try to find someone that can explain it to you."

"No need," Da Silva interrupted as she stepped forward. "I'm Officer Da Silva. I assume you must be the family of Mr. William Marino."

"Yes." Aurora nodded. She reached over to place a comforting hand around the shoulder of the man standing next to her. "My father, Radley Marino. William was his brother and my uncle. Please, ever since we received that call, everyone has refused to answer our questions and—" She stopped short as her eyes suddenly drifted over to Holm. "Oh." The expression of confusion on Aurora's face only grew more pronounced as she looked back and forth between him and Marston, neither of whom had said anything yet. "You're here."

"Do the three of you know each other?" Da Silva spun around to look at Holm and Marston in surprise.

"Yes," Marston replied before Holm could. "Actually, we do. What a weird coincidence."

He sounded incredibly suspicious, which Holm couldn't blame him for. It *was* a bizarre coincidence. Too bizarre, actually, because what were the odds that a random woman they just happened to rescue back in New York happened to be related to a suspect in their case all the way out here in the Caribbean. Usually, Holm would have been suspicious as well. This was Aurora, though, and even though they'd spent only an hour together back in New York, Holm's gut was telling him that they could trust her. A beat of silence passed after Marston's comment, and then Aurora broke it with an angry, broken bubble of laughter.

"Is this some kind of sick joke?" she snarled as she looked back and forth between Marston and Holm. Her eyes were alight with fury, and her slim, delicate shoulders rose and fell rapidly as she breathed. "Some kind of trick to get me to come down here? What are you doing here? Are you some kind of con artist? Is my uncle even here?" She was looking directly at Holm, her expression a mix of anger and pain.

"It's not a joke," Holm replied softly as he looked back at her. "And I'm sorry, but William Marino really is dead."

The fire went out of her eyes then, and her shoulders slumped as she crumpled in on herself. It was like she'd been clinging to the possibility that this was all just a joke, and knowing it was real had snuffed out the light in her eyes.

"Why don't we find somewhere quieter to talk?" Da Silva suggested, the confusion she felt still evident in her voice. "Come on. There's a room we can use just over here."

Aurora nodded silently before placing a gentle hand against her father's shoulder so the two of them could follow after Da Silva. Holm and Marston trailed behind, and together, the small group filed into a conference room just a few steps away from the lobby.

"Alright," Da Silva began once everyone was inside the room. "I think we all need to talk about what exactly is going on here." She roved her gaze over every person in the room.

"We met back in New York," Holm explained as he turned to look at Aurora.

She glanced up at him for just a second, her expression unreadable, before she quickly looked away.

"Some men on the street were harassing Ms. Marino," Marston added. "We just happened to be around when it happened."

"Harassed?" Radley Marino snapped his head around to stare at his daughter in shock. "Stellina, you never told me about that. O-Or about meeting these men!"

"Papa, it was nothing, really," Aurora hurried to assure him. "I didn't get hurt. The agents arrived just in time to help me." She snuck another peek at Holm before averting her gaze again. "I didn't see them again until today."

"So, what exactly is going on here?" Mr. Marino looked at Marston pleadingly. "I got a call early this morning telling me my brother was found dead this morning. I ask for details, and I'm told that the police can't reveal any information connected to an active case." He scoffed. "I tell them I'm the family of the victim! They can't give me information!? But then they tell me that they're talking about a different case. A case in which my brother is a suspect! And now I find out that the detectives investigating know my daughter! Somebody, please explain it to me!"

"I'm sorry about the confusion," Marston replied. "It seems like things have gotten a little messy. To begin, my partner and I aren't detectives. We're federal agents with an organization called MBLIS. We investigate crimes that span international borders. We're currently investigating a case involving the kidnapping of multiple homeless men. These men are being snatched off the street and transported to St. Vincent. After that, they are taken onto a boat and out into international waters, where they are forced to fight one another to the death for the entertainment of a group of party guests."

Aurora gasped. Her eyes went wide with horror as her hand flew up to her mouth.

"I'm very sorry to hear that," Mr. Marino replied, and though he didn't sound as distressed as Aurora, his concern seemed genuine. "But I don't understand what any of that has to do with my brother."

Marston pursed his lips together, and it seemed to Holm that he was reluctant to explain further. Judging by their reactions, it seemed like neither Marino nor Aurora knew anything about what had been going on, so Holm could understand why Marston was reluctant to reveal to them that their family member had possibly been one of the people hurting the victims.

"We think that William Marino might have been involved," Holm explained. "We aren't yet sure who killed him or why, exactly, but we have strong reason to believe that it's related to the fact that he was participating in these fighting events."

"No!" Aurora gasped, stumbling over to one of the chairs in the room. She fell into it weakly, shaking her head as she looked up at Holm. "No, that's not possible.

Uncle Will wouldn't do that. You've made some kind of mistake. He was just with us in New York! Just a few days ago!"

"A few days ago?" Marston parroted sharply. "So, he left? Did he tell you where he was going?"

"Well, he said he was... meeting some friends," she replied, her gaze going vacant as a single tear rolled down her cheek. "He said he was meeting up with some friends down in the Caribbean." Holm could see the gears turning in her head as the dots began to connect. "No." She shook her head again weakly as she looked up at Holm with bright, wet eyes. "This is some mistake. He comes down here all the time. He likes boating. It must be some horrible coincidence."

"It's not," Mr. Marino cut in quietly, and every eye in the room turned to look at him.

"Papa?" Aurora gasped in shock.

"I think the agents are telling the truth," he sighed sadly as he reached up to run a hand through his salt-and-pepper hair. He suddenly looked ten years older, the bags under his eyes dark as he looked up at Marston and Holm. "To be honest with you, I knew that my brother was up to something untoward down here."

"What?" Aurora asked him weakly.

"I wasn't sure what he was doing," Mr. Marino admitted. "Prostitution was my guess. He's been cooking the books, skimming off the top, and doing a poor job covering his tracks. We co-own a wine business together, you see. He didn't think I knew, but I knew." Mr. Marino smiled sadly. "He was my brother, though. I figured he was out here doing drugs and partying. I was ashamed of him for lying and stealing like that, but he was still my brother. I turned a blind eye and pretended that he really was down here just going fishing with his old buddies." He sighed. "Maybe if I hadn't, this wouldn't have happened."

"What he did isn't your fault," Holm assured him quickly.

"This can't be real," Aurora muttered as she buried her face in her hands. Holm thought that she was crying, but when she lifted her head suddenly, her eyes were dry, and rather than sad, she looked pissed. "He said something to me, back in New York, before he left." She bit down on her lip before letting out a small, bitter laugh. "We were outside the hotel one morning, waiting for our taxi. A little old man was digging through a trash can at the corner of the sidewalk. I said how terribly sad it was how many homeless people there were in New York City. I'd seen so many since we'd gotten there, and it always broke my heart. Do you know what he said to me?"

She turned to look directly at Holm. "He said, 'you shouldn't feel so bad for them. They barely count as people. They don't contribute to the world. There's hardly any point to them.' I was so shocked, but he laughed and said he was only joking. I remember thinking it wasn't a very funny joke, but I turned a blind eye just like Papa. I ignored it." She bit down on her lip and looked around the room nervously before suddenly getting to her feet. "I need some air."

She suddenly took off, past Da Silva, and through the door out of the conference room. Holm was up on his feet before he'd even made a conscious decision to stand up, and he raced after her before he could think twice about it. Holm looked around as he stepped into the hallway and caught sight of her auburn-colored hair just as she rounded the corner toward the front doors of the station. Holm followed after her.

Aurora finally came to a stop on the sidewalk just outside the station, her arms folded over her chest as she looked up at the sky.

"Are you okay?" Holm asked as he approached her slowly.

She jumped as she spun around to look at him, as though she hadn't heard him approaching. She visibly relaxed when she realized that it was only Holm.

"I don't know," she replied with a slight shrug. "I'm not sure what I should feel or think right now. I just know that I feel like throwing up."

"I know it must be a shock," Holm offered sympathetically.

"That's putting it mildly," Aurora scoffed as she leaned back against the front wall of the station. "I just... I can't believe it. But at the same time, I can, I suppose."

"What do you mean?" Holm frowned at her as he moved to stand beside her along the wall.

"It's like Papa said," Aurora replied sadly. "I loved my uncle, and *to me*, he was always kind and gentle. But I think, deep down, I always knew there was something bad about him. That comment he made about the homeless man wasn't the first time he'd been cruel. I guess we all turn a blind eye when it comes to family."

"I'm sorry," Holm muttered, unsure what else to say.

There was only silence between the two of them for a few moments.

"My father's a weak man," Aurora suddenly spoke up as she turned to look at Holm. "I don't mean that he's foolish or weak-willed, just that he's kindhearted. Too much, in fact. That's why he didn't do anything, even though Uncle Will was stealing from the business." He'd rather suffer himself than upset anyone else." She shook her head sadly. "That's also why I was so angry earlier in the lobby." Her face flushed red at the memory. "Sorry about that, by the way. I don't usually lose my composure like that, but I just couldn't stand to see my dear father cry, and I knew he wasn't going to stand up for himself."

"I don't think there was anything wrong with it,"

Holm replied, though he had to admit that the force of her rage had been quite the intimidating sight to behold at the time.

"Well, I appreciate your understanding," Aurora replied. She smiled at Holm warmly for just a moment before the expression slipped off her face. "I'm disgusted to admit it now, but I used to think that I quite resembled my Uncle Will. He and my father worked together to run the company. While my father was always the brains behind everything, he lacked the assertiveness needed to be the head of a company that large. That's where Uncle Will came in. I've always been more like him than my father. I'd rather take matters into my own hands than wait in the wings for someone else to get things done." She frowned. "I'm not sure how I should feel about that now."

"You and your uncle are different people," Holm hurried to assure her. "Just because you both share certain personality traits doesn't mean that you're the same."

"I certainly hope not," she grumbled bitterly.

After that, she fell silent for a moment before glancing up at Holm from the corner of her eye.

"I have to say," she snickered. "I didn't think we'd be meeting again like *this*."

"I wasn't sure we'd be meeting again at all," Holm admitted before he had a chance to realize how rude that might sound.

He opened his mouth to apologize, but Aurora cut him off before he could.

"Is that right?" Aurora asked slyly as she raised an eyebrow at Holm. "And why is that? Do you think I go around giving my things away to just everyone I meet?"

"Oh, well, no," Holm replied quickly, feeling flustered at the way she was looking at him and babbling a little as a result. "Of course not. It's just, well, you were back in New York, and we were already down here in St. Vincent, so—"

"So?" She grinned impishly up at Holm. "Papa flew us down here at a moment's notice. Do you think I wouldn't have done the same if you'd actually called? How do you think I felt, waiting by the phone every night, wondering why the handsome agent who'd saved my life had suddenly left me waiting like that?"

"I, uh, well—" Holm stammered, unsure which part of that statement he should address first. His face was burning, and the sly way that Aurora was looking at him was not helping him think straight. "You were waiting by the phone for me to call you?"

"Well, maybe that was a bit of an exaggeration," she admitted. "Still, it's not every day that someone comes to your rescue like that. I would have come."

"Marston was right," Holm muttered, equal parts amused and shocked that Marston's joke about Aurora flying to him on a private plane had actually been right on the mark.

"Hmm?" Aurora furrowed her brows at him in confusion. "Marston? Your partner?"

"Yeah," Holm chuckled as he rubbed the back of his neck awkwardly. "He'd made a joke about you flying all the way to St. Vincent if I called."

"Did he?" Aurora smiled devilishly as she tossed a glance over her shoulder through the window into the station. "He sounds like a wise man."

"He's not," Holm deadpanned in response, decidedly ignoring the tiny twinge of panic that bloomed at the back of his mind just at the notion that Aurora might be in any way interested in Marston.

Holm loved his partner like a brother, but the guy was an absolute playboy when it came to women. The last thing he wanted to do was send Aurora in his direction, and that sentiment had everything to do with Aurora's wellbeing, and absolutely nothing to do with Holm's interest in her.

Nothing at all.

"He's not?" Aurora asked before shrugging. "Oh, well, I suppose I can stay here and talk to you some more then." She smiled at Holm, who felt himself smiling back without even thinking about it. "Then again, I suppose right now isn't the best time for us to be having a chat. You're in the middle of investigating, aren't you?"

"Yeah, we are," Holm admitted reluctantly.

Now that he had finally gotten the chance to meet

up with Aurora again, the thought of cutting their time together short made him feel miserable.

"I understand," Aurora murmured as she looked off into the distance. "I just wish that there was something I could do to help those poor—" She suddenly gasped as she snapped her head around to face Holm, her long, silky hair whipping around her face as she did. "That's it! I can help you!"

"What?" Holm looked back at her in alarm and confusion. "What do you mean?"

"I can get you onto that boat!" she exclaimed, the fire in her eyes back in full force.

Holm looked back at her in confusion, still unsure what she was talking about. He was sure of one thing, though. There wasn't a chance in hell he would let Aurora become involved in the case, not when there was the remotest chance that doing so could put her in danger. Before he could say a word in protest, though, the station's front door suddenly burst open with a bang.

"There you are!" Da Silva exclaimed as she ran outside. "We need to go. Another body's just been found."

24

ETHAN

HOLM HAD COMMENTED EARLY that morning that the case hadn't let up since the moment we'd landed, and as we raced toward our latest crime scene, it struck me just how true that was. We really hadn't gotten a moment's rest, and now Holm and I were in the car, following closely behind Da Silva as the three of us rushed to the ocean-side restaurant where the latest body had been found.

Well, "found" was really a mild way of putting it, I supposed. After Holm had followed Aurora outside, we'd continued our conversation with Mr. Marino, though there wasn't much else for him to tell us. Though I'd been a bit suspicious at first, it quickly became evident that our chance encounter with Aurora really *was* just a coincidence and that she and her father didn't know anything about what William

Marino had been doing. Not long after that, Captain Larose had come down from his office to tell us that someone had just been murdered in broad daylight in an upscale restaurant just a few minutes from the station. So, it wasn't really that someone had "found" the body. Rather, several people had actually watched as the man in question was brutally killed.

"The guy walked in, killed one of the guests, and then just walked on out?" I murmured as I followed closely behind Da Silva. She was able to weave through traffic with the help of her lights and sirens, and so long as I trailed just behind her, I should be able to do the same.

"So, it was definitely a targeted attack," Holm replied. "Whoever did this knew exactly who he wanted to kill and had no interest in hurting anyone else."

"Thank goodness for that," I remarked. "Do you think maybe they know about their men being arrested? If they found out that we found the other victims, they might be scrambling now to do damage control. Cull the ones they think might talk and spill their secrets."

"I don't know," Holm muttered in response. "I feel like if they knew we were onto them, they'd try to lie low instead of brazenly taking each other out like that. That reminds me, though, Aurora said something kind of weird about—"

I slammed on the brakes as Da Silva's police car came to an unexpected and sudden stop in front of mine. I could see the restaurant just up ahead, but we weren't quite in the parking lot yet. It wasn't until I rolled down my window and craned my head out to have a look that I realized it was because the parking lot outside was swarming with both people and vehicles as everyone attempted to leave. Da Silva backed up just slightly before turning the wheel of her car and setting it off to the side of the road.

"Everyone, calm down!" she yelled as she got out of the car.

Holm and I got out after her, and the three of us raced into the parking lot.

"What a disaster," I noted as I took a look around at the scene.

Some of the people in their cars leaned out through their windows and yelled angrily as we walked past, arguing with others to get out of their way.

"They're panicking," Da Silva remarked. "I might, too, if someone walked into a restaurant where I was eating and murdered one of the other diners."

We walked past the mess of people and through the front doors of the restaurant. I noticed that one of the glass doors was broken and wondered vaguely how that had happened.

Though the parking lot outside was filled to bursting, the restaurant's interior was almost entirely empty. Small, intimate tables filled the large dining areas, and it only took me a second to spot the body slumped over at one of the tables, a massive spot of red staining the crisp white tablecloth beneath.

At the front of the restaurant, near the host booth, a woman was wailing, trembling as she babbled something about a murderer. Two employees wearing uniforms bearing the restaurant's name were speaking to her. One of them, a woman with short brown hair, looked up at us in relief as we approached.

"Thank goodness you're here!" the woman exclaimed as she looked toward Da Silva.

The crying woman turned around to look at us, and she started screaming afresh when her gaze landed on Da Silva.

"The police!" she moaned as tears rolled down her face. "You need to do something! M-my husband! Please! Someone—someone killed him!"

She broke down into sobs as she fell to her knees. Da Silva crouched down with her.

"We're going to help," Da Silva assured her gently before looking up at the two employees. "Can someone tell us what happened here?"

"That guy came out of nowhere," the woman with short brown hair mumbled as she clasped her hands together. "I remember when he came in. I was worried because he looked like he'd been crying. I asked if he had a reservation, but he just ignored me and walked inside. I tried to tell him he couldn't just go by himself, but it was like he didn't even hear me." She hugged her arms tightly around herself as she glanced over at the table where the body was still lying.

"I was taking their order," the other employee chimed in. He was a younger man, with choppy dark hair and pimples on his face. "I was asking them what drinks they wanted, and suddenly, that guy walked up to the table. He was looking right at them, so I thought he was their friend or something, and then..."

"And then?" I prodded him to continue.

"He picked up the vase on the table," the woman on the ground mumbled darkly.

I looked over at the table and noticed that each one had a large glass vase of brightly colored flowers set in the center. I couldn't be sure without picking one up, but they certainly looked pretty sturdy and heavy. As I glanced over to the table where the body was, I noted immediately that there was no vase to be seen.

"Why don't we go speak somewhere else?" Da Silva asked pointedly as she looked up at the two employees. "Somewhere not in the dining room?"

"Oh!" the brown-haired woman replied as she understood that Da Silva wanted the victim's wife moved away from where the body was. "Sure, we, uh, we have a break room in the back! It's just through here." The woman pointed back toward the kitchen.

"Come on," Da Silva spoke to the woman gently. "Let's go find somewhere for you to sit down."

The woman did as Da Silva suggested silently, getting to her feet and allowing Da Silva to guide her gently toward the kitchen. As Holm and I trailed after them, I looked back once more at the body, then turned to the young man.

"Maybe sure nobody else comes inside," I instructed. "I'll call for some backup, so until then, just watch the door, okay?"

"Uh, yes, absolutely," the young man replied seriously.

"If anyone tries to force their way in, though, don't fight them, just yell for us," I clarified.

"G-got it," the kid replied, suddenly looking nervous after my warning.

I nodded at him in thanks and then slipped my phone out of my pocket to call the station. After reaching Captain Larose, I asked him to please send some more officers to secure the scene while we spoke to the witnesses and then hurried to find where Da Silva, Holm, and the others had gone off to.

It didn't take me very long to locate them, sitting in a small room just off the kitchen. The victim's wife was robotically smoothing out the wrinkles on her white and pink floral sundress where she was sitting at a small round table.

"Ms. Sanford," Da Silva addressed the woman. I assumed she must have asked her for her name in the few minutes that I was on the phone with Captain Larose.

"Oh, please, honey, call me Grace," the woman replied as she blew her nose into a tissue.

"Grace, then," Da Silva corrected herself. "Could you please explain to us exactly what happened?"

"I..." Grace muttered before biting down on her lip. "We were having such a nice morning. Gavin, he's been busy all week. I know it's a business trip, but I didn't think he'd be gone so often! But today, he surprised me, brought me out to this lovely little restaurant. He knows I love the ocean. I could see it from our table. It was so romantic, being able to look at the waves while we had our tea." She sniffled and wiped her nose again.

"Can you tell us about the man who attacked him?" Da Silva asked.

"I don't know who he was," Grace mumbled anxiously as she absentmindedly scratched at the surface of the table with her fingernail. "He walked right up to us, and before either of us could say or do anything, he picked up the vase and hit Gavin over the head with it."

She scratched harder against the table. I could hear the low rasping noise her nail made as she dragged it across the rough plastic.

"He didn't say anything to you?" Da Silva asked her gently.

"No." Grace shook her head. "He just kept hitting him with that vase, over and over. Gavin couldn't even fight back. He was already lying on the table. And then suddenly that—that *monster* threw the vase down and took out a knife and—" She cut herself off as she scratched hard against the table with enough pressure that she left a gouge in the cheap plastic surface.

"And you have no idea who this man was?" Da Silva asked.

"No!" Grace cried out as a fresh wave of tears came streamed out of her eyes. "I already told you! I've never even seen him before!"

"What about your husband?" I asked tentatively. "I know you must not know all of your husband's friends and acquaintances, but is it possible he was someone your husband knew? You said that he was here on business?"

"Well, yes," she replied. "But there's no way my husband would have known a lunatic like that! My husband works with some of the most intelligent and capable people in the world! The man that attacked us was filthy and smelled awful. His hair was dirty and messy and—look, there's just no way that my husband could have known someone like him!"

"Okay, alright, Ms. Sanford, um, Grace," Da Silva hurried to calm her down as she continued to cry.

I took a few steps out of the room to let her work since it seemed like my words had really upset Grace. A few seconds after I left the tiny break room, the brown-haired employee stepped out into the kitchen after me.

"Um, hey," she whispered to me before looking over her shoulder toward the room where Da Silva was still trying to soothe Ms. Sanford.

"Yes?" I answered.

"She lied about not knowing that man," the employee whispered.

"What?" I looked down at her in surprise before motioning for her to follow me to another part of the kitchen where we wouldn't be spotted or overheard. Once we were out of the way, obscured behind a metal rack, I turned to her again. "Okay, why do you say that?"

"W-well, maybe I shouldn't say she's lying, exactly," the employee muttered nervously. "But when you asked her if the killer said anything and she said no, that wasn't true. I heard him. He was yelling the whole time."

"Is that right?" I asked as I glanced back toward the room.

If that were true, it didn't necessarily mean that Ms. Sandford was lying. After all, the shock of seeing her husband viciously bludgeoned to death in front of her might have caused some glitches in her memory.

"And what was the killer saying?" I asked.

The employee hesitated for a moment as her expression twisted into one of fear.

"He kept saying that Mr. Sanford 'deserved it,'" she admitted quietly, as though she didn't even want to speak the words out loud.

"That's what he said?" I asked. "He told the victim that he deserved to die?"

"Yes." The woman nodded her head. "He kept screaming 'you know what you did' and 'you deserve this' and stuff like that. I didn't know what to think. I still don't, but..." She paused for a moment as she looked back toward the break room. "I think even if Mrs. Sanford didn't know the killer, her husband probably did. He sounded serious, and I mean, why would he say that unless he knew the guy, right?"

"Right," I agreed as a chill ran down my spine.

Suddenly, I felt as though a missing puzzle piece had clicked into place and a picture that had been so difficult to understand before suddenly became clear.

This was so bad.

"Thank you for letting me know that," I whispered.

The woman smiled nervously at me before nodding and walking out of the kitchen. A moment later, Da Silva and Holm stepped out of the break room with Mrs. Sanford. She threw me a dirty look as she came out.

"Why don't I walk you out through the back?" Da Silva suggested.

"I would appreciate that very much," Mrs. Sanford sniffed.

Da Silva smiled at her and then looked at me before turning to head out the back with Mrs. Sanford, presumably so she wouldn't have to pass by her dead husband's body on the way back out again. Holm waited until they were gone before walking up to me.

"She was not pleased with the implication you made that her husband was involved with 'that kind of filthy riff-raff,'" Holm informed me. "And those were her exact words."

"Well, sorry but not sorry," I replied dryly. "Especially since it turns out that I was right. The hostess came to speak with me just after I left."

"Yeah, I noticed her leaving right after you," Holm replied. "What was that about?"

"Apparently, the killer yelled something to Mr. Sanford right before killing him," I explained. "Something about him 'knowing what he did' and 'deserving to die.'"

"Damn." Holm blinked up at me in surprise. "Sounds vengeful. I wonder—" He stopped short, his eyes going wide as his jaw fell open.

"I think you're thinking the same thing I am," I sighed. "I think our killer is one of the victims."

"Oh, damn," Holm muttered again.

"I hear that," I muttered.

This really wasn't good because as bad as I felt for anyone who had gone through such a horrible ordeal, that meant that we now had a crazed vigilante to deal with on top of just finding the group themselves.

"So, someone is going around killing off the people who did this to him," Holm muttered. "So, does that mean that someone else escaped besides Roy?"

"Roy did say that someone else was with him, remember?" I reminded him. "In fact, the whole escape plan of jumping overboard was this other guy's idea. Wesley, that was his name."

"You think he's the one going around killing off his former captors?" Holm asked me.

"It's possible." I shrugged. "All I know for sure is that everything so far points to the idea that a former victim is the one behind the killings."

"What?" Da Silva called from the entrance to the kitchen. She looked at Holm and me in surprise.

"The hostess told me that the killer shouted something about Mr. Sanford deserving to die for what he did." I quickly explained my theory to her. "That, coupled with the fact that Marino was also killed recently, makes me think we've got a revenge-fueled serial killer on our hands."

"Which means he'll likely strike again," Da Silva replied. "And soon, if he's already taken out two men in three days." She sighed heavily as she crossed her arms over her chest. "Okay. We can work with this." She looked up at Holm and me. "Let's go take a look at the body, and then we can get back to the station and figure out where to go from here."

Holm and I followed her out as she turned on her heel and stepped out into the dining room. A few shattered glasses and plates of food lay smashed along the ground, probably casualties of when the other diners had panicked and rushed out of the restaurant in the wake of the attack. The closer we got to the body, the more I realized just how badly he'd been beaten.

Like Marino, it was clear that there had been rage in the murder. The back of Sanford's head was completely smashed in, the gray matter of his brain visible beyond the bloody, matted hair that was splayed over the crater in his skull. And then, as if that weren't enough to end the man's life, his back was riddled with stab wounds as well.

"What do we know about Mr. Sanford?" I asked Da Silva as I crouched down to inspect the body without touching it. I couldn't quite see his face from the angle that he was lying, but from what I could see from his general build, hair color, and what little I could see of his face, I would estimate that he was in his late forties or early fifties. "Did his wife say anything?"

"Well, she mentioned that he owns several casinos and hotels in Las Vegas," Da Silva replied. "She said that they usually just vacation there, but that he insisted on coming down to St. Vincent this time around."

"What a surprise," I muttered as I stood back up straight. "So, he has a lot of money, and he was really eager to come down here, huh?"

"Wait," Holm frowned in confusion. "Didn't she say that her husband was down here on business?"

"She did say that, didn't she?" I muttered as I recalled her saying something like that as well.

"That might have just been the story he fed her," Da Silva replied. "Nevertheless, I'll call the officer taking her home and tell him to keep an eye on her hotel, just in case."

"You guys think she might have been a 'guest,' too?" Holm asked.

"It's definitely possible," I replied. "Roy said he remembers seeing people in fancy suits and *dresses,* so I assume there were women there as well. That, coupled with the inconsistencies in her story, makes me think maybe she knows more than she's letting on."

"Maybe we shouldn't let her go back to her hotel, then," Da Silva murmured, her voice tinged with alarm. "If she's involved, she might tip off the rest. I'll call and let him know to reroute to the police station. If we're wrong, and she's innocent, then I'll apologize and take the blame personally." She whipped her phone out of her pocket and took a few steps away to make the call.

"If she is involved, though..." Holm hummed. "Then why didn't the vigilante kill her too?"

"Maybe he didn't recognize her." I shrugged. "Imagine you're being held captive on a boat."

"I do not want to imagine that," Holm grumbled.

"Not the point," I snorted. "Anyway, you're on a boat, confused, probably malnourished. There're all these people around you, maybe a dozen, maybe two or three times that. How many faces do you think you could remember?"

"Me?" Holm glanced at me sideways. "Probably most of them, same as you. The average person, though? I can see how it might become a jumble. You're right. It's possible he remembered the man's face and not hers. He let Ms. Halshire go, after all. He might have assumed that Mrs. Sanford was just a random, unrelated woman as well."

"We'll have to ask him whenever we finally catch him," I muttered as Da Silva finished her call and tucked her phone back into her pants pocket.

"Okay," she declared as she walked back toward us. "He's bringing her to the station now. Lucky for us, she was already in the back of a police car."

"I'd like to be a fly on the wall when she realizes he's driving her to the police station instead of her hotel," I muttered.

"I'm sure she will be less than pleased," Da Silva replied flatly. "In any case, we should be getting back there as well. We need to be ready whenever Chen gets that call, and we need to come up with a plan in the meantime."

"Oh, there's something I've been meaning to mention," Holm suddenly spoke up as Da Silva turned to leave.

"What is it?" She looked at him. I did the same, curious what he could have to say that he hadn't already.

"Sorry," he muttered sheepishly, as though reading my thoughts. "I tried to tell you back in the car, but we kept getting distracted. Anyway, Aurora said that she wanted to help us."

"Aurora did?" I asked, curious as to where he was going with this.

"Yeah, back at the station, while we were speaking together outside," Holm explained. "I didn't even want to consider it at first because I didn't want her doing anything that might put her in danger, but with this new murder, and what we know about the vigilante... maybe it's the best way to find them."

"What is?" I asked impatiently. It wasn't like Holm to beat around the bush like this.

"Aurora said that she might be able to get us onto the boat," Holm revealed. "She might be able to get on board the yacht where the fights are taking place."

25

HOLM

"Just hear me out," Aurora insisted eagerly, her eyes sparkling with excitement as she spoke, and Holm cringed.

This had been such a stupid idea. Sure, he had been the one to suggest they hear out Aurora's idea back at the restaurant, but now that they were standing here, in her hotel room, Holm felt nothing but regret.

"It's too dangerous," Holm replied firmly from where he was sitting on a chair just a few feet away from where she was perched on the edge of the bed.

His words did nothing to dim the fiery, determined light in her eyes, and he hated himself for finding her brave determination so attractive.

She's going to get herself killed, the rational part of his brain screamed at him even as he looked into her bright hazel eyes. *Get it together, Holm!*

"It'll be fine," Aurora insisted. "Look, they won't hurt me. I'm one of them, as nauseating as that feels to say." She scrunched her nose up as she grimaced in disgust. "You said my uncle was one of the guests, right? So, it's not a huge stretch to imagine that he might have told me about these little parties. And maybe I decided I wanted to go too. Are women allowed in?" She turned to look at Da Silva and Marston.

"We... have heard accounts of women being among the guests," Marston replied honestly from where he was leaning against the wall, and Holm shot him a murderous look. "But I agree with Holm." Marston hurried to add that statement as he caught sight of the expression that Holm was shooting him. "I think this is too dangerous to involve a civilian in, especially out in open water. There's literally nowhere to run if things go badly."

"I don't know," Da Silva chimed in as she crossed her arms over her chest. She was sitting in one of the other chairs, and she bit her lip pensively as she spoke. "I think Ms. Marino has a point. She is 'one of them,' as she states. And there must be some way that people are invited to be guests of these parties, right? I think this could work."

Marston shot Holm an apologetic look. Though Marston could back up his partner, there was nothing either of them could do to stop Da Silva from agreeing with Aurora, who grinned at the officer's response. Holm was about to launch into another protest, but before he could, Mr. Marino spoke up.

"I think Aurora is right as well," he muttered from where he was sitting on the other side of the bed, facing down at the ground.

"Y-you do?" Aurora asked him, surprise evident in her voice.

"Yes, Stellina, I do," he sighed wearily as he stood up and turned to face the group. "As much as I hate the idea of you being there, I think you're right that this is the best way for us to help the agents onto that boat. And I know there's no way that you'll stay here if I go."

"Absolutely not," she replied immediately, her voice hard and curt.

"I thought so," Mr. Marino chuckled before turning to look at Marston and Holm. "This is the least we can do to atone for what my brother did, so please allow us to help you."

"No, wait a minute," Holm responded. "This isn't your responsibility to atone for."

"I know," Mr. Marino replied somberly. "But, to be honest, I wouldn't be able to sleep at night knowing what I do now if I were to just stand by and do nothing. There are innocent men out there suffering because of what my brother did. He used the money we earned together to hurt people. I know it's not my responsibility, Agent Holm, but I feel the need to atone all the same."

Holm would have been lying if he'd said that he didn't feel moved by Mr. Marino's speech, but he still couldn't help but be worried about his and Aurora's safety.

"We'll be okay," Aurora assured him, as though reading his thoughts. "Papa's smart. He'll figure out a way to convince them. All we have to do is get an invitation. We'll find out where they are, and then we'll lead you there."

She bit her lip as she looked nervously between Holm, Marston, and Da Silva, waiting for their approval. Holm wanted to say no. He wanted to scream it, even. He knew that she was right, that this was the fastest and easiest way for them to find the kidnappers and rescue the victims. Still, Holm was selfish, and even more than he wanted to save the kidnapped men, he wanted to keep Aurora safe.

"Fine," he forced himself to utter before he could convince himself otherwise.

Aurora's eyes lit up with excitement at his response, though Mr. Marino looked decidedly less enthused by the idea.

"As much as I wish you'd just let me go in your place," he sighed as he looked at his daughter. "I'm certain there's no way I can actually convince you to stay behind, is there?"

"No," she replied with a huff before turning to look at the agents. "So, how exactly do we do this? And when?"

"As soon as possible," Marston replied as he crossed his arms and looked up at the ceiling thoughtfully. "Originally, our goal was to wait until Chen received a call from the organizers, but it might be better if we contact them first." He turned to Mr. Marino. "We can pretend that William gave you their contact information. Do you think they would buy that?"

"I'm sure they would," Mr. Marino replied. "I'm confident that I can convince them, so don't worry about that."

"That's one less thing to worry about, then," Marston muttered. "Really, our biggest problem right now is getting this done before word gets back to them about Sanford and William Marino. If they find out that one of their former victims is hunting them down, they're likely going to scatter like roaches."

"I can make the call right now," Mr. Marino stated firmly as he took a few steps toward Marston as if to prove his determination.

"Whoa, wait," Holm spoke up as he suddenly stood from his chair. "Let's hammer out a few more details before we jump right in. For one, who all will be going?" He paused as he took a look at the gathered group. "You and Aurora are one thing, but I imagine it might raise some suspicion if you bring a trio of strangers with you."

"That's a good point." Mr. Marino frowned. "Maybe one or two, I can excuse as being a pair of business associates, but you're right. Too many will raise eyebrows."

"The two of you can go," Da Silva offered at once as she looked between Marston and Holm.

"Are you sure?" Marston turned to look at her.

"I'm sure," she replied. "The two of you have more experience with this kind of thing than I do. In any case, someone needs to stay behind on the ground as backup in case something goes wrong. I'll monitor the situation from afar with a few other officers. Should you need help, we'll be standing by to move in."

"That's a good idea," Marston agreed. "Speaking of help, it might not be a bad idea to pull the Coast Guard into this as well. This is all going to be taking place out in international waters, so it would probably be a good idea to clue them in to what's happening."

"I agree," Da Silva replied with a nod. "I can contact them as soon as we get back to the station."

"We should go there now then," Marston declared as he stood up as well. "You said that we need to move quickly before they find out what's going on, right? So, we should hurry."

Holm almost flinched at the jolt of anxiety that coursed through him. Once again, he knew that she was right. The faster they moved, the higher their chance of success as far as infiltrating one of the parties. However, the thought of her participating in the operation made him nervous, and he found himself wanting to put it off for as long as he could.

"You're right," Da Silva replied before Holm could say anything to the contrary. "We should get back anyway before Chen gets that call and messes up our new plan."

And just like that, all five of them left the hotel and headed back to the station. For the most part, there weren't any words exchanged between Aurora and Holm on the drive there, but Holm was intensely aware of her presence just behind him in the car. He told himself that he was acting a little ridiculous. Sure, she was a civilian, and sure, it was normal for him to be concerned about the safety of a civilian during their mission, but was it really necessary for him to be this worked up about it? In the end, she was just a woman he'd met a few days ago. It was barely enough time for him to even consider Aurora his friend, so why was he so invested?

Holm hopped out of the car as soon as they pulled back up to the police station, all the talk of their plan having left him feeling anxious. Da Silva led the group into the station and up through its winding labyrinth of corridors before coming to a stop outside one of the doors.

"We can make the call in here," Da Silva explained as she opened the door into what looked like a typical conference room. "It's quiet and out of the way enough that we won't be bothered. I'll go and see about getting Chen's phone so that we can get the contact number."

She pivoted and headed quickly down the hallway then. It seemed she didn't want to waste a single moment of precious time.

"I'll call Diane, then," Marston muttered as he sauntered through the open door and into the room. "She can see about getting the Coast Guard's assistance."

Mr. Marino stepped in after him, and Holm was about to step inside as well but paused when he felt something soft press against his arm. He snapped his head around instinctively but relaxed when he realized that it was just Aurora.

"Agent Holm," she addressed him as she moved her hand away from his arm. "You don't want me to go with you onto the boat." It wasn't a question as much as it was a statement and an accusatory one at that. "You don't have to deny it. I could tell as much just from the face you made when I suggested it."

Holm clamped his mouth shut for a second, unsure what he should say in response.

"This is dangerous," he finally sighed after several moments of silent hesitation. "I know that you and your father think that it'll be fine, but—"

"It *will* be fine," Aurora insisted. "As I said earlier, I'm one of them." She grimaced as the words left her mouth, as though just saying them left a bitter taste on her tongue. "They'll probably welcome Papa and me in with open arms. And the person who is killing them is one of the victims, right? Not one of the other guests like you first thought."

"That's true," Holm replied reluctantly.

He and Marston had given Aurora and Mr. Marino a brief rundown over the details of the case. She was right that their initial theory about the party guests turning on each other had turned out to be wrong, but that didn't mean it couldn't happen. When backed into a corner, he doubted that the perps would hesitate to kill Aurora and her father just because they happened to be cut from the same cloth.

"Besides." Aurora smiled up at him warmly as she took a flirtatious step into his personal space. "You'll be there, right? So, I haven't got anything to worry about."

Holm felt his face grow uncomfortably warm as he looked down at her. Her eyelashes were the same pretty shade as her auburn-colored hair, and he felt his mouth go dry as he looked into her eyes.

"That's a lot of faith to put in someone you barely know," Holm replied, surprising himself with how smooth his own voice sounded to his ears, especially when his heart was thrumming as fast as it was.

"What can I say?" Aurora shrugged slyly. "I'm an impulsive person."

"Yeah, I can tell." Holm sighed. The frustration of having Aurora leap head-first into danger was still at the forefront of his mind.

"I hate to interrupt," Da Silva's voice suddenly cut through their conversation like a sword.

Aurora took a quick step backward, and Holm froze as he realized just how close together they'd just been standing.

"But I have the phone." Da Silva held the device up in her hand. "We can make the call whenever everyone's ready." She was holding some kind of bulky black device in her arms, and Holm could see a shiny silver phone clutched in her hand.

"We're ready," Aurora replied as she turned away from Holm, her attention suddenly entirely on Da Silva.

Holm frowned unconsciously and refused to dwell too long on why the loss of her attention suddenly left him feeling so bereft.

The three of them walked into the room where Marston and Mr. Marino were already waiting for them. Marston was standing just inside the doorway, and he flashed Holm a smirk as he stepped inside. Holm's frown deepened in response, but he didn't have time now to analyze what that smarmy look meant or to ask Marston about it. Holm was sure that Marston would have some sarcastic comment to make later, though.

"Chen wasn't pleased when I told him the plan had changed," Da Silva informed us as she set the device she was carrying down in the center of the conference table. "He seemed to think that he wouldn't be getting his end of the deal anymore. As tempting as it was to watch him squirm, time was of the essence, so I assured him that the deal would still stand so long as he confirmed the phone number for us. I hope that's okay." She turned to look at Marston and Holm.

"I guess that's fair," Marston replied as she took a seat at the conference table. "We are using his phone, after all, and he is the reason we have a means of contacting them in the first place."

"That's what I thought as well," Da Silva sighed as she fiddled with some settings on the device. Holm looked on curiously as she did. "Though it would have been satisfying to watch him fall apart as we snatched his deal away from him. Oh, well. In any case, this device will allow us to record the call. I can try to trace it as well, but I'm not sure how successful that will be, especially if whoever answers is out on the water right now." She picked the phone up off the table and pressed something on it before holding it out toward Mr. Marino. "Besides, if everything goes well, we'll know exactly where to find them by the end of this call."

Mr. Marino took the phone in his hand delicately as though he was holding something made of glass. He looked down at it pensively before reaching into his pocket to pull out his own phone.

"May I?" Da Silva asked as she reached a hand out for Mr. Marino's phone. He handed it over at once, and Da Silva quickly hooked it up to the machine before handing it back. Holm watched as Mr. Marino read the phone number off of Chen's phone before punching it into his own. Because it was connected to the device, Holm could hear it ringing. The sound filled the otherwise empty room, almost abrasive against his ears as it rattled through the recording device's speakers. It continued to ring for an unusually long time, and Holm was worried for a moment that the call might go unanswered. Then, finally, the call connected with a low click.

Beside him, Aurora let out a small gasp as the call connected. She bit her lip and clasped her hands together, and Holm fought the urge to reach out to place a hand on her shoulder or back. For several tense seconds, nothing followed the sound of the call connecting.

"Hello?" Mr. Marino finally spoke calmly into the phone.

Still, there was no answer, and Holm tensed as he realized this might go very, very badly. Maybe they should have just waited for them to call first, after all.

Mr. Marino, by contrast, carried on calmly as though nothing was wrong.

"For goodness' sake," he mumbled as he held the phone a little away from his ear. "Did I call the wrong number? Or did Will give me the wrong number? My goodness, let me see..." Holm was shocked at how calm he sounded. He was doing an excellent job of pretending he was alone, just making a regular call.

"Who is this?" a low, lightly raspy voice finally answered.

Holm could hear the suspicion dripping from his voice.

"Oh! Hello, I was worried I'd dialed the wrong number," Mr. Marino replied cheerfully. "This is Radley Marino. My dear brother Will told me about the, uh... the *parties* that he's been attending recently." Mr. Marino lowered his voice into a conspiratorial whisper as he spoke, and Holm almost wanted to shudder. If he hadn't known that Marino was only acting as their agent, he might have believed that he was genuinely interested.

"Oh!" the voice on the other end of the line replied, the raspiness suddenly gone, as if whoever was speaking had been deliberately altering their voice to make himself sound more intimidating. "Mr. Marino! I'm surprised to hear from you. Ah, but pleased, of course. William made it seem as though our *activities* were not something that would be to your taste."

"Well, my dear brother is always trying to make decisions for me," Mr. Marino laughed. "I think he sometimes forgets who the elder one is here. Will probably wanted to keep all the fun to himself and decided to keep it a secret, but I always get what I want, in the end. One way or another."

There was a threatening edge to his voice as he spoke that last sentence, and Holm could tell from how the person on the phone fell silent that he had noticed it as well.

"O-of course," the voice replied stiltedly. "Well, if you're calling me, then that must mean that you're interested in participating. You're in luck. We're actually having a little excursion tonight."

"Tonight?" Mr. Marino repeated, and for just a second, his mask of impassivity fell as a note of surprise crept into his voice. Holm was concerned that the man on the other end of the line might have heard it as well, but Mr. Marino recovered quickly. "How fortuitous. I suppose I called at just the right time, then."

"Yes," the man replied slowly. "I'm surprised William didn't mention it to you."

Aurora swore quietly beside Holm, and he knew that she was thinking the same thing that he was. The man *had* heard the hesitation in Mr. Marino's voice.

"Well, as I said, he didn't seem very eager to invite me along," Mr. Marino amended his error smoothly.

"Actually, I only found out about his little proclivities while I was doing an audit of our records. It seems dear Will was having a little too much fun at my expense." Mr. Marino laughed, and again, the underlying threat in his voice was evident. "Of course, I can't fault my brother for that. After all, once I found out what it was he was spending that money on, I got a little curious myself."

The man on the phone laughed as well, but Holm could tell from the hollow tone of his voice that Mr. Marino's words had made him nervous.

"Well, of course," he replied. "There's no entertainment in the world quite like ours."

"I'm inclined to agree," Mr. Marino replied, his voice as upbeat, as though he were talking about a new Broadway play and not an illegal, transnational fight club. "In any case, I'd be delighted to join in the festivities tonight. Is there anything I should bring? Party favors, perhaps?"

"Oh, nothing like that," the man assured him. "Of course, there is a small betting fee if you care to make any wagers while you're on board."

"Well, of course, I will!" Mr. Marino laughed so raucously that Holm wanted to shiver. He knew that Mr. Marino was only bluffing, but the notion that all the other guests really did feel this dismissive about betting on the victims' lives made his stomach churn. "After all, what's the fun of a game without a little gambling, eh? Don't worry about that! Oh, and what of the dress code? I wouldn't want to show up under-dressed."

"Nothing *too* formal," the man replied. "Mostly black tie for the gentlemen, though the ladies tend to get a little competitive when it comes to their attire."

"As they do," Mr. Marino chuckled.

"Will you be bringing—ah, how rude of me," the man suddenly cut himself off. "My apologies."

"Please, don't worry yourself," Mr. Marino replied graciously, though his face fell for just a moment.

Beside him, Holm noticed that Aurora went stiff as well, and he wondered vaguely what the deal was with both of their reactions to the man's question.

"Well, um, whatever you feel most comfortable in, of course," the man clumsily barreled on. "I'm certain that a man of your caliber has impeccable taste."

"Well, I like to think so," Mr. Marino replied, his lofty, nonchalant attitude firmly back in place.

"Of course," the man replied. "Anyway, we'll be setting sail tonight at midnight. As for the location, normally, I would send that information out via a text message about an hour before departure, but as it's your first time, I'll tell you now."

"Well, how very kind of you," Mr. Marino replied as his gaze slid over to meet Marston's and Holm's.

The entire room held its breath as the man on the

phone rattled off the address of the dock from where the boat would be departing.

"Please, feel free to call me if you have any trouble finding it," the man offered. "I wouldn't want the party to leave without you."

"Thank you," Mr. Marino replied. "I'll keep that in mind."

"I look forward to seeing you," the voice replied one last time before the call ended.

Mr. Marino looked down at his phone as if to make sure the call really had disconnected before letting out a big sigh of relief.

"That was nerve-racking," he breathed as he set his phone face down on the table.

"You did amazing, Papa," Aurora insisted as she rushed to her father's side. She threw one of her arms around him as she crouched down beside him.

"She's right," Holm agreed. "I'm stunned at how collected you stayed that entire time, especially when it seemed like he was starting to get suspicious."

"Well, I wasn't so calm on the inside, believe me," Mr. Marino chuckled as he patted his daughter's arm. "Years of having to do business with those kinds of people had steeled me to this kind of thing, I suppose. As long as you give off an air of confidence, it's not that hard to convince them of whatever you want them to believe. Money helps too, and whoever I was speaking to definitely recognized my name. His entire tone changed the moment I told him who I was."

"I noticed that as well," Marston added as he sat down. He'd remained standing during the call, likely too nervous to sit. Now that it was all a done deal, he looked more relaxed. "Do you have any idea who he might have been? He definitely knew who you were."

"I have a few ideas," Mr. Marino replied as he reached a hand up to stroke his beard thoughtfully. "His voice definitely sounded familiar. I can't say for sure, though." He frowned at Marston. "I'm sorry. I work with a lot of people. I just can't put a face to the voice right now. I know I've heard the voice before, though." His eyebrows knitted together as he scrunched his face up in frustration.

"It's alright, Mr. Marino," Da Silva was quick to assure him. "You've done more than enough to help us already."

"That's true," Holm added. "If it weren't for you making that call, we wouldn't have a way onto the ship now."

Aurora smiled up at him, and Holm felt his heart seize in his chest.

"About that, though," Aurora muttered as she frowned at her dad. "You didn't mention anything about Agent Marston or Agent Holm or me." She took a step backward away from him as the frown on her face deepened. "Papa, you aren't thinking of trying to do something foolish and go in on your own, right?"

"Nothing like that, stellina," Mr. Marino replied. "I just figured it would be easier to just show up. Better to ask forgiveness than permission, you know." He grinned cheekily over at the agents. "If I don't ask for permission to bring Aurora and the two of you, then he can't say no, can he?"

Holm had to hand it to the man. He really had nerves of steel. Holm couldn't imagine showing up to a party with three extra guests in tow. Then again, this wasn't exactly an ordinary party, so he supposed that the standard rules of decorum didn't really apply.

"Well, we should get going then," Mr. Marino declared as he stood up from his seat at the table. "After all, if we're going to do this, then we'd better do it right."

26

HOLM

"THIS IS WEIRD," Holm muttered to himself as he took a look at the man in the dressing room mirror.

To be honest, suits had never really been his thing. It wasn't like he minded wearing them if the occasion called for it, but they weren't something he would reach for if given a choice. The tuxedo he was currently wearing was a step above even that, though. The tight collar and cuffs felt stiff and uncomfortable and, frankly, impractical. He quickly twisted around as if he were reaching for his gun and winced as the collar dug uncomfortably into his neck. Sure, tuxes probably weren't designed with gunfights in mind, but still. This just wasn't convenient.

When he and Marston had first landed in St. Vincent, the last thing he would have imagined doing was spending the afternoon before a mission inside a fancy boutique store near the hotel where Aurora and her father were staying, trying on tuxedos. Mr. Marino had insisted that it was necessary, though.

"Appearances are everything to these people, believe me," he'd said as he'd led the two agents into the store. "I can convince them that you two belong there, but only if you look the part. If you walk in wearing something shabby, they'll chew you up and spit you out."

Though Holm had been felt mildly affronted by Mr. Marino's description of his clothing as "something shabby," he did have to admit that his usual tactical pants and boots were pretty lackluster in comparison to the slick tuxedo slacks and leather loafers that he was currently wearing.

"You doing okay in there, Holm?" Marston snickered from outside the changing room that Holm was in.

Holm rolled his eyes and pushed the heavy, velvety curtain aside to step out.

"It looks lovely," Mr. Marino declared from where he was sitting on a small, cushioned bench just a few feet away.

That felt weird, too. Having Aurora's dad tut and fuss over the fit of the tuxes as he and Marston tried them on felt... bizarre, like he was a kid getting ready for his high school prom with his dad. Mr. Marino stood and walked over to Holm, his mouth pressed into a thin line as he inspected the length of the shoulders on the jacket.

"Of course, a bespoke one would look nicer," he muttered. "No time for something like that, though, so we'll just have to make do with what we can find off the rack."

"I think it looks pretty good," Marston added as he fiddled with the tie of his own tux. He was wearing a similar one to Holm's, though with slightly differently shaped tails.

"Are you sure we should even be wearing tuxedos?" Holm asked as he pulled at the collar of his shirt. "I mean, it's a party on a yacht. Wouldn't, I don't know, swimsuits make more sense?"

"One would think." Mr. Marino shrugged. "But our friend on the phone did say that it was a black-tie affair. I imagine there wouldn't be much swimming going on, especially as it's an evening party."

"I think the only reason it's even on a boat is that it makes it harder for us to track them," Marston added as he finally gave up and let the two ends of the tie dangle over his shoulders. "If they were keeping the victims in a fixed location somewhere on land, it would only be a matter of time before we found them. This way, they can move around all they want, and at a moment's notice."

"I think you're exactly right," Mr. Marino sighed as he sat heavily back down on the bench. For a long moment, he just stared anxiously down at the patterned carpet of the dressing room. "I still can't believe that Will—It was sickening, you know. When I was on that phone call, it made me feel ill to have to pretend that I was actually interested in participating in such a horrifying game."

"You're a hell of an actor," Marston commended him. "The guy bought every word, luckily for us."

"I'm glad I could be of help," Mr. Marino replied sadly. "Nevertheless, it occurred to me that William really did feel that way. He really was eager to come down here and wager on people's lives like they were less than animals. My own brother..."

Holm felt a wave of hurt hit him on behalf of the man. He looked so broken there, hunched over on the bench. Holm couldn't imagine how he would react if he found out that his sister was doing something so evil. What were you supposed to do when you found out that one of your own family was a monster?

"Anyway." Mr. Marino cleared his throat as he looked up at the two agents. Holm could swear that he saw the man's eyes shining brightly, but then he blinked, and the wetness was gone. "We should discuss what we'll say when we arrive. Of course, Aurora's my daughter, so she'll be allowed on without protest. As for the two of you—" He pursed his lips as he looked back and forth between the two agents. "You're an employee of mine." He nodded at Marston. "I'm getting on in years, and it's about time I started to train up a new successor. That's believable enough, and giving off the impression that we're close enough that I would consider handing the company over to you will explain why I would trust you enough to invite you to the party."

"Sounds good to me," Marston replied easily.

He'd always been pretty adept when it came to lying and playing a part, so Holm wasn't surprised by how undaunted his partner seemed.

"You, Agent Holm," Mr. Marino continued. "You'll attend as Aurora's date."

"I, um, what?" Holm stammered intelligently as he failed to process what Mr. Marino had just said.

"Well, it wouldn't do for a woman like Aurora to attend a party like that alone," Mr. Marino sniffed. "This way, it'll keep any other sharks on that boat from trying to get too close. And besides, I hardly think such a task will be a problem for either of you."

He flashed Holm an impish smile for just a second before it was gone, and Holm felt his face getting red.

"Sure, no problem," Holm replied stiffly, doing his best to keep his voice steady and willing his face to cool down.

"Well, if we've got that all squared away, I'll go and pay for everything," Mr. Marino stated as he got back to his feet.

"Um, you don't have to," Marston attempted to stop

Marino as he suddenly made to leave the dressing area. "We can expense this back to the office. We need it as part of an undercover mission, so—"

"Please, it's no issue," Mr. Marino insisted calmly. "And in any case, I can't imagine your boss would be too pleased to see an expense report that hefty. Don't mind me, and just make sure those don't get too wrinkled before the party tonight." Then he turned and left before either agent could put up a word of protest.

"This feels weird," Holm muttered again once Mr. Marino was fully out of earshot.

"Yeah, it does." Marston snorted as he sat down on the bench that Mr. Marino had just vacated. "This *is* the best way for us to get on that boat, though. Once we find the perps and locate the rest of the victims, we can drop the act and get this all settled."

"You think it'll be that easy?" Holm raised an eyebrow at him.

"I mean, hopefully?" Marston replied before heaving a sigh. "Not likely, though. Still, I have a feeling most of the party guests won't be much of a threat themselves. They hire guards for protection against the victims, remember? So long as we take out the hired muscle, we'll probably be able to gain the upper hand."

"That's a good point," Holm replied. "Let's just hope we can pull that off before anyone figures out who we really are."

"Hello?" a familiar voice called from the doorway into the fitting area, and Holm's head snapped around reflexively.

"Aurora," he greeted her as she stepped into the dressing area.

"Wow, you two look so nice!" she gushed. "Papa told me that you were finished getting your clothes ready. Are you heading back to your hotel now?"

"This is the men's dressing room," Marston informed her dryly, a small smile tugging at his lips.

"Yes, I know," Aurora countered without hesitation or a hint of shame.

Marston let out a snort of laughter at her straight-forward response.

"I'm gonna go change out of this tux," he informed the two of them, tossing Holm a knowing look before he walked over to the dressing room furthest away from where they were standing.

"Is everything alright?" Holm asked her with concern once Marston had disappeared into the dressing room cubicle. What had prompted her to come all the way down here?

"I'm fine," she replied quickly, but her voice wavered even as she said it. "Well, no, actually, I guess I'm not." She crossed her arms over her chest as a frown settled over her face. "Everything feels so surreal right now. Like I might suddenly wake up and realize this was all some really horrible dream."

"I'm sorry," Holm muttered. "I can't imagine how you must feel."

"You don't have to be sorry," Aurora sighed. "You're only doing your job. And besides, now that I know what's happening, I want to help as well. I can't rest knowing that there are innocent men out there being forced to participate in such an atrocious... event." She pulled a face and shuddered as she spoke the last word. "I'm glad that I found out what was happening now, while we can hopefully still do something about it. If Uncle Will hadn't been killed... I might have gone my entire life not knowing what was happening, the awful things he'd done." She paused as she lifted her head to look Holm directly in the eyes. "I'd rather know the truth than live in ignorance."

"That's a very noble outlook to have," Holm commended her.

"Hardly," she chuckled beneath her breath as she suddenly reached her hands out toward Holm's face.

He froze as she did, surprised and confused at what she was doing.

"This isn't tied correctly." A small, teasing smile broke over her face as she deftly unknotted the tie that Holm had around his neck.

"Oh," Holm stammered as he realized that she was just trying to fix his clothes. "Yeah, I'm not used to wearing bowties. Regular ties are about as much as I'm used to."

"Well, I'm not that experienced myself," Aurora admitted sheepishly as she attempted to redo the bowtie correctly. "I've never actually worn one, but I've been to enough black-tie events that I'm familiar with how it's done."

"Are you sure?" Holm asked teasingly as Aurora continued to struggle with the tie.

"Well, it looks better than how you had it," she countered as she hastily undid the bowtie again to start over. "Maybe you should just forego it. A lot of younger men do that these days. Pretend it's a fashion statement."

"I don't think so," Holm replied as he pictured how ridiculous he would look if he were to show up with his clothes so sloppy. Sure, maybe rich kids could walk around like that without batting an eye, but Holm already felt out-of-place enough as it was just wearing the thing properly without trying anything experimental. "I think the idea is for Marston and me not to stand out while we're there."

"I suppose that's a good point." She laughed as she continued to work the tie into place.

Their conversation had been so lighthearted and easygoing that it hadn't even occurred to Holm just how close she'd been standing to him for the last couple of minutes. She wasn't looking at him because she was still focused on the tie around his neck, but her face was just inches from his, so close that he could smell the light floral fragrance emanating from her hair.

"Aha!" She beamed triumphantly as she finally got the bowtie done correctly. "It looks perfect now! Only took a few tries."

She grinned up at Holm, and his mouth immediately went dry at the full force of having her gaze set directly on him. The smile slowly slipped from her face as they continued to look at each other in silence, and Holm was gripped by the sudden, overpowering urge to close the distance between them.

"Well!" Aurora cleared her throat as she stumbled backward away from him before Holm could act on the temptation. "I, um, I should go get ready as well."

She fell silent for a moment and looked up at Holm with a torn expression, as though she had more she wanted to say. She didn't speak another word, though, and eventually just nodded awkwardly before turning and leaving the dressing area. Holm watched her go with mounting disappointment. Had he done something wrong? She'd turned and fled like he'd done something to offend her, but he hadn't even gone in for the kiss yet when she suddenly pulled away from him.

Maybe it's for the best, he thought to himself as he sauntered over to one of the changing rooms to pull the tux off. It was ironic, in hindsight, that Aurora had put so much effort into fixing his bowtie when he was just going to take it off again, and for a second, he hesitated before undoing her work. In any case, maybe right before a dangerous mission wasn't the ideal time to be engaging in romantic encounters with a suspect's family member. For now, at least, he would shelf whatever thoughts and feelings he had toward Aurora. Once everything with the case was said and done, Holm was determined to continue his conversation with Aurora exactly where they'd left off.

27

ETHAN

THE TAXI RIDE over to the marina was silent, eerie, and uncomfortable. I'd told Holm as much earlier, but the last thing I could have imagined myself doing when we'd initially landed in St. Vincent was getting all dressed up for a ritzy party. It seemed that we never could know what to expect while on a case, though, because here we were.

Aurora had changed into a silvery blue dress that slunk down from her narrow shoulders and exposed her back. She'd also done up her hair and put on some jewelry, and the complete picture made her look like a movie star about to walk the red carpet. Holm obviously thought the same because he'd barely been able to take his eyes off her since we'd all met up in the lobby of the hotel to leave. Usually, he was a lot better at being subtle about things, but the glances he was throwing in her direction every couple of seconds were so blatant that I had to fight the urge to laugh.

Aurora, surprisingly, didn't seem like she'd noticed it. She'd barely said a word at all since we'd met back up, and it was pretty obvious that she was too caught up in her own thoughts to think about anything else. Not that I could blame her, considering she'd just found out that morning that her uncle had been complicit in the kidnapping and deaths of several innocent men. She hadn't hesitated to come forward and offer her assistance, though, which was incredibly admirable.

After gathering in the lobby, Mr. Marino had arranged for a luxury cab to pick us up and transport us to the location that the voice on the phone had given to us. It would be better than driving ourselves, he'd said, to completely pull off the act we were putting on. The car he'd arranged for was a large, sleek black SUV that probably guzzled an excessive amount of gas, but it definitely looked the part. Da Silva and three other officers would be following behind us in a pair of police cars so they could wait on standby. The Coast Guard had been notified and would be monitoring the situation as well. The moment we located the victims, they would move in to help with the arrest.

Everything was in place, so all that was left was to get there. It seemed that the reality of the situation was setting in the closer we got, though, because both Mr.

Marino and Aurora were solemn and quiet as they sat in the back of the cab along with Holm and me.

"Alright, here we are," the taxi driver declared as we finally pulled up to the marina.

Beside me, Mr. Marino took a deep, steadying breath before reaching over to push open the door of the taxi. I followed out after him and was immediately hit by soft, gentle notes of music coming from somewhere in the distance. It didn't take me long to realize that the music was coming from an absolutely massive yacht docked just a few yards away. It was a pure, glittering white and so big that it could practically be considered a houseboat. The beastly thing loomed over the rest of the boats docked along the water like a monster. Soft, warm lights emanated from the upper deck, and just beyond the music, I could hear the sounds of laughter and the low hum of conversation.

"That's it," Mr. Marino mumbled shakily. "Right there, on that boat. That's where—" He cut himself off abruptly, as though he couldn't even bear to say what he was thinking.

I heard the second-row seats slide up, followed by the shuffling of Holm and Aurora as they climbed out from the back of the SUV.

"Come on, Papa," Aurora said as she approached and put her arm around her father's shoulder bravely. "We can do this."

"You're right," he replied, his voice solid and confident. "Let's go."

The four of us walked across the marina toward the yacht. As we did, I took a glance out of the corner of my eye toward a pair of black, unmarked cars that were parked in the lot just a few steps from us. Da Silva and the other officers were in place and ready to monitor everything that happened. Of course, they wouldn't be able to do much to help once we were out on the water, but they would at least be able to direct the Coast Guard.

As we walked, I noticed other people dressed similarly to us, chatting and laughing as they made their way toward the boat as well. My stomach churned as I took in just how normal they all looked. There were men and women alike, of various ages. They didn't look like monsters or freaks. They were all just the kind of regular people that one might casually pass on the street at any time, and yet here they were, laughing and joking as they prepared to party it up and watch people beat each other to death. From the corner of my eye, I watched as Aurora slipped her arm through Holm's and murmured something into his ear. He said something back, and her shoulders relaxed right away as she moved closer to him.

Finally, we made it to the little ramp that led up to the yacht. Usually, I would have taken the lead as far as talking my way into somewhere I wasn't supposed to be, but on this occasion, I decided to fall back and allow Mr. Marino to deal with the guard standing just at the front of the ramp. The guard was stocky and broad-shouldered enough that the suit he was wearing made him look like a literal square. He eyed us suspiciously as we approached, the mean expression on his face growing more unfriendly as we walked toward him.

"Name?" he asked simply once we were standing in front of him.

"Radley Marino," Mr. Marino replied easily as he turned to Aurora. "Oh, and my daughter, Aurora, as well."

"Hmm," the guard grunted as he looked down at a tablet he had clutched in his meaty hand. It looked tiny in comparison to his large sausage-shaped fingers. "List only has a Mr. Marino on it. No women or any other guests." He looked up and eyed Holm and me with distrust. "Who are they?"

"My boyfriend," Aurora replied before Mr. Marino could, pulling Holm's arm closer to her as she did. "And he's one of Papa's employees. Sorry, what's the problem here?"

She raised an eyebrow at the guard, and I had to restrain myself from letting the surprise show on my face. In the entire time I'd known her, Aurora had always struck me as being very calm and serene, not including that moment in the police station. Right now, though, she looked and sounded a bit like a spoiled brat as she stared down the guard in challenge.

"Listen, I don't make the rules—" the guard attempted to argue.

"'Listen'?" Aurora scoffed in mock disbelief. "Did you just tell *me* to listen? Who do you think you are?"

"It's so hard to find decent help these days," a woman standing just behind us tutted as she overheard Aurora's complaint. She and the man she was with were standing just behind us in line to get onto the boat. "No respect at all, speaking to a lovely young woman that way!"

"Now, now, it's alright," Mr. Marino said kindly. "The man is just trying to do his job, after all. There's no need to get yourself worked up, Aurora." He turned to smile at the guard. "We'll just get out of your way now. We don't want to hold the line up any longer."

"But, I..." the guard muttered, looking around helplessly. He was outnumbered and clearly worried about getting in trouble.

"Of course, if you'd rather I call someone out here to confirm our identities, I'm sure that can be arranged," Mr. Marino suggested, the same easygoing smile still plastered on his face. There was an unsettling edge to it now, though, and the threatening tone in his voice certainly didn't help.

"N-no, that's not necessary," the guard stuttered as he stepped aside. He'd certainly heard the threat in Mr.

Marino's voice, and he knew that he'd be the one in trouble if he were to embarrass a guest like that.

"Thank you very much," Mr. Marino replied as he led the way onto the boat.

Aurora kept up the conceited princess act by rolling her eyes and turning her nose up at him as she passed, and I noticed that the guard deliberately looked away from her as she did. I allowed myself to breathe a sigh of relief once we were on the deck, but whatever slight relief I felt was short-lived as I took a look around and realized just how many people were on this boat. Dozens, easily, all dressed to the nines and acting as if they were at a regular get-together and not in the middle of a modern-day gladiator arena. I felt physically sick as I watched them sip from wine glasses, lounging around on cushioned couches and chairs as they all waited for the night's entertainment to begin.

"Papa, look!" Aurora gasped as she reached out to grab her father's arm.

She pointed over at one of the tables set up along the sides of the yacht, and I realized immediately what she was talking about. Several wine bottles were set on the table, all bearing the Marino brand name and label.

"I guess now we know why Will was such a fan of these parties," Mr. Marino mumbled. He clenched his fist at his side for just a moment before stumbling over to an empty couch at a corner of the deck. "I need to sit down."

"Are you alright?" Aurora asked as she sat down beside him.

"I'm okay," Mr. Marino replied quietly. "It was just a shock, I suppose, to see that. It means that Will wasn't just participating in this. He was profiting from it. Profiting off of—" He shook his head as he reached a hand up to rub at his temple.

"Maybe this was a bad idea," Aurora sighed. "Maybe you shouldn't have come."

"No, I'm fine," Mr. Marino insisted as he suddenly sat up straight. "Just give me a moment. I did pretty good back there with the guard, right?" He let out a small, hollow laugh.

"You did," I agreed. "I was worried for a second when you offered to call someone down to confirm our identities."

"I was, too, to be honest," Mr. Marino admitted. "We might have been in a pickle if he'd taken me up on that. I had a feeling he wouldn't, though. He was too scared that he'd get in trouble for daring to question one of the guests. Aurora's little act certainly worked in our favor."

"Well, I figured the easiest way for us to get past him would be to pitch a fit." She smiled devilishly. "I was hoping he'd prefer just letting us through than having to deal with me."

"It was smart," Holm commended her, and she smiled shyly up at him.

Now that we were safely onboard, I decided to take the opportunity to reach up to my lapel, where I'd hidden a bug. I turned, so my back was to the deck full of people before muttering quietly into my jacket.

"Da Silva, can you hear me?" I asked.

"Loud and clear, Agent Marston," she replied into the tiny earphone I was wearing in my right ear. It was small enough that it couldn't be seen from the front, and anyone who caught sight of my ear from the side would likely just assume it was some kind of hearing aid. "That guard sounded like he was suspicious, though. Is everything alright?"

"Yeah, I think so," I replied as I turned to look over the side of the boat where the guard was still standing on the deck, checking names as more guests arrived. "Mr. Marino and Aurora did a good job getting us past him."

"Good," Da Silva replied. "Just make sure they don't get hurt, okay? I'm still worried about the fact that they're there at all."

"Yeah, I am, too," I replied. "Anyway, I'm going to stop talking before someone notices. Bye."

"Bye," Da Silva replied, and I quickly turned back to face the deck. A quick scan was all I needed to know that nobody had noticed. No one was looking in my direction, so it seemed I hadn't been caught.

"So, what do we do now?" Holm asked quietly enough that he wouldn't be overheard over the sounds of the party. "Should we go and look for the men, or should we wait until they're about to start fighting and then reveal ourselves?"

"It would be ideal to catch them in the act," I replied. "Then no one would be able to have deniability and claim that they didn't know what was happening. Then again, the longer we wait, the riskier. Someone could actually get hurt if we wait until then, and if we go now, we might be able to find the victims before the boat even leaves. Da Silva and the other officers can help if we're still docked."

"That's true," Holm muttered. "So, maybe we—"

"Someone's coming," I cut him off brusquely as I caught movement out of the corner of my eye.

I pretended that I hadn't noticed and maintained my composure, but inside, my heart rate was rapidly climbing as the figure moved closer to the quiet corner where we were gathered.

"Marino!" the man exclaimed in a low, thickly accented voice. "What a pleasure to see you here at last! It always struck me as a little strange that William would never invite you along, but now I see that he was just trying to keep the fun all to himself, the rascal."

"Zakharova," Mr. Marino replied kindly as he stood up to greet the man with a firm handshake. "I thought that was you on the phone. It's been a while since we spoke, old friend."

"It's been too long!" the man replied with a hearty laugh. He was a rotund man, with a thick, bushy beard and a round stomach. He might have looked like Santa Claus if his hair had been white instead of dark brown. "And I see you brought Miss Aurora with you tonight. How lovely."

There was an unpleasant, leery expression on his face as he turned to look at her that made me uncomfortable. By the way that Aurora shrunk back beneath his stare, it made her feel uncomfortable as well.

"Yes, well, she was curious to see what the fuss was about," Mr. Marino replied. "As was I, to be honest."

"Well, don't worry, the festivities will begin soon enough!" Zakharova replied gleefully. "Where is William, by the way? You didn't come together?"

"I'm afraid not," Mr. Marino laughed. "He had a little too much of the bubbly last night. He's been feeling under the weather all day. He really wasn't up to partying tonight."

"Ha!" Zakharova cackled. "I know all too well what that's like. Poor William, he must be sick as a dog! Well, he can just join us next time, then."

So, they don't know about the deaths yet, I thought as Zakharova's obnoxious laughter echoed in my head.

"Miss Aurora," Zakharova suddenly stated as he turned his attention back to her. "I've recently acquired quite the collection of impressionist paintings, some of which I've hung up here on the boat. You're a fan of art, are you not? If you'd like, I could—"

"Ah, how rude of me," Mr. Marino interrupted as he deliberately moved so that he was standing between Aurora and the man. "I've yet to introduce our guests. This is Ethan. He's one of my best men. Currently in line to succeed me as CEO. I figured it would be good for him to come out and have a look at how things work in our world."

"Ah, yes, of course," Zakharova replied, barely paying attention as he struggled to look past him toward where Aurora was still sitting.

Holm was glaring daggers at the man, and I knew that it was taking every inch of his self-control not to jump up and punch the man in the face.

"And *this* is Mr. Holm," Marino continued. "He's an investment banker from New York. He's here as Aurora's date tonight." Aurora slipped her arm through Holm's again as soon as her father finished speaking, and Zakharova looked like he was about to blow a fuse.

"Is that right?" he asked. His face had scrunched up into an unpleasant grimace, and he was glaring at Holm with venom in his eyes. "An investment banker? In this climate? My, but that does sound stressful. What's that like?"

For just a split second, Holm's expression wavered, and I knew it was because Holm didn't know a single thing about investment banking. It was just a random detail that Mr. Marino had come up with on the spot to make Holm's presence alongside Aurora seem more believable. My heart thrummed with anxiety because all of a sudden, we were on the verge of being found out.

"Now, Kristoff!" Marino laughed jovially. "This isn't the time to be talking about work. We're here to party. Why don't we go and have some of that wine I saw on the table back there? It sure did look familiar."

"Oh, no need to get up," Zakharova insisted the moment that Mr. Marino leaned forward as if to get out of his seat.

Zakharova lifted his hand and snapped his fingers, and just a second later, a sharply dressed man bearing a tray full of glasses appeared to dole out drinks to the group. "I'll have to thank William whenever I see him again. He always gives us quite the good deal on our refreshments."

"Well, our family has always believed in making sure our customers are happy," Mr. Marino replied.

"An excellent standard to live by," Zakharova agreed before suddenly turning on Holm again. "What's *your* family like, Mr... Hold, was it?"

"Holm," Marino corrected before launching into a made-up explanation about Holm's family lineage.

It was actually kind of impressive how easily Mr. Marino was able to lie and spin stories like that on the fly. Obviously, Zakharova was angry about Holm's presence at Aurora's side, but no matter what questions he lobbed at Holm to try to trip him up, Marino was there to hit back at him with some excuse or explanation. He was managing to keep Zakharova at bay, but it was quickly becoming apparent that Holm wasn't going to be free for a while, at least not until the nosy man got tired or bored enough to leave. If we wanted to find these victims before the ship departed, I would have to do this solo.

I glanced over at Holm. He looked up and met my eyes, and I offered him a slight nod before slowly backing away from the group. Zakharova was so absorbed in the passive-aggressive conversation he was locked in with Marino that he didn't even notice me quietly walking away. Once I was alone, though, I suddenly felt incredibly exposed. It was one thing to walk around alongside Marino and Aurora. This was their territory, and so long as Holm and I stuck with them and blended in, no one really paid us any mind. Now that I was on my own, I started to feel uneasy, like everyone would suddenly know I was a fed.

I grabbed a wine glass from a tray a nearby server was carrying and took a sip from it as I casually walked down the length of the deck. I told myself that this was nothing. I'd played roles plenty of times before in the course of an investigation. Going undercover was second-nature to me, and there was no reason this had to be any different. All I had to do was stay calm and pretend I belonged here, and no one would be any the wiser.

"I hope they have Lucas fighting tonight," a woman sitting nearby gushed, and I nearly spat out the wine I'd just taken a sip of. "He's *so* handsome, and when he uses those biceps—oh, I could just die!"

I could barely believe what I was hearing. It made it a lot more challenging to stay calm and blend in when the people I was trying to blend in with were casually discussing which man they hoped to see fight to the death next.

"How many times has he been up?" another older woman wearing a dark green, sequined dress asked. "It's been three or four now, hasn't it? They don't usually last much longer than that. If he does go up, this will probably be the last time you get to see him."

"Oh, that would be so sad," the first woman whined as she slouched back in her seat and swirled her wine around in her glass. "You're right, though, usually by then, they're all worn out. He's done well, though! Hey, I don't suppose they'd let me buy him off of them."

"My dear, why would you want to do a thing like that?" the older woman giggled as she took a sip of her glass. "You're talking crazy."

"Well, it just seems like such a waste for a strapping man like that to just die, you know?" the first woman grinned impishly.

"You are too much, my dear," the older woman replied before the two of them burst into a fit of giggles.

I blinked in shock and forced my legs to move as I realized that I'd been standing still there for far too long already. It was beyond unnerving, the way they'd literally laughed about buying the victims like that. My stomach churned as I made my way blankly across the deck. I'd been struck dumb by what I'd heard, but I needed to keep moving. The victims were somewhere on this boat, and I needed to find them fast.

I knew that they'd most likely be somewhere below deck, so I casually walked toward the stairway entrance leading to the boat's lower level. To my surprise, there weren't any guards standing outside the door, though that didn't necessarily mean that it was safe for me to go down. I stayed on alert as I calmly made my way down the steps, and my suspicions were proven correct when I made it to the bottom of the steps and was instantly greeted by a large man dressed in black. His right arm was in a sling, but he still looked like he would be able to stand his own in a fight, especially with the gun that was hanging at his hip.

"You can't be down here," he informed me.

"Ah, sorry, I needed to take a leak," I muttered, stumbling slightly to give off the impression that I'd had a little too much to drink. "You know where the bathroom is?"

"There's one up on the main deck," the guard informed me politely. "If you go up and head toward the back, near the helm, there's one—" He stopped suddenly, his eyes narrowing at me.

"Huh?" I raised an eyebrow at him. "There's one where?"

"I know you," the guard replied instead of answering my question, and my blood instantly ran cold.

"What?" I murmured as I took a step backward away from him, still maintaining the charade. "Look, I'm just trying to find the bathroom."

"In New York," the guard growled as he bared his teeth at me angrily, and suddenly I realized that I knew who he was as well.

Back near the harbor in New York, Holm and I had set a trap with the help of the two homeless men. They'd been attacked, just as we'd expected, and we'd barely managed to rescue the two men from being killed. Though we'd managed to kill one of the assailants in the struggle, the other one had managed to get away, though not before I'd shot him in the arm. My gaze slid over to the sling that the man had his arm in.

The guard reached for his gun, and I immediately dropped the drunken act to lunge toward him. I tossed aside the wine glass I was still holding as I tackled him to the ground. I couldn't afford to let him get his gun, but I couldn't fire mine, either. A sound like that was sure to alert everyone that was up on deck, and if that happened, it would be only a matter of seconds before everyone realized what was happening, and our plan would be ruined.

The guard let out a guttural yell as he fell, and I punched him hard in the face. He tried to hit me back, but his blows were clumsy and weak as he attempted to fight me off using only one hand. I punched him again, then decided to pull a dirty trick and elbowed him hard in his injured arm. It was a low blow, but I didn't have time for a clean fight right now. The guard went still and opened his mouth as if to scream in pain, but I punched him again before he could, first in the nose and then again in the jaw. The last blow hit him with enough force that his eyes rolled back in his head, and he went limp as he lost consciousness. I breathed out a sigh of exhaustion as I climbed off of him. My shirt and jacket were a mess, but I didn't have time to fix them now. I hopped to my feet, ready to go and find the victims before anything else could happen, but before I could take a single step, the floor suddenly shifted beneath me.

"Dammit," I muttered as I realized that the boat was moving.

I was too late, and now Da Silva and the other officers wouldn't be able to help. We'd have to rely on the

Coast Guard to move in and back us should anything go wrong.

"Ladies and gentlemen, are we all ready for the night's entertainment?" a voice called from up on deck, and a heavy sense of dread pooled in my stomach. Were they starting already? The boat had literally just set sail, and they were already about to start a fight. I panicked as I heard footsteps coming down the steps and quickly reached down to grab the unconscious guard. I dragged him toward the first door I saw and silently prayed that it would be unlocked. I could have cried in relief when I turned the knob and realized it was open. It led into a closet that was filled with sheets, towels, and cleaning supplies, and there was barely enough room for me to stuff the guard and step inside myself. I pulled the door closed as much as I could but found to my horror that it wouldn't shut all the way, not with both of us in here. In the end, I crouched down and pulled the door shut as far as I could by force and just held onto it tightly, barely managing to conceal myself before two men appeared at the base of the stairs. I could see them through the tiny sliver of space left between the edge of the door and the wall.

"Where the hell is Jordan?" one of the men grumbled as he scanned the hallway at the base of the stairs. "Isn't he supposed to be down here?"

My heart seized in my chest as I watched him in

fear that he would suddenly spot me here in the closet. The door was only slightly open, with less than an inch of space for me to look through, but I still worried one of them would notice that it wasn't completely shut.

"Who knows?" the other man grumbled. "He's been off ever since he screwed up a few weeks back. Honestly, I'm surprised they didn't just get rid of his sorry ass after he messed up so badly, and twice in a row."

"Yeah, well, lucky for him, *and us*, this isn't a job that has a lot of takers," the first man chuckled darkly. "If they get rid of us, then they gotta find someone else willing to do all this crap, you know?"

"I wouldn't feel so confident if I were you," the other man muttered. "There are a lot more people willing to do this kinda stuff than you think. Money's money, after all."

"Yeah, right," the first man snorted as the two of them moved off down the hallway.

The muscles in my arm were burning from keeping the door pulled closed against the weight of the unconscious guard, but I didn't dare let go or move. The two would likely come back at any moment, and once they did, I'd be able to step out behind them without being spotted.

As I had guessed, the two men returned just moments later, though this time they had two other men with them: two victims, I assumed, judging from their physical state and appearance. Both looked dirty and exhausted. One of the two looked decidedly worse than the other, though. His clothes were torn and caked with dark, dried blood, and he was covered in dark bruises in various states of healing. I wondered if he was the "Lucas" that the women from before had been discussing. I waited until the four of them had gone up the stairs before slowly opening the door to the closet.

The guard's limp body crumpled down to the floor unceremoniously, and I stepped over him as I slowly crept my way to the base of the stairs that led up to the deck. It occurred to me that this was actually an excellent position for me to be in. With me behind and Holm in front, we'd have the guards surrounded up on the deck. Hopefully, if everything went smoothly, we'd be able to get them under control and keep them that way until the Coast Guard arrived.

"We're about to move," I leaned my head down to speak into the bug under my lapel. "Is everything in place, Da Silva?"

"Ready," she replied at once, her voice coming through clearly in my earpiece. "I'll alert the Coast Guard now."

"Thanks," I replied before beginning my ascent up the stairs.

"The show is about to begin!" someone called from above, as though he was announcing the beginning of a play and not marking the start of a grotesque death game. It sounded like Zakharova speaking.

I walked quickly but silently up the steps, drawing my gun as I went. As I finally came back up onto the deck, several of the guests' eyes turned to look at me. Some of them narrowed their eyes in confusion as their eyes drifted down to the gun I had clutched in my hands, but, fortunately, no one spoke up. The guards were both still facing away from me, though, too focused on getting the victims into position to notice me. I quickly scanned the crowd for Holm and found him just a few seconds later, standing near the front of the group alongside Aurora and her father. He had a horrified, repulsed expression on his face as he looked down at the victims. Aurora was standing close to him, an equally horrified expression on her face as she watched the scene unfold. The guards had pushed the two men into a small opening formed in the center of the deck. There was nothing physical to mark where the arena was, but the crowd itself had formed a tight circle around the area where both men were now standing, each avoiding making eye contact with the other.

I noticed at once that both men looked utterly defeated. Neither was doing anything to fight back or put up any kind of resistance at all. They both just stood there, shoulders sagging and heads down as the two guards looked on. It seemed to me like both of them had lost any will they had to push back against their captors and were just resigned to their fate at this point. It made a chill run down my spine for a moment, and I felt a surge of fury well up inside me as I looked up at Zakharova, who was presiding over the spectacle like the ringleader of a circus.

Holm lifted his gaze and caught sight of me, and I only needed to look at him for a second for him to understand what I was thinking. He turned to Mr. Marino and pushed Aurora gently toward him before reaching down to where his own gun was hidden beneath the jacket of his tuxedo.

"Has everyone got their bets in?" Zakharova called out to the crowd excitedly. "Because the fight will be starting in just ten... nine... eight—"

"Everyone freeze!" I roared as I stepped closer to where the guards were, unwilling to let him continue for even a second longer.

Around me, several of the guests gasped or even yelled outright at my exclamation. Zakharova spun around to look directly at me, his face going pale with fear and shock as his eyes landed on the gun I had clutched in my hands. He turned to look at Mr. Marino and then back at me, the betrayal he felt evident on his face.

"What is the meaning of this?" Zakharova uttered as he looked back and forth between the two of us. "What is going on here?"

"You know exactly what's going on here," I sneered at him. "My name is Agent Marston, with MBLIS. You and everyone else on this boat tonight know exactly why we're here." I took a look around at the guests, several of whom were literally shaking with fear as they realized they'd just been caught in the act. "It's over for all of you."

28

HOLM

"Don't even think about it," Holm called as one of the guards suddenly reached for something.

Several nearby guests screamed as Holm raised his gun and pointed it directly at the guard, who froze before begrudgingly lifting his hands.

"Everyone, sit down, now!" Marston yelled. "The Coast Guard is on their way, so no one try anything stupid."

Some guests didn't even try to argue and immediately got to the ground. When they realized what was happening, most of the other guests decided to follow suit and behave as well. Zakharova and the two guards, however, seemed less inclined to cooperate.

"Y-you can't do this!" Zakharova stammered angrily, his face turning red as he ground his teeth. "There are more of us than there are of you!" He turned toward the other guests. "You're really going to just roll over and do what he says! There are only two of them! Come on, if we all band together—"

In a flash, before Holm could react at all, Mr. Marino strode calmly over to Zakharova and punched him in the face.

"Papa!" Aurora gasped as Zakharova stumbled sideways from the force of the blow.

"Why don't you get your head out of your ass already?" Mr. Marino shouted, his voice louder and more aggressive than Holm had ever heard it. "It's over, don't you get that? Just listen! The Coast Guard's already here!"

As he stopped speaking, Holm realized that he *could*, in fact, hear the sound of a boat motor quickly approaching. That seemed to be enough to cow the two guards into submission because they dropped their guns and fell to the ground as well.

"What did he say?" Da Silva's voice suddenly rang out in Holm's earpiece. He flinched in surprise, having been so relieved by the sound of the motor that her frantic voice caught him off guard.

"Who?" Holm asked in confusion.

"Marino!" Da Silva replied urgently. "Did he just say that the Coast Guard was there?"

"Yeah," Holm replied. "I can hear the motor. What's the problem?"

"Agents, the Coast Guard is *not* there! Their ETA is still approximately three minutes out."

A cold sensation dropped into the pit of Holm's stomach as he heard that because the boat motor was definitely growing even louder now. He looked up at Marston, and the two exchanged a confused glance before Holm rushed over to the side of the yacht. They were pretty close to the shore, and just a few feet away now, Holm could see a boat rapidly coming closer to them. The small, gray thing definitely wasn't one of the Coast Guard's unmistakable orange boats, though it certainly seemed to be going as fast as one. It came to a stop beside the yacht, close enough that Holm could make out the shape of someone walking out of the helm, but before Holm could make out any distinct features, something suddenly came flying toward him. Holm ducked out of the way as the object soared over him and smashed onto the deck behind him, exploding into a wave of heat and flames as it did.

Holm swore as the heat from the fire reached him, warm now but rapidly growing hotter. He blinked against the smoke that was quickly filling up the deck, and the cold feeling in his stomach grew worse as he realized that the shards of glass and bits of fabric scattered on the deck where the object had landed were the remnants of a Molotov cocktail. He spun around just in time to catch sight of another object being lobbed toward the boat, and this time, he turned and jumped toward Aurora, shielding her as the second homemade bomb hit the deck and instantly doubled the number of flames onboard the boat.

It only took a second for all hell to break loose after the second bomb hit. Everything on the deck was quickly catching fire, including several guests, who screamed and launched themselves overboard in a panic to put out the flames.

"Are you okay?" Holm turned to look at Aurora. Her head was bleeding, and she was shaking, but she nodded at him.

"I'm fine," she muttered as she frantically looked around. "Where's Papa?"

Holm helped her to her feet before scanning the deck for Mr. Marino. He couldn't find any sight of him, or Marston, for that matter. It didn't help that thick black smoke was obscuring his vision.

"Holm!" Marston's voice called out from some-where behind him.

Holm spun around and was relieved to find Marston standing near the helm. Mr. Marino stood beside him, clutching his arm against his chest.

"Over there!" Holm yelled to Aurora. The two made their way over to Marston and Marino.

"Stellina, you're bleeding," Mr. Marino fretted as he gingerly reached up to touch the injury on his daughter's forehead.

"It's nothing," she insisted quickly. "What about you, Papa? Your arm!"

Holm realized then that Marino's arm was severely burned, the skin between his shoulder and elbow raw and red.

"It's alright," he assured her. "It barely even hurts." He winced and hissed in pain just after he finished speaking.

"We need to get out of here," Marston declared as he looked around for an escape route. "What the hell is going on? Who threw those bombs at us?"

As if to answer his question, someone hopped over the railing at the edge of the boat just then. His shoulders rose and fell visibly as he looked around, an expression of pure loathing and disgust stretched over his features.

"I'm going to kill all of you!" the man screamed as he pulled a knife from his waist and began waving it around. "Every single one of you is going to pay for what you did!"

"Marston," Holm gasped as he suddenly realized who the man must be. "I think that's our vigilante."

"And he's just decided to up his game," Marston muttered in response. "Why go after them one at a time when he can just take everyone out at once? Crap, this is bad."

"Everyone, stop!" The crazed man continued to

scream even as the guests scrambled away from him and the flames. "I said stop!"

He reached out and grabbed the next person to pass by him. The guest turned to look at the bomber with wide, fearful eyes as the bomber's hand closed tightly around his wrist. Then the vigilante lifted the knife he was holding and brought it down onto the guest, over and over, into his face, head, neck, chest, and anywhere else he could reach. The guest screamed for a few seconds before finally letting out a low gurgle and falling to the ground.

Beside Holm, Aurora let out a terrified scream, and suddenly everyone on the deck went still as every eye turned to look at the killer.

"Don't you look at me like that," the madman sneered as he waved his knife toward Aurora. Holm stepped in front of her instinctively. "He deserved it. You all know that he deserved it. It's what you all deserve for doing what you're doing here! You're playing with people's lives! You all deserve to die!"

"You don't understand!" Mr. Marino stepped forward suddenly. Aurora tried to lung ahead after him, but Holm reached out an arm to catch her before she could move. "These men are here to help. We know what's been happening, but—"

"Don't try to trick me!" the armed man replied lowly. "Just stay where you are. Don't come any closer."

"He's telling you the truth," Marston tried to reason with him. "Look, my name is—"

"I don't care what your name is!" the armed man screamed, his voice cracking. "I don't care about anything anymore! It's not fair! I never asked for any of this! This isn't the way my life was supposed to turn out! You all did this. You all did this, and you all deserve to die!"

He lunged toward Marston, swinging the knife as he went. Marston took a step back as he reached forward to grab the man's arm. He managed to stop the blade just inches from his face, and the two became locked in a power struggle.

"I don't want to hurt you," Marston muttered through gritted teeth. "I know you're a victim in this. Please, just calm down, and we can all talk about this."

"I don't want to talk!" the crazed man screamed.

It was evident to Holm that he was too far gone right now to listen to reason. They needed to get him under control now before he hurt anyone else.

"Stay here," he turned to look at Aurora and her father.

He was about to go and aid his partner when Marston suddenly got the upper hand and managed to twist the knife out of the attacker's grip before throwing him down into the ground.

"Just calm down!" Marston yelled as the man crumpled to the ground. "We don't have time for this! We need to get off this boat before we all burn to death!"

The man looked up at Marston in fury, but then, his eyes slid over to something else. Lying just a few feet away was one of the guards. He was lying on his side, clearly dead. From the looks of his charred skin and clothes, he'd likely been killed in the explosion. The guard's gun was still sitting in the holster at his hip. Holm knew what the man was thinking before he even moved.

"Marston, watch out!" Holm screamed as the man reached over to yank the guard's gun out of its holster before turning it on Marston.

Marston, who was still holding the knife, jumped out of the way as the armed man suddenly fired in his direction.

"No, stop!" Mr. Marino yelled as he rushed toward the armed man.

Aurora screamed, and an intense fear gripped Holm as he watched the deranged man turn the gun away from Marston and onto Mr. Marino instead.

In the next instant, several things happened so quickly that Holm couldn't say with certainty in which order they each occurred. Aurora screamed as she rushed to her father, who had gone still with fear as he suddenly looked down the barrel of a gun. Holm couldn't remember moving or even making the conscious decision to move. He only knew that suddenly there was an intense pain in his chest, right in the center, between his ribs. It was funny how the brain focuses on tiny details like that in really intense moments.

Holm looked down at his chest from where the pain was radiating. A small, round spot of red sat directly in the center of his crisp white tuxedo shirt, almost as though someone had placed a target there. He wasn't wearing a bulletproof vest. They couldn't, not with the tuxedos on. It would have been a bulky, obvious giveaway that they were law enforcement. Going undercover was always a little extra risky, particularly because of things like this.

Holm tried to remember what he knew about anatomy and first aid as his knees buckled beneath him. The bullet hadn't hit his heart, right? The heart was off to the side of the chest, not in the center. He hoped that was right, anyway, not that his chances of surviving a gunshot to the chest were very good, to begin with. Aurora was still screaming, which upset him. He'd jumped in front of the bullet because she'd screamed, because she'd been scared that her father would be hurt, so why was she still screaming? He was fine.

Then, he was on the floor, his head hitting the deck with a painful thump. He could still feel pain. That was good. He could hear Marston's voice now, too, beneath the sound of Aurora's yelling. He was saying something, but it sounded muffled. Suddenly, Holm felt like he was drowning. There was liquid in his throat, and when he coughed, the water that came out was thick and warm. It felt better for a second, but then his throat filled up again, and the drowning sensation came back.

Holm tried not to feel scared as blood continued to spurt from his mouth. He knew this was bad. He knew that he was probably dying, but he didn't want to think about that. He wasn't done living yet. He wasn't ready to die. As he fought to keep his eyes from closing, his final thoughts were of how he wished he'd kissed Aurora back when he had the chance.

29

ETHAN

"No, DAMMIT!" I yelled as I willed Holm to remain conscious. "Come on, don't do this right now."

He was out cold, though, blood pouring from the wound in his chest and trickling out of his mouth. It was a dizzying sight.

"What can I do?" Aurora sniffled as she knelt beside me. "What do I do?"

She looked at me pleadingly, her eyes red and shiny with tears. I looked past her, back at where I'd last seen the deranged man lying on the ground right before he shot Holm. He was gone, and as I frantically scanned the deck of the boat, it only took me a second to spot him again. He was rushing down the stairs that led into the cabin below deck, but I didn't have time to worry about him now. Maybe I should have. As a federal agent, perhaps I should have prioritized catching the killer before he managed to shoot anyone else. I wasn't about to just abandon my partner, though.

"Go get that tablecloth." I nodded toward the table at the other end of the deck where all the wine was set up. It had, miraculously, survived both the bombing and the ensuing fire.

Aurora nodded and snatched off the heels she was wearing before running to the table. She knocked all the bottles on the table to the ground in a single sweep with her arm before pulling the sizable white cloth from the table, balling it up in her arms before sprinting back to where I was still crouched on the ground beside Holm.

"Here," she muttered as she handed me the cloth.

She reached up and roughly dragged her hand over her eyes to wipe away the tears. As she did, I reached down to rip open the buttons holding Holm's shirt closed. I winced as I saw the uncovered bullet wound. It was ragged and still bleeding heavily. I quickly ripped a long strip from the tablecloth before folding it several times on itself to form a makeshift compress. I pressed it down onto the wound and pursed my lips together when it immediately became soaked through with blood. I repeated the process several times until it seemed to be staunching the flow and then ripped another long strip from the cloth to tie the entire thing down into place. It was a messy job, but it was better than nothing.

"What now?" Aurora asked me, her voice shaking as she looked down at Holm.

"Keep pressure here," I instructed as I took her hands and showed her where to press down onto the makeshift bandage.

"Okay," she replied with a firm nod.

I'd slightly expected her to be squeamish, but she remained calm as she pressed down on the wound to keep the blood from flowing out. I leaned down to speak into the bug hidden in my jacket.

"Da Silva, how far out is the Coast Guard?!" I yelled into it. "Holm's down. We need help now!" However, no one replied, and my heart rate began to climb as my pleas for help were met with silence. "Da Silva! Hello!?"

When she continued to stay silent, I reached up to touch my earpiece and realized only then that it was gone. My heart sank into my shoes. I must have dropped it somewhere during the explosion.

"Dammit!" I screamed as I yanked the transmitter off my lapel. "Da Silva, if you can hear me, I need you to send for medical help. Holm's been shot. I don't know where my earpiece is, so I can't hear you. Just— Send help, okay?"

I dropped the transmitter helplessly as I looked back

down at Holm. How had everything gone so wrong so quickly? The plan had been going exactly as we wanted it to. Everyone had even been cooperating, and the next thing we knew, bombs were flying, people were dead, and now Holm was bleeding out on the deck of the boat.

"The Coast Guard is here," Mr. Marino suddenly declared as he knelt beside us. "For real this time. I just saw them." He paused as he looked down at Holm. "How is he?"

"Still breathing," I replied grimly as I got to my feet.

Now that I knew that both Aurora and Mr. Marino were watching over Holm, I needed to go and find the man who had shot him. Victim or not, I couldn't let him continue on his deranged killing spree, especially now that he'd injured Holm. I'd scarcely taken a few steps, though, when he suddenly appeared again from the stairway that led down below deck. I froze when I saw him and reached for my gun but stopped when I realized that he wasn't alone. Behind him, over a dozen men were trailing up the steps. Their clothing was all dirty, and most of them were sporting injuries and bruises of varying degrees of severity.

"He let them all loose," I muttered to myself as I took a step backward, and all at once, the men all attacked. They went after the guests who hadn't yet jumped overboard, clawing, scratching, and punching at them with their bare fists.

I raced back to where Holm, Aurora, and Mr.

Marino were. I knew that it was only a matter of time before the men set themselves upon us as well. They were blinded by fear and rage, just as the man who'd shot Holm had been. They were too out of their minds right now to think clearly, and they would probably just assume that we were all just more party guests.

"Stay low," I cautioned Aurora and Marino. "Don't call any attention to yourselves. I'll try to hold them off."

Aurora nodded, her eyes wide with fear as she looked out at the men all pouncing on the guests. I stood before the three of them with my badge in one hand and my gun in the other. I was hopeful that brandishing my MBLIS badge would be enough to deter any of them from attacking, but on the off chance that they decided to come at us anyway, I needed to be ready. I didn't want to hurt any of them since they were victims, but I couldn't let them hurt Holm or Aurora and her father, and I couldn't go up against so many unarmed.

I turned to face the men, only to come face to face with Zakharova instead.

"This is all your fault!" he shrieked as he took a threatening step toward me.

I quickly put my badge away since I knew already that he wasn't going to be intimidated because I was a federal agent.

"Please don't be an idiot," I warned him as he continued to walk aggressively toward me.

The man was waddling as he stepped toward me, and he looked like he couldn't throw a punch if his life depended on it.

"I'm going to kill you!" he screamed as he lunged toward me, his hands outstretched as though he wanted to wring my neck with them.

I didn't even bother getting out of his way and instead chose to brace my legs against the deck as he came at me. As I suspected, there was no force behind his attack. This was a man who had spent his entire life paying others to fight his battles for him, and it clearly showed in his physical movements. After stopping him in his tracks, I reared back and punched him in the face with enough force that I felt his nose buckle and crack beneath my knuckles.

"Ah!" He let out a scream as he reached up to cradle his wounded face.

I followed up my first punch with another to his chest. He gasped as the blow caused him to buckle and bend over in half. I was about to knock him to the ground, so I'd be able to cuff him, but before I could, one of the released victims suddenly ran in between us, brandishing an unopened bottle of wine like a club. He brought it down forcefully over Zakharova's head, and though the bottle didn't break, Zakharova crumpled to the deck.

"Stop!" I cried out reflexively as I yanked my badge out of my pocket.

As much as I detested Zakharova, I still couldn't let one of the victims bludgeon him to death. I held my badge out to him, and I watched as a look of confusion flashed across his face.

"Y-you're a cop?" he mumbled as he looked at the badge.

"Yes," I lied, figuring it would be better just to say yes than to explain the difference between the police and a federal agent at a pressing time like that.

The man slowly lowered the bottle but then lifted it back up again as his face twisted into an expression somewhere between horror and fury.

"You're a cop, and you still did this to us!?" he screamed as he swung the bottle at me.

"No!" I yelled as I dropped the badge and dodged the bottle.

I lifted my gun to shoot at him but hesitated. I couldn't do it. Even if he was attacking me, I knew with disturbing clarity the kind of hell this man had been put through. I couldn't bring myself to shoot him, knowing that he was just acting out of panic. I dodged to the side again as he swung the bottle before shoving against him with my shoulder. He stumbled to the side, and I brought the butt of my gun down against his head. He fell to the ground in a heap, and I breathed a sigh of relief that I was able to get him under control without fatally wounding him.

At least, that was the case until one of the other men spotted the man at my feet and misunderstood the situation. He ran toward me, and, like the first victim, he was brandishing a bottle, though this one was broken and ended in sharp, jagged points. I prepared to take him on as well, but before he could get to me, one of the other victims jumped between us.

"He's a cop," the man who jumped in to defend me informed the attacker.

"Huh?" the other man frowned at him before glaring up at me.

"He's a cop!" the man standing between us exclaimed, and I realized that he was one of the men who'd been about to fight when Holm and I broke up the party. "He came here to help us. He stopped them right before they were about to make Lucas and me fight."

"But... Wesley was the one who let us out," the attacker protested.

"Yeah, he got here after," the other victim grunted. "Look, just back off, okay? They didn't do anything. And look!" He nodded toward the side of the boat.

I turned to look alongside the attacker and nearly collapsed with relief as I saw about a dozen Coasties all clambering over the side of the yacht.

"Just lay off, man, it's over," the guy concluded.

Just like that, it was like all the wind went out of the attacker's sails, and his shoulders slumped as he dropped the bottle to the ground. The victims stopped their attack as they turned to look at the Coast Guard officers storming the boat all around us.

"It's really over," the man who'd been holding the bottle muttered as he turned to look at me, and suddenly, he didn't look angry or hostile at all. In fact, his eyes were red, and it looked like he wanted to cry.

I lowered my gun and finally allowed myself to relax. As I did, I took a look around the deck of the boat, which was in utter chaos. Though the tables and chairs at the center of the deck had burned, the fire had mostly died down by now, except for a small bundle of debris near the fighting ring. The bodies of the guests who the escaped victims had slain were strewn about the deck, mixed in with those who had died in the explosions. Several of the escaped men turned vigilantes were crying in sorrow and relief as they reached out to the Coasties, who were now swarming around the boat and trying to maintain order.

It was all so much to deal with, but right now, the only thoughts on my mind were of Holm and whether my partner was going to live to see the light of another day.

"He's bleeding!" Aurora screamed at the top of her lungs, and I spun around to look at her. "The bandage isn't holding the blood back! What do I do?" She turned to look at me, her eyes wide and frantic. "Agent Marston, what do I do?"

I ran over to Holm and fell to the deck beside him. My knees hit the hard surface of the deck with a painful bang, and I winced as pain radiated down both my legs. I pushed through it as I examined Holm. Aurora was right. He'd completely bled through the makeshift bandage we'd constructed out of the table-cloth. The blood was everywhere now, soaking through the white of his tuxedo shirt until the entire thing looked red. The color seemed especially horri-fying in contrast to how pale and waxy his skin looked.

"He's losing too much blood," I muttered, as though stating the obvious would do anything to help. I turned to look at the Coasties. "Hey! I need help here!"

They couldn't hear me, though, or they were just too busy to pay attention. Hadn't Da Silva heard me earlier? I'd told her that Holm had been shot. The fact that there was an agent down should have been relayed to the Coast Guard. He should have been their priority!

I jumped to my feet and rushed toward them, determined to make them listen if I had to. I was about halfway across the deck when the tiny bundle of flames that had still been burning suddenly burst into a complete inferno that engulfed half the deck and cut me off from where the Coasties were. I could hear them yelling from the other side about getting water to put it out and rushing to help the victims who were still trapped onboard the boat.

"Hello!" I screamed over the roar of the fire, desperate to get their attention. "We're here too! We need help!"

The fire was loud, though, crackling and popping louder than I'd ever heard any fire. From behind me, Aurora started to scream again.

"He's not breathing!" she screeched, her voice so shrill that it cut through me like glass.

It felt as though every drop of blood in my body turned to ice as I heard that. A cold, horrifying, sinking sensation washed over me as I rushed back to where she and Marino were still gathered around Holm. He looked even paler now, almost blue, and the pool of blood around him had doubled in size. It occurred to me that he couldn't possibly have any blood left in his body now with how much had leaked out. That was why he was so pale because he'd already bled everything he could, and there was just nothing left inside him.

"Do something!" Aurora screamed at me, grief and fury mingling together in her voice.

I fell to the deck beside Holm, hating myself for how powerless I felt because what could I do? I reached down to touch his face and recoiled when I felt how cold his skin was. Cold and hard, stiff like rigor mortis had already set in. It was a sensation I'd felt before when Holm and I had encountered dead bodies during our cases. Cold and lifeless, just like Holm was now.

Dead.

30

ETHAN

DEAD, Dead, Dead...

The word bounced around in my mind almost mockingly as my partner's cold and lifeless face drifted in and out of focus. It wasn't possible. It wasn't true. It couldn't be. I clung to that desperate hope like a lifeline, and as I did, my eyes suddenly flew open.

I gasped so sharply as I sat up that my throat stung. My eyes were bleary, and it took me several seconds of blinking before I regained my vision completely and was able to take in my surroundings. White walls and marbled tile floors. Wires and machines and fluorescent lights and the smell of antiseptic. I was in the hospital.

I'd had that dream again.

It had been two days now since Holm and I had put on those stupid, impractical tuxedos to sneak onto the party boat where the kidnapped men were being held hostage–tuxedos that were too thin and closely fitted for us to hide any kind of body armor underneath. It had been a risk, but one that we thought would be worth taking. We weren't rushing into a crime den full of hardened criminals, after all. Of course, we'd quickly discovered how naive that thought had been. A rogue, unexpected variable had arrived at the last moment to literally drop a bomb into the middle of the situation. Holm had put his own life on the line to protect Mr. Marino. He had been rushed to the hospital immediately afterward, and after a nail-biting eight hours in surgery, he'd finally been transferred to the ICU for observation.

"He's in critical condition."

That's what the doctor had told me when he'd finally come out of the operating room after nearly half a day. Though they'd claimed that the operation had been a success, they'd also said that they couldn't provide any guarantees for the time being. I knew what that meant. There was still a solid chance that Holm was going to die. Gunshot wounds like that were highly likely to be fatal. I'd been a federal agent for long enough and seen enough gunshot injuries that I knew damned well that the likelihood of surviving a gunshot wound to the chest, from nearly point-blank range, was so slim that you'd have about as much chance of winning the lottery.

So, I'd waited. For over forty-eight hours, I'd sat in the hospital as I waited for someone to get me an update on Holm's condition. Da Silva had been by to give me updates on the case a few times. All the surviving guests had been taken into custody. The kidnapped men had all been taken into protective custody as well. Though some were arguing that they should also be punished for having attacked the party guests at the end, Da Silva was arguing vehemently on their behalf. It was a messy situation that I usually would have been invested in, but I couldn't focus on any of it right then. Not when I was half expecting someone to walk out into the waiting room at any moment to inform me that Holm had finally died.

At around the thirty-six-hour mark was when fatigue really started to hit. I couldn't sleep, though. The fear that I might wake up to find that Holm was no longer alive weighed heavily on my mind. Worse than that, though, was the fact that any time I did doze off, I kept having that same horrifying dream where I was too late to save Holm, and he ended up dying right there on the deck of the ship.

I nearly collapsed then, when right around the forty-eight-hour mark, a nurse in a set of pale yellow scrubs walked out of the ICU to inform me that Holm had made it through the worst of it and was being moved to a regular inpatient room.

"You can even go and wait in there with him if you'd like," she'd informed me brightly.

I'd taken her up on the offer and immediately followed her up to the room that Holm had been moved to. I'd settled into a chair by his bed, and it hadn't been long before the relief I felt took over, and I dozed off again, only to jolt myself awake, yet again, after another nightmare. I swore as I dragged a hand down over my face. I was exhausted, and the lack of sleep was beginning to make me cranky.

"Whoa, language," a raspy voice drawled from beside me, so low and hoarse that it took me a moment to realize it had been Holm that had spoken.

I shot to my feet and looked at him, shock and relief both flooding through me in waves.

"Hey, brother." I smiled down at him. "How are you feeling?"

"Like hell," he replied, grimacing with pain. "I got shot, didn't I?"

"Yeah, you did," I replied. "How much do you remember?"

"All of it, I think," Holm replied. "I remember the vigilante pointing his gun at Mr. Marino, and then..." He frowned. "Actually, now that I think about it, I don't really remember moving. I was just suddenly standing in front of him with a hole in my chest. Wait, how is Marino? And Aurora? Are they okay?"

"They're fine," I assured him as he began to cough.

"Settle down before you bust open your stitches, and they kick me out."

"So, she wasn't hurt at all?" he pushed past the wheezing to ask. "Aurora, I mean?"

"No, your girlfriend is fine," I sighed. "Seriously, chill before you hurt yourself. You've got stitches on your lung right now."

"I've got stitches where?" Holm looked up at me in shock before looking down at himself.

"Yeah," I snorted. "As it turns out, you really can't get shot in the chest without sustaining some pretty severe damage. You should be happy it was your lung and not your heart. We probably wouldn't be having this conversation in that case."

"Well, when you put it like that, I guess you have a point," Holm chuckled. He took a long, deep breath before speaking again. "Damn, I really came that close to dying, didn't I?"

"I have to admit," I replied as I sat back down. "I really wasn't sure if you were going to make it for a minute there."

"You had that little faith in me?" Holm sniffed, pretending to be offended. "Is that why you were cursing like a sailor just now?"

"Something like that," I replied vaguely. There really wasn't any need to clue Holm in on the exact details of my dream about him dying. "Anyway, what do you want to do about the guy that shot you?"

"The vigilante?" Holm turned to look at me as much as he could manage. "I'm not sure, to be honest. I mean, I guess we can't just let him off completely scot-free, but..." Holm frowned, his eyebrows knitting together in thought. "I wouldn't feel right if we completely threw the book at him, either. He was a victim. They forced him to *kill* other people just to survive. I can't really blame him for losing it like that, you know? He wasn't in his right mind."

Of course, I could count on Holm to feel sympathy for the man who had landed him in the hospital, mere inches away from death. I understood where he was coming from, though. The man hadn't killed the guests because he got some sick thrill out of it like they did. He was just reacting to the horrible things they had done to him. Of course, we couldn't just forgive vigilantism either, especially not when his actions had nearly resulted in the loss of a federal agent's life.

"We'll have to talk to Captain Larose and Diane about it," I sighed as I leaned back in my seat. "Maybe some kind of psychiatric program would be more fitting than jail."

"I think so too," Holm replied. "Ultimately, Zakharova and the rest of those monsters are the ones that need to be held accountable for what happened. What's the news on them?"

"Zakharova is in custody," I informed him gladly. "Da Silva was by earlier to tell me about it. He and all the rest of the guests were arrested and are currently being held down at the station. She's been working through doing interrogations and getting statements from all of them, but it's slow going with so many people."

"Well, you should get down there and help her," Holm grumbled. "I'm awake now, so stop lazing around here and go do some work."

"That's the thanks I get for waiting, *anxiously*, to see if you were going to pull through?" I asked in mock indignation.

"Yep, get the hell out of here," Holm replied as he made a shooing motion at me with his hand. "Go finish this up so we can go home as soon as I'm discharged. I'm ready to get back to Miami."

"I'll get right on it," I replied with just a hint of sarcasm as I stood back up. I wasn't really upset, of course. If anything, I was glad that Holm was apparently feeling well enough to crack jokes. "I'll come back as soon as I finish up Zakharova's interrogation."

"Okay," Holm called back lazily as I stepped out the door.

I shook my head as I walked down the narrow hallway toward the elevator. It seemed like it was more and more often now that one or both of us ended up in the hospital during cases.

"We should try asking Diane for some hazard pay," I thought to myself as I got into the elevator.

I could just imagine her face now if I were to go through with something like that, and the image was enough to have me snickering to myself all the way into the lobby. As I was heading toward the entrance, I spotted someone familiar.

"Aurora," I called her name as I approached her. She was standing stock still right in front of the hospital doors as if rooted to the spot. Her hair was pulled back into a loose bun, and her face looked a bit pale. She had a bandage on her forehead, and she had been staring fixedly off into space until she heard me say her name.

"Oh, Agent Marston," she muttered as she looked up at me. Her eyes were wide, and she looked nervous.

"Is everything alright?" I asked her, immediately on edge.

"Yes, it's fine," she replied, flashing me a small, weak smile. "Everything's fine. I, um, I came to see how Agent Holm was doing, but... I was worried it might bother him if I just dropped in."

"It wouldn't bother him," I replied at once, knowing that Holm would likely be ecstatic to receive a visit from her. "Trust me."

"Are you sure?" she asked me, still looking uncertain. "It's just..." She paused as she looked up at me, her expression torn. "He got hurt taking that bullet for my father. And I'm so, *so* grateful. But I was worried that maybe he might not want to see either of us, since it's kind of Papa's fault that he got hurt, and—"

"Yeah, no," I hurried to assure her. "He's not mad at you. Honestly, he isn't even mad at the guy who shot him."

"Really?" She looked back at me in surprise.

"Really," I replied. "He's not the kind to hold grudges. And I promise he'd be happy if you went to visit him."

"Okay." She smiled with relief. "Thank you, Agent Marston. I'll see you later, then."

"Bye," I replied, and a moment later, she was off.

I laughed to myself as I stepped out of the hospital. Part of me would have liked to be a fly in the room during their reunion, but I had things to do now back at the station. I would just have to get the details from Holm later.

31

ETHAN

WHEN I GOT BACK to the station, Da Silva informed me that someone else wanted to speak to me before we interrogated Zakharova. Apparently, the vigilante had stated that he wanted a chance to say his piece before facing whatever consequences were laid out for him and had explicitly asked if he could speak to Holm. After being informed that Agent Holm was in the hospital, Da Silva had suggested that he talk to me instead.

"I hope you don't mind," she said as she led me down to the interrogation room where the man was waiting. "To tell you the truth, I think he wanted to apologize. He seemed really upset when he heard about Agent Holm being in the hospital, and I supposed that speaking to you would be the next best option."

"It's fine," I replied. "I would have liked the chance to speak with him either way."

We kept walking in silence until we reached the door to the interrogation room, at which point Da Silva came to a stop and turned to look at me.

"His name is Wesley Bransen," she informed me.

"Wesley?" I repeated. "So, he's the man that was kidnapped alongside Clearwater. He was the other escapee."

"That's right," Da Silva replied. "We ran his prints, but even if we hadn't, he told us everything himself. He's in his late twenties, and he moved to New York about two years ago. He was in a car accident about a year after that. Apparently, it cost him his job and left him in debilitating pain. That's how he ended up on the street."

"And wound up all the way here," I sighed. "Tangled up in all of this. Damn, he was dealt a bad hand."

"That's an understatement," Da Silva replied. "In any case, he hasn't been combative or difficult in any way since he was brought in, so I don't think we'll have any problems speaking with him."

"Alright," I replied. "Let's see what he has to say then."

Da Silva nodded and pushed open the door. This interrogation room was a little less intimidating than the one we'd used earlier on the other suspects. There was no two-way mirror, and though the walls were windowless and the room still felt a bit claustrophobic, the simple plastic and wooden furniture in this room was somehow less scary than the metal table and chairs that had been present in the other.

Wesley was sitting calmly at the table. He wasn't cuffed or chained down in any way like the other suspects had been, but he didn't try to get up or do anything as Da Silva and I stepped into the room. Actually, he looked embarrassed as he glanced up at me before quickly looking away to stare down at the table.

"Mr. Bransen?" I addressed him as I sat down at the low table across from him.

"Yeah, hi," he muttered nervously as he slowly looked up at me.

"I'm Agent Marston," I introduced myself as Da Silva sat down as well. "I heard that you wanted to speak with my partner, Agent Holm."

"Yeah, I did," he muttered in response as he anxiously fiddled with his hands. "I mean, I do, I still would like to. I-I wanted to say sorry about the, uh, about what happened."

He was a stammering mess, and for a moment, I found it very difficult to believe that this was the same man who had climbed on board the yacht and declared that he was going to kill everyone before ruthlessly unleashing his fury upon all the guests he could get his hands on.

"About shooting him, you mean?" I asked dryly.

Wesley flinched.

"Yeah." He nodded slowly. "I really didn't mean for that to happen."

"You didn't?" I cut him off brusquely. "Because it certainly seemed to me like you meant to do it. You were shouting it to everyone within earshot, after all. Mr. Marino was just trying to talk some sense into you, and you reacted by trying to kill him."

Wesley curled in on himself. Maybe I was being a little too mean. I'd walked in here feeling sympathy for the guy, but now that he was actually sitting in front of me, I couldn't help but feel angry as well. He was the reason that Holm had almost *died*, and even if he was a victim, I couldn't put aside the fury I felt at that.

"I know," Wesley mumbled. "I know, and I did mean that, it's just... I thought that man was one of *them*. One of the people that forced us to fight and beat each other to death like a bunch of rabid dogs!"

Wesley slammed his fist down on the table as he finished speaking. He ground his teeth together, and there were tears in his eyes.

"Why don't we start at the beginning?" Da Silva suggested. "Let's go back to when you were on the boat. We heard from another victim that you managed to escape by jumping overboard and swimming all the way to shore. That sounds very impressive."

"I wasn't about to die there," Wesley muttered, "after they made me—after they made me kill Logan!"

His voice caught in his throat as he buried his face in his hands and let out a noise that was halfway between a sob and a growl. It was the type of sound that was borne from pure pain, and once again, I felt a surge of sympathy for the broken man sitting in front of me.

"He let me do it, you know," Wesley muttered as he let his hands fall limply onto the table in front of him. "Once he realized what was happening, he told me to 'give it my all.' I didn't want to do it. Logan was a wacky guy, not always all there, but he was nice to me. He was a decent guy, and I didn't want to kill him. But he told me that one of us had to make it out of there and that it would have to be me. Then he started taunting me, trying to piss me off to get me to hit him. I knew what he was doing. I knew he was just trying to get me angry so that it would be easier."

Wesley sighed as he leaned back in his seat. "He was a tough old bastard. I hit him over and over until he was black and blue, but he kept hanging on. Finally, he went still, and I heard them say I was the winner. They pushed me back down the stairs into that cage, and I just felt dead inside." Wesley paused as he looked down at his own hands. "They all stood around and laughed and cheered while I beat my friend to death."

"I'm sorry you went through that," I replied, at a

loss for what else I could say. It was bad enough that he'd been forced to do that to anyone, but to do it to someone he considered his friend was unthinkable.

"You wanted to get back at them," Da Silva concluded, and Wesley let out a bubble of broken laughter.

"I wanted them to feel pain," he gritted out through clenched teeth. "I wanted them to feel just a fraction of what Logan had felt, of what *I* had felt, as they all stood around and clapped while I killed him. I wanted them to suffer." He looked up at me viciously. "That's what they deserved. So, after that kid and I escaped, I decided that's what I was going to do. It wasn't all that hard to do, to be honest. I could remember their faces, most of them. They were seared into my mind like a branding iron. So, when I got back to town, I decided I'd try to hunt them down. I had no idea how I would do it, to be honest, but then, like a message from the universe, one of them just strolled right in front of me."

"William Marino," I guessed, as he was the first victim.

"That was him," Wesley snarled. "He walked right past me on the street, coming out of some fancy seafood place. He didn't even look in my direction, even though, just a few nights before, he'd been making bets on whether I would win or die." Wesley snorted. "Damned bastard didn't even recognize me. That was good for me, though, because it meant I could follow him all the way to his hotel. I watched him for a while. I thought maybe it would be better to wait until he headed back to that boat, and then I could take them all out simultaneously. I couldn't wait, though. I had this urge to make him hurt, and the longer I waited, the stronger it got."

He sighed. "So, that night, I snuck into one of the kitchens and took the biggest knife I could find, and then I waited until I saw him come out again. He was with some woman, but I couldn't wait any longer. I followed them down to the beach, and once I was sure there was no one else around, I killed him." He took a deep, raspy breath as though just telling us about what he'd done was a weight off his shoulders.

"You didn't harm the woman, though," I noted.

"Well, no, of course not," Wesley replied, looking confused by my statement. "Why would I hurt her? She didn't do anything to me."

"You weren't worried that she might go to the police?" Da Silva asked.

"Oh." Wesley suddenly flushed. "Well, I did kind of tell her not to. I wouldn't have actually hurt her, though! To be honest, I figured I'd be caught eventually, anyway. At that point, I just wanted to take as many of *them* out as I could."

"Mr. Sanford was next," I added as I crossed my arms over my chest. "You killed him just a day and a half later and in front of a restaurant full of people."

"Yeah," Wesley replied flatly. "As I said, after what happened with that woman, I knew I was going to get caught, eventually. I decided that before that happened, I needed to do the world a service and get rid of as many of those monsters as I could."

"How did you know where he was?" I asked. "Was it just another coincidence?"

"No," Wesley replied. "I took Marino's phone after I killed him. He had quite a few text conversations going on, and I knew I'd hit the jackpot. A lot of the people he was talking with mentioned the fights, and one of them, in particular, mentioned that he was taking his wife out to that restaurant that morning. That's how I knew he would be there. That's how I found the boat, too."

"What do you mean?" I asked.

"Well, I got a text a few hours before midnight," Wesley explained as he began to fiddle with the hem of his shirt. "Technically, Marino got a text, but I had his phone. Anyway, it was a little after ten, and all that was in it was an address. It was from someone named 'Z.' When I looked up the address, I realized that it was right by the marina, and I knew that it might be the invitation to another one of those sick parties."

Wesley ground his teeth together and took a deep breath before continuing. "I went out and stopped by the nearest liquor store. I grabbed a bunch of bottles and then ran out. I knew they would call the police, but I didn't care. If everything went well, then after that night, every one of those monsters would be dead, and I'd be fine with going to prison then."

"You took the alcohol bottles to make the home-made bombs," I surmised as I leaned forward with my elbows against the table.

"Yep," Wesley replied proudly. "You'd be shocked at what kind of information you can find on the internet. All I had to do was Google how to make a Molotov cocktail, and boom! About a hundred different results popped up."

Actually, that didn't surprise me at all. The last case we'd worked on before this one had dragged us into the deepest and most disturbing bowels of what the internet had to offer. In comparison to some of the horrifying things I'd seen, instructions on how to turn a bottle of alcohol into a flaming projectile seemed mild.

"Anyway," Wesley continued with a shrug. "That's basically it. Oh, I stole a boat, too. It didn't seem like a very big deal after I robbed that liquor store. Whatever." He heaved a long, sad sigh. "I really didn't care anymore then. All I could think about was giving them what they deserved." He clenched his jaw and looked up at me. "I'm sorry about what happened to that other agent, honestly. I never wanted to hurt anyone who didn't deserve it. I'm not sorry about the rest, though.

Those people, those *monsters,* they deserved to hurt, and I don't regret hurting them."

A hush fell over the room as he finished his speech. As I thought about what he said, I decided that I couldn't really blame him for feeling that way. Being kidnapped and forced to kill several people, including his own friend, all for the entertainment of a bunch of soulless maniacs, had broken something in him. He'd broken the law by trying to take justice into his own hands, but I couldn't bring myself to fault him. Of course, I couldn't say that. My job wasn't to decide what he was or wasn't guilty of, after all.

"Thank you for being honest with us, Wesley," I told him.

"Yeah, of course," he replied calmly, and though he seemed sad, he also looked relieved, as though telling us about his ordeal had somehow lessened the burden of it. "So, uh, I guess I'll be going to jail now, right? I mean, I killed a lot of people."

Da Silva and I exchanged a look.

"Well, first off," I sighed as I turned to look at Wesley again, "I highly recommend you stop admitting to things now." Maybe I shouldn't have told him that, as a member of law enforcement, but the man was really not doing himself any favors. "I can't tell you what's going to happen now. You're right. You did make some bad choices. That being said, I'm sure the circumstances and everything you went through will be taken into account."

"Really?" Wesley looked up at me with surprise in his eyes. "Oh, uh, thanks. Thank you."

He smiled awkwardly at me, and I offered him a small smile in return before standing up.

"Come on, Mr. Bransen. Let's get you back now," Da Silva prompted him gently as she got up as well before turning to look at me. "I'll be right back."

I nodded in response and watched as Da Silva led Wesley away. Once they were gone, I left the small interrogation room as well, my head full as I went over the interview in my mind. Da Silva wasn't gone long, and by the time she came back, I'd made up my mind about Wesley.

"We need to make sure he doesn't rot in prison," I muttered as Da Silva walked up to me.

"He got to you too, huh?" She sighed as she leaned against the wall just beside the door to the interrogation room. "It's awful what he went through."

"Yeah, and it's all Zakharova's fault," I spat angrily. "Him and the rest of those lunatics who attended those parties. I know we can't just let people run around killing in revenge, but—"

"But Bransen wasn't in his right mind," Da Silva finished. "That much is certain. I'll have a word with Captain Larose as soon as I can. We'll have to see what the best course of action is for something like this."

"Alright," I agreed as I made a mental note to do the same with Diane. "In the meantime, let's go speak to Zakharova."

I was incensed after our meeting with Wesley. Ultimately, every action he'd taken had only happened because of what Zakharova and his ilk did, and I couldn't wait to rip him to pieces.

"Right this way," Da Silva replied as she led me further down the hallway and past one of the special metal doors that could only be opened with a keypad. "He's actually been in there for a while now. I figured I'd let him stew while we spoke with Bransen, make him sweat a little."

"Good call," I replied. Frankly, I had no sympathy for the man, so the more uncomfortable he was, the better.

"His full name is Kristoff Zakharova," Da Silva explained as she continued past a series of doors. "He's the owner of a large fur trading business up in Russia."

"Russia?" I repeated as we came to a stop in front of one of the rooms. "That's a long way from here."

"And all so he could watch people die," Da Silva remarked distastefully. "No priors that we could find, although, with the kind of money he has, it wouldn't surprise me if he just bought his way out of trouble."

"I'd like to see him try to use his money to get out of this," I scoffed as Da Silva reached up to unlock the room.

We'd caught him red-handed with a boat full of captive victims. Try as he might, he wasn't going to wriggle his way out of facing the consequences.

As we stepped into the room, I noticed immediately that this interrogation room was much more austere than the one in which we'd spoken to Wesley. It was a harsh, cramped box made of flat, gray walls and a cold, concrete floor. The rugged metal table and chairs that comprised the only furniture in the room really completed the unwelcoming picture.

Zakharova was sitting in one of the chairs. I was slightly taken aback to see bandages obscuring a portion of the top of his head, but then I recalled the way one of the victims had struck him with an unopened wine bottle back on the boat. I'd been so preoccupied with Holm and everything else that had gone down that I'd completely disregarded Zakharova. He turned to look at us as we entered, and I could immediately tell that he was nervous. He opened and closed his mouth before swallowing, and he kept moving his hands. First, he clasped them together on the table, then he crossed them, and then he just set them in his lap, all in the span of just a few seconds.

"You can't keep me in here!" he yelped as Da Silva and I sat down. "Do you have any idea who I am?"

The chairs *were* uncomfortable, which I knew was a deliberate choice meant to get suspects to talk, but it was always a shame that we had to sit in them too.

"Kristoff Zakharova," I replied bluntly. "And I'm Agent Marston. We met briefly back on the boat."

"Oh, I remember you," he sneered as he looked me up and down. "I knew from the moment Marino introduced you as a supposed employee of his that you couldn't be trusted."

"Did you?" I cocked an eyebrow at him as I leaned back in the chair. "Because it seemed to me like you were a little too preoccupied harassing Aurora Marino to notice much of anything else."

"How dare you!" Zakharova blustered, his cheeks glowing red as he looked at me indignantly.

"Too busy to notice me sneaking down below deck and straight into your guard," I continued, unperturbed by the sad man's glare. "Tell me, what was it that you were so desperate to keep guarded?"

"Oh, well, I—" Zakharova stammered, his face growing even redder at my question.

"Don't worry, that was rhetorical," I pushed forward. "I know exactly what was down there. I was the one who broke up your little party, remember? What I want to know, Zakharova, is *why*."

I stopped there and looked at him expectantly. Zakharova stared back at me for a moment before tutting and averting his gaze.

"To think that Marino would associate with the likes of *you*," he scoffed, clumsily sidestepping my question. "I once admired him so much, the traitor.

Was William in on this as well? I assume so. That's probably why the little turncoat wasn't there that night."

"William Marino is dead," I informed him flatly, and the look of shock that flashed across his face filled me with satisfaction. "He was killed by the same man who firebombed your boat that night, Wesley Bransen. Mr. Bransen was one of the men you forced to participate in your sick games for the entertainment of your friends."

Zakharova gaped at me.

"He was one of the two that got away that day," he mumbled as all the color drained from his face. "Those idiots! I told them to make sure they were dead!"

"You run a pretty sloppy operation, don't you?" I narrowed my eyes at him. "Did you even notice several of your men had already been arrested? Or is everyone just expendable to you?"

"W-what?" Zakharova looked at me in surprise. "No, that isn't true!"

"Oh, it is," Da Silva added. "We intercepted a boat just a few nights ago that was carrying a fresh load of victims."

"We've got plenty of statements," I informed him. "So, please don't get the idea that any of this is going to just go away. We don't need a confession from you. All we really want is an explanation because no matter how I look at it, I just can't fathom a reason why anyone would want to do something this disgusting." I paused and waited for him to answer, but Zakharova just blanched and clamped his mouth shut.

"Was it the money?" Da Silva asked him in mock concern. "Doesn't seem to me like fur is very popular these days. A lot of people are against it, actually. Maybe your business was suffering. Is that it? You were hard-up for cash and decided that human cockfights were the answer?"

"Absolutely not." Zakharova bristled at her accusation. "My business is going very well, I'll have you know. As if I'd have to stoop as low as something like that just to earn money!"

"So, if it wasn't for money, then why?" I glared at him. "Just for the fun of it?"

"Precisely," Zakharova replied, as though it was an obvious answer, and for a moment, I was stunned into silence. "That's all it was from the beginning: entertainment. Those people, if you can even call them that, serve no other purpose in life. You tell me, what were they doing before they were brought on board my boat, hmm? Languishing on the streets. They didn't work, and they didn't contribute anything positive or useful to the world! At least here they were useful!"

"Useful?" I stared at him in disgust, barely able to contain the unbridled fury I felt toward his cavalier attitude.

I was about to ask him to elaborate, but I clamped

my mouth back shut before I could say anything. Really, what was the point? It was clear that Zakharova felt no remorse about the things he'd done. On the contrary, it almost seemed like he thought he'd done something honorable by making the victims "useful," as he put it. Anything more he had to say on the subject would probably just piss me off more, so instead, I would just focus on extracting the answers to the few little questions I still didn't have answers to before ending this interrogation and putting this vile man behind me once and for all.

"What did you do with the bodies?" I asked him.

"Well, we'd bury them, of course," Zakharova replied.

"Where?" I asked calmly.

"Here and there." Zakharova shrugged. "You can't expect me to remember the exact locations of all of them, can you? We'd just stop at a nearby island and have the men take them out and bury them. A lot of those smaller islands aren't even inhabited, you know. I'm not sure I could find them again if I tried."

"Don't you have an ounce of empathy in your body?" Da Silva snapped at him. "These are human beings you're talking about. You stole their lives from them, and now you're telling me that you can't even be bothered to remember where you dumped their bodies? Don't you have any shame?"

"W-why should I care about them?" Zakharova

muttered boldly, though his voice quavered beneath Da Silva's hateful glare.

"So, what happened to Logan Clearwater?" I interrupted before things could get more heated between the two of them. I could practically feel the anger radiating off Da Silva, and I really wanted to just get my answers and get out of here before either of us did something to Zakharova that we would regret.

"Who?" Zakharova furrowed his eyebrows at me in confusion.

"One of your victims," I replied curtly. "An older gentleman. You forced Wesley Bransen to kill him."

"Ah, that old geezer." Zakharova rolled his eyes. "He hardly made for an interesting fight! He just stood there while that beastly man attacked him. They were both duds, to be honest. The other one had a crippled leg and was hobbling around the entire time. It was quite a pathetic display. I wasn't even sure which of the two would win—"

"You didn't bury Clearwater," I cut him off. "Obviously, because we found his body washed up on shore."

"Ah, that," Zakharova muttered. "Well, the fight was so dull that we decided to have another. We couldn't just have the old man's body in the way, so I had some of the men weigh it down and toss it overboard. Normally, I wouldn't have been that lazy about it, but after such a boring fight, we needed a little something extra to make our night worthwhile."

Suddenly, Da Silva was on her feet, her arm reaching across the table in a flash to grab Zakharova roughly by the collar. Zakharova let out a short, frightened cry as she yanked on the fabric of his shirt.

"You're an awful, sad little man," she hissed at him as she leaned down to look him in the eye. "You're going to spend the rest of your life rotting away in a prison cell, and I'm going to make sure your time in there is as absolutely miserable as it possibly can be."

She released him suddenly, and Zakharova fell forward and onto the table. Da Silva brushed her hands clean as if she'd touched something filthy and then calmly turned and walked to the door.

"Well, thank you for answering my questions," I added almost robotically.

To be honest, I was itching to throttle Zakharova myself, but I needed to maintain my composure. It was in everyone's best interests for me to just wrap this up now. Zakharova just muttered and curled in on himself as he rubbed his chin, which he'd bumped on the table when he fell. I got up and followed Da Silva out the door. She slammed it shut the moment I was outside, and just being away from Zakharova felt like a relief.

"Wow," Da Silva sighed as she took a deep breath. "I'm not even sure what to say about that."

"I think you said enough," I noted. "He certainly seemed at a loss for words there at the end."

"I meant what I said, too," she muttered darkly. "Someone that foul needs to be behind bars. I'm going to make sure he isn't given a single concession, either. No amount of money is going to make his stay in prison any more comfortable for him."

"He might end up getting extradited to the US," I remarked as I tried to work through which country would wind up having ultimate jurisdiction to try him. He was a Russian citizen who'd committed crimes against American victims in international waters, off the coast of St. Vincent. It was a mess. "If he does, I'll make sure the same applies there."

"Good," Da Silva replied as she reached up to pull her hair down out of its ponytail to run her hand through it. "Anyway, I've got a headache, and I want nothing more than to stop thinking about this case. You up for a drink?" She turned to look at me expectantly.

"Yeah." I smiled at her. "I could use a drink about now as well, actually."

"Let's go then." She smiled back at me. "You can get the first round."

32

HOLM

HOLM FLIPPED LAZILY through the channels. There was a small, outdated TV mounted in the corner of the room that he'd turned on as soon as Marston had left. The channel selection really left something to be desired, though, as there were only about a dozen in total, at least half of which seemed to be running infomercials non-stop. He'd finally settled on a program about the supposed mysteries of crop circles when he heard a knock at the door.

He turned toward the open doorway and nearly jumped in surprise when his eyes landed on Aurora. She was standing at the edge of the door, peeking inside so that only half of her body was visible. She looked as though she wasn't sure if she was allowed in.

"Hey!" Holm greeted her as he reflexively

attempted to sit up, immediately regretting the decision when pain shot through his torso.

"Oh, don't get up!" Aurora called as she rushed into the room, any and all bashfulness gone in an instant. "Are you okay? Should I call a nurse in here?"

"It's fine," Holm insisted, though there was still a dull, pulsing pain in his chest. "That was dumb. I was just excited to see you here."

"Really?" Aurora smirked at him smugly. "That excited, huh? Well, I suppose I shouldn't be surprised. That is the reason you're here in the first place." The smile slipped off her face slowly. "I wanted to apologize about that, actually. And thank you, of course. You saved my father's life. But you got injured in the process, so, I'm really sorry, Agent Holm."

"No, stop," Holm held a hand up in protest. "First, you can just call me Robbie. And second, you don't have to apologize. You and your father are the only reason we were able to find the boat in the first place."

"You ended up in a hospital bed because of it," Aurora insisted, biting her lip anxiously. "You could have died. You almost did die. You were in surgery for hours."

"That wasn't the first time I've almost died." Holm shrugged dismissively.

"What!?" Aurora looked at him in alarm.

"It's all part of the job," Holm replied. "And in any

case, I don't regret taking that bullet. I'd do it again, without hesitation."

Aurora's face grew pink as Holm looked up at her sincerely. She looked beautiful like that, and Holm deeply regretted that he wasn't in any position to get out of bed right now.

"Oh, I brought you something," she suddenly proclaimed as she sank into the chair that Marston had vacated.

She reached into the oversized tote bag she had slung on her shoulder. Holm's eyes went wide with surprise as she pulled out a full-sized wine bottle from inside.

"I'm sorry it isn't more," Aurora said sheepishly as she set the bottle down on the small table next to the hospital bed. "I thought about bringing snacks, but I don't know your preferences. My father happened to have a lot of samples with him, though. This is our very best product."

"Oh, wow," Holm muttered in surprise as he recalled what they'd learned about the company when they were researching William Marino's identity. If he remembered correctly, the bottle Aurora was gifting him was worth an unbelievable amount of money. "That's very kind of you."

"Really?" Aurora beamed, and Holm felt his heart seize. "I'm glad. I was worried you might say that you don't drink. And, um, actually—" She reached up to brush a loose strand of hair behind her ear. "I thought maybe we could drink some of it together. We never did get the chance to get together after New York."

"Yeah," Holm answered, maybe just a little too quickly. "Yes, that would be great. I'd love to."

"Perfect," Aurora replied before reaching back into her bag to retrieve two stemless wine glasses.

"Oh, you meant right now?" Holm looked at her in surprise.

Aurora smirked at him again before looking over her shoulder into the hospital hallway.

"Well, I won't tell if you won't," she replied as she set the glasses down on the table beside the bottle. "Besides, the last time I left it up to you to call me, you left the country."

"It sounds terrible when you say it like that," Holm grumbled as he awkwardly tried to move up into a seated position without causing himself too much pain.

"Here, let me help," Aurora offered as she stood back up and then leaned over to help readjust the pillows at the head of the bed to allow Holm to sit up more.

Even moving around this much sent jolts of pain through his torso, but he honestly barely noticed it. He was too shaken by just how close Aurora was to him.

"There," Aurora declared triumphantly when she

felt satisfied with their work and Holm was sitting up enough to drink without choking.

To Holm's surprise, she didn't move away from him as she spoke, just continued staring at him with that cocky smirk. He moved at the same time that she did, lifting his hand to curl into her hair as the two of them pressed their lips together.

Aurora moved away from him far sooner than he would have liked, her cheeks flushed scarlet as she cleared her throat.

"We should have that wine," she murmured as she smiled shyly at him. "Before someone comes in and yells at me for agitating a patient."

"Okay."

Holm grinned back at her. His heart thudded almost painfully in his chest, though in that particular moment, the sensation had nothing to do with his injury and everything to do with the way that Aurora was looking at him.

EPILOGUE

I PAUSED to take a long swig of my drink. The last remnants of my beer quenched my thirst as I brought the story to a conclusion.

"And then we came back home," I stated as I set the thick pint glass down on the table. "I had to wait for Holm to heal up a bit, of course, since it really wasn't safe for him to travel while he was recovering from a gunshot injury that severe. Not that I minded, of course. Of all the places to be stuck waiting, a gorgeous Caribbean island wasn't a bad spot."

I grinned as I recalled how I'd wound up taking a mini-vacation for a few days out in St. Vincent while Holm got well enough to fly. I could have gone back, but it seemed a little mean to ditch Holm by himself while I went home.

"So, you got to take it easy while Holm was stuck in the hospital?" Jeff shook his head at me in mock disapproval. "Sucks to be him."

"Well, it's not like he was *alone* in there," I countered, my smile growing even wider as I fondly recalled how smitten Holm had been with Aurora back then, like a lovesick teenager.

"Did Aurora stay with him the whole time?" Mac asked as she raised her eyebrows in surprise. "That was nice of her. She must have liked him a lot if she hung around in a hospital room with someone she'd only just met."

"Well, he *did* take a bullet for her dad," Jeff argued as he absentmindedly rolled an ice cube around his empty glass.

"She was extremely grateful for that," I replied as Nadia stopped by the table to collect the empties. "As was Mr. Marino. He ended up taking over the family business completely after that since his brother William was no longer in the picture."

"That's so messed up," Ty grunted. "I feel bad for Marino, finding out his brother was doing something like that."

"I'm amazed that he and Aurora had the stones to go through with that plan," Mac added. "Most people would be falling apart after getting news like that, not jumping at the chance to help a couple of feds infiltrate an illegal fight club."

"They're tenacious," I started before being quickly caught off by a loud blare of music.

I snapped my head around to look in the direction of the jukebox, which was now lit up and blasting at full volume. Charlie stood in front of it proudly, a screwdriver in his right hand and the floor around him littered with different-sized drill bits and tools.

"I fixed it," he proclaimed proudly as he looked over at the jukebox.

"Great," Ty called back over the sound of the music. "Now turn it down, will you?"

"Sorry," Charlie replied, his smug smile still firmly in place as he reached over to adjust the settings on the jukebox back to their normal levels.

I sighed with relief when the volume went back down to a mellow hum, the notes of a guitar riff drifting across the bar.

"Well done," I commended Charlie happily as he knelt to gather up all the tools off the ground. "Where'd you get the screwdriver?"

"I gave it to him," Rhoda informed me as she walked up to Charlie with a tall pint of beer in her hand. "Here, on the house, as thanks for fixing it up. I can take these back to the backroom."

She took the screwdriver and the rest of the tools from him in her arms before turning and heading back to the room behind the bar.

"Thanks," Charlie beamed as he traded the tools for the drink and walked back over to the table.

"What was wrong with it?" Ty asked as he nodded toward the jukebox.

"One of the internal components melted," he explained with a shrug. "It's not crazy uncommon for it to happen. Something overheats, and over time, the wiring can start to melt. It's okay for now, as I managed to rearrange some things and stripped back the damaged wire, but you still might need to get a new one sooner rather than later."

"Well, that's a shame," I grumbled as I looked over at the machine with a frown. "At least it's working for now, though."

"Yeah," Charlie agreed with a nod. "If you want my advice, you should replace it with an older model. The new, high-tech stuff is great and all, but you see the same thing with electronics as you do with cars. Stuff just isn't built to last anymore. You could probably find an older one that's still up and running like the day it was made, and it'd still last a long time to come, too."

"But then Ethan couldn't program it not to play any top tens pop," Nadia teased as she returned to the table with a tray of freshly made drinks.

"Damned right," I muttered as I pulled the pint of beer toward me. "Last thing I need is someone blasting some obnoxious, repetitive crap all through my bar. Charlie's got a point, though. They don't make stuff how they used to. Just take a look at some of the stuff in here." I paused as I gestured around at the various collections of antiques I had on display around the bar. "A lot of this stuff is hundreds of years old, and some of it was found at the bottom of the ocean. And it's still here."

"Speaking of stuff found at the bottom of the ocean," Ty changed the subject tactfully. "You didn't tell us anything about the *Rogue* this time. Whatever happened to that note you got from Ava?"

"Oh, yeah," Mac hummed as she narrowed her eyes at me. "Last time we were all in here, you mentioned something about her giving you a sextant. Whatever happened with that?"

"Ah, well, she did end up giving it to me," I explained. "When we finally did get back home from St. Vincent, Diane let me know that a package had arrived for me while we were gone." I laughed as I recalled that particular incident. "When I heard that, I assumed that it must be a package from Ava."

"But it wasn't?" Charlie asked as he drained his beer, having clearly worked up a thirst while fixing up the jukebox.

"No." I grinned. "It was something a lot bigger than a little sextant. In hindsight, I should have figured something would be weird about the package when it was delivered to me at work instead of home."

"Was it something bad?" Ty asked in concern.

"No, not at all." I smiled at him. "Actually, it was a piece of the *Rogue.*"

"No way," Charlie replied as he leaned forward, elbows against the table as he looked at me. "So, what was it?"

"A door," I replied simply.

The kids all looked back at me in confusion.

"A door?" Mac repeated as she looked toward the front entrance of the bar. "Like an entire door, full-size door?"

"Actually, it was probably a little bigger than a standard, modern door," I replied after thinking about it for a moment. "It was the main door to the captain's quarters on the ship."

"And it just arrived, without warning, in a package addressed to you?" Ty looked at me with a perplexed expression.

"Well, there was a note," I explained, unable to hold back a grin at the looks on their faces. It *was* a pretty weird package. Even I'd been stunned when I'd received it and realized what it was. "An old friend of mine just happened upon it while he was on a case and thought to send it to me."

"That's lucky," Mac remarked. "So, he found the *Rogue*? Or was it just the door?"

"Well, that's the complicated part," I replied. "And something I really wanted to know too, back then. Lucky for me, the spot where he found it wasn't terribly far from where our next case ended up taking place."

"And where was that?" Charlie asked me before gulping down the rest of his beer.

My thoughts drifted a little as bits and pieces of our case there floated to the forefront of my mind: a missing ship, unexplained disappearances, and even talk of voodoo and witchcraft from the locals. It had been a while since I'd thought about it, but the moment I did, the memories came flooding back all at once.

"The Bermuda Triangle," I replied, and Charlie nearly choked on his beer.

"*The* Bermuda Triangle?" he coughed as he tried to clear his throat. "Like the place where ships and planes and stuff disappear?"

"That's just a myth," Ty rolled his eyes.

"It's true, actually," I corrected him, and Ty snapped his head around to look at me in disbelief. "Now, I'm not saying it's because of something paranormal or anything, but the area does see an unusually high amount of wrecks."

"Is that what you were there for?" Mac asked me somberly.

I nodded.

"A missing ship," I replied. "One last radio signal for help, and then it was gone."

"The whole ship?!" Charlie exclaimed in alarm.

"The whole ship," I confirmed as I took a long sip of my beer. "And Holm and I were the ones tasked with finding out what happened to it."

AUTHOR'S NOTE

Hey, if you got here, I just want you to know that you're awesome! I wrote this book just for someone like you, and if you want another one, it is super important that you leave a review.

The more reviews this book gets, the more likely it is there will be a sequel to it. After all, I'm only human, and you have no idea how far a simple "your book was great!" goes to brighten my day.

Also, if you want to know when the sequel comes out, you absolutely must join my Facebook group and follow me on Amazon. Doing one won't be enough because it relies on either Facebook or Amazon telling you the book is out, and they might not do it.

You might miss out on all my books forever, if you only do one!

Here's the link to follow me through e-mail.

Here's the link to my Facebook Group.

Made in the USA
Columbia, SC
27 May 2025

58559475R00295